“WILL YOU LET

His fingers were steady and warm as they traced her lips. The brute heat of his flesh fervid and masculine and so . . . tempting.

Min closed her eyes, and as she did, the teasing heat on her lips was replaced by the confident press of Chance's mouth. Surprised and shocked by his daring, her conscience stabbed at her, but she had no desire to voice her inner concerns.

Ha! her conscience scoffed. *You want this man in all his valiant glory. His touch is enchanting, his lips divine madness—*

Min sank into Chance's embrace as his strong arms wrapped about her. Her body felt weak and hot, as if a fever had overcome her.

He opened her mouth with his tongue and pressed a wet warmth across her lips. She felt Chance's hand move up her back and cross over her arm with measured stealth. The spinning warmth in her stomach surged upward in response. Saints, this man had an irresistible command over her!

“No!” Min pulled away and twisted the robe openings in her fist. “We—we cannot do this.” She was not his courtesan. “It's . . . well, 'tis not proper.”

“Proper?”

“I am a lady,” Min protested.

“A lady?” Chance smirked and waved a hand through the air. “You, Mademoiselle Imp, are a lady only when it is convenient for you.”

“I *am* a lady!” Min said forcefully. “I shall always be a lady, whether I choose to wear breeches or a dress.”

Chance regarded her with a sharp glance down her robed figure. “Or undress.”

BOOK YOUR PLACE ON OUR WEBSITE AND MAKE THE READING CONNECTION!

We've created a customized website just for our very special readers, where you can get the inside scoop on everything that's going on with Zebra, Pinnacle and Kensington books.

When you come online, you'll have the exciting opportunity to:

- View covers of upcoming books
- Read sample chapters
- Learn about our future publishing schedule (listed by publication month *and author*)
- Find out when your favorite authors will be visiting a city near you
- Search for and order backlist books from our online catalog
- Check out author bios and background information
- Send e-mail to your favorite authors
- Meet the Kensington staff online
- Join us in weekly chats with authors, readers and other guests
- Get writing guidelines
- AND MUCH MORE!

Visit our website at
http://www.zebrabooks.com

TAME ME NOT

Michele Hauf

Zebra Books
Kensington Publishing Corp.

http://www.zebrabooks.com

ZEBRA BOOKS are published by

Kensington Publishing Corp.
850 Third Avenue
New York, NY 10022

Copyright © 1999 by Michele Hauf

All rights reserved. No part of this book may be reproduced in any form or by any means without the prior written consent of the Publisher, excepting brief quotes used in reviews.

If you purchased this book without a cover you should be aware that this book is stolen property. It was reported as "unsold and destroyed" to the Publisher and neither the Author nor the Publisher has received any payment for this "stripped book."

Zebra, the Z logo and Splendor Reg. U.S. Pat. & TM Off.

First Printing: October, 1999
10 9 8 7 6 5 4 3 2

Printed in the United States of America

For Ashley.
Don't allow your dreams to be tamed—
follow them to the stars

And for Marian Enerson and Violet Svedahl,
the best grandmas in the world!

Chapter One

France—1660

Apprehension setting her high on the saddle, Mignonne Saint-Sylvestre looked to her brother, Adrian. He remained cool and calm, in complete control, while her own hand clutched the leather reins. Excitement caught and curled about her bones like a hot flame, a flame laced with fear.

"Now!" Adrian commanded in a low hiss.

With a spur to her horse's flanks, Min was off through the hazy fog that shrouded the French countryside in a veil of ethereal whiteness. The previous night's rain had softened the road, but the horses took the pliable surface well, their hooves spitting up stinging clumps of pebble-laden mud.

Min's pockets were full of tonight's booty. Her blood raced with the rush of success. Laughter pushed over her lips and dispersed through the fog. She had to admit that joining her brother on his midnight raid was a thrill to match no other.

But such cunning play would never dissuade her from her goal of a more honest profession.

The twosome did not stop until they reached home. The grounds behind the Saint-Sylvestre château glittered with an assortment of thick ivory cathedral candles placed on heavy iron bases and nestled in the dewy grass. Mignonne and Adrian slowed their mounts to a walk.

"He's at it again," Adrian said of their older brother, Alexandre. "God only knows what the man does with his flowers in the dark of night."

Min dismounted and exchanged the bundled reins that Adrian had cut from their victim's horses for the lumpy suede pouch of jewels she held.

"Clever," she said as she tapped the curled reins against her wrist. "Makes it rather hard for a coach and four to follow, eh?"

With a knowing wink, Adrian stuffed the pouch inside his vest and nodded towards the reins. "Save those." His words were exhilarated gasps. "Alexandre will have use for them to secure those seedling lindens out back. But if you value your freedom, you'll not let Armand see."

"I won't," Min said. Armand, the eldest of the four siblings, would surely be outraged should he discover her venture into criminal activities this evening. "I'll be along soon. First I want to see what Alexandre is doing."

Pulling off her leather gloves and tossing them to Adrian, Min sprinted across the clover-dotted lawn to the large garden where she could always be assured of finding the middle brother sitting amongst his flowers with drawing paper and charcoal in hand.

The oblong flower bed sparkled like a fantasy fairyland in the candlelight. Colors took on a jewel-like brilliance, nearly rivaling the booty that jingled in Adrian's pouch.

Red roses became rubies; tissue-thin morning glories, their petals shut for the evening, were sapphires winding up the trellis; the soft summer moss beneath Min's boots, a carpet of emeralds. Tender, fragrant petals were tipped with diamonds of moisture from the fog. The garden never failed to seduce her; inside, she became lost within the heavy fragrances and lush textures.

Min stopped just behind Alexandre, observing over his shoulder as he sketched.

"You look a mess," he muttered, his attention barely straying from his drawing.

"I've been riding." Min straightened and looked over herself. Mud splattered her leather doublet and chamois breeches, both hand-me-downs from Adrian. Both suede boots were mottled gray with caked mud. Her left boot had slipped down to reveal her water-soaked hose and the silver-handled dagger she always kept hidden near her ankle; the dagger was a gift from Armand. She reached down and tugged on the wide brim of her boot.

"You've been on the prowl with Adrian," he said. "Our brothers are extremely fortunate they have never been caught, Mignonne. I pray every time they leave Saint-Sylvestre land they are not. But what of you?" The narrow stick of charcoal lingered over his drawing pad as Alexandre turned and tossed long strands of ebony hair from his eyes, meeting Min's matching dark gaze. "I am a bit surprised. I know you do not want the same life that our brothers have chosen."

He knew her well. Alexandre was the only brother Min trusted with her most private dreams and secrets.

Save one.

"I went along with Adrian thinking we might have a chance to talk. I so wish he and Armand would give up the road and become the musketeers our father wanted them to be."

"And you thought you could convince Adrian of this? A man who lives with a wench in one hand and her purse in the other?"

Min matched her brother's smirking grin with a gentle chuckle. "I thought it would be far easier than trying to convince Armand. I thought if I could see what it was that made the life of a highwayman so attractive, I'd better know how to change it."

"And did you succeed?"

"Well . . ." She toed the mounded dirt that circled a newly planted rosebush. "It was rather exhilarating . . ."

"Mignonne!"

Min spun around at the familiar voice. "Armand!"

It had been nearly a fortnight since they'd last spoken. Cocking her arms akimbo to look him over, Min's tiny frame was shadowed by her eldest brother's statuesque build. He'd regrown his mustache since his last adventure. She liked it because it covered the thin, silvery scar that trailed from his upper lip to his nose. A lucky man he was that his opponent's sword had not cut deeper than it had.

"Come from LaChaize?" Alexandre said with nary a glance toward his brother. His charcoal resumed its long brushing sweeps.

"And many thousand *livres* richer, dear brother." Armand tousled a broad hand through Min's hair, shaking dried crumbles of mud from the mussed queue.

Min had listened to Armand plot and plan this escapade for all of a month in hopes of snaring great riches from the widowed LaChaize sisters. Besides working the high roads, Armand was an excellent pretender. Judging from the stories Min had heard from Adrian and Alexandre, Armand could move himself into a person's life to charm and seduce the very shoes from their feet.

"Ah, but what of you, Alexandre? How go your studies?"

"Oh, yes." Min suddenly remembered she was not the

only one with aspirations of an honest lifestyle. "How goes it?"

"I've an appointment with Le Nôtre in two days at the Louvre." Alexandre's eyes beamed with a child's delight. "He's very interested in my botanical studies and wishes to incorporate my findings into the gardens at Vaux-le-Vicomte. If all goes well, I may be granted a commission."

"Magnificent!" Armand placed a congratulatory kiss on his brother's cheek.

"It is late, Alexandre," Min said. "Come inside, and we'll have a celebratory toast on your behalf. Then we'll sit around the fire and interrogate Armand about his exploits."

"Always the one for intrigue." Armand took his little sister under his arm. But his hand slipped down to her waist before Min could stop him. "What's this?" He held up the cut reins and they uncoiled to the ground like a sun-dried snake carcass.

"Er—"

Armand's dark eyes grew wide beneath the spray of fashionably curled hair that washed over his shoulders. He clenched the leather as tightly as his teeth. "These are carriage reins. Where did you get them?"

Min flinched at Armand's look. She cast a pleading glance toward Alexandre in hopes that he would speak for her. But he remained silent as he gathered his drawing tools. He was always so irritatingly impartial.

"I asked where you got them."

Don't tell Armand . . .

Min bit her lower lip. "I, er, well . . ."

"You've been out with Adrian!" Armand's voice boomed in the still of the fog and candle flame. "Have you not?"

She wanted to simply whisper "not," but she was never good at telling lies. Especially when her eldest brother was looking so sternly at her.

"I know you have. Always, he cuts the reins!" Armand turned and stalked towards the château.

Min followed on his heels, her spurs kicking up tiny tufts of grass behind her. She couldn't let Adrian take the blame. He had never planned the robbery. Heaven knew, she had only wanted to talk to him. But when the opportunity had presented itself . . . well, she had pressed Adrian to let her try her hand at thievery. Odd how the heat of the moment provided for irrational thinking.

"It just happened," she pleaded to her brother's back as she scrambled after him. "He's not to blame, Armand. I begged him! I wanted to know what it was like."

Armand's furious pace took him through the house and to the bottom of the stairwell, where a great path of faded emerald carpeting began its snaking journey upwards. "Adrian!"

Their housemaid, Camille, scurried in to take Armand's black woolen cape and leather gloves, then quickly sped away.

Off in the hearth room, the cries of a tiny baby matched the incessant coos of a frantic female voice. Min ground her jaw, knowing from the wails that her sister-in-law was still up nursing the twins. It was just what Sophie enjoyed most—seeing her in trouble, and lots of it.

Adrian appeared at the top of the stairs in a paisley dressing gown and slippers, his wet hair resting limply on his shoulders. He smiled to see his oft-absent brother. But the smile fell from his face when he saw the fury in Armand's eyes.

"You've taken her with you!" Armand shook the severed reins before him, the signature of Adrian's highway robberies. He cut the horse's reins to ensure that his victims would not take chase.

Min cringed as she caught Adrian's cruel glance. She could hear his silent accusation: *How* could *you?*

"I never planned it," Adrian defended himself.

"He didn't," Min offered feebly.

"She was just there—"

"Just there?" Armand whipped the reins against the bottom stair and the loud crack made Min jump. "Why did you do it at all? Have I not told you many times before that you were never to bring her along on any of these—these midnight prowlings of yours?"

Adrian chuckled and casually passed his brother, walking into the hearth room where Camille had started a fire. "They are your midnight prowlings too, Armand," he called over his shoulder.

"I was well disguised," Min pleaded to Armand's damasked back.

"We were very discreet," Adrian explained. "No one will know."

"No one will know?" Armand threw the reins at Adrian's slippered feet and reached behind him to grab Min by the shoulders. Min felt like a string of sausage on display at a butcher's shop as she was thrust forward for all to examine. "She's but a girl! A very young and misguided girl who does not need to become a criminal like her brothers." Min twisted her shoulders in protest, but Armand's firm hold persisted. "Look at her! What do you see?"

Sophie, one twin still at her breast, stood and sauntered across the room, her wrinkled heather skirts dusting the floor. Min felt her fingernails dig into her palms. Oh, how she despised Sophie! The woman had not once been kind to her since marrying Alexandre a year ago. A displaced Parisian tart sulking in the country air, she was.

"I see," Sophie drawled, her dark-circled eyes falling cruelly upon Min, "a bespattered little *garçon.*"

"Exactly!" Armand agreed. "We've turned the little ragamuffin into a boy! This body has never seen fine lace or known the elegant manners of a refined lady."

"I don't like those stuffy dresses," Min chimed in her defense. "You'll never get me to wear one."

"You see!" Armand looked to say more, but finally he could only shake his head and pace before the fire, his back to Min and her cohort.

"You promised you wouldn't tell," Adrian whispered while keeping a keen eye on his brother's stiff shoulders.

"I didn't," Min hissed. "He saw me with the reins. I didn't know what to say."

"She means"—like a grass snake, Sophie appeared over Adrian's shoulder, her golden eyes glinting with a gleeful menace—"she never has been a good liar."

"Coming from an expert?" Min spat sarcastically.

Sophie smirked at Min, the satisfaction at seeing her under such vicious scrutiny turning her thin lips into a semblance of a smile.

"What is all the commotion?" Alexandre appeared, pushing a dirt-smeared hand through his flyaway hair, which released a sprig of green leaf to the floor. He pressed a fatherly palm to the head of the infant nursing at Sophie's breast, though his retraction was a bit too quick for Sophie's eager fingers to grasp his.

"It seems Armand has had a change of mind regarding our dear Mignonne," Adrian offered. "What's fit for the gander is not fit for the goose."

"He wants me to start wearing dresses," Min complained.

Alexandre's eyes widened beneath bushy brows, though he couldn't disguise his mirth.

"She means"—Sophie slithered up behind Alexandre—"he wants her to become a member of the female population. How else will she ever be considered for betrothal?"

Armand swung around. "Thanks to the LaChaize widows, I've now enough money for her dowry—"

"Dowry?" Min had known it was coming. But not so quickly!

"Yes," Armand said. "I've been talking to the Montesquies of Bigorre. We may be able to make your betrothal yet this summer. That is . . ." He did nothing to disguise his disgust with her appearance. "If you can ever learn to act as a lady. The Montesquies are of the *noblesse de epée.*"

"Bosh! And so are we, if you remember. But I see the years of thievery have clouded your memory. I don't want to be a lady," Min proclaimed. "And I will not marry a man I have never seen, nor one I do not love. I want freedom. The same freedom I've had since birth. Ladies do not have freedom. Their entire life is a sacrifice." She cast a disgusted glance towards Sophie. "They are imprisoned by their clothes, by the expectations of society, by their men. I won't have it, I just won't!"

A burst of pride shuddered through Min, lacing her voice with a brave confidence. "I seek a far more honest profession than you or Adrian have chosen. I want to become a musketeer!"

Deafening silence filled the room. Sudden regret stiffened Min's neck. She jerked her gaze from one opened-mouth face to another. *Fools,* she thought. *They will never understand this desire that burns deep within me. Why did I tell?*

"A musketeer? *You?*" Armand broke the silence with a rash of sarcastic laughter.

"Madness," Sophie hissed.

"You could never."

"I can." Min matched Armand's defiant poise as well as she could. The fact that he towered a head above her own petite figure made it a challenge. But a thrust of her chin made her feel a bit taller.

"You," Armand spat at her, "obviously have not looked in a mirror lately. The musketeers would have you in their ranks," he said, grinning, "but not for fighting purposes."

"Armand," Alexandre reprimanded.

Armand waved his brother off with a curt hand. "She needs an education in domesticity. Mignonne must learn how to be a lady. She needs a man to take care of—"

"A man?" Min pulled away from Armand's grasp and smeared her hands down the front of her breeches, leaving a dirty trail on the studded tan chamois. "Whatever should I need a man for? I can do anything a man can do. And even better than most! I've no need to be taken care of, thank you."

"And do you think Adrian and I can work the high roads forever?" Tension pulsed Armand's jaw and fire flashed in his coal-dark eyes. "It's hard enough that we have the twins to support. 'Tis high time we secured a betrothal for you. But that will never happen in your present . . . condition."

"My con—"

"First," Armand continued, "you need some taming. And I know just the thing that will do it." He thrust his hands before him, as if presenting a great gift to the king, and laid his revelation upon the family. "We shall take her to a convent."

"What!" Min felt as if her jaw would touch her neck.

"A convent?" Adrian and Alexandre both chimed.

"Oh, yes," Sophie chuckled.

" 'Tis the only way. Do you not see what we've done?"

Too shocked to react, Min felt her body move against its will as Armand placed firm hands on her shoulders and turned her towards her other brothers for inspection in the glowing light of the fire. Clots of dirt fell at her feet as she felt her brother mess about with the fragile pins tangled in her hair.

"Look here," Armand said. "Who will have her? She is a savage. She is unmarriageable. She eats, acts, thinks, and sleeps like a man. She rides horses astride, fights like an alley cat, and can out-fence any master I know. Over the years, we have been so busy with ourselves that we've been completely blind to our *petite* one. And now this musketeer nonsense."

"But Father was a musketeer!" Min managed to snap.

"Perhaps it isn't nonsense," Adrian meekly interjected. "We could—"

Armand stifled his younger brother's words with an icy glare. "I won't have you bring that up again. It's over. The tradition died with our father."

Swallowing, Adrian acquiesced with a regretful nod and stepped to Alexandre's side before the hearth.

Armand turned his gaze on Min. "Father was a man. Men serve in the king's guards. Not women. You, my untamed spitfire of a sister, must now look to domesticating yourself—"

"I won't go to a convent!" Min declared and crossed her arms over her soiled clothes. "You'll have to drag me behind a herd of cows to make me go. And even then I would rather die."

"Don't you think a convent is a little harsh?" Alexandre interjected. "Perhaps if we leave her to Sophie—"

"Oh, no." Min cast a glare at the smirking woman. Sophie returned the look with deadly daggers.

Armand pushed a hand through his hair, ending in a sharp slice through the air. "No. I have thought on this for months now. There is Aunt Huguette."

"Aunt Huguette?" Min cried. "But she's—"

"She is Mother Superior at Val-de-Grâce," Alexandre finished, in shock.

"Yes, that is it! She can help us."

"Aunt Huguette is a vicious old witch. My knuckles still ache to recall that cane of hers."

"Well, if you had stayed out of her rose garden . . ." Adrian said on a chuckle.

Min stomped her boot. She couldn't believe they were actually holding this inane conversation. She'd grown up running in the footsteps of her brothers. Hers was a life of freedom and discovery, each day bringing new wonders and yet another task she could learn and perform better than any male. She knew nothing else. And now, all of a sudden, they thought to change her? In a pig's eye!

"Whatever can some frumpy old nuns teach me that I cannot learn by observing my brothers or the maids?"

Sophie opened her mouth to speak but was silenced with a look from Min.

"Manners," Alexandre interjected thoughtfully. He counted off on his green-stained fingers. "Writing, Latin, embroidery, obedience—"

"Obedience?" Min stalked over to Alexandre. "You approve of this? How can you? And you, Adrian." She turned on her brother. "Stop him. This is preposterous!"

"She does know a few things," Adrian said with a shrug. "Even I do not know the meaning of preposterous."

A spew of delirious giggles erupted from Sophie, but stopped abruptly when Min flashed her another silencing glare. "She could use some taming," the bedraggled mother pouted.

"It is settled," Armand announced. "We leave for Val-de-Grâce at daybreak."

Chapter Two

A spur to Petit Feu's flank took Min across an ankle-deep stream. She figured she had a good four hours on her brothers, for their midnight excursions made them late sleepers. Unless, of course, Armand was serious about his daybreak announcement and was hell-bent on delivering her to Val-de-Grâce before drinking his morning chocolate. Armand would be leading the trio with fire in his eyes and a chastity belt in hand when her escape was discovered.

But she had been given no other option. It was ridiculous that Armand should suggest such a thing. The convent? God's body, where had that come from? 'Twould be a fate worse than the Bastille. If she were to marry—a fate she had not entirely ruled out—the man would have to accept her as she was, lack of feminine graces and all.

Besides, no musketeer had ever broken morning matins to fend off the enemy and then made it back to the chapel in time for evening prayer.

She pulled out a folded piece of vellum from inside her doublet. The blue wax seal had long fallen away, and one corner was burned to a serrated black border. Though addressed to Armand Saint-Sylvestre and tossed with little regard into a simmering hearth months ago, the letter was her key to securing a position in the King's Grand Musketeers. She could still recall Armand's sullen decision just over a year ago, on the eve that Alexandre had announced his plans to marry. . . .

"Alexandre will always do what he deems the right thing," Adrian had said, as Min listened from the hallway, unannounced to either of her brothers.

"It is unfortunate for him," Armand said as he tapped his upper lip with a folded letter. "I truly hope his studies do not suffer because of the added responsibility. Damn that city whore for trapping him in such a ruse!"

"You know a man is as much to blame in such a case."

"Yes, well . . ."

Min had peeked around the doorframe to see Armand squat before the hearth. She cringed to see him hold the letter over the glowing coals, a letter he had read aloud to her upon its receipt weeks ago. Sent by Captain d'Artagnan, it granted Armand a commission to serve in the king's household troops.

"With these new additions to the family," Armand said, "I've more work than ever before me. I'll have to use the money I've saved for our sister's dowry for the wedding and the forthcoming infant. I don't think I'll be needing this anymore."

Min watched the letter fall to the sooty brick of the hearth, just out of reach of the sizzling wood.

"A musketeer's wages will barely feed one, as we have already learned from the great riches that never did befall Father."

Her back to the wall and her eyes shut tight, Min had

listened as both brothers strode out of the hearth room. She peeked around the corner, saw the room was empty, and dashed across the room just as the folded letter took to flame. . . .

Now Armand's words were a heavy burden to bear when all Min could think to do was carry on the tradition of serving in the king's musketeers. Her sigh pierced the fresh morning breeze as her thoughts turned to her own desires. To become a musketeer . . .

Musketeers were dashing, brave, sword-wielding heroes who fought without fear for the honor and glory of their king. So regal and chivalrous they were!

Her father had been a musketeer like his father before him, and before *him* . . . The tradition dated back to the inception of the musketeers. Commissioned by the king, Antoine Saint-Sylvestre had served his holy ruler to the death. Min had not seen much of her father after her fifth birthday due to his duties to Louis XIII. But he held a strong place in her heart. The image of her father, home on leave, dressed in the musketeer mantle festooned with cross and fleur-de-lis and wielding a sword, was like a religious icon Min revered and honored.

Ah, to be looked upon with such pride.

Antoine Saint-Sylvestre's death was still a mystery to her. Most likely, cutthroats had overtaken him, for his pockets were bare and his sword and musketeer mantle stolen, along with his boots. At least that was what Alexandre had explained. Captain d'Artagnan sent his regrets, and months later, his commission offer arrived for Armand.

Unfortunate as Father's death was, it was not uncommon for a lone traveler, even a trained musketeer, to fall victim to cutthroats. Min would miss him always, and to honor Antoine Saint-Sylvestre's memory was the only future that filled her thoughts and dreams.

"But there will always be the one thing standing in my way," she muttered.

It was unthinkable for a woman to join a regiment. Indeed, it was positively suicidal. Even if a woman were able to infiltrate the ranks of the military, society would be scandalized. Not that Min gave a whit for society and their foppish standards regarding manners, dress, and social standing. That was Sophie's calling.

"I can do this," she declared, drawing a proud breath through her nose, though she hadn't really planned a course of action; she'd been pressed to leave quickly or lose all chance of ever fulfilling her dreams.

She pressed a kiss to the folded letter and slipped it inside her doublet, next to her heart. "I will do this. I can accept marriage—even a loveless match—but never the convent. Before such a fate befalls me, I'll show Armand and the others that I have what it takes to follow in our father's footsteps. The life of a highwayman is not for me. You'll see, Armand—it is not the life for you, either."

"It is the gypsy blood from Mama's veins!" he'd once told her.

Bah! Min knew otherwise. Armand had adopted that excuse as a means of justifying the brothers' new occupation. Early on, thanks to their father's frequent campaigns and meager wages, Armand had had no choice but to put aside his aspirations of becoming a musketeer and take to the high roads to steal for a living. It was either that or work the fields and send Min and Adrian off to the orphanage. Fortunately, at the time Armand had been firmly against subjecting his family to such drastic separation.

But Min knew it was not their mother's blood that had lured the brothers to the road. At first it was need. Antoine Saint-Sylvestre had bequeathed more glory than wealth to his children. It was to be expected. His duties were to the king, not his family. And after his death, all Saint-Sylvestre land, save a few acres and the château, had to be sold to appease the tax collectors. Armand and Adrian had had to work the roads four or five times a month to achieve that goal.

But now thievery was no longer necessary to eat and survive. They lived well, the twins were clothed, and the servants were paid. Min believed that it had become a kind of sport, a game her brothers played to prove it still possible.

And now Armand had enough for her dowry, a carrot to wiggle under some fop's nose to secure her betrothal.

"Please, not a fop," she whispered. "If marriage befalls me, pray the man offers a challenge to my heart."

The sun was high in the sky by the time Min came upon the chance to put some food in her grumbling stomach. Ivory windmill sails flapped in the July breeze, and a sparkling splash from a fresh water pond kissed the stones along the shore. A delicate giggle, quite unexpected this far from a village, caught Min's ear. She walked Petit Feu beneath the dark cover of a twisted walnut tree and peered between the green foliage.

There, on a sloping bank below the windmill, a young couple picnicked in the shifting shadows of the sails. A gentle breeze carried the heady aroma of dark pumpernickel bread Min's way. The smell of baked bread always gave her a warm, safe feeling. And the wine, the sweet smell of deep, blue grapes . . . Oh, she could practically feel the thirst-quenching liquid slip down her throat.

Min pressed her hand to her stomach to stifle the incessant groans. " 'Twas foolish not to pack a meal."

A blanket had been spread across the grass, and on that, a young rake dressed in ribboned petticoat breeches and slashed doublet, lay on his back, while his lady fed him bits of the bread with her teeth.

Her teeth? Min blew a tickling leaf from her cheek and nudged her nose through the surrounding frame of leaves for a better look. How absurd. Shoving food into a man's mouth when the woman could be gobbling up the loaf herself.

Min squinted to better assess the situation. The dress the woman wore was sewn so tight, her bosom was almost in her face—or more truthfully, the man's face. The plump mounds were less than a hand's width from his eyes. Suddenly, the bread was forgotten. Throaty chuckles saturated the air. The first lacing was undone from the woman's stays thanks to the man's deft hands. Roaming fingertips encircled the jiggling globes with lusty intentions.

"Hmmph. I would never behave so ridiculously for a man," she muttered.

But she couldn't resist lingering over the silly, romantic frivolity.

I wonder what it's like? To kiss a man.

Would the touch of a lover's lips steal her very breath away, as Adrian so often put it? Would she long for one kiss and then another? Were a man's lips as soft as her own? What would a kiss taste like? Would she even know how to return the kiss?

The man, quite unaware of Min's observations, smoothed his fingers over the mounds of flesh that hung before his face. The woman let out a strange gasp and tossed her head back, as if she enjoyed the man's scandalous touch.

What of a man's touch upon her breasts?

Min cupped her hands to her chest. Her heart beat faster and a tickle of sweat trailed down her stomach. Though her breasts were generous, she wore a scarf to flatten them so that under a billowing shirt, leather vest, and doublet they would hardly be detected. A necessary masquerade, if she hoped to secure a position in the musketeers.

She ran her tongue over her lower lip, wondering, fantasizing the feel of the rogue's lips on hers. She might like to try a kiss sometime. . . . With a handsome soldier. After he had defeated the enemy and rescued her—

A jerk of her neck snapped Min out of her roaming thoughts. What was this? No, no *no!* After *she* had rescued *him.* Yes, indeed. She needed no man to come to her aid. Ah! What was she doing? Did such a scene make her weak in the stomach? Here she sat fantasizing and wishing she knew the touch of a man's lips!

"Nonsense," she muttered, brushing the back of her hand across her mouth, unconsciously wiping away her fantasy kiss. "I am merely starving. I need to know the touch of bread on my lips."

Pulling the long black scarf she wore around her neck up over her nose, Min dashed from her hiding spot and mounted Petit Feu. With sword in hand she spurred her horse onward and galloped over to the two. The lady gave a frightful cry and gripped the remaining half loaf, weaponlike, in her fist. Her suitor jumped to his feet and, with a comical struggle, finally managed to unsheathe his rapier from the gaudily beribboned swordbelt he wore.

Stupid fop, Min thought.

With a deft flick of her wrist, Min's sword pierced the hilt of his rapier and sent it flying. It landed with a plop and a splash in the pond behind them. The lovesick rogue stared incredulously at his hand. Quickly, she procured her dagger from her boot and held that, too, on the man.

"Oh!" the woman cried. "Please, take my jewels. We want no trouble." She began to unfasten the emerald brooch at her breast.

"Geneviéve," the man hissed. Under the threat of Min's sword he was reluctant to move. He held his hands before him, casting a discerning gaze over Min, as if to memorize the features he could see above her scarf.

Min lowered her voice. When she spoke it came out as a harsh whisper. "I've no need of your jewels, mademoiselle."

Hearth-roasted pumpernickel tickled Min's nose. The aroma of bread and wine was too strong to resist. Sure the fop would remain still, Min leaned forward and expertly speared the loaf of bread the woman held with the end of her sword. "This will do."

Chapter Three

At the unexpected sound of a lady's scream, Chevalier Chancery Lambert lifted his head from the sun-warmed stream and gave it a good shake. Set into motion after years of being constantly at the ready, Chance grabbed his thin lawn shirt and slipped his arms through the sleeves. Urgent fire rushed through his veins, setting his instincts to a sharp edge. He stuffed his feet into his boots and grabbed his sword. As much as he preferred to tend to his own duties, he was a soldier.

Toujours prêt! Always ready!

He shook his head vigorously, sending a spray of droplets across his horse's flank. "Barely a moment to myself," he grumbled as he mounted the charcoal Friesian. "So it goes." He pulled his plumed beaver hat down over his brow and spurred on the stallion.

Words escaped him as Chance came upon the situation. He reined his steed to a halt. The cause of the scream was a small-boned young thing, a mere child. Yet he held his victims at sword point. *No pistol?* How original. Most highwaymen were never without a pistol. Must be a naive urchin with dreams of great riches and no more sense than a beheaded cock running about the farmyard.

With a spur to his horse's flanks, Chance headed in for the rescue.

"Throw down your weapon!"

The highwayman startled at his surprise, but kept his dagger trained on the dandy in the beribboned lilac doublet.

"Settle your hat, monsieur, he means us no harm," reassured the dandy's paramour as Chance rode up alongside her. Her beau hissed at her.

Chance couldn't help but do a double take. The woman's tightly cinched bodice exposed her assets well. No wonder the fop's face was so red. Though there were signs of a picnic, it was evident the dandy had been sampling something much tastier.

Chance narrowed his eyes against the bright sunlight. There was something speared upon the end of the robber's rapier. A . . . loaf of bread. What the deuce? This was certainly an original *modus operandi*. Starve your victims as well as robbing them?

Clumps of soil and grass flew into the air as the robber spurred his mount and sped away.

"Did he harm you?" Chance asked, but he did not remain to hear a reply. He'd had enough of the criminals that ravaged the countryside. They were like a vat of slippery eels spilled across wet sand, slithering about in a great twist of foul darkness. They deserved to die a cruel death, as an eel did in the heat of the sun. For it was highwaymen who had committed the ultimate betrayal against him.

Bittersweet memories invaded Chance's subconscious without warning. *Justine. Pensez à moi,* came her sweet whispery voice. *Yes, I always think of you.* His sweet, vindictive

Justine. Perhaps that had been the worst betrayal. She'd played him for a fool, but not before stealing his heart.

Determined to spend no more memory on her wicked ways than necessary, Chance pressed his jaw tight in determination and focused on the retreating criminal. That one was going to pay if he had to hound him all the way to Spain.

The robber's horse was a black roan mare with agility and speed, but it was no match for the mount beneath Chance's legs. A gift from King Louis XIV, his was a fine destrier bred for speed, strength, and battle prowess. Chance dug in his spurs and gained the other. Soft green leaves flicked across his cheeks and exposed chest as he raced through the forest in close pursuit.

Chance reached for his pistol, but his fingers hooked in an empty hip belt. "Damn!" He must have left it by the stream. He had taken it out to prime. But he was never without his sword; it was like a third arm to a man of his profession. He pulled his steel free and thrust it across the headstall between his mount's ears, gifting his steed with a vicious, horn-like weapon. "Stop! I demand in the name of the king!"

The robber's horse whinnied and suddenly misstepped, sending the rider over its head.

Chance jumped from his horse and raced to the tangled heap of limbs lying on a carpet of tight moss. The robber's legs lay spread wide, one arm stretched above his head, the other tucked near his hip. He'd been knocked out cold. He wore a black leather doublet slashed once on each arm to reveal a shirt with fine gold stitching poking out at the cuffs. On his folded leather boots were mud-spattered spurs, and his hat, to Chance's amazement, was still pulled tightly over his head.

Chance smoothed his fingers across his mustache and rubbed a thumb over his smudge of beard. Fine clothing, though not garish in any way. Not an outfit a petty robber would wear. It had to be stolen. The urge to draw his sword and ram it through the robber's heart tensed the muscles in his neck and coiled about his heart with vicious disregard.

Somewhere overhead, a crow cawed, and a gentle breeze sifted a few moist summer leaves to the ground. And with it came Justine's voice . . . *I always loved you, Chancery. But it is so difficult to remain exclusive to one man. I am so bored. I shall do as I wish. You cannot stop me.*

"No," Chance whispered, reining a tight rope about the vengeful anger that always rose with the memories. "She did love me once. Violence is not the way to erase her betrayal."

Chance bent to pull the scarf from the robber's face. But the slash of sharpened steel sent him stumbling backward.

Min sprang to her feet like a fairy taken to air. Though her spine ached, she stood prepared to defend herself, showing no signs of injury from the fall. Sword and dagger held steady before her, her eyes darted from the man's face to the nearby horses and back to her pursuer.

She hadn't expected him to be fool enough to follow her. Pray to the saints, he was not as skilled with his sword as he was on his horse.

"You are under arrest in the name of the king," he proclaimed in a gruff bark. "Surrender your weapons."

Min's eyes darted over the man's disarray, the deep vee in his opened shirt, the tense muscle pulsing in his jaw, and the short, wet hair that sprang up at odd angles all over his head. The feet of his boots were wet, the knees of his breeches, as well. "You do not resemble a king. You jest."

With that she lunged forward, delivering a close call to his left shoulder. Their swords clashed in a ring of steel and hissed through the air with blinding speed. When their blades engaged, Min quickly prepared her next move. As taught by Armand, she had learned to gauge her opponent's reactions and judge his next move by the subtle tremors felt in her blade.

Chance backed his opponent across a large jagged rock. Dammit, he was impressed. The boy hadn't even had to look back to sense the obstruction; it was as if he had eyes in the back of his head. And still, he never failed to parry every move Chance pressed on him. His movements were small, precise, and deadly. For a miscreant, he fenced so gracefully.

No simple country urchin would know such moves and fight with obvious skill. Perhaps he was not so young as he appeared. Chance stole another glance at his masked face. Not much to see in the shadow of his hat-brim save dark, dancing eyes, almost—

A great whoosh cut the air and Chance felt a searing heat burn across his forearm. Crimson bloomed on his linen shirt. "Fie!"

How had he let his guard down for that? He was rarely bettered by any man, let alone such a puny thing as danced before him now. An imp he was; the devil's pitchfork was his weapon.

Setting his jaw, Chance delivered a thrust above his opponent's dagger, only to have it halted. He thrust again and again, each time the robber matching his movements with the greatest ease and glittering eyes. It was as if the boy were taking great joy in this duel. In fact, he laughed!

"You give your lunge away, monsieur."

"What?" A country urchin giving him, a king's musketeer, fencing advice? "How dare you!"

"You tilt your head," he said with a laugh. "Such an obvious signal."

"Blast!" Signal his lunge? He did not! *Did he?*

Chance pressed his opponent closer to the forest border,

where tall grasses would impede his steps. He wished he could get a better look at the face behind the kerchief. There was something about this child. So delicate his mirthful eyes, and the lashes so long. And so tiny his frame! Despite his skill, he had to be a mere boy, for surely a man's shoulders would be wider and his legs and arms much thicker. As it was, his slight figure put him at the advantage, allowing him to easily dodge Chance's best advances.

"I took nothing from them other than food," the boy suddenly proclaimed.

Yes, surely he was quite young. His voice was still as soft and fine as a lady's. Fie! A mere child dare challenge him?

His anger renewed by the boy's audacity, Chance fended off a deadly lunge to his chest. He was in no mood to go easy on his opponent simply because he was a senseless brat. "You have stolen. An offense punishable by the removal of the offending body part."

"Ha!" The boy lunged and succeeded in slicing through the thigh of Chance's chamois breeches. He bit down on the inside of his cheek. Damn, this insufferable child! He'd had enough!

Chance acted quickly, his abandonment of the fight surprising the miscreant. Plunging forward into the boy's chest, Chance knocked the frail thing to the ground. "That'll serve you." He lay atop the robber, his hands pressed to his chest to keep him at bay, his legs struggling to pin down his opponent's. It was when Chance suddenly squeezed his hands that he realized something very odd. The boy, er—*What?*

Like a demon spat forth from hell's bowels, Chance sprang upright.

The boy scrambled to his feet amidst an amazing stream of curses. He snatched up his hat and quickly pulled it over his generous piling of hair. "Bastard! You might have broken my bones! That's not how a gentleman duels at all!"

Chance stood frigid, blindly ignorant of the boy's ranting. He examined his hands, quite shocked over what he had just touched. The child's chest was surely *plump.*

"Insolent buffoon!" proclaimed the robber in his weak, girlish voice, and then ran for his horse.

How confusing. Who or *what* was this strange creature with the foul mouth and raging eyes? He fought with the agility and experience of a master, yet his body was that of a . . . a . . .

Dumbfounded awe held Chance to his place. He squeezed the air before him, imagining the flesh of a—woman?—between his fingers.

As the boy mounted, he jerked his head towards the dumbstruck musketeer. A few clumps of long dark hair had fallen from behind his hat. For a moment, Chance saw a lovely young woman with dancing eyes instead of the foul-mouthed creature that had succeeded in disarming him.

A woman? *"Impossible."*

The robber turned his mare and galloped off, leaving behind a slip of darkness. Chance stepped over to retrieve a ribbon from the carpet of moss. Black moiré.

Absently threading the ribbon through his fingers, Chance watched the robber's retreat. A *woman.* An exceedingly feisty, strong-mouthed woman. Hmm . . .

His musketeer's intuition told him to forget this incident. He had other things to worry about. *Mount your horse and return for your things by the stream.* But his male voice, a lusty one deep within him, couldn't resist wondering. Was he truly . . . a *she?*

* * *

Deep jutting shadows from towering poplars grew across the cooling blades of summer grass. The air was heavy with the perfume of greens, dirt, and horse sweat. Petit Feu's gait slowed to a walk. The mare needed water and rest. Indeed, Min also needed something to appease her growling insides. She had been on the road since early morning, and her stomach still would not let her forget that she had left the bread behind after her robbery attempt had been thwarted by that insolent man.

That man.

Min found that if she closed her eyes, his face appeared before her like a ghost haunting her thoughts. A face of steely determination, with thick lips framed by a thin mustache and goatee of the same sun-burnished brown as his short-cropped hair. Odd that he did not wear his hair long, as was the fashion; but it was not unattractive.

He had been dressed in black from boots to breeches, his plain white shirt unlaced to reveal sun-bronzed flesh. Min still could not shake the startling warmth she'd felt as her hand had grazed over his chest when struggling with him. Were all men so firm and hot, like fire-honed steel? And the smooth, dark hairs that covered his chest—they were so fine and soft. Her brothers had none of this tantalizing softness on their chests.

And when he lay on top of her, pinning her, for a brief moment of madness she had fallen captive to his mystical gaze. He had eyes of sky blue, flecked with darker spots of cobalt.

He'd appeared almost frightened before he'd sprung from her. As if she were fire itself. And then he'd stood so confused, staring at his hands as if she had really singed him.

He couldn't know he had dueled against a woman. Could he?

Ah, but maybe she had sparked a flame. It certainly felt possible to Min. Her heart beat at a thundering pace. Her toes curled inside her boots. A delicious warmth prickled her cheeks. . . .

Min bolted upright on the saddle, her rambling thoughts shocking her to alertness. *Mon Dieu,* she must stay on her guard! What was it about this man that she could not shake from her thoughts?

Min turned on Petit Feu and scanned the horizon for the silhouette that had been following her for hours. He was there. It was madness that he followed her, never gaining, nor falling too far behind.

What did he want of her? Round two? Death?

She smiled and spurred Petit Feu. "Perhaps he likes to play with fire."

How the boy/girl creature had slipped from his sight he would never know.

Chance's thoughts ran the gamut. He could not think straight, let alone see correctly. It was not a mere girl! Impossible. Women simply hadn't the strength or skill to fight as the robber had. It had to be a *garçon,* if a rather oddly shaped one.

Avoiding the open high road, Chance rode his stallion along a copse of fragrant orange pine, eyeing carefully every movement from within the thick brush that grew up around the trees. His senses were honed to pick up anything out of the ordinary. Off in the distance, farmers worked their fields, their long scythes clicking in soft rhythm. The sweet scent of burning peat carried for leagues. Branches snapped at the leap of a squirrel and leaves rustled against one another. But there was no sight or sound of the robber.

It would be dark soon; the sun was but a sliver of gold on the horizon. Confound it, he was slipping!

His fingers curled about the stallion's reins. This was insanity. How had the miscreant been able to give him the slip? He, Chancery Lambert, lieutenant of Les Mousquetaires Noirs!

"I need to return to Paris," Chance muttered. "Two days away from the king and I have become a lackwit."

But he would not return until his personal mission was complete. It was fortunate that Captain d'Artagnan had persuaded the king to allow him a fortnight's leave. He needed this time alone. Time to think. Time to rebuild and restart after . . .

Justine.

Much as her cruel indifference to his emotions had ripped the very heart from his chest, her abduction and murder by a band of highwaymen could not go unpunished. Justine had been a human being. She deserved as much—at least a proper burial. Though the carriage she'd been traveling in had been found, the interior spattered with blood and scraps of her clothing, her body had mysteriously been missing.

Why anyone would want to take a dead body along after such a hideous act was beyond Chance. But he was determined to find her murderer, or murderers. Thanks to a scurrilous night questioning the inhabitants of the Bastille, Chance had narrowed his search down to a band of highwaymen that called themselves the Notorious Ones. Their leader was rumored to be a small man of dark hair and eyes. Some said he was an Italian, others, a Spaniard. All agreed he was most likely to acquire a dead body. Why, no one cared to wager. Nor did Chance care to know. But he would find him. For Justine's sake.

My wicked Justine.

Why he gave her even a moment of thought was beyond him. He had been so desperately in love. She had been so cruel. But for as much as he reasoned her deserving of her fate, he would forever regret his final words to her: "I consign you to rot in hell!"

Chance felt a swallow catch in his throat. He straightened in the saddle, thrust his shoulders squarely back, and spurred his horse onward. He was thirsty, dammit, that was all. He would never let his emotions interfere with a mission.

But his mission would never begin until he saw to it that damned bread-stealing urchin was put away or seen safely to his father's home. He was too young to be running wild, robbing as he pleased, and possibly harming innocent folk.

But was the *garçon* really a boy?

Chance recalled the soft mounds he had pressed beneath his palms. Boys were never so fleshy as that! And the strangely dulcet voice and dancing eyes—surely it was a female in disguise. And if so, then truly he must see to her safety. The dark roads were no place for an unescorted young woman. Especially with the likes of the Notorious Ones riding rampant.

But where to find her? After returning to the stream to retrieve his pistol, he had easily picked up her trail and kept her in his sight for the next two hours. One simple sneeze had blackened his vision for mere seconds. When he looked up, she had disappeared.

Where was the pitchfork-wielding imp?

Chance let out a yelp as his shoulders took on a falling weight and he toppled from his horse.

Chapter Four

Chance had the sense not to struggle. Instead, he swallowed—carefully. Each shallow breath pushed his Adam's apple against the sharp blade of ebony steel expertly wielded by his aggressor.

The flight from above had sent the highwayman's hat flying. Great masses of thick, curling hair tumbled over narrow shoulders. Suddenly Chance saw things with perfect clarity.

"I knew it," he managed with the utmost delicacy.

"Silence!" The robber dared to drag the tip of her dagger across his flesh.

Chance felt his skin split. A trickle of blood wound a hot path to his shirt. Damn the imp! What the hell was she up to? *She!* Blessed mother, this was not happening. To be overtaken by a—why, a mere *woman.*

"Why is it that you follow me?" she hissed in her altered, husky voice. "Hmm? Are you mad?"

Chance held his tongue. The creature's eyes were of

darkest chocolate, as black as the bittersweet confections he so hated. But there was a sparkle of white in the centers, a bit of sugar to sweeten the bitterness. His attention grew fierce as she sized up her prey, running her tongue over her lower lip. A lip as plump as a meadow-fresh peach and deserving of a bruising kiss. So curiously enticing. Most certainly not a boy as he had once thought. No boy had such soft skin and such a delicate jawline, like a finely crafted Dresden doll. But no doll had ever attacked him from above and then dared hold him at knifepoint!

"I asked you a question," she barked, becoming impatient. Her eyes were vivid beacons, not missing a single flinch or cocked brow.

She *was* that feisty. Chance couldn't help but smile. He rather liked a feisty woman— What was he doing? Thinking with his cock instead of his brain. He'd allowed himself to care for a woman of such nature once before. And that had produced horrendous results. Never again!

Although, on the other hand, there was nothing wrong with appreciating a beautiful woman. Why, it was a military tradition. *Just look, don't indulge,* he coached that lustful organ that tended to lead him into danger more often than his common sense.

"You begged my silence, mademoiselle," Chance said, taking great care not to rile her. "What is it you want? My silence, or my confession?"

Her eyes flared, glistening with passion. Chance held his breath. Longing stirred in his loins, a reaction he could not, for all his frustration, control. Perhaps he should give the bittersweet chocolates another try?

The robber stood and unsheathed her rapier with such speed that Chance hadn't a second to blink. He now found himself staring down a narrow blade of ebony steel to a hilt of interlaced silver. A fine sword—for a man.

"May I stand?" Chance asked, holding his hands spread open in surrender.

The robber stepped from between his legs and gave a jerk of her head, which set her curls swinging across her shoulders. Oh, yes, not a thing wrong with appreciating beauty. And with some wine and candlelight . . .

"Only if you tell me why you've been following me. What is it you want? Revenge for the paltry morsel of bread I stole from those ridiculous lovebirds?"

"Ahah!" Chance carefully rose to his feet, keeping his hands raised at his sides so she could see he would not reach for his weapon. He wasn't stupid, though his fingers itched to hold his sword to the woman's throat and silence her foolish bravado. "So you admit to your thievery."

"You are delusional, monsieur. I'm the furthest thing from a thief."

"And the furthest thing from a man," he said with a long glance at her attire. "Though you wear the breeches well, I must say, the hair isn't quite right. . . ." His words ended in a hush as he was suddenly taken in by the creature's face. A single thick curl of darkness fell across one bittersweet eye, dangling just above parted peach-sweet lips. Chance forgot his next word. His eyebrows rose, his eyes softened, and his lips parted as if to allow the next fly easy entry.

What he wouldn't pay for a taste of those lips. *Forget the wine and candlelight, on with the debauchery!*

She pushed a hand through her hair, drawing out the strands in search of something. "What is it? Why do you look at me that way?"

Jerking out of his titilating thoughts, Chance narrowed a dark brow on the creature. "What way?"

"That way! Like . . . like . . . I am a pastry under the baker's glass!"

"P-pastry? What? Oh, no, no, my little fool, you've got it all wrong—"

"Have I now?" She backed him across the uneven ground, the blade of her sword pressed to his stomach.

"You have! Pastry, you say? No thank you, I've already eaten today, mademoiselle." He stumbled across a dried clump of mud, but maintained his footing. It was obvious she had no intention of letting him off with so feeble an explanation.

"It seems you've a wandering eye, monsieur. I should warn you, I've three brothers not far behind. They've pistols and are fiercely protective of their sister."

"Mademoiselle! Whatever it is you think you saw in my eyes, it most certainly was not—" He pulled his shoulders straight and stepped back from her sword. "It is only because I, a man, as all can plainly see—"

She thrust an impudent lip at his gesture to himself.

"—am confounded as to why a *petite fille* should choose to masquerade as a boy. Furthermore, why is it that you ride the countryside alone? These brothers three you mention are nowhere in sight." A derisive chuckle welled deep in his throat. "Or is that just a story concocted to protect you from the danger you sense?"

"Danger? From you? Ha!" She batted a nuisance curl from her face and thrust her sword proudly between them. "I can take any man, any day, and he'll be the sorrier for having met me."

Chance crossed his arms and allowed a deep-throated chuckle to escape. A boastful hell-sprung imp, she was. He'd love to take her, that was for sure. But not with the sword he carried in his shoulder belt. "Is that so?"

"Yes, that is so!"

"And that is the reason this tough little spitfire chooses to ravage poor, helpless people for food?"

"They were neither poor nor helpless! The man was a

fop; he could not have defended himself for the deuce. And the woman all but threw herself into my arms."

"I see. So that is the sort of man you can take? A fop?" Chance could not help but laugh. The more infuriated she became, the wider and more enticing her dark eyes grew. Oh, yes, he would purchase a morsel of the bitter-sweet kind as soon as he set foot in Paris.

"No! Oh, you infuriate me, monsieur!"

"As you do I." Chance's gaze wandered down the luxurious carpet of her hair, detouring when he reached the smooth softness of her neck. The warmth that spread through his groin threatened to reveal his debauched thoughts to all. *Keep your wits about you, man. She's a thief, remember? You need not involve yourself with another impetuous, self-serving woman.*

"Pray, tell me where your family is so I may escort you into their hands. The country is no place for a woman. Especially alone! It is swarming with cutthroats and villains of such a nature I dare not even mention them to you."

" 'Tis none of your concern regarding my family. Oh!" The air was sliced with a stab of her dagger, the ground pummeled with a stomp of her foot. "None of this would even be happening had we never robbed that coach!"

"What?"

She flashed him a twisted grimace, her eyes wide with an unrecognizable fury. Or was it fear?

"You admit to robbing a coach?"

"No. Now you will kindly—"

"You just did!" Chance persisted.

"A fantasy, monsieur." She twirled dancing fingers near her ear to illustrate her crazy thoughts. "Sometimes my mind plays tricks on me. I am merely a simple bread thief. Though as you can see, the item in question is painfully absent."

"Because you ate it," he snapped.

"I did not!"

Fury brightened her cheeks to a delicious cherry-stained softness. Much as he should not, he did enjoy this one. Such a temper. Hot-blooded sass just begging to be tamed. Chance wondered briefly if her wild-eyed pride was evident in everything she did. Such as . . . lovemaking?

"I will thank you to leave, monsieur. Unless you plan to arrest me for pilfering a morsel of bread?"

"Chevalier."

"What?"

Bestowing on her his most chivalrous bow, Chance grandly drew his plumed hat along the trampled blades of grass. "Chevalier Chancery Blaise Lambert, mademoiselle. Oh, and I've no plans to arrest you."

"Hmmph." She could not disguise her curious summation of him from head to foot. But just as quickly she snapped her chin up and plopped her hat upon her fallen tresses. With a decisive nod, she said, "Very well, *chevalier.* Hand over your weapons and I shall be off."

Wasn't she the strong-willed sprite? Thinking she could demand that a musketeer hand over his weapon. Of his own volition. Chance's fingers curled about his sword hilt. "No."

"You don't expect me to leave you fully armed so you may attack me later, do you? I don't know what your game is, *chevalier,* but I do not trust that you'll turn and leave after following me nearly eight leagues thus far."

Chance followed her gaze to his horse, and then snapped his eyes back to her. She was a sneaky one.

"You are right there. I have plans to keep you in hand until you are safely returned to your father's side, or your brothers', as the case may be."

"I think not. My brothers would not like it were they to find me in the company of a man."

Chance cocked a brow. She thought to intimidate him

with threats? "I am sure they will not mind. In fact, they will most likely thank me for my attention to your safety."

"This is an exquisite horse, *monsieur le chevalier.*"

"I—" Chance followed her to his horse. Now what was she up to? Hadn't she heard that he was not going to let her out of his sight?

The smooth length of her rapier slid along the Friesian's thick mane. "Yes, he is," he started cautiously, trying to guess her next move. He couldn't shake the sense of mischief that seemed to cloak his opponent like fairy dust. "A very fine horse. Given to me by the king."

She glanced at him, her lithe, graceful fingers smoothing absently over his horse's reins. "The king? Really."

"Given to all in the black regiment."

"The Blacks?" she uttered, her voice fleeing in a fearful whisper. For a worried moment her eyes danced with his before quickly darting away, like an elusive butterfly sprung from the net. "So you are a musketeer."

"Indeed."

"Then are your duties not to the king? I find it most curious a musketeer should stray so far from Paris."

"I am on leave. And at the moment, I find myself with the duty of your protection."

"Protection? Bosh!"

"Yes, protection. Ladies should not be carousing about the countryside in breeches and doublet, pressing an ill-wielded sword to the throat of a stranger who only wishes to offer his kindness." He gripped her by the chin, directing her bewitchingly defiant gaze toward his. "Where are your needle and thread? And pray, tell me your father's name so I may see you safely home before you hurt yourself."

"In a pig's eye!"

"Damn!"

Chance turned and paced across the uneven earth. It

was all he could do to keep himself from rushing over to the imp and gifting her with a crushing kiss. *You did it again! Don't look into those eyes. There is where the real danger lurks. It happened once before . . . with Justine.*

He pressed two fingers to his pulsing temple. Yes, he needed to avoid her eyes and keep to business. But to convince her she needed an escort would be a task. It would be so easy to simply throw her over his shoulder and be done with it. But then what would he do with her? He had no idea from where she had come.

"Follow me now, chevalier!" she called as she mounted her horse and sped away, her long tresses whipping in the wind behind her.

Chance leapt to his horse and reached for the reins. Two short stubs hung from the leather harness. "Blast!" He shook an angry fist above the stallion's head. "You are a vexing one, *petite fille*. But if you think this little prank can hold me off, you'd best think again." Mounting, he pushed his fingers through the Friesian's thick black mane and spurred his horse's flanks.

The cunning schemer would not get away with this. She was crafty and wicked and—blast!—she reminded him of Justine!

Ah, but Justine had never pranced about in such attire. This petite imp was a little girl in boy's clothing. Soft and delicate beneath the tough-talking exterior. She wouldn't be able to fool everyone. And when she did run into trouble, who would help her?

Cursing himself for caring, Chance galloped across the rolling hills in pursuit of the elusive *fille*.

Unrestrained laughter and shouts filled the air. The night was young, and the *fêtes* had begun. Soldiers on leave from campaign were enjoying their freedom, and farmers smelling of manure and laborious sweat had come to town for a tankard of ale and a plump, promiscuous woman.

Min tied Petit Feu up beneath an elm at the edge of the village, Remalard. Across the way a tin sign swayed in the breeze, each creak of the jagged-edged metal setting the hairs on her arms upright. On the sign, a great pink pig rolled in a puddle of mud—The Laughing Sow. Though the creature looked more as if it were drowning than laughing.

Min removed her beaver hat, the black plume shivering with motion, and scratched her fallen curls. She didn't like wearing her hair down. It flowed to her elbows in thick, wavy circlets that either strayed in her eyes or mouth, or landed in her food. It was very bothersome. She would much prefer to cut it all off and be rid of it. But Adrian had always stopped her, saying she must never cut such a treasure.

Treasure? Bosh! It was nothing but a bother.

For safety's sake, she twisted her hair into a chignon and tucked it up under her hat, wondering futilely where she had misplaced the moiré ribbon. But at the moment she was too hungry to care whether all the strands were hidden away.

Sneaking up behind a free-standing stall of horses, Min eyed the commotion across the packed dirt marketplace. A hearty bonfire spit hissed orange sparks into the air. A handful of men milled around it with pewter tankards, fistfuls of roast pig, and legs of greasy fowl. At the sight of the food, Min drew in the smells. Smoke and dust masked any aroma of sustenance. Just as well, she thought glumly, or she would begin to drool.

Women in all states of *déshabillé* draped themselves across the men, quite unmindful of exposed limbs. Others traipsed in and out of the tavern carrying beer and food, which was quickly devoured by the men.

Mmm . . . to devour that man. Tall and confident, handsome and brute.

Min shook off a sudden shiver. How odd. She wasn't cold. What was this?

That man again! His image kept appearing in her mind without her bidding. Yet it wasn't such an awful image. That determined set to his wide jaw. His regal bone structure. A mustache that did not hide but instead highlighted deliciously thick lips and surprisingly white teeth.

Min's blood raced with thoughts of the gallant cavalier, the hairs on her arms prickling to attention beneath the thin linen sleeves. It was an exciting feeling, unexpected and different, clinging about her toes in tingling whispers and dancing up her veins to shudder through her entire body. And *he* made it happen.

That self-assured smile had seemed almost mocking as he'd gently defied her. But it was his deep, rich voice that plunged to the very depths of her being. It was as if each word he spoke was a warm drop of summer rain. And then there was the *pièce de résistance;* his bewitching blue eyes seemed to look right through her own and into her very soul. It was as if his eyes were the heated embers that lay after the fire, smoldering, drawing in air in hopes of blazing yet a moment longer. All-consuming. Those glistening, hungry eyes . . .

Hungry for what?

Min felt sure it most certainly was not pastry that had occupied his thoughts. Though why he'd given her such an odd look was beyond her reckoning

And he was a musketeer! *Mon Dieu,* what would she do now? She had to be very careful not to run into the chevalier again, for her plans would never succeed if he were to discover them. She did not need a musketeer shadowing her every move. Even if he was heart-stoppingly handsome and had a voice that made her toes curl.

"Oh." Min jumped as her self-inflicted pinch brought her out of her crazed thoughts. "What am I doing?"

It would not do to be thinking such things when she had to be on the alert. At the moment there were more important things with which to concern herself. Like eating. And the only place to serve that desire stood across the way. She had to enter the Laughing Sow, as a man. It shouldn't prove a problem. Adrian had always said she could curse and duel as well as the next. And when dressed in men's clothing she could go virtually undetected, walking through a tavern with little or no notice.

But there was one thing—she couldn't swagger. She hadn't taken on the walk of a man, confident and cocky at the same time. Her swaggers always ended up a drunken farce. Not proud and brave, like . . . *him.*

There was no way around it; she had to try, or the men outside would be suspicious. Soused or not, they would see through her disguise.

Min took a step forward, but a little voice inside her head brought her to a halt. *How the deuce do you plan on paying for this glorious meal?*

"Merde," she muttered. She hadn't thought of that. Planning was not her virtue. She'd lived her life as each moment came and enjoyed it, heartily embracing the many challenges that arose. Her brothers had unknowingly honed her life to parallel theirs. Though at the moment, as her stomach groaned unmercifully, she wasn't much up for a challenge.

Min pressed her forehead to the splintered hitching post. One of the horses nudged her cheek with its warm velvet nose. "I'm so hungry I could eat you right now," she whispered, while glancing cautiously over to the tavern. No one had taken notice of her. Perhaps if she waited long enough, she could poke through their scraps. A turkey leg lay beneath a trestle table with a tempting amount of meat still clinging to the bones. Even the dirt, glistening with grease, seemed appealing.

Min absently ran her palm across the nose of the horse, her attention wandering along the tavern front and back to where she hid. Drawing her eyes up the length of the horse's nose, she matched its gaze.

"How interesting." Min leaned back to examine the curious beast, who was amazingly calm and unaffected by her close presence. It was a lovely horse, finely muscled and strong in leg. Its coat was brilliant white, with not a speck of dirt on its legs. Snow on a cloud. Amazing, considering the foul weather France had seen lately. Surely a prize to whoever owned it. But its eyes, instead of a solid black, were foggy gray and surrounded by a wide rim of white. She'd never seen such a curiosity.

A thought struck Min as she stared into the beast's disturbing gaze. Perhaps the horse could help fill her stomach. The men outside the tavern looked to be road travelers. Their dress was not so fine as a gentleman bourgeois, their demeanor rowdy and ill-mannered. Surely they would have supplies with them.

Cooing gentle reassurance, Min ran her hand across the stallion's back and slipped her fingers inside the soft leather saddlebag, feeling around for anything that might be edible. She grasped upon something small and round and pulled it out.

Damn. This would not serve her needs. She dropped the ruby brooch back inside the saddlebag. So they were thieves. Perhaps they'd cut her a bit of slack if they knew she was of the same ilk. Then again . . .

"Seize him!"

Min's fingers slipped off what she'd thought to be a chunk of dried jerky. "Double damn!" She pulled out and ran from the approaching band of men, her boots kicking the dirt up in billowing clouds behind her. Heartbeats worked like a drummer's fist against her ribs. They would be on her in seconds!

Pressing her hand to her hat, Min ducked under a low-hanging elm branch and quickly swerved to avoid an over-turned wine keg. But she misjudged the distance. Cursing her stupidity, she stumbled, her cheek grazing the dirt road as she fell. She swallowed a good helping of dust and spat out a few pebbles.

Her pursuers were on her like flies on a rotting carcass. Thick fingers dug into her thighs and arms as three men lifted her over their heads and carried her, kicking and screaming, to the fire by the tavern.

"A wiggly little worm, we've got!" one yelled. The others whooped and raised their tankards in a crashing cheer as she was dropped on the ground.

Min's heart beat a furious tattoo against her ribs. Her fears of being discovered as a woman threatened to come full circle. She dared not look up. She was thankful her hat was still in place, though the black plume had broken in the fall, drifting across her cheek. Min closed her eyes. It was unbearable to think what they would do to her should they discover she was a woman.

Struggle was futile. But she wasn't one to give up when Death stood tapping its bony finger against his jaw. Min strained against her captors' hold, but their thick, rough hands pinched into the flesh of her upper arms.

A deep, whiskey-laced voice hissed near her ear. "Do you know what the punishment for thievery is, boy?"

Yes, she knew the punishment. But she wanted to keep all her body parts, thank you, blessed Mary.

"Perhaps the boy's already lost his tongue?" one countered from the circle.

More hoots and hollers. She flinched as someone spat at her boots. A spray of vinegar wine splashed her cheek.

But the crowd froze in stunned silence when someone shouted for quiet.

Min stared at the firelight dancing across the polished jackboots of the man who stood before her. More black leather curled about his thin legs. His sleeves, as high as she dared look up, were a billowing burgundy linen, edged in soft black lace around the spotless burgundy leather gloves.

For a heart-pounding moment, Min wished to God she had never left home. But the image of a nun's robes and daily vespers quickly wiped that thought away.

And then another thought came to her. Where was the chevalier? He had been following her since their first meeting. Surely he had not given up so easily? He had been adamant about seeing her to safety. Where was he now, when she really needed him?

"Secure his hand!" the leader barked.

Sharp pebbles ground into her knees as Min was pushed to the ground. A leather strap circled tightly about her right wrist. Min's other hand was wrenched behind her back. Her shoulders were forced forward by two strong arms, and the leather strap was pulled across a tree stump, her secured wrist slipping through a spill of strong-smelling ale.

They were going to cut off her hand!

Min struggled fiercely, twisting her shoulders and digging her heels into the dirt in an attempt to lever herself free. She'd be damned if her spurs bent; there was no way she could let this happen. A musketeer could not fight with but one hand! Nor could a woman embroider a damned tapestry if she ever lived long enough to succumb to that horror. This was preposterous! Where was the justice?

"I did not take a thing!" she squeaked hoarsely, barely remembering to disguise her voice.

"You should have thought of that before you touched my horse," the stranger hissed in his slow, accented drawl.

"A damned ugly beast!" she yelled and squirmed to no avail. The men who held her were just too strong. Maybe it was time to change her plan? She could reveal the highwayman skills Adrian had taught her. Honor among thieves? Wasn't that the way it worked?

The man with the deep voice bent before her. Min saw the edges of long, straight black hair against the burgundy linen. The strong scent of brandy filled her nostrils, followed by the sweet taint of fragrance. Lilacs? Finally, Min was eye to eye with the deepest, darkest black voids she had ever seen. Not even a gypsy could possibly be as dark.

His voice was like a sword pulled slowly down her spine. "You touched my horse," he said, his head nodding slowly to reiterate his point. "No one touches Luciano's horse."

"No one," the men around her echoed.

The whine of steel pulled from a metal scabbard set Min's heart to a wicked pace. She clamped her jaw tight.

Please let the chevalier come! I need him!

"No!" Min pulled hard against the leather strap, fighting her inner voice as much as her captors. With all her might, she whipped her head back in an attempt to lever her hand away from its bloody fate. Her hat fell to the ground, releasing her hair in a great cascade across her shoulders.

"Halt!"

Min froze, her feet braced against the stump, the leather burning around her wrist. The executioner's sword hovered above her in a glistening taunt. All was silent save the intake of breath about her.

"What is this?" Luciano twisted a thick skein of her hair about his hand and jerked her head back to examine her face. "A *petite fille* masquerading as a *garçon*? Ha!"

An ear-shattering cacophony of laughter rose about Min. With the release of her wrist, she fell to her backside. She sat alert, watching for a way out, an unguarded moment, even a space between the fence of legs circling her in. The laughter was maddening, their jeering looks even more so. She guessed her fate before Luciano barked out his new orders.

"Bring her to my room! Tie her to my bed." His evil gaze swept across her face, his sneer revealing a glint of gold between his snake-thin lips. "Let her contemplate her punishment for a while."

Chapter Five

As each minute sifted by, her fear raced towards the sharp-edged cliff of pure panic. Each tiny creak, every unrecognizable sound, sent her heart flying through her ears. Each time, Min felt sure the gravel-voiced Luciano was on his way up the narrow stone stairway.

"Well, this is certainly a spot."

Much as she tried to calm her nerves, the sound of her own faltering voice did nothing but increase the tension. Min twisted her hands within the ties they'd used to secure her to the wooden bedposts. The rough leather burned across her wrists and itched like a hive of bees with every movement she made. The band of four men who carried her up had left her, reluctantly, saying that the boss man wouldn't like it if they touched his property.

His property!

Min had screamed and shouted every curse she knew at the men, but they had only laughed and rudely mimicked her words before slamming the door. She could hear them now. They were outside, on the other side of the Laughing Sow. Their raucous hoots and jeers echoed through the night.

Let her contemplate her punishment.

"You'll never touch me," she hissed, and then sank against the bed frame, her bravado losing its fire. "I hope."

Somehow all those times Adrian had tied her to a tree and played Prisoner's Base didn't seem so funny anymore. He'd always set her free, and then they'd rolled about laughing beneath the canopy of elm boughs. Matters as they were, Min didn't even want to contemplate what Luciano had in mind for her. But it was difficult not to. Her hand had been spared, but what of her virtue?

As sudden and shocking as a bolt of lightning, a twinge of pride straightened Min on the bed. *This is not the time to be feeling sorry for yourself!*

The devil's toenails, she had been raised better than this. Adversity made the man. Life without a challenge was not a life at all.

Glancing around, Min spied her sword a mere two feet away on the floor. They'd secured only her wrists. The dagger in her boot, after an ill attempt to wrench her foot up near her fingers, was of little help. If she could just loosen the ties! Min scanned the room. Next to the bed sat a bleached wood armoire, and beside that, a surprisingly spotless chamber pot.

Concentrate. Think of a plan. Min bit her lip so hard she jumped. "Fie! Oh, what am I going to do?"

"If you say 'please,' I might think to help you."

The familiar voice sparked a surge of hope in Min's breast. She jerked her head as far as she was able. Her self-appointed shadow sat on the window ledge, one leg stretched along the sill, the other dangling inside the room. Darkness shrouded his face, though the dancing flames from the bonfire below glowed across his smirking lips. She'd never been so thankful to see a man in her entire life.

But the smug look on the man's face only infuriated her. Why wasn't he moving? Luciano could be on his way up the stairs at any moment.

"Get me out of here! Hurry, before that fiend comes for me."

"Really?" The musketeer jumped to the floor in a jingle of spurs, one hand smoothing the plume on this hat. He stopped, placed the hat on his head, one side cocked roguishly over his right eye, then casually examined her situation with a finger to his lips. "You couldn't wait to get away from me before. And now all you can think to do is order me around?"

"Oh!" He was a smug bastard.

A damned attractive smug bastard.

What? What are you thinking? Stop it, Min, he's no different than any other man.

So why did her blood rush to her heart every time she looked at him?

"I'm waiting."

"For what?" she snapped.

"Say 'please'?"

Please? She'd never gift him with such submission. And she wasn't about to start improving her manners, especially when she'd so narrowly escaped that fate last night.

Who was this man that he thought himself her own personal guardian angel? And to order her about as a man does a wife?

He's a musketeer, her conscience reminded her. *And you must get away from him if you are to accomplish your goal. But first . . .*

"Cut me loose," Min hissed. "Then I shall say what you wish."

"Ah, ah, ah." The chevalier waggled a playful finger at

her. "You must say please first, er—what is your name, my unfortunate little imp?"

He was taking great joy in prolonging her agony. His self-indulgent smile made her want to kick in his lower lip. But matters as they were, that would have to wait. Besides, it was a rather nice lip; she'd hate to bruise it.

"Mignonne." Her arms stiffened at the sound of boots pounding up the steps, the sudden icy clink of a wine bottle against the plastered wall. "Hurry! He comes."

"Mignonne, eh?" The musketeer paced before her, his hand moving ever so casually across his sword hilt. "What sort of name is that? Gascon? Frank? No, it most certainly must be Gascon. I have never seen such a headstrong young thing before. Definitely Gascon. Now about that 'please.' "

"Oh! You infuriate me, monsieur!"

"Chevalier."

"What does it matter! I shall tell you when we are gone and out of here. Now—"

A rugged, drunken voice called from the other side of the bedroom door. "You will be wishing you had taken the sword after I am through with you, my little *garçon.*"

Min froze, staring hard at the offering of escape. Just one touch of that broad, muscled hand was tempting enough. But what would he want in return? She had no desire to have the chevalier tailing her again, in hopes of seeing her safely to her family—a family that would lock her up in some barren convent and throw away the key if they ever got their hands on her.

Keys rattled on the other side of the door.

"Hurry, he's coming!"

"I can hear that," he offered casually. "Do you know what I've been doing for the last hour?"

"I do not care!"

"I've been purchasing new reins for my horse. Seems an imp slashed her pitchfork across them."

The click of iron in the door lock did not dissuade the musketeer from his idiotic speech.

"The shopkeeper wasn't all too pleased to be roused from sleep either, I'll tell you that—"

"Can we discuss this later?"

"Why? Have you more pressing matters, Mademoiselle Imp?"

The door swung wide and Luciano staggered inside. He cracked a sparkling grin, brandy still dribbling down his chin. Min thought no longer on her dilemma.

"Please!"

The chevalier's sword slashed through the leather bindings.

"Come." He climbed onto the window ledge and held out his hand.

She scrambled off the bed, grabbing her sword belt in the same instant.

Luciano stumbled forward, the liquor reducing his gate to a wobbling stagger. He looked up just in time to see Min salute him, and then quickly disappear. "Seize them!"

Min followed the chevalier across the slatted rooftop of the Laughing Sow. Smoke drifted up from the bonfire. Her boots slipped across the red slate tiles, but she kept a firm hold in the grooves with her fingertips. When they came to the edge, there was another roof ten feet lower.

Below, Luciano's men had started to organize. Shouts of "What has happened?" "Where is Luciano?" "Where's my wench?" echoed up to Min.

"It's an easy jump," her rescuer coached, keeping his voice low. "Take hold of my hand, and I'll lower you gently."

Min eyed his fingers, the digits gracefully long, yet strong and scarred on the knuckles. His hand would swallow hers whole should she place it in his.

He gave a reassuring nod and a quick wink. "Come, mademoiselle."

Ignoring his chivalry and the irresistible half-smile that pushed up the left side of his narrow mustache, Min took the jump with a brave leap, landing deftly on the slanted roof of the next tavern. The air chuffed out of her lungs, but she turned her head quickly so the chevalier would not see her wince.

He leapt and landed by Min's side. "I am at your service, mademoiselle. Believe me when I say I'll not let you out of my sight until I've seen to your safe return home. *Tout mon possible.*"

She turned to him, finding his words little more than bravado. "Everything in your power?"

He nodded, setting the frothy plume on his hat to a gentle quiver. "My personal motto. Always ready and everything in my power. It is a code I live by."

"Is that so. Chancery, wasn't it?"

"Chance," he offered with a confident wink and a bob of his head.

Min knelt and tucked her hair into the stiffened collar of her leather doublet. She fixed her sword belt over her shoulder and smoothed her fingers across her burning wrists. Escape had been so narrow.

"Chance." She liked the feel of his name on her lips. It didn't sound like a Frenchman's name, though it mattered not; French, or other, his lips still looked irresistibly kissable. But enough of that. " 'Tis a chance I don't believe I shall take. I ride alone. Adieu, chevalier."

She sprang to the next roof before her self-appointed guard dog had an opportunity to protest. But he followed. Min was aware of his overwhelming male presence, as if a great fortress loomed on the horizon, protecting all who sought shelter below. Not that she hadn't expected it. It would be a task to shake this man.

From her position on the middle of the roof, Min scanned the grounds. Luciano's animal growl echoed up to her.

"The girl has escaped! Quickly! On the rooftops."

Adversity, she thought. But she didn't need quite this much.

"You are a stubborn fool, mademoiselle," Chance called in a forceful whisper as he leaped into the air. He let out a grunt as his foot missed the edge.

Min turned to see him dangling from the roof. Scarred fingers struggled for a good hold on the smooth tiles, but she could see he was slowly slipping away.

The roof tiles were cool beneath her palm. But nervous perspiration was beginning to build. Min felt her body turn as her mind struggled for control. *No, I won't do it. I've my own hide to worry about.*

"Go on," Chance called, his jaw disappearing below the roof border. "It won't be long before they answer their leader's call. I can fend for my—"

"Ahah!"

A spiked hiss of steel alerted Min to the ground below Chance's dangling figure. Luciano, though staggering at best, taunted Chance with his sword. She glanced to the roof edge. The white knuckles of one hand clung desperately to the eave while Chance fought off the villain.

Min turned away. Petit Feu stood just below, tied beneath the cover of a sheltering elm. She worried her lower lip between her teeth. Freedom. Her dream awaited.

But her legs would not move.

Go! This is your chance.

Min pressed her palm to her breast, confused at the strange sensation stirring within. Never in her life had she been so at odds with herself. Something deep inside clicked. Feelings altered. Sides were changed.

And her will was defeated by heart's determination.

Her body had already made a complete turn. Min dashed across the rooftop, secured her boot toe behind the field-stone chimney, and stretched her arm out. "Grab hold!"

Chance's sword clattered across the slates as he grabbed her delicate fingers in a secure grasp. She strained, not pulling so much as holding firm as he struggled to lever himself up, while at the same time he kicked at Luciano's taunting sword.

"Oof!" Chance's body landed next to Min, the two of them instantly springing to their feet.

"Confound it, I've a band of fools!" came Luciano's cry from below. "Get off your drunken asses!"

Min picked up Chance's sword. A gush of heat flooded her breast. Three words were carved into the steel blade. *Mousquetaires du Roi.* Many times she had traced the same words impressed in her father's sword.

Someday I shall wield a sword just like this one, she thought.

"Come, mademoiselle!"

Min jerked out of her hopeful reverie and followed Chance, jumping from the rooftop to a conveniently placed cart of hay and landing at the hooves of Petit Feu.

The two silently sped out of Remalard, leaving behind the raucous yells and confusion of Luciano's men.

When they had ridden for perhaps two leagues at a good, steady pace, Mademoiselle Imp slowed her horse and allowed Chance to come up alongside her.

"Why this madness?" he asked, punctuating his question with an exhausted huff. "And the disguise? Who are you running from—besides me and those bastards we left behind?"

Reining her mount to a halt, she stopped in the moonlight. It fell across her hair, making it gleam in the rich darkness.

She met Chance's inquiry full on, her eyes staring brazenly into his. What Chance saw there stole his breath away. Danger. Intrigue. Temptation. What was it about a woman's confident gaze that always landed him in trouble?

Look away!

But he could not. Dammit, he didn't want to.

"I seek only the freedom I have had all my life." It was a mere whisper in the still night air. "I've a mission. And I won't stop until it is fulfilled. Do not interfere with my dreams, chevalier."

"A mission, eh?"

"Yes."

"And may I ask what sort of mission finds a young woman in such dire circumstances?"

"I am en route to Paris."

"A rather lengthy journey." He glanced north, knowing that the great city lay tens of leagues away, the highroads fraught with danger, the city even more dangerous to a lone woman. "What great temptations does the city hold for a country urchin? You are aware of the dangers? Where is your final destination?"

"I go to . . . visit relatives. That is it. Relatives. My . . . my Aunt Huguette."

He did not miss the unsure catch in her voice. "And your family sees fit to allow you to leave on your own? Have they no worry over such a pretty young thing?"

"Pretty?" One elegant eyebrow rose above her surprised gaze.

Had she never considered the word before? Even dressed in breeches and mud-spattered boots, beauty blossomed in the soft plum of her cheeks, the confident lift of her chin. He was forever cursed to be compelled towards beauty no matter what the outcome. For good or for ill, he did enjoy a gorgeous woman. "Yes, pretty. A pity you choose to hide it behind such vulgar dress and manners."

"You think me vulgar, chevalier?"

"I didn't exactly mean—"

"It is all well and good for you to speak of something you know little about. You do not know me."

"I do know that you are a headstrong ball of fire who thinks she can handle more than her weight. What would you have done had I not rescued you from that bastard?"

I would have been violated, Min thought. *And then tossed to the others for dessert.* A chill shudder traced her spine. *But I wasn't. Never look back. Yesterday was; today is.* "I thank you for your assistance, chevalier, but I feel quite sure I'll not be in further need of your protection. We have not been followed. Surely you must have other, more pressing matters than guarding me?"

Moonlight shone across his face, highlighting the throbbing muscle in his jaw. The tingling Min had felt when spying on the rogue and his bread-wielding lady returned. *So strong. And so . . . alluring.* Min quickly looked away.

"You are right there. I've my own mission."

Min followed Chance's gaze as he scanned the dark horizon. A copse of pine was jagged against the pearl-gray sky, thrusting up like the devil's twisted spine.

"I am in search of the Notorious Ones," he offered. "A band of vicious highwaymen who are wanted for robberies and murders across the countryside."

Min stiffened in the saddle. All senses snapped to a rigid alert. The Notorious Ones? A band of highwaymen? She tried not to think what she was thinking, but it was impossible. Though she had never heard Armand or Adrian mention the 'Notorious' sobriquet, she couldn't be sure. Was it *her* brothers this man could be after?

But they were hardly vicious! They were quite gentlemanly; she knew that from her own experience with Adrian the night before. Their victims had freely given up their jewels. In fact, the women had swooned upon receipt of Adrian's seductive charms. And murder? Never! Of course, the grapevine had a tendency to exaggerate any criminal's actions.

Curious to glean more information, she leaned forward, threading her fingers through Petit Feu's mane. "Er, how many in the gang?" She didn't want to appear too interested, but this was her family. No matter what their misguided intentions regarding her welfare, she must protect them at all costs.

"Not sure." Chance clicked his tongue and the charcoal stallion stepped lightly beside Petit Feu. "Perhaps four or five. But it could be as few as two. At least that is what I've gleaned regarding Justine's murder."

His swallow was audible even from a distance. Justine? He whispered her name with such conviction. Such . . . passion. Was she a woman the chevalier had loved?

"One struck just last night, as a matter of fact. Took only jewels. Left in a blaze of gunpowder."

Gunpowder? Her brothers never used their pistols unless it was to protect themselves. Adrian had fired once last night, straight into the air—scare tactics only. As for leaving in a blaze—

"So I am off then." Chance tipped his hat at Min.

He was actually leaving? After following her this far and vowing he'd not let her out of his sight? And when he believed such vicious criminals to be riding the highroads?

"Wait!" Min called as he turned away. There was no telling what would happen when Chance met up with Armand and the others. Like it or not, she had to keep him with her to ensure her brothers' safety. Or at least until she was sure it was not her brothers the man sought.

But how to keep him with her? It seemed he'd tossed his plan to protect her for a more compelling destination. He sought Justine's murderer.

Her heart twisted. Min could not place the feeling, though she felt sure she'd never felt the odd emotion before. Almost as if her heart were being prodded, poked with an intrusive finger.

Perhaps if the chevalier had something to protect?

"Yes, of course."

"What was that, mademoiselle?"

Aware of her less-than-feminine apparel, Min took to the challenge with sly assurance. She lowered her head and looked up through her long dark lashes, trying her best to look like a lost, helpless woman. Her voice could be very delicate if she tried. "Perhaps you could escort me. At least to Châteauneuf. I am a bit shaken after our adventures on the rooftop." Figuring this would be a good moment for one of the pouting looks Sophie often gave Alexandre, Min did her best. "If you could, chevalier, I would be most grateful."

The musketeer's stallion stepped over to Min. Chance leaned forward, the darkness forcing him to lean close.

"You have a nice smile, mademoiselle."

His breathy comment caught Min off guard. Concentration gave way to an utterly silly open-mouthed gasp.

"Ha! When it is in use."

The imp had finally come to her senses. Not that Chance had planned to allow her to ride on to the next village unescorted. He'd intentionally revealed his search for the Notorious Ones, thinking that no woman should like to be riding alone when there were criminals on the loose. If she hadn't fallen for that one, he would have followed her from a distance. But he was relieved she had come around and asked for his help. It made up for the embarrassment he'd felt when she had successfully disarmed him earlier.

In all his days, Chance had never thought to run into such a vexing, confounding, maddening woman.

Twice.

This woman angered him almost as much as she enticed him. So had Justine. Yet, unlike Justine, Mignonne was totally unaware of the strong allure she possessed. The unknowing power of seduction in the hand of a masquerading little sass. She possessed a spark. And that spark had jumped from the fire and branded a lustful desire across every muscle in his body. Chance could not keep thoughts of her from his mind. And that was a problem. He had more important matters to deal with. Lust, and the raw emotion it encompassed, was a drain on any man's system.

But if he could not allow himself to lust, the least he could do was protect. For he had not been able to protect Justine.

They were exhausted by the time the horses sidled up to the sign of the Bare Moon. There, Min and Chance received warm bread, carrot-leek soup, and a welcome goblet of freshly pressed wine. All of which, Chance noticed with fascination, his traveling partner inhaled with gusto. She was already on her second loaf of rye bread by the time Chance had finished his first.

"So they starve you? That is the reason you've left home?"

She glanced up from her feast, a crumble of bread falling from her lips. "I've not eaten since yesterday eve, chevalier. And if you'll remember, a nosy musketeer kept me from a feast of bread earlier. Do you plan to eat that apple?"

Chance nudged the badly bruised fruit across the table. At least she wasn't a frail piece of porcelain who fainted at the mere mention of real meat. The fashion in Paris of late was beef essence. Essence? That was like drinking the air about the vine and not biting into the grape. Heaven forbid a person should eat real food anymore. Delightfully pleased with his companion's voracious habits, Chance settled back against the tavern wall and continued his observations.

After eating, they discovered there was but one room available. A slew of travelers headed for Paris occupied most every room in the area—Countess de Maurepas's party, according to the innkeeper. The name meant nothing to Chance. A *fête* sure to be talked about for weeks afterward, the innkeeper's wife had raved. Bah! Chance hated festivities. The only way he would attend a party was through a direct order from his captain. And he knew that would never happen. All he wanted was a place to rest his road-weary bones.

The myopic innkeeper eyed the pair suspiciously, his bottle-thick spectacles lingering on Min.

"Er, he's . . . my brother," Chance managed.

"Wha—"

Chance held Min off while the innkeeper tried to get a look over Chance's shoulder at the struggling brother in question. "Settle down," he hissed to Min. "Do you want to sleep in the stables?"

"No," she whispered, ceasing her struggles and huffily jerking her doublet down. "But I believe you shall."

"After all I've done for you," Chance said as they followed the housemaid up the stairs. "You would have me sleep beneath the fly-infested tail of a horse?"

If he were a gentleman, he would have offered to sleep elsewhere. But damn if he didn't need a nice, soft place to rest his bones tonight. If Mademoiselle Imp argued, *she'd* end up in the stables.

"You've no need to worry," he reassured her as he

flipped the housemaid a sous and closed the door after her retreat. "I've no intention of doing any more than sleeping. I'm far too tired to even think of assaulting your person."

The tip of an ebony dagger hit dangerously close to the wound on his neck she'd given him earlier. "I'm not too worried about that." With a defiant cock of her brow, she sheathed her dagger and stepped aside.

"Wench," Chance muttered under his breath.

The room was small and boasted but one pallet with stale straw and a thinning coverlet. *Most likely teeming with lice,* Chance thought. He drew his eyes up and down the walls. They seeped with rank moisture, and the window was yellowed with dirt and other unthinkably foul substances. Not suitable for a lady, but then . . . he wasn't quite sure what to call this fascinating creature who'd fallen from the trees into his life.

Seemingly indifferent to the disgusting arrangements, Mignonne went immediately to the pallet and sat down to pull off her boots.

Alone, and in such confined breathing space with a female, Chance began to feel as if the walls were suddenly closing in, pushing him towards the girl. Teasing voices sounded inside his head. *Go to her. Touch her. You know you want to. Take her in your arms. Pull her close and press your body against hers. Lose your troubles in debauchery. . . .*

With a loud scrape of spurs, Chance's left boot skidded out from under him, nearly toppling him had he not recovered quickly. "Er—um, I must thank you."

"Whatever for?" She pulled off her mud-soaked hose with a grunting tug and began massaging her toes, quite blind to his growing interest in her bared parts.

"For allowing me to stay in the room with you." By the bloody gods, look at those pink little toes!

She gave an indifferent shrug. " 'Tis not as if you are allowing me a choice."

Not for a thousand *livres* could Chance tear his gaze from her toes. Sweet, delicate pink buds that could scarce have come from inside such hideously dirty hose. He felt his own toes wiggle inside his boots. What he wouldn't pay to see the imp all done up in laces and shimmering satins, her hair pulled up from those delicate shoulders, her arms encircled in soft silk and those toes . . . those precious little buttons covered by silk slippers and ribbons. All to be unlaced and undone by him.

"Chevalier?"

"Huh? Oh, what?"

"You're doing it again."

Chance nervously smoothed his hand along his goatee, ruffling the sharp bristles against the raised scars on his fingers. "Doing what?"

"I do believe you're giving me the glad eye."

With hands on her hips and her chin thrust upward, she looked prettily disgruntled.

"I beg pardon, mademoiselle, I am doing no such thing."

"You are."

He drew in his upper lip. Blast, she was a vexing one. Perhaps he would have been better off bedding down in the stables than to spend the entire night in this small room with her. She stared at him, awaiting an explanation. "I was just thinking . . ." Thinking what? About doing unspeakable things with her toes?

Perhaps he *had* been giving her the glad eye? Fool!

"Er—we should get you some new things in the morning," Chance spat out. "I can inquire if there's a dressmaker about."

"A dress?" She gave a dismissive chuckle and a casual toss of her hand. "I am in no need of a dress. As you can plainly see, I am quite comfortable in my chosen mode of attire."

"You *purposely* dress as a man?"

Mignonne shrugged.

Chance pushed his fingers though his shortly cropped hair. "You are the most confounding female I've happened upon. And believe me, I've happened upon many a woman in my days."

"Is that supposed to impress me, chevalier?"

"I feel sure it would take much to impress the likes of you."

"The likes?" She drew her back straight and tilted her head curtly. Fury had never looked so seductive as when beaming at him from two bittersweet chocolate eyes. "Meaning?"

"Well, just look at yourself." *As I have not been able to stop doing.* "How can you ever hope to attract a man in that guise?"

"And what makes you think I wish to attract a man? Besides"—she looked down her nose and assumed her seductive tone again—"what you don't realize is that I already have."

His mind caught in an erotic fantasy of naked toes and silks and satins, Chance nodded absently. It was only when the woman's eyes flared wide that he shook his head and scanned his immediate memory for the words she had just spoken.

"What?" Chance pressed unbelieving fingers to his chest. "Me? I am only here—"

"In my chamber!"

"Blast the Bastille!" Chance slammed his hat against his knee, setting the plume quivering. "You know as well as I that this is the last room. And if it hadn't been for my quick thinking—"

"My silence, you mean! Your brother? I could have said something."

"That wouldn't have been smart." The long hours on the road were starting to catch up with him in a most disagreeable way. "I've been riding all day. I am already half asleep on my feet. You invited me to escort you, and I'll be damned if I will let you chase me away now. Especially after it was I who paid for the room! Have no worry, I've no intention of assaulting your"—He looked over her dirtied costume, seeing only the sweat and dirt and haggard condition of her tousled hair rather than her tempting toes or her sparkling gaze—"your person! I prefer to wear the breeches in my relationships."

"Oh, so it is a relationship now, is it?"

"I did not say that!"

"You did—"

"If you wish it, mademoiselle, then so be it."

With that, Chance could no longer contain his fury, nor could he fight the odd, vexing temptation he felt towards the sassy spitfire who challenged his every personal value regarding women. Plunging to one knee on the floor, he took her chin in his hand. She hadn't time to protest before his lips silenced her soft, rose-petal mouth. She squirmed as he stole her surprised breath into his mouth. She fought him, and yet at the same time, her greedy fingers curled about his doublet and dug into his shirt. Her lips pressed equally hard to his, and her fingers pulled him closer.

Chance's kiss curled into a smile. She wanted this too!

Cautious to keep one hand against her back so she could not suddenly slip away, Chance let his other hand stray down and over her breeches, slipping them under her thigh to squeeze. Heaven forbid, he should ever see himself in such a position with a person dressed as a man. But oh, she was far from male. The soft curves crushed against his chest were making things so . . . hard.

"It seems Mademoiselle Imp is not strong enough to resist," Chance whispered into her mouth.

She sighed, her mouth parting at his command. "Hmm?"

Capturing her whimper with another kiss, Chance smiled against her lips. Oh yes, she could be tamed. And he had just discovered how to do it.

"What?" Those bittersweet eyes were but inches from his. But it wasn't desire or infatuation that made them wide with shock. His little vixen seemed suddenly struck by what she was doing. Mignonne pushed back across the pallet, wedged her feet against Chance's chest, and kicked. Hard. Chance's tail bone met the wall with a crack.

"You are quite mistaken, monsieur!" Min stood on the pallet, a pixy fist thrust before her in declaration of battle.

Chance massaged his aching chest. "And here I thought those toes so delicate and sweet."

"You did?" Quick as her rage had surfaced, Mignonne was suddenly all softness again. Her fist fell to her side and her mouth pursed into a sweet red bow. She resembled a bespattered doll. Dragged through the mud and tossed about, but still a precious beauty.

When she realized she'd let down her guard again, her mouth drew tight and her fingers balled into white little fists. "I mean, you *did!* I'll thank you to keep your lecherous eyes from my naked body parts, chevalier. And . . . please refrain from placing your lips on mine."

"You mean kissing you?"

"Yes!" She crossed her arms firmly. "I'll not stand for it. And if that is what you intend, then you most certainly shall sleep in the stables tonight."

Chance could only muster a soft chuckle, thanks to the pain in his backside. Maddening was the only word to describe her. First she pulled him closer, devouring his kiss as much as he hers. And now she threatened him if he laid another hand on her. Women. They were so damned . . . difficult!

"As you wish, mademoiselle." So the stables it would be. A bed of straw was quite tempting when compared to the hard floor. "A momentary lack of concern on my part. It will never happen again."

"Never?"

Her abandonment of bravado made Chance prompt hopefully, "Unless you wish it?"

Wild-eyed pride returned. Min held her jaw firm. "I shan't. Now, if I may go to sleep without worry of further assault from your person?"

Chance nodded. What else could he do? He would never force a woman. And he'd be damned if he would beg for her attentions. He could not let himself become involved; it would only bring heartache. Women did nothing but serve themselves, totally oblivious to the damage they caused.

He stood and made for the door. "Chivalry is certainly not all it's been said to be."

Chapter Six

That kiss . . .

"You want this, do you not?"

Min looked up into the chevalier's blue eyes. His breath hushed across her lips, warming them with a tickling desire. She drew in the scent of his presence, so male and virile. "Oh, yes," she moaned, and pulled him down on top of her.

Hard muscle pressed along the length of her body. His body was both steel and sinew, so powerful a force she did not want to resist. Everywhere, her body was pressed and touched by his lingering hands, searching, seeking, mapping out her responsive spots. He teased her mouth open with his tongue and dove inside, transferring his passion in a long, slow kiss that mined her deepest emotions. She could sense his every desire pulsing within her, his every need with each subtle move of his lips or caress of his fingers. To be kissed by him was a dream realized, commanded so that her senses wanted only his hot touches and whispered desires. To be possessed by a man's passions . . .

Min stretched out her bare toes and turned her head, allowing

Chance free rein along the side of her neck, where his tongue traced a burning map down to her shoulders. Soft grass, fragrant with dew, tickled her cheek. She laughed out loud because it felt so good to be touched by this exquisite man.

"Mignonne!"

Her lover looked up from his fervid ministrations and squinted his eyes to see who had spoken. "Who is that?"

"It is Armand."

"Armand?"

"My brother!"

"The devil take me!" Chance looked about for escape, as did Min, but the landscape closed in on them, the trees swallowing them into a tight circle, Alexandre's prized yellow roses growing high, their thorns woven into vicious barbs.

"Petite one!"

"Another brother?" Perspiration trickled down Chance's forehead.

"Yes, and another!" Min pushed him off her body. "Hurry, they'll kill you if they can lay a hand on you!"

Min bolted upright upon the pallet. She wiped her hand across her eyes to remove the sleep and stared into the room's early-morning darkness. Something, some horrible notion, had woken her from a well-deserved sleep.

You can't be with him.

With whom? Her eyes moved across the seeping walls and around the scuffed pine floor. He wasn't there.

Frustration keeping her from a peaceful sleep, Min stood and kicked the tiny bedside table into the wall, breaking one of its fragile legs into a splintering spray.

She had to get away from this man if she was ever to gain Paris and become a musketeer.

* * *

Breakfast of salted side pork and boiled goose eggs had served him well. Chance plucked yet another twig of wilted straw from his breeches and closed his eyes, his mind at rest.

But not for long.

What a mess he found himself in. This woman would certainly be the death of him. He felt responsible for her safe return home, but would she ever trust him enough to reveal where home was? And would it happen within the fortnight he'd been granted leave?

Damn it, he had things to do.

Chance cursed himself for not paying closer attention in Remalard. He'd been too worried for Mademoiselle Imp's safety to check around for men who might fit the description of the Notorious Ones given him by the prisoners he'd grilled in the Bastille.

Why hadn't he paid closer attention?

Because you only had eyes for the sassy-lipped vixen! Fool.

Yes, the Notorious Ones could have easily been close by. He might have walked right by any of them without being the wiser. Why, Justine's killer could have been the very man with whom Chance had clashed swords.

Chance loosened his boots off his heels and tipped his chair against the roughly plastered inn facade. He would struggle with his ineptitude later. Right now, he wanted only to relax before heading to Paris. The ride was but five hours, a mere day's travel. The sooner he got rid of the girl, the sooner he could return to the task at hand. He didn't believe the Aunt Huguette story for a moment. He decided it would be easiest to stow her away at a convent until he could locate her family. There she would be safe.

Yes, he needed to protect her from—

From you! You know that is the truth. Lock her away in a convent before your lustful desires carry you away and you take her yourself.

"So true," he muttered. "Why the hell is it so difficult to keep such thoughts from my mind? Think of Justine," he coached himself. "No woman could be more cruel. You must not allow yourself to fall victim to a pretty face ever again."

He still found it hard to believe that she had helped him in Remalard. Why? When she'd been so adamant that she wanted only to get away from him? And then her apparent change of heart regarding his offer of escort. Chance lowered his hat over his eyes and closed them in the shade. If there was a heart beneath that tough, crazed exterior of a woman, she hid it well.

How the hell had she come to be such a feisty character? Women simply didn't act like . . . *that.*

Women were supposed to be feminine and dainty and smell good and. . . . And that was the kind of woman he liked, dammit! Soft, demure, and innocently attractive. Not like her.

He'd heard enough curses in the past day from her lips to beat any man under the table. Yet those lips, those soft, pink rosebuds . . . They were the most delicious things, weren't they?

Chance sat up with an abrupt snap of his head. How could he think her delicious?

It was her lips, lackwit, you were dreaming about her lips.

"Oh, yes." He settled back against the chair.

And her eyes. As dark as bittersweet chocolates, and sparkling with freedom and excitement.

There *was* a woman beneath the man's clothing, wasn't there? Beneath that tough exterior there was a soft and feminine creature just waiting to be held and caressed . . . and kissed. Ah, yes, that kiss. Chance licked his lips, recalling the sassy taste of Min's kiss. So brief, yet provocative that kiss had been.

She wanted me.

Chance struck the side of his head with his flat palm. "The deuce! You're going soft, man." His aching ribs reminded him of his flight across the bedchamber. When most women wanted a man, they did not kick him away.

A small keg behind the tavern held a meager offering of water. Whether remainders from the guests' baths or week-old rainwater, Min did not care. She scooped the surface free of grass and dead bugs, then splashed the cool liquid on her face.

"I do believe my lover dipped his feet in that very bucket before coming to bed last eve."

Spewing water, Min turned to the vision of burgundy damask perched in the tavern doorway behind her. A leech-drained complexion studied her from beneath dancing blond ringlets. Eyes of steel widened in challenge, and ropes of pearls clicked as she propped a lace-covered hand on one panniered hip.

"But don't let that dissuade you from breaking your fast," the ice-princess offered.

A primped-up courtesan, Min decided, as her eyes strayed to the powdered mounds of bosom barely concealed by the heavy damask. Powdered and curled and cinched and perfumed. And all for her lover's dirty feet. "You are en route to the countess's ball?" Min wondered, though it mattered not if the woman answered.

"She is a darling companion of mine." Her pearls clicked once more as she tossed her curls. "I judge from your attire that you will *not* be attending?"

Min snorted out a laugh. "Not unless she needs a stable-mucker, or so I presume that to be your opinion of me."

"I would never be so cruel."

"You would never be anything but."

"Now you are the one making presumptions, you there with a rich man's discarded bath water running down your chin."

Swiping the trail of water from her face, Min fought against the urge to release her anger with a fist across the woman's smirk. She glanced to the stables. Chance had risen early, unfortunately for her. How to slip out of his sight was the only challenge she must concern herself with now.

"If I offend you so, then you may leave," she offered. "And take your silly pearls and powder with you."

"It would serve you well to consider my pearls and powder. Or is that layer of dirt I see coloring your face as permanent as your scowl? Come, come, my angry young thing, if only you would decorate yourself with a bit of pearl and lace, then perhaps you wouldn't be so disgruntled at your lack of a man."

"My lack—! See here, madame!" Her fists rattled at her thighs. Min wasn't quite sure how to control her raging temper. "Why must everyone I speak with insist on my need to attract a man? I am quite content without one. I shall never need one. And if I should wish one, then believe me, I could catch one!"

"So who is he?"

Min released her breath in a gush and cocked a disbelieving gape at the woman. "He?"

"This man who has stirred such a fiery rage of passion in this pintful of female I see simmering before me."

"Passion? I—" Min snapped her jaw shut. She wasn't sure what to answer to that. Passion? Her? Impossible. "You see things that simply do not exist." She jarred a boot against the keg, setting its contents to a splash. "Did your lover really wash his feet in this last night?"

The woman nodded.

"Joy." Min swallowed the sick feeling that bubbled up her throat.

"He's exceedingly fussy about cleanliness," the woman offered as she toyed with the pearls that swayed from the center of her breasts to her right sleeve, where a large ruby brooch secured them just above her elbow. "I've been forced to abandon my lighter dresses for the darker shades, for the dusty roads tend to discolor them. And it causes him such a great amount of bother when my hems are stained."

Oh, to have such problems.

"I wonder if the tavern maid would appreciate my satin gown. It's pink. Dreadfully difficult to keep clean."

Min tapped her boot against the convex base of the keg, a sneaky idea sparking inside her head. "A pink dress, eh?"

Three riders rode up to the neighboring inn, the Widow's Peek. Chance looked them over from beneath the curled brim of his hat. The tallest, the one in the lead, was a broad-shouldered, dark-complexioned man, with midnight-black hair curling over his shoulders. Chance had worn his own hair in the same fashion before joining the musketeers, but the rampant spread of lice within the ranks demanded his current choice of closely trimmed hair. The man wore fine lace at his collar and matching lace on his boots and gloves. He gestured to another, who possessed a wild mess of hair that floated about his face in the breeze. The third seemed to be youngest, with dark eyes and the same dark skin and hair as the others.

The first tipped his hat to Chance and the others followed his lead as they entered the nearby inn. Chance had never seen such dark eyes before . . . Before *yesterday*.

Chance startled upon his chair, catching his spurs in the dusty ground.

Could they be the brothers the spitfire had proclaimed earlier? It was a possibility. She had said they were three, and they did possess the same bittersweet eyes and the exotic skin tone.

Or perhaps, the Notorious Ones? No. They seemed too well-mannered and finely dressed to be highwaymen. Most likely not. But he'd keep an eye on them just the same. Highwaymen were notorious pretenders. They wielded manners and charm the way a murderer wields his weapon. Yes, he would check out these riders. It was high time he started acting the soldier.

About to go over to the Widow's Peek and introduce himself, Chance was cut off as a gilded coach arrived in front of the Bare Moon, stirring up a cloud of dust beneath his nose.

He tipped his hat to the coachman. Behind him the inn door swung wide, and a woman dressed in silver-laced pink skirts, wearing a bolero hat adorned in dancing pink fringes pulled down over her velvet-masked eyes, stepped out.

Chance inhaled. An aura of scent surrounded her like a mist, pure and white as a snow-kissed mountain. He loved a woman who smelled of flowers. Justine had worn lilac, a scent he'd remember forever—unfortunately.

Figuring this to be the countess who planned the ball, Chance bowed and offered his hand. "Your Grace."

"Monsieur," she offered in the tiniest wisp of a voice. She did not look at him. All he could see were her reddened lips beneath the silly fringe. Her hand quivered beneath a generous fall of crisp silver lace, awaiting his move. Always one to oblige a lady, Chance assisted her into the carriage, inhaling her heady scent as he did. Damn, and he smelled like the foulest part of a horse.

"*Merci,* monsieur," came her delicate reply.

Bowing grandly, Chance replaced his hat and stumbled most ungracefully backward into the tavern. The swinging door cuffed his shoulder on the return. Chiding himself for acting like a whipped puppy dog, Chance glanced over the top of the door to assure himself that she had not seen. Ah, but it was those lovely, soft women that always muddled his senses.

It seemed he might never learn his lesson regarding women and their ways. Ah, well, there was no harm in looking.

Forgetting his previous intention to investigate the neighboring inn, he skipped up the stairs with only the scent of the lady's perfume on his mind. Now that was what women were supposed to be like. Soft and feminine and smelling like a garden. With a gentle voice that sounded like a hummingbird's flutter in the Tuileries.

Not like the imp behind this door.

Chance pushed the chamber door open and the pleasant scent of woman was quickly replaced by an ugly clutch in his stomach. She was gone. He stepped frantically about the tiny room, lifting the pallet and checking out the window.

"The deuce! How has she managed this?"

A trace of fear squeezed his heart when he spied the broken table. Had she been taken forcefully? God's blood, the man who kidnapped her had returned and somehow managed to spirit her away from under his very nose! And he with his eyes fixed on a pretty lady. What had happened to *toujours prêt?* Always ready, indeed.

He took the stairs two by two, nearly toppling a housemaid in the process. She shuffled her grease-spattered skirts down and adjusted her bodice, which pushed her generous breasts up just below Chance's nose.

No time for the appreciation of beauty now. "Have you seen a *garçon?* About so high, and quite dirty?"

The girl shrugged and sauntered over to the bar. At the same time Chance noticed that the three riders had come inside the Bare Moon. He nodded acknowledgment to them and resumed his questioning.

"It was not really a boy. He was a girl. I mean . . . she wore men's clothing. . . ."

"What?" The tallest rider, with the fine lace, turned at Chance's statement. "A girl in men's clothing?" He approached him, his eagerness stretching his strides. "Really? Have you seen her?"

"Why . . . yes. I've been watching over her. I feared she would stumble into trouble." *And now she has, no thanks to you!* "Do you know her?"

"Where has she gone?" asked the youngest.

"I am Armand Saint-Sylvestre," the tall one offered. "My brothers, Adrian and Alexandre. If we speak of the same person, then the girl in question is quite possibly our sister. Her name is Mignonne?"

"Min," Adrian offered from over Armand's shoulder.

"Min. Yes, it was she." What a relief to find her family! "I thought perhaps you might be the brothers she had mentioned. I am Chevalier Chancery Lambert, Lieutenant of the Blacks."

"A musketeer?"

Chance noticed the brothers exchanging glances. Something was up, but what he wasn't sure.

"Can you tell us where she is?"

"Yes," Adrian said. "Where is she?"

Chance scanned the expectant stares of the three men. *Damn.* He had been escorting her specifically to see her safely into her brothers' hands. Now here they were—and Min was not. Oh, he had failed miserably on this one. He was a musketeer; his job was to protect the king and queen with his life. Yet he wasn't even able to keep an eye on one petite, vexing woman.

"Lieutenant?"

"I am sorry, messieurs." He found it hard to look any one of them directly in the eye. "She has eluded me. I was keeping watch, but somehow she managed to escape. She's a slippery one. Beg pardon, but she is a handful, that girl."

"That would be our Mignonne," Alexandre sighed, blowing a cloud of dark hair from his eyes. "When did you last see her, chevalier?"

"Hours ago." Chance pointed over his shoulder up the stairs. "Before she kicked me out of our room."

Armand's eyes widened.

Alexandre choked on his breath. "*Our* room?"

Adrian drew his rapier, placing it expertly at Chance's throat.

"Oh, no, messieurs," Chance carefully directed Adrian's sword away from his throat. It quickly swung back, finding its mark on the narrow cut he'd received from Min's dagger. He gulped. What was it with this family? Did they have it in for musketeers? "It is not what you think."

"Then tell us how we should think," growled Armand, his right fist working around his sword hilt. "For I have just heard a stranger confess to sharing a room with our sister."

"I was keeping watch over her. She had been attacked—"

"Attacked?" Alexandre's sword now joined Adrian's.

Chance stepped back from the double attack. He made to reach for his own sword, then thought better of it.

"She is fine. Or at least . . . she was. She was not harmed. Earlier, I mean. But I fear the same man who held her captive before may have returned and purloined her right from under my nose. We must find her," Chance pleaded.

"She was held captive?" Armand's sword now joined the others. "What is going on, lieutenant?"

"D-do you really think she's in trouble?" Alexandre fumbled with the lace at his cuff.

"Perhaps. If it is the highwaymen I have been after, the Notorious Ones, she could be in serious trouble. I am surprised that her family would allow her to travel alone."

The brothers looked from one to the other. They exchanged the same glances as earlier, an unspoken code among the three of them that Chance could not decipher. Finally Armand gestured that his brothers sheathe their swords.

"It is not your concern, lieutenant." Armand offered curtly.

"You are aware she is destined for a certain . . . um . . . aunt, I believe."

"Aunt Huguette?" Adrian could not hide his surprise. "But that's impossible, Min would never—"

"We thank you for looking over our sister," Armand interrupted. "We will take matters into our hands now."

"She was here." All four men turned at the sound of the housemaid's shaking voice. She twisted her grease-stained apron between her fingers and shuffled from foot to foot on her wooden clogs. "She left the mare here in our stables. In trade for the—"

"What?" Chance stepped over to her. "What do you know about Mademoiselle Saint-Sylvestre?"

"Forgive me, messieurs, but—oh!" The girl broke into a storm of tears.

"Out with it, woman," Adrian prompted. "You know where our sister is?"

"She . . . slipped out . . . a little while ago," she managed between sniffs.

"Unescorted?" Armand averted his eyes to Chance, not hiding the fact that he might have expected more from a musketeer.

"Yes, alone."

"How!" Chance yelled, amazed that he had missed her, but relieved that she had left of her free will and not at the hands of a villain.

"It was . . . quite clever . . . really." The maid shrugged and drew a long, loud sniffle through her nose. "You helped her yourself, *monsieur le chevalier.*"

"What?"

"The lady you helped into the carriage." The maid wiped away her tears and gave a weak smile. "The one in the pink dress."

"Dress?" the brothers said simultaneously.

"Our Min?" Adrian scratched the side of his head with his sword hilt.

"The deuce!" Chance slapped his forehead. "I thought she was a countess."

"Countess?" Alexandre could not hide his amused disbelief.

"What a brilliant disguise for the girl who fears to wear a dress. Come, gentlemen." Chance made haste for the door. "The coach was destined for Paris. We must be off!"

Luciano watched from the shade of the Widow's Peek as the four men mounted their horses and took off in a cloud of billowing dust. He'd overheard everything. "Paris, eh?"

"What thoughts are brewing in your head, lover?"

"Ah, my pet." Luciano received his woman under his arm, crushing her crisp skirts against his leg and savoring the fragrance of her body. "You're up rather early. You should rest when we ride the roads. All that traveling will line your fragile skin."

She nuzzled her nose beneath his ear. "You fret over me so. I do adore your attentions, lover. But why do I find you speaking to yourself?"

"I've just been working out some things. I'm to ride on myself."

"But—"

"No argument." He stepped forward, sensing her need to cling to him, but taking gratification in the fact that she withdrew and remained behind him. Always obedient, his pet. Just as she should be. "There is a situation I need to rectify."

"But I can help."

"It has nothing to do with you. You ride on to Paris this eve as planned and purchase your dress for the ball—and anything else that catches your wicked eye."

"Anything?" Her masterful fingers caressed him from behind, squeezing his backside in a most wanton way.

"Anything. Be sure to purchase it, though . . ." He cocked his head back to see that she was paying attention. "Keep those swift fingers of yours gloved, pet. I don't wish the *garde* on my back while I'm in Paris."

"There's no joy in paying for what I want," she pouted. "Just a few things? Small? Jewels?" She spread her hands over his shoulders and hugged him from behind.

Luciano pressed a kiss to the back of her hand. "Perhaps something small. Now, back inside for you. It's far too hot out here for your delicate complexion, and my departure will stir up the dust."

A shrill whistle brought his servant and snow-white Andalusian to him as his lover skirted inside. "Where to next, boss?"

Luciano examined the flanks of his horse. He brushed his fingers over the hide, sniffed them, and looked to his servant.

The servant's face went white as the horse. He curled his fingers into a ball. "Forgive me, master. It is so hard to keep my hands clean. This red dust!" He fell to his knees, blackened fingers clutching his hat to his chest. "I am so sorry."

A firm rub of his fist removed the dirt from the horse's flank. Luciano rolled his dark gaze at the miscreant. It would be too easy to kick him in the ribs, and not at all satisfying. He wrapped his fingers around the braided leather secured at his waist.

The boy saw his actions and began to plead. "No, master, please!"

If there was anything Luciano hated more than a dirty horse—and oh, did he hate a dirty horse—it was a whining man. A deadly cobra unleashed, his whip snapped through the air and sliced the boy across the back, leaving behind a deep trench of bloody flesh.

Without so much as a scream, the boy fainted.

"Now." Luciano stepped over the servant to mount his horse. "I've got a debt to settle with a fair maiden in pink."

Chapter Seven

The coachman called from his wobbling perch; they would arrive within the hour. A wave of relief washed over Min to know that Paris was within reach. And with that, her dreams. She settled back against the ill-padded red-damask seats, her thoughts focusing on the pain in her ribs.

She hadn't dared more than an indiscreet wiggle before the eyes of the other three passengers, two men and a young girl. But by the holy saints, if she didn't want to just rip her stays apart and run free and unrestrained. The maid at the tavern had pulled them so tightly she thought sure her breasts would never again regain their proper shape. No scarf had ever been so cruel.

And then there were her toes. Min wiggled them, or at least tried to. The shoes the pearl-festooned woman had given her felt two sizes too small. It had been a feat just to walk from the inn to the coach.

But oh, it had been such a joy to see how easily Chevalier

Lambert could be fooled. He'd almost swooned when she laid her hand in his. And his silly gushing words; he had thought her a countess. Ha! Such fools men became around a fancily dressed lady. If only he had known what had really been beneath the torturous disguise.

Min's heart sank. Yes. *If only.*

Sudden anger boiled just beneath the surface. He'd paid her more attention when she wore laces and frills and smelled of an entire garden. The deuce!

Why should it matter to you whether or not he pays you any attention?

It doesn't, she silently snapped at the irritating voice inside her head. But all the attention had been . . . well, nice. For once she had felt special. Important. Not just one of the "boys." Not that she minded being one of the boys. But for the first time, she'd actually experienced what it was like to be singled out, even admired. Why, she now knew what it felt like to be a woman!

And she felt it every time the seductive musketeer cast his eyes over her. Bewitchery it was, for she knew not how to answer these feelings inside. She knew only that they confused her. Never in her life had she felt so out of sorts. But 'twas a good confusion. She rather liked receiving the chevalier's hungry stares. And his kiss last night! Bless the angels, it had been divine. So much more than she could have ever imagined. What a surprise that she had known how to respond. Reaction had been quick and demanding. She hadn't wanted the connection between them to end, though, for her own sake, she had broken it. It wouldn't do to become sidetracked.

No, she had a mission to fulfill.

The horses began to slow. Min pulled the patterned damask curtains aside to scan the road. They'd passed a windmill grinding flour, the great slatted sails creaking in the wind. An undercurrent of manure wilted the scent of fresh pine, and a pollen-loaded bumblebee buzzed aimlessly past her window. She saw no signs of a village, nor did she see the Porte Saint-Jacques, which opened into Paris. They were stopping in the middle of nowhere.

"Stand and deliver!"

The chilling command stiffened Min's bones. Everyone in the coach sat erect. The girl clutched her father's leg with narrow, white-gloved fingers, her blue eyes wide with apprehension.

The hairs on the back of Min's neck curled as a pistol shot whizzed through the air. From her window, she saw the coachman fall to the ground and land in a crumpled heap, his livery stained with a flower of crimson over his heart.

Min dropped the curtains. What was this? *She* was being robbed? The nerve.

Fumbling about for her sword within the folds of her skirt, Min cursed herself for allowing the tavern maid to talk her into hiding it. She could feel the long needle of steel but it was irretrievable. As was her dagger, secured beneath her stays and pressed tightly against her hip. The only way to get at either weapon was to stand and lift her skirts. And standing was impossible in this crowded carriage. Fie!

The girl began to whimper. Min figured her to be no more than ten, perhaps twelve at most. Whispering gentle reassurances, her father hugged her tightly, his eyes fixed to the carriage door in horror.

"Do as he says," the man sitting next to Min whispered. "I'll not let harm come to you."

Min noticed his bony fingers quivering beneath the gold-stitched lace that fell over his hands. He would swoon before the man laid a hand on him. From the corner of her eye she could see his powder-laden eyelids grow wide as the robber flung open the carriage door.

"Depart the coach one by one," came the robber's command. "Keep your hands where I can see them. This will be simple if you follow directions."

The man who had been sitting next to her stepped out and was clunked on the back of the head with a pistol.

Min listened hard; that voice was so familiar. It was so low and deep, like the devil himself come to earth.

Like the voice that had threatened her just last night.

"Mon Dieu," Min whispered. "Luciano." Her heart scaled her throat in less than a breath. The one man she dreaded seeing again stood less than five feet away. What would he do to her now?

"Please," the other man begged as he stepped from the carriage, his daughter firmly in hand. "You mustn't harm her. She is still a babe."

"Silence!" roared the robber. He smashed the butt of his pistol against the side of the man's face, sending him to the ground next to the other.

The girl screamed as blood spattered her yellow satin skirts. Min feared the child would be the next recipient of Luciano's violence if she could not quiet her. Unmindful of her plans to fish her sword from the many folds of her skirt, she clambered out of the carriage and pulled the girl to her, hugging the child's face tightly to her chest to stifle her sobs. "Hold your tongue, precious one. Your father is not hurt. He will wake up."

I hope, Min thought, as she glanced over the two fallen men. The father had taken a blow to his cheek, the flesh was split open, but she saw his chest rise beneath his limp fingers.

"Ah, *ma petite garçon.* We meet again." Luciano snapped his pistol on aim with Min's heart.

Her instincts jarred into motion, Min quickly took in the situation. Two leather pistol straps crossed over Luciano's burgundy shirt. He had fired once. That would leave him with only one loaded weapon. Then she noticed the pistol at his hip.

"What do you want? I've no money. There. Take their purses and the girl's jewels and be gone. But do not cause this child harm." She felt the child clutch her skirts, and her whimpering shuddered against her stomach.

Luciano reached out and smoothed a burgundy-leathered hand over Min's cheek. The setting sun shone across his face, sparkling in his dark eyes. The devil's eyes. Min flinched from his touch, but that only angered him. He wrenched her away from the child, twisting her hand behind her back.

"You are the only jewel I am interested in, my pretty." He jerked her around and forced her face towards him with the barrel of his pistol. "You fare a trifle better in a dress."

Min cringed to feel his hot, garlic-laced breath shudder down her chest, excruciatingly aware that her breasts heaved from the low-cut silk.

"Exposes your assets well." He ran a hand down her left side, a slow creep that examined each and every inch of her body, and then down her right, stopping, Min knew, when he felt the hard steel dangling beneath her skirts. "I thought as much."

"You bastard!" Taking a chance, Min jerked her elbow backward, crushing it deep into Luciano's ribs. He released her with a surprised grunt.

She dashed a few yards away and, with her back to the man, lifted her skirts.

"Ahah! I see she is as eager as I!"

Min's sword slashed through the air, abruptly halting Luciano's advance. The girl screamed, but Min ordered her to hush and keep back.

"If you wish to make a fool of yourself," Luciano reached behind his hip with measured slowness, "by all means, a little physical combat can be substituted for foreplay. It is all the same to me."

A sharp thwack ignited the air near Min's ear. She jumped and looked about. What was that? It hadn't been a musketball; they generally made a shrill, whizzing noise. She felt a sudden burn on her shoulder, like a bee sting.

"Ah-ha!" Luciano wielded a bullwhip high above his head. A smile cracked his pale countenance, revealing a glimmer of gold. "Take care, *petite garçon,* you do not charm the snake, for its bite is deadly." His whip cracked again, this time near her toes.

Her instincts told her to move and not stand still, make his target a hard one. And fight for her life. Her fragile sword was no match for his whip. She would have to close the distance to reach him, while he was at an advantage where he stood.

Inhaling a breath of bravery, Min lunged forward. Another crack and the whip snapped her skirts, tearing a serrated gash down the front of them. Silently she thanked the tavern maid for insisting she wear two petticoats instead of one.

The girl screamed again and fainted against the carriage, falling to the mud by her father's inert body.

Hampered by her skirts, Min stumbled backwards across the uneven ground, wishing vainly that at least one of the two men would wake up and help her.

"Snake!" she cried at Luciano's approaching figure. "I'll not let you touch me, or the girl."

One more crack and her sword flew from her fingers. Pain stung across her hand. Blood oozed from her knuckles. She swiped her fist across her skirts and gave her injury not another thought. Rushing to the girl's side, she shook her awake. "Get inside the carriage. Do not come out!" With a wide-eyed look over Min's disarray, the girl obliged, and Min spun around to the sound of snapping steel.

Luciano held up two pieces of her sword. His cauldron-bubbling chuckle echoed across the grounds and died in Min's heart.

"That was a gift from my father," she gasped, fighting the smothering rage in her chest. If one person in the world knew that she was capable of becoming the musketeer she so wished to be, it had been Antoine Saint-Sylvestre. He had known without words that the blaze in Min's eyes was that of determination and pride and said as much when he'd given her her very own sword. Now her father's confidence in her had been cruelly destroyed.

"You'll pay!" Min tried to scramble up but her legs were tangled in yards of hideous pink silk. One ankle was twisted within constricting petticoats, while the other slipped in the mud. Thoroughly frustrated, she beat her fists in the air. "Damn these skirts!"

"Would the mademoiselle be in need of assistance?" Luciano snapped his whip once again, catching Min in its squeezing embrace. Her hands were pinned to her sides. She gripped the braided leather and tried to pry it loose, but her fingers were slick with her own blood.

"Release me, you beast!" She gasped against the squeezing snake. "My brothers are not far behind. They'll kill you if you lay one dirty hand on me."

"And would those brothers be three?"

"Three?" She gulped. It was getting harder to draw breath from her squeezed midsection. "You've . . . seen them?"

"Ah, so it was not only the musketeer you were trying to elude back at the inn, eh?" One jerk of his wrist pulled Min over to Luciano. Charmed by the snake, Min was held firm against his thin, bony figure. Spidery fingers curled about her arms. She was momentarily blinded as the setting sun flashed across his gold tooth.

"Fear not, mademoiselle, you have eluded them all.

The musketeer has gone off on his own and the brothers stopped at the last village, for one of their horses was lame. I've you all to myself now, see?"

No one to help you now. You're on your own.

"No!" Min's struggles were in vain. Luciano succeeded in wrapping her skirts about her kicking legs and hoisted her over his snow-white horse. She lay stomach down, wriggling and screaming, the bullwhip clenched about her gut.

Luciano pulled himself up behind her and gave her hindquarters a sharp slap before spurring his horse. "We're off!"

"What now?" Alexandre wondered as he paced impatiently back and forth across the grease-laden floor of the tavern.

Adrian paced by the hearth, nursing his second tankard of ale, while Armand brushed his fingers back through his hair before slamming his fist down onto the trestle table. "We were so close!"

"She's headed for Paris." Adrian replaced the salt cellar that had toppled courtesy of Armand's outrage. "There is no doubt."

"You go on without me," Alexandre said. He splayed his hands across the table, leaning into the half-circle of anxious faces. "I've an appointment at the Louvre tomorrow. I'll have to leave you anyway. My horse is lame. It'll have to be shot. I'll wait and take the next coach to Paris. Two of you should be more than enough."

"Yes," Armand agreed. "We mustn't delay any longer. We should split up when we arrive in Paris. Make it all the more difficult for anyone to track us. Damn, I hadn't wanted to enter Paris without thorough planning and disguises. I do not like being forced!"

"If we are careful, we can slip in and out of the city before wind of our presence ever reaches the *garde,*" Adrian said.

"Perhaps. God only knows where that girl is off to. Alexandre, did she give you any clue to where she might be headed?"

"Certainly not Val-de-Grâce," Adrian said with a chuckle. "It had to have been a ruse, her mention of Aunt Huguette to the chevalier."

"I don't know." Alexandre stomped his toe against the leg of the table. He should have anticipated something like this. She would never stand for the convent. Even if it was to only be for a few months. If only Adrian hadn't taken her along on the robbery. If only Armand had not seen the severed reins. Had she no idea the dangers Armand and Adrian faced entering Paris? They were wanted men!

He caught the nervous glitter in Adrian's eyes. He knew they were both thinking the same thing. They could not betray their sister's trust, but at the same time they both knew her foolishness could endanger the entire family. He remembered the letter. Alexandre had looked through Mignonne's things before leaving yesterday morning, hoping for a clue to her mind-set; it was missing.

"There is a possibility. But a dangerous one, at that," Alexandre offered weakly. "You could check musketeer headquarters."

"Musketeer?" Armand eyed Alexandre. "She was serious?"

"She carries your letter."

"Letter?"

"The commission in the musketeers granted by d'Artagnan."

"But I burned that letter. Months ago!"

"Min rescued it before it burned. It's not as if she could

read the thing; she thinks it is a welcome to the musketeers."

"It is! But not if my crimes are ever discovered! It is merely bait, awaiting my bite. Any Saint-Sylvestre's bite! Who's to say the king will not demand our sister be held for ransom until either Adrian or I appear to face justice for our crimes? How could she do such a thing?"

"She's always looked up to you, Armand. And father. Well, we all have our dreams, haven't we?"

"Dear God." Armand pushed splayed fingers back through his hair. "Our sister wishes to become a musketeer. I thought it only a foolish boast. Besides being a girl, she's just . . . damn!"

Knowing there was no right time to say what Mignonne had told him many times before, Alexandre felt it best to get all things out in the open. Armand must know sooner or later. "She wishes to restore honor to the Saint-Sylvestre name."

"Honor?"

"She sees her brother riding the high roads every day. Lying, deceiving, stealing—"

"But I have no choice!"

Armand's words lingered about the brothers like a foul odor, settling heavily upon their shoulders as they each exchanged knowing glances.

"We've more than enough to support the family now," Alexandre stated. "Even with the twins. And you know that I shall take complete control over my children's needs as soon as I've secured a job."

"No, Alexandre, you mustn't worry about that." Armand waved a dismissive hand before him. "I will support your family until my dying days if I have to. They are no burden. You are my brother. But I must still ride the high roads. I know no other life. But where did I go so desperately wrong with our sister that she should attempt such a ruse?"

"You mustn't be so hard on yourself, Armand." Alexandre laid an arm across his older brother's shoulder. "Perhaps if mother were still around, she would have seen to it that our *petite* one had been raised correctly. We are all equally to blame."

"Yes, but the musketeers will never have me now. Save to see me hang. Do you actually think our sister plans to impersonate me?"

"I imagine so. It is your name on the letter."

"But they will discover she is not a man!"

"And then what will become of her?" Adrian wondered with a foreboding glance to his brothers. They could all guess her fate.

"I shall not rest until our Mignonne is safe in the hands of the sisters of Val-de-Grâce. I know this is the best thing for her. For then she will learn the graces and manners that will procure her a good husband. A man to look after her and treat her as a woman should be treated. And if we should not find her before she attempts this foolish ruse . . . well, pray God she does not."

He hadn't been able to get the vision of the lovely woman in pink out of his mind. So light and graceful her hand had been in his. The scent of flowers had floated about her like a ghostly summer mist. So sweet and musical her voice. Her lips, brazenly red beneath the black velvet demi-mask, had been a perfect bow. It was impossible to believe that she was the same foul-mouthed imp/woman who had cursed at him with such vigor.

This only proved that there was yet hope for Mignonne Saint-Sylvestre. She could be delicate and feminine if she wished. Not that she would ever wish for such things.

Chance chuckled as he spurred his horse into a canter. Min must be cursing herself about now for donning such a disguise. There was no way she could ever be comfortable in a dress after all the swordplay he had witnessed and the race across the roof. Why, the gown would be a virtual prison with all the stitching and whalebone reinforcements and layers and layers of frivolous laces the women so adored.

Ah, but wouldn't he love to help her out of it? To slip the pink satin from her shoulders, release the tight laces that crossed over her breasts, press his hand flat to her bare back and entice her into his embrace, holding her close so he could feel her timorous heartbeats. Taste her kisses . . .

A gray squirrel scampered across his path with all the dodging speed of a fox on its tail.

Alerted to possible danger, Chance drew rein, listening for sounds, anything unnatural. He hadn't ridden back to Remalard in search of the mystery man who had plans to rape Mignonne. He would be gone by now. And even though Chance was now sure that all three of the Saint-Sylvestre brothers were in pursuit of their sister, he was still uneasy.

They had seemed quite unaware, in fact, disbelieving, of her intentions to visit the aunt, a feeble excuse that Chance had never quite believed himself. But what was her real reason for fleeing her family? Her real destination? Did the brothers mean her harm? No, no. They had seemed concerned and compassionate towards their sister's plight. Quite eloquent and quick-witted was Armand. The makings of a fine musketeer. And the other one, Adrian, might have a chance, too. Though Alexandre had freely told him he was on his way to Paris to work in the king's gardens. Ah, well, every man had his vocation.

And Chance's vocation was to know and suspect danger at all possible turns. To anticipate a foul outcome and crush and stifle it before it became true. He lived by the sword and the honor of his king. He had many times risked his life to protect his holy ruler.

And now . . . that nagging feeling. A minute tingle in the back of his neck. Chance sensed all was not right. He would not rest until he saw Min back in the hands of her brothers. Safe and protected from all danger. Including himself.

Tout mon possible.

"Everything in my power."

Chapter Eight

Min hit the ground with a bone-jarring thud. A fallen elm branch cracked beneath her skirts and dug into her thigh. She accidentally bit into her tongue, but controlled her scream. Coppery blood swirled into her saliva, but she swallowed with a grimace. She had no time to grow queasy. There were more important things to worry about.

Like freedom.

Kicking her legs, Min began to pry them from the twisted mess of silk. Thankfully, the fall also succeeded in loosening the bonds around her wrists. She rolled to her back to hide her newfound freedom while Luciano casually tethered his horse to a tree.

"Where shall we begin, my little thief?" Luciano stood brushing the dust from his horse's legs. He obviously hadn't noticed the blood on the other side.

Min could barely make out Luciano's features until he stepped closer. At any other time she might comment on his beauty—the smooth, pale skin, the deep dark eyes, framed by a straight fall of midnight hair. But not this time. His constant smirk and garlic breath sickened her.

"For the last time, I did not take anything of yours!" Min screamed. "You are an evil man to want to punish someone for nothing." She had begun to bend her knees beneath her skirts, slipping the back of her skirt up with her toes. Just a little more and she could jump to her feet.

"And how can I be so sure you took nothing?" He looked off beyond his horse, pensive in his chilling beauty. His jaw pulsed once and he twisted his lips into a cruel sneer. "There was intent. You had your dirty fingers in my horse's saddlebag. Thieves, by nature, are dishonest and liars."

"Look who talks!" she cried. "You take so much, and with so little regard for human life. You yourself can probably not recall every piece your filthy hands touch."

"First," he said, bending down on one knee and grabbing her wrist, showing little surprise at her unbound hand. "My hands are never filthy. And you, besides being a master of disguise, are a quick-tongued wench. But I promise you, I shall remember *this* piece." His hand dove beneath her inched-up skirts, his fingernails scraping across her thighs, alerting Min deep in her breast. She had to get away from him before he started what he hadn't been able to begin at the inn.

Min pushed away with her bent leg, and spread her other leg to lever herself up. But the awkward position did not serve to her advantage. Luciano dove, pinning her left wrist to the ground by her head, pressing the length of his body down the one leg she had not succeeded in bending.

"You are readying yourself for me?" His chuckle was sepulchral and chilling as his free hand found the softness between her legs. "Good girl. Let us not waste another minute."

Silently rejoicing, Min pressed a pistol to the man's lips,

stopping him dead in his tracks. He'd been too busy digging his way through her skirts to notice her slip the weapon from the holster at his waist. She held the weapon steady, and prayed that this was not the one he had already fired. "Get your hands where I can see them."

He obliged, slowly dragging his fingers the length of her thigh before bringing them into her sight.

"Stand up," she demanded in a steady, cool voice. Her insides were a crazy mess of jitters and nerves, but she could not let them win over now. Always look your enemy straight in the eye, Armand had once said during fencing practice. It's like one dog facing down another; sooner or later, one will back off.

Min drew a deep breath in through her nose. "Get up, or I'll blow your lips off. Won't be so easy to take your pleasures then, will it?"

Luciano's expression relaxed and his lids fell heavily over his eyes. When he opened his eyes, a thin smile spread behind the barrel of the pistol, exposing a golden glint. Min could not believe the man's nerve. Did he not care? Did he have a death wish? For she was not beyond dropping the cock to ensure her own safety. Not that she had ever killed a man before, but if need be, she would do just that to protect herself.

Reluctantly, Luciano released the hand he had pinned over her head, retreating slowly, until he held it near his ear. Securing the pistol with both hands and pressing it firmly to his mouth, Min concentrated on the man's eyes. A sparkle of hunger shone brightly in both orbs, but so very different from the hunger she had seen in Chance's eyes. They never wavered. Yet his smile grew larger behind the pistol barrel. Madness!

A rush of air drew past her ear. The cool press of metal touched her forehead and dug into her temple.

Luciano cocked the trigger on the pistol he'd pulled

from the shoulder strap behind his back. He nudged his lips until the barrel of the gun Min held rested in the curved flesh just below his nose. "Now," he hissed. "Which one do you think has the ball? Come on, wench, do you think you've won? Or perhaps it is I who holds the loaded weapon? Ah, such a dilemma!"

Min closed her eyes. Her blood pounded hard in her temples, pressing unmercifully against the steel barrel. She rubbed a sweaty thumb over the cock of the pistol she held.

"This is foolish." She tried desperately to hide the nervous quiver in her voice. "If we both fire, then only one shall die. Unless we both have a loaded pistol. Which would be doubly stupid, for then we would both be dead. But if not—if I have the ball—then hurrah for me, but if you have the ball, your fun is already done. I'll be dead."

The glint of gold in Luciano's mouth and the white sparks in his eyes were the only things discernible in the shadows where they lay. "Who says I still won't take my pleasures? It takes a while for the body to cool."

Min swallowed. *Merde.* He would kill her one way or another, and have his pleasures, too. The thought made her stomach flip-flop.

"Very well," she countered, struggling to maintain eye contact with the very devil himself, while at the same time fighting the revulsion brewing in her throat. "But you'll allow me the advantage of firing first, since I am the lady. And if you are a gentleman, then it is only fair."

"I've never claimed to be a gentleman. But . . . very well, go on."

Not what she wanted to hear. There was no ball in her pistol. Min's thumb slipped from the trigger.

Time for a new plan.

Drums beat loudly. Somewhere. So close. Inside it seemed. Min realized it was her heart that pounded a vicious beat against her ribcage. *Use the fear,* Adrian had directed just before their midnight raid. *Without fear you become cocky, make mistakes.*

"Well then, I shall just have to take the chance that you would prefer a live body to a cooling one." Min rammed her pistol into Luciano's mouth, and at the same time brought up her bent leg and crushed it into his groin. The villain's pistol exploded by her ear. Her vision blurred into a sparkling daze. The heavy gun dropped from her fingers, and she groped haphazardly into the foggy blur of stars before her.

Bone-chilling yowls served to bring Min to her senses. Not her own, thank God. She dragged her legs from under Luciano's moaning body and was able to pull herself to her feet.

Luciano rolled about on the soft thicket of fallen maple leaves, clutching his groin with one hand and his bloody mouth with the other. A barrage of foreign curses filled the air. Min dashed for the pistol she had held, pointed it at his leg, and released the cock. Nothing. "Fie!"

She ran to the waiting horse and fumbled through the saddlebags. Another pistol. And it was primed. She cocked the trigger and aimed. Luciano's bloodcurdling whine scraped the air as hard steel merged with his flesh. He rolled to his back, the blood spitting from his thigh with each curse. He screamed, "You'll die for this, wench!"

Min prepared to dash away when a flash of gold caught her eye. She dove to the ground near her captor's shoulder and snatched up the bloody tooth. "*Merci,* monsieur, but I believe you're in no position to bring death upon anyone at the moment." She gave Luciano a hearty slap on his wounded leg, then tossed the tooth into the air and caught it with a snap of her wrist. "This shall serve me well."

The villain yelped and cursed her as a ruthless bitch.

Sure that her aggressor would be incapacitated for a

time, Min switched her thoughts to escape. She could run, but there was no telling how soon Luciano would be able to pull himself up on his horse.

She spun around and eyed the horse. It practically glowed in the hazy darkness. "Yes!" Min ripped her skirts up the front, kicked off her hazardous high heels, and mounted the Andalusian. She wiped her hair from her eyes, her hand slipping through something sticky at her temple. Further study of her forehead found a shallow wound. The pistol ball had grazed her.

Not enough to worry.

Min wiped her fingers over her skirts and then, satisfaction growing inside, she smeared them across the horse's pristine coat, painting it with serrated trails of red.

"I'm touching your horse, Luciano!"

"Damn . . . you . . ." he choked.

She jabbed the horse's flanks with her bare heels and left her conquest groaning in the grass.

The horse was a feisty one and hard to control. A white demon, luminescent against the darkening sky, racing towards the raging bowels of hellfire. Min had ridden perhaps two leagues when the beast finally succeeded in throwing her into the cool, algae-caked waters of a millpond. The Andalusian gave a laughing neigh and galloped off.

Her dress had started to dry. Which proved to be an instrument of torture. For as the silk dried, it also shrank, pulling the whalebone reinforcements in the stays tight to Min's breasts, clamping her ribs in like a vise.

She had thought to remove the overskirts, but she didn't want to deal with the situation of wandering about in only a chemise and petticoats should someone discover her. Instead she tore the sleeves off, which had begun to bind under her arms. As soon as she stepped through the gates of Paris she would find suitable clothes, preferably men's, and a weapon.

"Damn him!" She cursed Luciano for so mercilessly breaking her sword upon his knee as if it were a trifle and not the valued treasure it was. It was the only tangible memory she had left of a brave and gallant man. A man Min knew would have been proud to see her in the ranks of the musketeers.

Her forehead burned. Min studied the serrated flesh with a dirty fingertip. The pistol ball had skimmed her temple, opening it into a shallow wound. It had bled for a while but was now stopped thanks to the length of pink silk Min had torn from her dress and wrapped around her forehead. She wrapped another strip of silk about her knuckles and jerked it into a tight knot with her teeth.

Night had come, and with the hazy darkness, an inkling of fear simmered in her nerves. Now what would she do? She had no sword, no clothes, no money—

Wait! She spat into her hand and the golden nugget toppled across her palm. It was small, but should bring a good price. "Hope he doesn't come looking for this."

A chill shuddered up the back of Min's neck. It made her queasy to even picture Luciano's leering smirk in her mind. If there ever were a Notorious One, it had to be him. She prayed she was right, and that her brothers would be safe from Chance's vengeance. As far as she knew, the chevalier was off in search of them at this very moment. "God protect them," she whispered. "May the night keep us safe."

She ripped away the rest of the lace petticoats and the bottom of her skirt, leaving only the outer silk, ripped to her ankles, to allow ease of walking. Imagining she looked a trifle worse than any of Paris's busiest whores, Min wasn't too terribly worried. If she was careful, and stayed off the high roads, no one would see her until she'd obtained some better clothes. Balling up the torn petticoats and silk sleeves, Min tossed them to the side of the pond.

One of a plethora of windmills dotting the countryside offered solace and rest. And time to plan. It would not be wise to walk out on the road for fear of being discovered by her brothers or Luciano. If Armand were to see her in such a state, she'd never see the light of day from behind the doors of Val-de-Grâce. And if Luciano should find her, well . . .

A chilling shudder returned to embrace Min's shoulders in its icy claws. The brandy-voiced villain would most certainly not give up on her now. Of course, it would be a good time before he was able to stand and walk after the damage she had done. She hoped.

Tossing her mud-caked, drying hair over her exposed shoulder, Min rounded the windmill; her plans, to walk the last few leagues to Paris. Yes, it would be wisest to travel in the dark of night, with hopes that any who pursued her had decided to call it a night—or was bleeding to death in the grass.

The sound of hooves picking slowly across the way alerted her. Min pulled her skirts to her waist and pressed her back to the mill, ensuring her concealment.

She listened with vigilant patience. Rhythmic sprays of sand scattered behind the horse's hooves. *Plish. Plish.* There was only one rider. He rode at a casual gait. Not in any hurry, probably keeping an eye out for something, or maybe *looking* for something. Min drew in her breath. Could it be Luciano?

Already? No, he had to still be rolling about on the ground. Of course, it had been over an hour. And if his horse was as faithful to him as he was to it, the beast might have plucked him up and thrown him over its back itself.

The horse nickered and suddenly its footsteps ceased. Min held her breath, inhaling deeply through her nose, trying to detect a hint of brandy in the breeze. She squeezed her fists and the gold tooth cut into her palm. Had he seen her? Were these damned pink skirts visible in the twilight?

She listened as a sword was slowly drawn, carefully, as if not to make a sound. The rider prodded about in the water with his weapon. Looking for what? Min dared a glance. The remains of her petticoats hung from the end of a gleaming broadsword.

She pressed her eyelids closed and prayed for mercy. That damn horse had returned to his master, and somehow Luciano had recovered from the damage she had done. But she wouldn't know for sure until she glimpsed the horse. *Mon Dieu,* but the glow of its white flesh alone should light up her shadowed hiding spot.

The murmur of air rushing through heavy fabric, and the sound of groaning wood as the sails turned about set her heart racing. *Be quiet,* she thought of the windmill. *I cannot hear if he approaches.*

As if her wish were granted, all became deathly still as she listened for the horse to move. It did not. Min's heart beat viciously inside her ribs. She willed it to be steady for fear Luciano would hear her anxiety. It was all she could do to remain still.

Chapter Nine

"Mademoiselle Saint-Sylvestre?"

Thankful for miracles, Min expelled her breath. Her knees let loose from their locked state. She grasped for the wall of the windmill behind her, but it eluded her fingers as her vision went black and she fell into the tangle of weeds and grass at her feet.

"Mademoiselle, speak to me."

Min could not verbally express the relief she felt at being in Chance's arms. Instead she fell deeper into his sheltering embrace, curled her legs up to her body, and clung tightly to his broad chest.

She did not cry. Only sissy fops cried, Adrian had always taunted her. But she did pant and heave and could not find her voice for the longest time. It felt so good to be surrounded by this man's arms. So strong, yet at the same time gentle. She burrowed her nose between his arm and chest and inhaled sweat and mud and the sensual smell of man. She closed her eyes to the gentleness of his touch as his fingers stroked across her bandaged brow and smoothed over her hair, soothing her as if she were a child.

"Tell me you are all right, mademoiselle, or I shall fear you have been harmed. Please, anything. Scream. Call me a buffoon. Do something."

Deaf to his worries, Min focused on the rise and fall of the warm chest near her face. Her fingers melded to his linen shirt, seeking out the steady, proud beat of his heart. So virile and strong, this lovely man. Living, breathing, all-encompassing in his nearness. Never had she been so intimately close to a man before. In all her dreams she could never have composed such a magnificent creature. But this was not a dream, it was gorgeous reality.

"*Merde,* someone's cut out her tongue. She cannot speak!"

Min smiled at Chance's frantic worry. "No, no, you buffoon."

"Ah, *merci,* mademoiselle." He hugged her gently. "Never has it felt so good to be called such a thing."

Min looked up into Chance's eyes. Their faces were inches apart. His breaths panted across her forehead. What happened next surprised even Min. It was as if some lever shifted inside her. Not unlike the odd turn her body had taken on top of the roof in Remalard. Her mind shrieked in crazy protest as she tilted her chin up and pressed her lips to his. *This is madness! Shameless!* But her lips did not heed her mind's screams. Chance's mouth received hers in a warm press. Fear and shame shattered into a surging force that conquered her weak limbs and took control, pushing, urging, making her body function at its own will.

Rising to her knees, Min straddled his legs. He, in turn, deepened the kiss, taking fiercely from her mouth and returning the pleasure with a slow dance of his tongue. A deep, wanting groan escaped her lips, spurring Chance's actions into a passionate quest for her heart.

When he reached around and clasped his hands across her back to pull her closer, Min thought surely she had fallen into the arms of an angel. His heavenly touch drew the pain from her wounds and numbed the terror. This was salvation. His kiss . . . the holy water that cures a dying soul. He touched her soul with his unspoken desires.

This man. This perfect man. She felt some emotion . . . an inexplicable compulsion to want to be with him, by him, inside him. Was this love? Could it possibly be?

If it was, then truly love was bliss.

But her bliss ended abruptly. Chance jerked away from her body. His blue eyes flashed wide as they scanned her face. "Mademoiselle?"

Suddenly aware of her actions, Min averted her eyes from his seeking surprise. She looked down at her fingers, pressed to his chest, his frenzied heart beating beneath her palms. Her own body had somehow snuggled close to his, leaving little room for propriety. Ah! How could she have done such a thing?

"Forgive me, chevalier." Min shuffled out of his grasp and rested on her knees in the grass beside him. "I am still a bit out of sorts." Most assuredly, if she were thinking about love! With a jerk of her head, she tossed her hair over her shoulder and smoothed a few stray strands from her face, relying on the simple movement to disguise her trepidation. "I am all right. I feared you were someone else, that is all. It was just relief that pulled me into a silly girlish swoon. That's it. I was not of my right mind."

"Really?" The sparkling glimmer in his eyes could not hide Chance's gentle humor. Though a glance over her bandaged head quickly brought him to his wits. "You are hurt?"

Min pressed her fingers over his, gently guiding them away from her forehead. If he were to continue to touch her, she knew not what she would do. She was completely at the mercy of her body's whims when in his presence, almost as if he were the sustenance her body craved and sought out against her will. " 'Tis nothing."

"Nothing? There is blood. And this." His large fingers cupped her bandaged knuckles as softly as if he held a peeping newborn chick.

"Long stopped bleeding," Min bravely replied. To fall weeping into a man's arms over so little a cut would be silly and so . . . cowardly.

"But why are you here? I thought you would be in Paris by now."

"And when did you guess it was me? I thought my disguise a clever one." She sat back on her haunches and looked over her dress. Thoroughly muddied and torn, it was no longer pink. She quickly pulled the front of her skirt together after seeing that she revealed far too much leg.

Chance cleared his throat, quickly shifting his gaze to her face. "The maid at the Bare Moon told me. Where did you get this dress?"

"From a lady dressed in pearls and silk. On her way to Paris for the ball, I believe. She was very obliging, felt it was necessary I had the proper attire. Besides she had no use for this, can you believe it?"

"You traded your horse?"

"I thought it a fitting payment."

"And your brothers—"

"My brothers?"

"By luck of fate, I met them at the inn after you slipped away."

Min felt her throat constrict. Mon Dieu, *does he know? Did he arrest them?* "Where are they now?"

"Looking for you."

"So you didn't arr—" Min pressed two fingers to her lips to stifle the betraying words. They were not the highwaymen he sought. They could not be. Perhaps he hadn't been privy to their occupation. Yes, just a friendly chat with three strangers. Well, not exactly strangers. He knew they were her brothers.

"Actually, you fooled them, too. You are a crafty trickster, I must admit." He stood and offered a dirt-smudged hand to her. "Tell me, why are you in such a fix? Where is the carriage? And how?" He gestured to her bandaged forehead, suddenly unable to find the words to express his dismay.

"Our carriage was robbed. By the same man who had me tied to his bed." Min pulled herself up with the aid of Chance's hand. To stand made her aware of her weakness. She felt so fragile and small next to him. He towered a good head over her petite frame. With the way her head spun from exhaustion and lack of food, she thought she might faint. "The bastard shot the coachman and knocked out the two men with whom I was traveling. We left behind a poor young child. I pray she is not hurt."

"We? Did he abduct you? But of course." Chance pushed his fingers over his shaved coif. "That is why you are in such a state." He jerked her around by the shoulders. Min thought she saw a niggling glimmer of worry in his eyes. "Mignonne, tell me, are you . . . safe?"

She followed Chance's eyes as they traveled nervously up and down her body, taking in the dirt and the bruises and bandages, and her general weary condition. She laid her hand across her breasts to try to hide the exposed flesh, well aware that his gaze lingered a bit too long. Were all men so obvious in their intentions?

"He did not have his way with me, if that is what you inquire." Pulling her shoulders straight, Min marched past him, her bare feet taking on the flour dust that surrounded the mill. She was suddenly quite angered that a man should worry for her safety when she so obviously was quite all right and had taken to the challenge with great success. No man could ever prove a match to her.

"You were damn lucky." Chance followed her to his horse.

"Lucky?" She spun about, wanting to punch the man in the gut, but she restrained her itching fist. "It was skill that saved me. Nothing but skill. I had neither sword nor pistol, and he was armed with three." She displayed three proud fingers. "I left him groaning and bleeding in the grass."

Chance crossed his arms and eyed her amusedly. "Really? And was he half lame and blind, too?"

"Oh!" Min stomped past Chance. The nerve of the man to think she could not look after herself. She had tricked death just hours ago, and he was making light of it. Well, she would not play the helpless woman to this *gasçon*. She had more important things to tend to.

Faltering against the side of the windmill, Min caught herself before Chance noticed. Her breaths came in deep gasps. Ignoring her failing energy, she pressed onward. The chevalier had no idea of her strengths. He most likely thought her a weak and frivolous female, just as most men did. Now was no time to let him see she was as drained as he thought. "Leave me. I am on my way to Paris."

"You are weak."

Just as she had thought.

"And damn stubborn! I cannot let you wander unescorted into Paris. You'll never get past the lecherous hands of the guards at the Porte Saint-Jacques this late at night." Mounting quickly, Chance rode up alongside Min, and drew rein to match her wobbling march. "Especially in your . . . disarray."

"I'll not turn my well-being over to you, Monsieur Lambert."

"Chevalier."

"Whatever!" Min spun about, causing Chance to jerk his horse to a halt. She gripped her fingers into tight balls. A wave of dizziness spun through one ear and out the other, twirling her brain into a confusing mix. Min caught herself against the horse's dark flank. "You could do the gentlemanly thing and offer your horse instead of allowing a lady to walk."

"So 'tis a lady now, is it? Hmm. And would I have you race off and leave me behind?" Chance chuckled. "Never. I'll bring you to Paris and keep you safe until I have located your brothers. After that I wash my hands of you, Mademoiselle Imp."

"Oh, don't call me that!"

Min wished only to wipe the smile from his face with a quick dash of her fist. But she feigned discretion. She was much too weak to deliver a good punch at the moment. And he did have a rather pretty face. It wouldn't do to be marking it up with bruises. And to think of drawing a fist across the very lips she had just kissed . . .

Oh, his kiss! Twice now she had tasted the power of this man's potent desires. It had been a heavenly treat that she wished to receive again. God's body, had she really straddled him and thrust her tongue into his mouth like a brazen courtesan?

Yes. And she wanted to do it again.

"It is just Min," she whispered, her defenses waning. "And I won't allow you to hand me over to my brothers so they may lock me up in a convent. I simply won't have it."

"Well, I don't believe you have much choice."

Before Min could answer, Chance lifted her by the waist and swept her over the saddle. Once again she found herself in the facedown position, her nose to horseflesh, her legs dangling, and her rump beneath the hands of a man. She opened her mouth to protest, but dizziness and fatigue finally succeeded in luring her mind into a silent darkness.

By the time they reached the refuse-scattered cobblestones of Paris, Min's ribs ached and her throat was dry from lack of drink and the dust that had billowed up from beneath the horse's hooves. Chance had eventually allowed her to sit upright, in front of him, but she was now quite sure she could detect a horse a league away just by scent, for it was so thoroughly entrenched in her senses.

She hoped her legs would take to ground easily after her dangling journey, because she had no intention of waiting to allow Chevalier Lambert to escort her to her brothers. Oh, no, much as his presence bewitched her and his kiss tempted her to . . . No. She just couldn't risk the chance of remaining the night.

Sequestering her away until Armand could jail her up in Val-de-Grâce was not something she would stand still for. Though the thought of staying near him and trying to change this handsome musketeer's mind was intriguing, she felt sure he would not sway. He'd pushed away from her kiss by the windmill. Had been shocked at her brazen actions. He most likely thought her a harlot or a crazed lunatic.

There was also that other notable item that lingered in the back of her mind. He had said he was on a mission. A mission to find the criminals who had murdered Justine. Who could this Justine be but a woman he had loved?

Shame washed over Min's shoulders. He had no interest in her when the need for revenge for his true love sat heavily on his shoulders. His kisses were merely an accident, a quick fix for some odd need his body wanted, a need she knew not. As muddled as her emotions were right now, she could not risk another shameless encounter like that. Fie! Every look, every touch from him only made her more confused as to what she really wanted.

Though it was dark, a high moon allowed partial display of her surroundings. In the distance the steeples of Saint-Germain-des-Prés stabbed the sky. Smoking chimneys did little to disguise the smell of the street filth. Rotten fish, overripe fruit, mud-soaked straw, and an incessant cloud of waste fumes were enough to make one gag. The narrow gutters that trailed down the centers of the streets were clogged and badly in need of cleaning. It was a far cry from the fresh, open air of the country.

They dismounted and Chance tethered his horse in front of a stone apartment building. "You become accustomed to it," he said, reading Min's thoughts.

"Perhaps if one spends his entire life with his head in a chamber pot," she snapped. She tested her legs by springing at the knees. Not so sore as her gut, they would do for a sprint.

"This coming from a woman hell-bent on getting to Paris and away from her safe country home? I should ask what the lure is, since you certainly do not seem pleased."

"I have my reasons." Reasons she could not divulge to a musketeer.

Min looked up the side of the apartment building. The cornerstone stated that they were on the Rue St. Antoine. Three stories of paned windows rose above her, a hideous black stain creeping from the second-story window. Refuse trails, judging from the dark stench that lay but a leap from Min's bare feet. A quick glance about her showed a narrow alleyway just to the left, and a few more down the way. All very dark, and most likely hiding street rabble of a sort she'd rather not encounter.

"I cannot imagine what reasons a young country girl would have to run from her family and flee to Paris, unescorted. You are aware of the dangers?"

Hands on her hips, Min cocked a defiant gaze towards the musketeer. "I believe I can handle myself, chevalier."

And she could.

Maybe.

He looked over her tattered state, stepping closer to enable his vision to adjust to the hazy darkness. "Yes, I'm sure you can handle yourself. Possibly. But you said you were to visit a relative?"

"Relative? Oh, yes, my Aunt Huguette." *Only when hell freezes over!* "Yes, I suppose I should be going then."

"In that condition?"

Min looked over her tattered facade. This ragged slip of silk would serve her no more than entrance to a cutthroat's murderous arms. New clothes were a necessity if she planned to walk the streets without worry of assault. She wondered if the chevalier had any to lend. Not that he'd approve . . .

"Come," Chance said. "We'll make you look presentable. And then I shall escort you to your aunt's door. No doubt it is past midnight. I'll not have you prancing about Paris alone."

"Chevalier Lambert!"

Min turned at the sound of a lone street hawker pushing his cloth-covered cart ahead of him. A tattered wisp of black cloth rippled in the subtle breeze, announcing to all that he bartered.

"Jean-Bob, it's a late night for you." Chance tipped his hat to the vendor. "Heading for the Rooster's Coop?"

"You know it! I see you've a dirty one there. A new recruit?"

"Bah! No recruit of mine . . ."

While Chance exchanged pleasantries with the hawker, Min took the opportunity to carefully inch toward the darkness of the narrow alley, all the while keeping her eyes on the hawker, who faced her, but was too caught up in speaking to the chevalier.

In a matter of seconds she was down the mud-slick alleyway, her dirty skirts held at her hips to prevent her from tripping. It was difficult to see more than the dull lines of buildings and shapeless blobs that lined the streets. Dashing beneath a high line of forgotten laundry that stretched from building to building, Min cleared two alleys by the time she heard the muffled shouts behind her.

"The deuce! She's done it again!"

Naughtily pleased that she'd once again given her musketeer the slip, Min dodged a cart of bundled faggots and slipped deftly between a stack of dirt-encrusted field potatoes piled on the ground and a cart which reeked of privy waste.

The streets were slick with filth and muddy water beneath her bare feet, but she slipped no more than a few times. It was just like running over slick rocks in the stream behind the château, though with a few more obstacles and no fish.

"Stop that woman!"

Min's heart jumped at the sound of Chance's voice. One street separated the two of them. Rushing blindly forward, her breath suddenly jerked from her lungs. The ragged hem of her dress caught on the corner of a splintered cart. "Once again proof that these damned dresses are nonsense!"

Chance called out again, his voice becoming closer. He would be on her soon enough.

Cursing her feminine attire with words that would make even Sophie blush, Min heaved, ripping the hem of her skirt, leaving a portion of dirty pink silk behind. Spying a flash of candlelight, she dodged into the nearest door and through the galley of a very surprised little old lady.

Chance slipped and caught himself against the cold filigree of an iron gate. He cursed the tricky imp under his breath. This was the third time she had succeeded in giving him the slip. And he was getting nothing more than angry!

When had finding the Notorious Ones taken second calling to chasing after an impetuous street rat?

He swiped the sweat from his brow. *I could just let her go. Her brothers will find her.* But did they even know her destination? What goal lay in Paris that could lure a woman such as Mignonne, without fear of the dangers of her solitary travel? And why did he feel this incessant need to watch over this particularly vexing imp? She had nothing of interest to offer him.

Really? So those stolen kisses meant nothing to you? And what was it about her eyes that you just couldn't stop thinking of them?

"All right, all right!" Chance cursed his conscience. At the same time his mouth watered for the taste of bittersweet chocolate. "So she does interest me. No! Do not be such a fool," he fought back at himself, gripping his fist before his heart. He did not want this. She would bring nothing but heartache. Justine was a lesson in the art of woman. She had proved to him what women were truly like.

No, not all women.

He knew as much. Mignonne was not like Justine. She would never purposely deceive him. Why, she hardly knew him. And it wasn't as if they were romantically involved—though he would never balk if opportunity presented itself.

Ah! With all his heart Chance did not want to fall victim to another pretty woman's charms. But it was the very same heart that forced the treasonous idea of pursuing the elusive Mademoiselle Imp. There was just something about her that he could not resist. Everything about her was so different from what he'd always desired in a woman. And that was beginning to frighten him. Had his taste in women been so odd all along?

Most certainly it had been when he'd said his vows to Justine.

Yes, Mignonne was the complete opposite of his departed wife. She was an innocent when it came to wicked ways.

Which—Chance gasped in a heaving breath—was exactly why he must find her. She needed protection. Whether she liked it or not.

He leaned over to catch his breath and spied a piece of torn silk hanging from the edge of a serrated board. "Mademoiselle Imp is not so deft in her more feminine costume." He looked around and spied an open door.

If you follow her, you know you can never stop. If you turn and run in the opposite direction, right now, your life will be all the easier.

Much as his conscience pleaded for attention, he could not—would not—listen. "Once again I step blindly into fire."

Embracing the challenge with a soldier's vigor, Chance dashed into the lighted kitchen, only to be greeted by the end of a broom.

"Vagrant!" the old woman croaked, wielding her broom as mightly as a sword.

Chance intercepted a blow to his kneecaps, but missed the return shot to his ribs. "Ouff!" The air chuffed out of his lungs. "Cease, madame, I am in—" Another blow to his already aching shoulder. He stumbled to the door, fending off a whooshing blow with his arm. "Where did the woman go?" he managed. "The one in the ragged skirts?"

"Keep your hands off that poor child! Beast!"

The broom cracked sharply across Chance's back, sending shock waves down to his toes. He lost his footing and stumbled out onto the street, his hands sliding through a mud puddle. The old lady followed, her broom waving valiantly above her head. Chance stumbled to his feet and limped away.

"And don't come back!"

"Insufferable hag," he muttered and leaned against the wall. "God's blood, I shall ache for days. And still the little imp eludes me. Blast! Is she a fox in disguise? This—this—Aggh!"

A shower of kitchen scraps pelted Chance's head and shoulders, splattering onion-laced liquid and slimy carrot skins across his face and hands. Thoroughly peeved, he slunk down against the wall, and spat a potato peel from his mouth. "Blast!"

Min stumbled through many more kitchens, frightening yawning, bleary-eyed children and a *marchand du vin,* whose walls were lined with casks of sweet-smelling wines, before finally securing a place in a tight alleyway that boasted a covered carriage. She squeezed inside the coach, held her breath, and waited.

Long minutes passed. No sound of Chance's footfalls. Good.

Maybe.

Releasing her breath, Min caught her forehead in her palms. She just didn't know what to think anymore. If he had ceased following her, did that mean he was no longer interested in her safety or that she'd actually given him the slip? No, she didn't need a man to protect her. And yes, she did need him out of her hair in order to achieve success.

So why couldn't she be more pleased with his absence?

Adjusting her weight and wriggling in the confines of the carriage floor, Min settled into a tucked ball to rest. As she closed her eyes, the image of Chance's dancing eyes appeared. She reached out but grasped only the edge of the seat cushion.

"I think I need you, chevalier," she whispered. And then, "But why?"

Sleep came moments later.

Chapter Ten

Sunrise forced its way into Min's cramped quarters. She rose, stretched out the kinks, and took to the streets. The rhythm of horses' hooves sang in every narrowly cobbled row. Sweet morning treats misted the air with their sugar and yeast aroma. The bleat of a mother goat and her kid made Min smile and reach to touch the silver bell that dangled from the little creature's neck. Paris was opening its eyes and yawning in yet another busy day.

A fine ebony-lacquered carriage charged down the cobbles at a pace that forced Min against the wall and into an inviting salon that was quite spacious and empty in the rich morning hours. Clutching her ragged skirts in her mud-spattered hands, Min looked about cautiously. Not a single face greeted her; not a sound echoed off the damask-covered walls. And so she dared to release an exhausted breath and allowed her shoulders to relax.

He had been so close last night. Mon Dieu, *what he might have done if he'd gotten his hands on me?* What might *she* have done if he had laid his big, muscular hands on her? Beg, plead, perhaps faint in his arms? All in the pursuit of further pleasures. Pleasures that she had only tasted in his kisses. And mere tastes were never satisfying; they only whetted one's appetite for the feast.

You mustn't think like that. Keep your mind on the task at hand. The king's household troops would never allow a love-dazed woman into their ranks. *Keep sharp. Stifle all thoughts regarding the chevalier.*

Really? And you actually believe the musketeers will allow a woman *into their ranks? Love-dazed or not?*

"Yes," Min answered firmly. "I'll give them no choice. They won't even see me coming. By the time they realize I'm a woman, it'll be too late. They'll beg me to remain."

With great reluctance, Min stuffed lustful thoughts of Chancery Lambert deep inside the back doors of her mind, replacing them with the Saint-Sylvestre bravado that she would need to fulfill her task.

Turning around, Min took in a grand staircase of turned mahogany. It spiraled up and around a great chandelier of gaudy, red crystal droplets. Everything had a touch of garish embellishment. There were scads of red damask chaises, lined in gold and emerald fringe. The floor was carpeted in loud emerald and dotted with red fleurs-de-lis, and the pictures on the walls were of scantily clad women. Min's jaw fell at the sight of the gallery of semi-nudes. The artist had captured his subjects quite unawares in the act of undressing. One plump lady pulled down her hose, quite unmindful that her left breast spilled from her chemise.

"Scandalous," Min whispered. But that did not keep her from scrutinizing the other, more enticing pictures. Her eyes fell upon that of a nude man bearing fruits for his lover. He quite resembled Chance, what with his broad, muscular shoulders. As Min's eyes traveled down his torso, her interest growing keen, she was suddenly interrupted by a hoarse cough.

A weary-eyed young woman greeted Min with a yawning welcome. "If you're looking for work, you'd best return after the noon bell. Madame d'Tournet does not rise until then." She stifled another yawn behind her bare arm. "I'm the only one fool enough to be up. Actually, I haven't yet gone to sleep," she said with a giggle and a wink. "My name is Lady Godiva."

"*Bonjour,* your grace," Min offered with a quick bow. "But I've no need of work."

"Then why are you here?"

Min glanced towards the door. "There is a man chasing me."

"Oh! Then we'd best close the door and secret you away!"

"What I mean is, there *was* a man chasing me. I eluded him. Last night. But I'm not sure if he'll pick up my trail this morning."

"Such adventure!"

Min glanced out the open doorway, wondering if her musketeer would be as set on finding her as he was on finding his lover's murderer.

Most likely not.

"Come," the woman said as she closed the door and trudged toward the stairs, "let's go upstairs, and you can fill me in on your adventures. Was he handsome? Brute? A fop?"

"Never a fop, please," Min muttered as she followed her bleary-eyed hostess up the winding stairs to a small room of lavish design and meager furnishings. In fact, there was but a bed and an armoire.

Min sat on the edge of the feather mattress, not wishing to muss the woman's bed linens with her mud-spattered boots. It was rather odd that she strode about in such *déshabillé.* Nary but a slip of chiffon covered her shoulders and her stays were completely revealed. And lounging about in but a thin skirt of petticoats!

Lady Godiva sat on the window ledge, her bright, red-lacquered toes pressed to the paned glass, yawning as she scanned the streets. Her hair hung past her thighs in rich waves of topaz and copper. The rose damask stays did little to contain her voluptuous curves, while her linen petticoats were wearing quite thin over the knees.

Min suddenly realized just what sort of work the woman had been offering her. *Mon Dieu,* the paintings downstairs . . . She was a courtesan! Adrian had told her of Paris's *maisons de joie.* Though he swore he did not frequent the brothels, Min could never be sure because he always seemed to know when Armand had been to one. Which was very frequently.

"Do you think he is still about, this man who must never be a fop?"

Min shrugged and released a heavy sigh. "Most likely not." After describing Chance, Min waited as the prostitute scanned the brisk morning bustle on the streets below.

"I see no man of such handsome design." Lady Godiva possessed a rich Parisian accent, so elegant and silver-throated compared to Min's rough country dialect. "Though why you would run from such a deliciously divine and virile man is beyond me." She stepped down and placed herself on the bed next to Min, as grandly as a queen would retire before her humble servants. "Why do you run? It would be me that did the chasing instead of the other way around. Is there something wrong with him?"

Min shrugged and leaned back on her elbows, which sank inches into the well-worn mattress.

Chancery Blaise Lambert. What *was* wrong with him? He'd only her best interests in mind since first meeting her, and he had rescued her twice thus far. Though his best interests seemed to be keeping her firmly in hand until he could deliver her to her brothers.

As for any physical attraction on his part . . . well, it wasn't there, she felt sure. His heart still belonged to Justine—though dead—for why else would he seek vengeance against her murderer? Obviously his kiss at the inn had meant nothing to him. He was simply taking pleasure without the emotion. Fie! She should never have reciprocated by kissing him under the windmill. He had pulled away from her. The deuce, he must have thought her a fool or wanton!

But she had to admit, it didn't matter how he felt, it was just too wonderful to finally know the heat of a man's lips on her own, something she had only dreamed of until now. Those two stolen kisses would serve as fuel to her fantasies for many nights to come.

"There is nothing wrong with him," she said with a melodramatic sigh. "He's . . . well, I've never met such a handsome man, and yet . . . one that bothers me so. I cannot stop thinking of him, and yet I know in my heart that it is foolish to do so. He—he vexes my soul. I cannot explain it any other way."

"Oh, I understand you."

"It's just that if I remain with him, he will bring me to my brothers. And my brothers have every intention of delivering me to Val-de-Grâce."

"The convent?" Lady Godiva drew in a gasp between pertly puckered pink lips. "Oh, *chère,* that is dreadful. Ghastly! We do not utter such words here."

"I feel much the same. My brothers have taken a holy name and turned it into a blasphemous thing in my eyes."

Lady Godiva's bloodshot gaze worried over Min's disarray. She plucked a portion of Min's muddied skirts up between two fingers. "Oh, but you must fix yourself up a bit. The man would not have in mind to let you out of his sight if you took better care of yourself."

Min ripped her skirts from the girl's fingers. A streak of pride straightened her back and lifted her chin. "I've no desire to attract a man, if that is what you mean."

"But why not? You do *prefer* men, do you not?"

Unsure what this meant, Min replied confidently, "Oh, yes, I do. But—well, I've other things to do in Paris. I haven't the desire or the time to run about pursing my lips and batting my lashes at every man who cares to look."

"There is only the one that you have told me about." Lady Godiva's thick lips curled into a delicious, knowing arc. "And he desires to chase you. Do you know how rare it is that a woman has a man chasing after her?"

Min let her head fall to the soft, beaten, feather mattress. Sweet perfume caressed her senses. "Is it truly?"

"If you've one chasing you, I'd spin about and lock him in my arms."

The image of Chance's sculpted body pressed close to hers, her arms locked around his broad shoulders, and his lips teasing across her mouth, was an enticing one. "He is very handsome. And I do rather like the way his voice drips across my body like a warm summer rain."

"Ah! The girl admits she loves him."

"Love!" Min bolted upright. "Oh, no, not me. Not . . . love?"

Lady Godiva's finely tweezed brow lifted slyly. "Whatever you say, Mademoiselle of the Tattered Skirts. But believe me, if anyone knows that look and sound in one's voice, it is I."

"What look?" Min flashed her eyes wide. She pressed a dirt- and bloodstained finger to her lips. "What sound?"

"The look of love," Lady Godiva cooed seductively, as she trailed a brilliant red nail down Min's cheek and then traced it along her bandaged brow. "It brightens your eyes and gives your skin a beautiful rose color—at least, from what I can tell beneath all this dirt." She flicked her fingers to shoo away any dirt that might have transferred itself from Min to her. "You have it, *chère.* You cannot deny it."

"I do?" Min nervously smoothed her palms over her face, feeling a blush heat her skin. That *was* what was causing the rose color Lady Godiva spoke of. Her embarrassment. Nothing else. She didn't feel anything that might resemble love. Not that she knew what love was supposed to feel like. "Bosh. That is nonsense."

Lady Godiva gave a dismissive shrug and a negative nod, her eyes rolled beneath thick lashes.

"The deuce! Love is not the answer for me." Min threw herself back into the mattress and blew out a big sigh.

"Then what is?" Lady Godiva leaned over her. Min found it hard to keep her eyes from the fleshy mounds that plunged from her loose stays. Her bosoms were almost ready to spill out.

Min tugged her own bodice together where it had torn during her debacle with Luciano. "I've come to Paris to join the musketeers."

"Oh, I love the household troops!" A child's unrestrained glee burst out in Lady Godiva's giggles. "Such ribald and dashing rogues! Don't pay much, but they are a wild bunch to play with. Very adventurous, I must say. Tire me out something fierce whenever they come around."

"Really?" Min could only imagine what the woman was talking about. It was sure her adventures took her no further than her own bed. Min squeezed the bedsheets in her free hand. The sheets were thin, the wooden bedposts quite worn, especially the headboard.

Exactly what did a man and woman do when naked and in bed? Adrian had always left off after the kissing part. You'll learn soon enough, he'd say, and then wander off, leaving her perplexed and more than a little curious. Oh, she had some idea. She had watched the horses after all. And what the stallion possessed . . .

Min covered her face with her hands. *Don't think such thoughts. It's just too scandalous to imagine.*

"Here," Lady Godiva went to her lace-covered vanity and tossed a moist cloth to Min. It felt good to smooth away the dust and grime. A bath would be ideal, but Min would take what she could get for now.

"I may have a gown you could borrow . . ." Lady Godiva tapped her jaw, obviously not sure whether she really wanted to make such an offer as she scanned Min's appearance.

"I have this." Min spat into her palm and displayed the gold tooth. "But I don't need a gown—"

"What?" The courtesan shrieked enthusiastically, her eyes widening and the drool nearly visible as she studied the gold morsel on Min's palm.

"Have you some men's clothes?"

"You wish to trade?" The woman's eyes were greedily glued to Min's palm.

"Of course. But you must provide me with suitable attire. Complete and suitable attire."

In less than a breath, Lady Godiva sprang to her armoire. "I think these will fit." She help up a pair of violet damask breeches. She noticed Min's dismay. "Some of my customers like me to dress as a man. Is that real gold?"

Understanding completely left Min. "They like you to dress as a man?"

Lady Godiva bent to pull the breeches up one and then the other of Min's legs. She motioned for Min to sit and pull her torn skirts to her chest.

"Fantasies, *chère.* Your ears would curl should I tell you—"

"Really?" Min stretched out one leg to allow Lady Godiva ease as she began with the white embroidered hose.

"But if you ask me, I'd much rather be in the company of a musketeer than some boy-loving old fart."

"Well, I don't really care to be in the company of either!" Min burst out, inadvertently dropping her soiled skirts over Lady Godiva's head. "Why is it that all women feel they must be with a man? Either on his arm or in his bed. I don't understand. It's just so . . . so . . ."

"Exciting." Lady Godiva pulled the skirts from her face to reveal bloodshot eyes flashing with bright secrets. "Might I have another look at that morsel in your fist?"

Min splayed out her palm.

"Seems to me, *chère,* that you are in dire need of a taste of the male specimen. You would not be saying such things if you had supped on one."

"Nonsense." Min stood to button her breeches. "Give in to a man and he will only dominate and order you around. You willingly become his slave, revoking all your freedom to please him. It's preposterous!" She crossed her arms over her chest, lifting each foot to allow Lady Godiva to slip on shoes. "There's so much more out there. Do you not desire to think for yourself, without worrying that your actions will be criticized by a man? Do you not wish to let loose your voice at high volume and just scream for no reason other than the release?"

"I release my voice many a time, *chère,*" Lady Godiva drawled seductively. "And believe me, it is ecstasy." She rolled the word from deep within her throat. Lady Godiva's attention focused inward suddenly, as her lids fell heavily and she seemed lost deep within herself.

"Lady Godiva?"

Pulling herself from some secret world, the woman redirected her attention up to Min. "What of you? Do you never desire *le grande passion?*"

The way with which Lady Godiva whispered the words

caused a shiver to shimmy up the side of Min's torso, like a lighted fuse sizzling toward the barrel.

"I don't know about passions and things. But I do know I will not allow a man to keep me from doing as I wish."

Lady Godiva tapped a brightly lacquered finger to her lips. "This musketeer thing?"

"Yes, I wish to become a musketeer!" Min proclaimed proudly, thrusting her hands into the air in a gallant gesture.

"Well, then, you know passion, for such a desire can only be pursued with passion. Another look at the nugget, please?"

Min took the courtesan's hand and deposited her booty in it. A joyous burst of energy overtook the woman and she began to twirl about, her fist thrust high above her head.

"Oh." She stopped dancing abruptly before Min. "You do know that only men make up the king's musketeers? Can't say I've ever seen a woman in the guards either. Well, it's simply barbarous to even consider. Playing with muskets and swords and getting dashed through, all in the name of the pompous boy king. Of course, if that is what you want . . .?"

Min's shoulders slumped, as did her spirit. "I do, but there is the one thing."

"What is that?"

"Well . . . just look at me!" Min jumped off the bed and spread her arms out to the side. She now wore baggy pantaloon breeches and matching damask shoes with deep purple ribbons crisscrossing over her arches, and still the shredded pink dress on top. "What is the one thing you notice on me that you have never noticed on any other musketeer?"

With a toss of her long hair, Lady Godiva stepped back and gave Min a careful perusal. "Well," she said, twisting her pouting lips decisively. "Your melons are a might big as compared to the ones I've seen on the king's guards."

"Exactly!" Min thrust out her chest. "And because I do have . . . er, melons . . . and I don't have a . . . er . . ." She fumbled for the proper word as she looked down at her crotch.

"A cucumber?" Lady Godiva gaily offered.

"Yes! A cucumber!" *A cucumber? Mon Dieu,* if her brothers could only hear her now. Armand would be appalled. Adrian would laugh. Sophie would have the time of her life.

But it was true!

"Because I am missing that most vital part, I am not allowed within the hallowed halls of *Les Mousquetaires?* An idiotic, nonsensical tragedy!" A burst of bravado rushed beneath her skin's surface, giving Min renewed hope in her task. "But I will show them. I've just as much balls as the next man. I shall infiltrate their sacred ranks and prove to them that a woman is just as brave and strong and capable as a man."

"I've always preferred melon myself," Lady Godiva added, as she casually picked her teeth with her pinkie fingernail. "Just sqwarsh them and chew off the insides. Though I would never refuse a cucumber if offered, if you know what I mean."

All this talk of food reminded Min of her hunger. She slumped down onto the bed, allowing her head to rest against Lady Godiva's shoulder. "I prefer them pickled myself."

"Pickled! Oh no, no, *chère.* You do not want them soggy and soft as a pickle floating in a barrel all day! You want them firm and hard!" She squeezed her fingers into a tight fist before Min's shocked eyes. "A good handful, you see?"

Min shrugged. A pickle would taste very good right about now. "I am quite hungry."

"You don't see, do you?" Lady Godiva tilted her head and narrowed her gaze on Min's blushing face. "You've never seen a cucumber before, have you, *chère?*"

"Of course I have." Min gave a careless sigh. "Alexandre has them growing in his garden—"

"You know what I am talking about."

Min looked into the woman's sparkling green eyes. Catty and playful, purveyor of fantasies to a world of men Min knew nothing about. Cucumbers, eh? Suddenly it hit her. Oh! She was talking about a . . . er, a man's—

"Now come, *chère,* you are a maiden, correct?"

"I am," Min offered proudly.

"Ah! Then it is no wonder you are so poor on the male of the species. You need to spend more time with them. Get to know them a little better."

"Get to know them?" Min jumped from the bed, taking the floor in great strides. The nerve of this woman to assume something so ridiculous. She spun around and dashed a finger through the air. "I've lived my entire life with three brothers. I know about men, their habits, their ways, their mannerisms. I love my brothers. But I do not see what that has to do with men and their . . . cucumbers."

Lady Godiva giggled. "You know . . ." She gripped Min by the ragged hem of her dirty skirts and pulled her closer. "You can tell a man's thoughts just by taking a look over his breeches."

"What?" Min pressed her hand over her groin.

"I mean, you look here." She touched Min's hand. "And if it is good and hard, then you know he's thinking of you. In a most intimate way, if you catch my meaning."

"Really! You mean, it . . . er . . ."

"Hard as a cucumber plucked fresh from a garden,"

Lady Godiva offered gaily. "It has a mind of its own. And most men I know follow *it* rather than their own thoughts."

Amazing. "I never knew that before." Min scratched her head. "That's good to know. But I cannot imagine actually looking *there.* I should be so embarrassed."

"Mademoiselle Independent and Strong, afraid of a garden vegetable?"

Min flashed wide eyes at the prostitute. Afraid? No, never. Curious? God, yes. But only of one certain man with speckled blue eyes and a delicious voice. She had been the one to kiss him first. That was brave!

"Let the man take charge the first time." Lady Godiva went to her armoire and shuffled around for the rest of Min's costume. She called from the depths of satin and lace. "He will teach you the way. Only takes once to learn the basics. After that . . ." She surfaced from her scavenging with a wide grin painted across her face. "If you want to learn more—well, then, you just come back to Lady Godiva. I will show you the ropes." She turned and kicked her bed, setting the mattress to a wobble upon the ropes. "And I do mean . . . ropes."

Goodness, they were terrible!

Min pulled the brim of her violet-plumed hat down to shadow her eyes and stifled a laugh with a gloved palm. The *Hôtel des Mousquetaires* had been her first stop. She'd discovered Captain d'Artagnan was the one to see regarding recruits, and that he was stationed at the Louvre for most of the month.

She thought to take a few minutes to get her bearings before marching inside, and so hiked a thigh up on a stone bench outside the Louvre and took to watching the cadets practicing in the courtyard. A regiment of lifeguards drilled off to the left, their lines precise, their gazes focused on the horizon. Within her immediate view were a dozen or so musketeers cleaning their muskets and practicing their fencing moves.

Fie! Did they need practice!

A young Gascon lunged towards his opponent, only to skid across the ground, his boot heel having lodged a small pebble into the leather. Min clutched her stomach. This was the sort of comical farce the king recruited for his musketeers? They were nothing more than young boys, so unskilled in the art of swordplay—she couldn't believe it.

Not that they would employ stringent fencing skills in the heat of battle. No, most likely their muskets were used, and if a sword or rapier was needed, no more than a stab or slash would serve their purpose.

But with a general understanding of the basic fencing moves, they could protect themselves so much better.

Min jumped from her post, her ankles stinging from the impact. Lady Godiva had only the heeled shoes instead of boots. Frivolous ribbons adorned the toes. Min felt like a peacock in a coop of chickens in her garb. Her doublet and breeches were of violet damask, embroidered about the slashes in wide silver stitching. The lace at her collar and wrists was of a wide, silver-stitched lace. She even wore a shoulder-length black wig of generous sausage curls. Quite the fop.

Min ran a finger along her fuzzy upper lip. *But a disguise all the same.*

An urge sizzled within her as she eyed the fumbling cadets. Without a second thought, she stood and drew her newly purchased sword from the garishly embroidered scabbard.

What could it hurt?

"Messieurs!" She ambled into the center of the comical spectacle. "Might I offer some assistance?"

* * *

In less than an hour, Min had gained the trust of two-dozen cadets by displaying her expert sword skills. An eager crowd of men milled about her now, each intent on gleaning what she had to teach them. The young Gascon who parried her lunges at the moment had learned to concentrate, thus allowing for a more graceful body carriage and a greater sense of his surroundings. Including small pebbles.

"And what of a man who signals his lunge with a tilt of his head?"

Min parried her student's thrust and followed with an immediate riposte.

"Monsieur," she called to the voice who had spoken behind her, her concentration focused on the Gascon. "As you see, I am in the middle of a lesson."

"Is that so? You've your own little *salle d'armes,* I see."

Min stopped abruptly. The voice. It sounded so familiar. Dripping over her shoulder like . . . warm rain.

Her opponent took a break from this interruption, stepping back to the line of observant cadets.

"Monsieur?" prompted the storm of summer rain behind her.

Damn. Dreadfully familiar. Did the man have a sixth sense regarding her? Was he a pigeon and she his dovecote?

Min's grip tightened about the sword hilt. It seemed lately that if it wasn't one thing, it was another. But she could handle this diversion. Oh, yes. She had added a little something extra to her disguise this time.

Pulling the brim of her hat low over her eyes, Min spun around and pressed her rapier to the man's neck, the point coming to rest on a day-old cut. Just as she had thought. Chevalier Lambert. His razor-edged grin took her slightly off guard. As did the glitter in his cerulean eyes.

Her heartbeats grew faster. For a brief moment, Min couldn't help but recall what Lady Godiva had said regarding men and their breeches.

Min swallowed. *No, don't allow your eyes to stray. Stay in control.* You don't want these men to know they've been taking fencing lessons for all of an hour from a woman.

"Monsieur," Chance started, but then stopped abruptly. Narrowing his speckled gaze, he made a discerning study of Min's stiff-lipped face. His journey over her features stopped curiously on her lips. Her upper lip to be exact.

He knows, she thought. The deuce! He has seen me in this disguise too many times not to know. Even if she was a damned fop. He knew.

But would he keep her secret?

Min held her jaw firm. She mustn't perspire; Lady Godiva had specifically warned against that. Else the glue would melt.

Chance squinted one eye shut, and when he did two tiny laugh lines radiated from the corner.

He smirked. "I'll be damned," he said in a hushed voice so that no other could hear. "You've a caterpillar on your lip, Mademoiselle Imp."

Not exactly a caterpillar, a strip of mouseskin, to be exact. Lady Godiva said she used them as false eyebrows when it was necessary to appear as a man.

"Hold your tongue, if you value your voice." Min judged his nerve by pressing her rapier deep into his flesh, though not far enough to break the skin.

Chance swallowed before speaking through a tight jaw. "You are a fool to think you can carry on this charade under the watchful eyes of Captain d'Artagnan."

"It seems I've already done that. He is nowhere to be seen. I've already many eager students. And believe me"—Min cocked a nod behind her—"these men need help. They know nothing. I can't believe they are musketeers."

"These men are my regiment!" Chance hissed, a sharp fury brightening his eyes to a vibrant sapphire. "You won't get away with this."

"*Your* regiment?" Min managed. His *regiment?* Her sword fell slack at her side. The damask doublet weighed heavily upon her shoulders. She felt a great void blackening in her gut. The emptiness rapidly expanded, as if she'd just been punched in the stomach by a brute fist. "Your . . . your men . . ." She had never deemed Chance more than just another cadet in the ranks of the musketeers. His men? These men were *les Mousquetaires Noirs,* the second company of the king's musketeers. Did he command the whole?

"You go too far." Chance shook his fist before her eyes. "This is foolishness. This charade of yours, it is madness!" He narrowed his eyes on her, as if searching for tangible signs of the lunacy he spoke of.

"Monsieur?" her pupil prompted from across the yard. "Ah, Lieutenant Lambert. It is good to have you back."

Lieutenant? Min gulped.

Yet her mind worked on automatic in an attempt to get out of this particularly vexing situation. *Don't let them find out you're a woman.* She stayed the cadet with a placating hand. "One moment, monsieur. Forgive me, your *lieutenant* has most intriguing things to say." She turned to Chance and hissed, "*Your* regiment? Why did you not tell me before. You? A lieutenant?"

"And do you have a problem with that, *monsieur?*"

"Well . . . no." Yes! She did. How could she ever join the ranks after this? "You could have at least told me!" This information threatened to spoil her plans regarding joining the musketeers. The Blacks had been her goal, the younger and smaller of the companies. A good starting point for an inexperienced fighter. "What were you doing out riding the countryside when you should have been here commanding your ranks?"

"I am on leave."

"Leave! You mean you're looking for the Notorious Ones?"

"You know that."

"Then what are you doing here, harassing me? It seems you've more inclination to tail me as a mongrel does a butcher."

That was the final straw. Chance pulled his sword from its scabbard and paced a few steps away.

"This will end right now," he hissed. "Observe, gentlemen," he raised his voice and all around paid attention. "This *man* who claims expertise of the sport, and who dupes you all—"

He was going to expose her! Min wasn't about to let Chance get the better of her this time. How dare he not tell her he was leader of these men? She would never have engaged in such a foolish endeavor had she known. But now, she had to protect her identity. Her only hope was to bring him down in front of his men—or run like hell.

Chapter Eleven

"En guarde, monsieur!"

Never one for running with her tail between her legs, Min matched Chance's salute and the two engaged swords.

"You see," Chance's voice carried across the stone courtyard, "while this *person* maintains a facade of expert swordsmanship and skill . . ." He missed Min's lunge and dodged quickly to avoid getting pierced in the arm with her rapier.

"A good example of bad style," Min quickly interjected, in hopes of waylaying the attention of the cadets between the two of them. "Gentlemen, this man may be your lieutenant, but his fencing skills hardly rival the most amateur of us."

"Observe the nervous banter he engages in," Chance threw in over her last words. "Only an impostor would be so worried about being exposed."

"Notice the obvious jerk of his head as he prepares to lunge." Min wasn't sure anymore what she was doing; she only prayed he would not skewer her in a mad rage. "There! You see?"

The onlookers agreed with nods and surprised gasps, as they truly did see the blatant signal Chance displayed.

"Sloppy give away, if you ask me," Min called, thankful for the diversion. "And he calls himself a musketeer."

"I have had enough of this!" Chance hissed through gritted teeth.

"As have I!" But Min hadn't enough time to think as she turned to the crowd and saw their shocked gasps and stunned looks. The Gascon dropped his rapier with a clatter. One of his fellow cadets stumbled backward and landed in a perfectly rounded yew shrub. What was wrong?

Min followed the wide-eyed stares and gasps of the cadets to Chance's rapier. Her wig dangled on the end! She reached for her hair. It tumbled in waves over her shoulders and down her back.

"*Voila!* Taking lessons from a woman now, are we?" Chance reproved the ranks that stood in utter shock about him. "Have the king's musketeers sunk to a new low?"

"You bastard!" Min hissed. She stomped away, the silly violet moiré ribbons on her toes flouncing about like beached carp. So he had won this one. Well, she was not about to stick around and listen to the laughter rising from the ranks.

Min marched across the courtyard, passing a tall, cylindrical yew, but was quickly cut off by Chance. "Going somewhere?"

"Wherever you are not!" She stomped her foot. "Ooow!" Needles of pain shot up her leg. She'd forgotten her frivolous footwear. *"Allez-vous-en!"*

Chance hooked an arm through hers and jerked her to his side, the two of them concealed from the cadets by the geometrical shrubbery. "Oh no, *petite* imp, not this time. I'll not let you out of my sight until your brothers have a firm hold on you. And even then, I may not rest until I see you shackled to the rooftop of a carriage with ropes and chains."

She looked him square in the eye. His in turn flared to brilliant beacons as he awaited her words.

"You would like that, wouldn't you? Restraining a woman so that you may laugh and have your way with her."

"Believe me," Chance ground through a tight jaw, "the thought has occurred many a time since I've run into you."

"Which?" Min pressed her fists to her hips. "Restraining me or having your way?"

"Both," he snarled. "Blast!" He jerked her into motion by her elbow. "Just wait until I get you home!"

"Oh? And is that when you will restrain me and have your way with me?"

"Just wait and see, mademoiselle. Just wait and see."

A water carrier followed the twosome up to the chevalier's third-floor apartment. Chance had flagged him down on the way. The hunchback plunked a huge copper basin on the floor and said he'd be right back with the water, the well he worked from being just down the street.

Pressed to the window like a fox-chased rabbit, Min inhaled, breathing in her own less-than-savory odor. A morning of matching swords with the cadets had only served to ripen her scent. Perhaps a bath would feel quite good after everything she had been through. Though—she looked about—there wasn't much privacy in this spare room.

"We'll be in need of a screen!" Min called after the vendor.

"Oui, madame," the water carrier called back.

"We've no need for a screen," Chance yelled. Then he hissed at Min. "That is an extra four sous!"

"*Oui,* chevalier," called the water carrier.

"Bring the screen!" Min yelled and then cast Chance a fiery glance. "Do you wish for me to bathe out in the open? Am I to provide the entertainment this evening? You've nothing but a bed and armoire—do you think I shall parade about before you as thanks for my humiliation?"

Chance's jaw dropped and then snapped shut. He pushed splayed fingers back over his head and nodded once. "Pardon, mademoiselle. Bring the screen," he muttered as the water carrier returned to pour the first bucket of water. "And some soap for the lady. She will need it."

"*Oui,* monsieur." He quickly lowered his eyes and bowed out, intent on another trip.

"*I* will need it?" Min crossed her arms and kept a keen eye on the chevalier. Who was he to talk? He most likely had not bathed for days. His odor was very probably as rank as hers. Which might explain why he kept his distance. "And what of you?"

"Is that an offer to join you?"

"Hmmph." Min turned to stare out the window. That comment did not even deserve an answer.

"I bathed just this morning. Had to get rid of the onion smell."

"Onions?"

He waved her off and went to hold the door for the water carrier. "A reward for chasing you last night. I shall add that to the welts on my back."

"Welts? But I don't understand—"

"It is no matter. You've a generous count of successes when it comes to eluding me. I'm sure you are nothing but proud."

"Hmmph." Min gifted the chevalier with her back.

They both remained silent as the water carrier brought up another and yet another wooden bucket. Min did not like the idea of bathing in the same room as a man. And who knew whom else.

"Your valet?" She glanced about the room. "Am I to provide entertainment for a crowd this evening?"

"Michel is with his family. I gave him a much deserved holiday with my own leave."

"Will you leave me alone?"

"Not in a million years, Mademoiselle Imp."

Min cast a longing glance over her shoulder at the rising water in the tub. Oh, but a bath would feel good on her weary body! Her tired bones felt ready to fall in a pile like a heap of dirty clothes. She didn't really care who watched, be it an entire crowd or just the one lusty man.

Lusty? Yes, she knew the meaning of the word now—the intense desire that curled beneath her skin and flushed through her heart and groin every time she laid eyes on the chevalier. Not an altogether unwanted feeling, but a dangerous one. Especially since she found herself alone in a room with a man, her fate to strip naked and bathe.

She turned slightly and out of the corner of her eye studied Chance. He stood over the tub, furtively running his finger along his jaw. It seemed he watched nothing in particular. His tall, elegant posture lent nobility to his appearance. A thin mustache flowed down around his lips to meet a smudge of beard on his chin. On his forehead were two worry lines, visible now as he frowned.

A dark silence hung about him. A certain sadness. He was gallant and yet . . . shadowed. This man possessed secrets. Dark secrets, she sensed.

Who was Justine? His mother? No, possibly a sister, or . . . as she had previously suspected, a lover. Min felt her heart catch. *Mon Dieu,* what was she doing here? This man had a mission, a very important mission to capture the man who killed his lover.

Chance looked up from his distant thoughts. "Mademoiselle?"

He ruffed his fingers through his short crop of hair and Min forgot her worries. His smile could charm a fox from the chicken coop. And a woman to her knees.

"Is something amiss?"

"No, chevalier, I just—" *I was thinking of falling to my knees, that's all.* "Perhaps I should not be here. You have more important things—the woman, Justine."

"Her murderer shall be found and justice served all in good time. Until then, I've undertaken the task of protecting you." He took a step towards her so that she would have to step around him to leave. The door closed for the final time behind him, as the water carrier quietly took leave.

"I don't—"

"I know, I know, you don't need protection. Fine. Be that as it may, you do need a bath."

Releasing her breath in a frustrated sigh, Min shrugged and nodded. She was much too tired to argue. And the lure of the water had become too strong.

"Very well. I shall bathe and then be off."

"Please," he offered. Crossing his arms over his chest he stood beside the tub like a proud sentinel.

Min waited, but saw that Chance had no mind to leave. "Will you allow me the decency of a little privacy?"

He nodded once and paced over to his high-legged bed, where he sat, back to her, eyes to the wall. "Very well, bathe away."

"How impossibly rude."

"I've learned better than to leave you alone, mademoiselle. Do not worry, I shall not turn around. Unless, of course, you give me reason."

Min stepped behind the screen and slipped off her doublet. She popped her head above the structure of thin blue serge and wood. "And what reason would that be?"

"I'll let you know when it happens." He gave her another fox-charming smile and turned his back.

Once within the depths of the cool water, Min's flesh prickled to a thousand goosebumps, reawakening her body with a blissful shock of sensation. Heaven had never been more close at hand. Tiny bubbles ran down her neck and shoulders, sliding through the valley between her breasts as she soaped up her hair with the thin sliver of lavender soap for which Chance had grudgingly paid an extra two sous.

"Are you going to tell me what happened to give you such nasty wounds?" he called as he stoked the fire in the brazier on the other side of his bed. Wisps of smoky ash carried across the room.

"I told you, the man who kidnapped me had three pistols." Min touched the wound on her forehead. A surface abrasion, more like a burn than anything. Shouldn't leave a scar. Not that it mattered to her. "One of them discharged during our scuffle. But I didn't take notice—I was too busy getting the hell out of there."

"A woman should not expose herself to such dangers!" Chance raged. "It is not—"

"Ladylike?" Min offered as she poured the tepid water over her hair. She shook off a shiver and dipped her cupped palms beneath the mirrored surface.

"Yes. Danger is for someone like me. A man!" She heard what she thought sure was a fist pounded against a firm chest. "I have been trained to live and die for danger."

"And just because I was unfortunate enough to be born a woman, does that mean I should be denied every right a man has?"

"Being a woman is not an unfortunate thing," Chance growled in a strange, husky voice. It reminded Min of the soft moan he'd given when kissing her at the inn and then beneath the windmill's slashing sails. "Women are . . . why, they are beautiful creatures. Elegant and graceful. They are a pleasure to behold, such as a great painting."

"If you are a man," Min retorted. "But as a man you've never been sewed into a dress, nor have you been forced to prance about on heels as high as your fist, nor must you sit about and wait for the salon to twirl some horrendous creation into your hair."

Sinking down until her chin was below water level, Min waited for Chance to reply with some snide comment. All was silent, save for the distant screeches of a vendor's cart being pushed down the street. An invisible wisp of smoke-tainted aroma curled above her head. "Chevalier Lambert?"

"Forgive me," he called. Metal clanked against the fire dogs as he poked and prodded. "It is just very hard for me to accept a . . . er, *you* as . . . well . . ."

Min knew what he wasn't able to say. He could not accept her as a woman. Not in the clothes she wore, nor from the manner she presented.

So what did she care what the man thought?

You care. You know you do. Have you been able to think of anything but the chevalier since first meeting him?

A shiver enveloped her bare shoulders. *These thoughts will get you nowhere. Have you forgotten Justine? She is the one he would risk his life for in pursuit of the Notorious Ones. Mon dieu,* but she had a dead woman for a rival.

Bosh! Here she was considering her rival, when she plainly knew the chevalier cared naught for her.

Min knew that she was only a distraction in his way, an affliction he must be rid of before he could tend to his real mission. Well, she would help him with that. She would be the thorn in no man's side. Min sat up in the tub, her breasts prickling to marbles. "Have you a robe?"

She heard Chance cross the floor. A soft Turkish dressing gown of royal blue and yellow silk floated over the top of the screen. Rather feminine. Justine's? The water splashed in singing droplets as Min stood and pulled the robe about her shoulders. No odor of perfume. Surely any remnant of Justine had died away by now, though Chance had not mentioned how recent her death had been. She tied the sash, squeezed her hair out over the tub, and then stepped around the screen.

Chance stood near the window holding a slip of ribbon, smoothing his thumb over a small portion of it. Min immediately recognized the black moiré as her own. "Where did you—"

"After your first brilliant escape," he whispered, his attention rapt on the small piece of ribbon.

"If you wouldn't mind, perhaps you could help tie my hair up?"

Min turned and allowed him to thread the ribbon through the heavy mass of her hair, the motion causing the right shoulder of her robe to slip down. She pulled the silk up to her neck, suddenly embarrassed at her lack of clothes. But it slipped down just as quickly.

"What is that?" He reached for her, his fingers stopped inches from her shoulder. "I thought you had only the wounds on your forehead and hand?"

"'Tis nothing." Min stepped back from his sudden urgency, but he followed her. He had seen the welt on her shoulder, the one from Luciano's whip.

"Let me see."

"No."

It seemed he had no regard for her modesty. Seeing that he wasn't about to back off until she gave in to his morbid curiosity, Min slid the robe down, clutching it even tighter to her breasts.

She drew in an unexpected gasp when his fingers

touched her skin as softly as a stolen glance. "It's very deep," he observed gently.

"F-from a bullwhip," she replied and shrugged the robe up, only to look up at a very changed man.

Chance's eyes were closed tightly, his lower lip quivering. It seemed he was troubled by some inward force. What could she have said to make him react so? It was a small wound. Though rather deep, it had already begun to heal.

"Chevalier? What is it?" He'd fallen silent suddenly and made no move to answer. "It doesn't hurt anymore. Chance?"

He held his fist clenched tightly to his chest. At her touch, Chance blinked his eyes open. He nodded, a confirming gesture that revealed nothing of his inner torment until he spoke. "Justine," came the breathless name, whispered as if it were a sacred prayer.

Min looked up into Chance's eyes. Burgeoning tears sparkled with golden flecks of the setting sun. Justine. Her faceless rival.

Could she really consider her a rival? When the chevalier had given her no sign of interest beyond a quick kiss? *Perhaps.*

"Did you . . . did you love her?" she asked softly, wishing suddenly that he had not.

He swallowed, releasing a great breath. "Immediately. Passionately."

Min's heart sank.

"Stupidly."

What was that?

"But always I gave my entire heart. No matter what portion of emotion she should care to serve me at the time, be it admiration or anger. I did love her."

Min couldn't help but feel a pang of jealousy. As if her heart were being squeezed and twisted by Luciano's whip. Why, oh why, did she feel this way?

Stop it! her conscience screamed. *This man is in pain, can you not see?*

Min pressed her hand over his. Yes, she had no right to jealousy. He was a man. A loving, caring human being. Of course he had loved. He had a life before meeting up with her. Though she had never given him reason to care for her, she cared deeply that he was now in such a state. "What happened to her? That is, if you want to tell me."

He drew in a sharp breath and then expelled it slowly. The wall caught his body, as he could not help himself from falling back.

"Justine," Chance said slowly. "The carriage was abandoned, destroyed, and . . . the interior covered with blood. Ah, I cannot speak of it now. Please, don't ask me to. She . . . she was my wife."

"Your wife. I am truly sorry. I don't know what to say, I—" This was a most disastrous position to be in. She standing between a man and the vengeance he sought against his very wife. He had married! And he had loved.

"Forgive me, I don't know why I allow myself to waste such emotion on the woman." He swept a hand through the air and clamped it gently on Min's shoulder. "No more talk of Justine. I mustn't."

Daring to invoke anything that might provide some solace, Min threw her arms about Chance and pulled him close. With a gentle press of her hand against the back of his head he succumbed to her ministrations, resting his face upon her shoulder. If she could ease his pain, she would. She would gladly be the sponge that would draw his pain, if only to make things better for him.

"That is why you seek the Notorious Ones," she whispered. "Oh, *mon Dieu,* I am such a terrible cad. I am keeping you from your mission." She pulled back and smoothed away the narrow trail of wetness slipping down his cheek.

"You keep me from nothing," he said, abruptly sniffing away invisible tears. "I have sworn to protect you, Mignonne. Until you are safely in your brothers' hands, I'll not let you out of my sight."

"But—"

Her protests were stopped with his finger to her lips. Chance reached up and trailed his finger through the wet strands of hair that had not been gathered by the ribbon, suddenly interested in her new, clean self. "You are a precious one, Mignonne Saint-Sylvestre. You are not like Justine in that I believe you would never be so cruel to another human being. But you, like Justine, are too impulsive for your own well-being. I have seen that you have a rigid streak of pride running through your body, one that blinds you to true danger. Skilled with the sword or not, you do need protection. I could not be there to protect Justine. *Mon Dieu,* if only I had been there . . ." He pressed his cheek to hers. His words were but a whisper. "You must think me deranged for professing love for a woman who toyed with my emotions as if they were a new strand of jewels laced around her neck. I loved her, and I hated her. And yet . . . I will always remember the first trust when I felt my love was reciprocated without falseness. I must continue to believe in that."

The power and conviction of his words wrapped about Min's very soul. Never had she so blindly wanted to be a part of another person's life until now. Chancery Lambert represented everything that had ever meant anything to her. His fierce pride, bravery, and undaunting beliefs made him a paragon among men. These were the same beliefs and convictions she strived for. The same reasons that pushed her towards the musketeers. He was so much like her father. . . .

"I shall protect you, Mignonne. I swear it."

His finger drew a gentle line down the side of her cheek.

Sadness lingered in his gaze as he slowly explored her face. Min's skin flushed and grew hot in his trail. Chance captured a perfect teardrop on the tip of his finger. He smoothed it between two fingers, bleeding her own confusion of emotions into his.

"Will you let me protect you?" His fingers were steady and warm as they traced her lips. The brute heat of his flesh fervid and masculine and so . . . tempting.

Min closed her eyes, and as she did, the teasing heat on her lips was replaced by the confident press of Chance's mouth. Surprised and shocked by his daring, her conscience stabbed at her, but she had no desire to voice her inner concerns. He was in pain and she his sponge. If this would ease some of his suffering, then she would make the sacrifice.

Ha! her conscience scoffed. *This is no sacrifice. You want this man in all his valiant glory. His touch is enchanting, his lips divine madness—*

Definitely divine, Min thought over her conscience's chiding.

Heedless of her struggling values, Min sank into Chance's embrace as his strong arms wrapped about her. Her body felt weak and hot, as if a fever had overcome her, while at the same time she felt it awaken and tingle at the new sensations this man stirred deep within her.

He opened her mouth with his tongue and pressed a wet warmth across her lips. She felt Chance's hand move up her back and cross over her arm with measured stealth. He gently caressed her breast through the silk robe, cupping it in his palm. The spinning warmth in her stomach surged upward in response. Min jumped as her nipples sprang to alertness. Saints, this man had an irresistible command over her! She could not control her own reactions. What would happen when she lay naked and he the same?

Naked?

Wait a minute.

"No!" Min pulled away and twisted the robe openings in her fist. "We—we cannot do this." She was his sponge, not his courtesan. The thoughts she had just been thinking! Things were getting out of hand. "It's . . . well, 'tis not proper."

"Proper?"

"I am a lady," Min protested, though she couldn't fight the lingering doubt that she was doing the wrong thing. She enjoyed the sensations Chance's touch awakened in her. And since when had she ever done the right thing?

"A lady?" Chance smirked and waved a hand through the air. "You, Mademoiselle Imp, are a lady only when it is convenient for you."

"I *am* a lady!" Min said forcefully. "I shall always be a lady, whether I choose to wear breeches or a dress."

"Or undress." Chance regarded her with a sharp glance down her robed figure.

"Oh!" Min stamped her foot and looked away from Chance's teasing eyes. Ripples of water sloshed against the side of the tub with each loud word. Rushing to the copper tub, she scooped up a wave of water with her cupped hands and sent it flying through the air.

Soaked from doublet to boots, Chance could only stand there, in shock, his fingertips dripping.

"There!" Min slapped her hands together, quite satisfied with her task. "That should cool you off."

"Blast it, woman!" Chance shook his head vigorously, sending a spray of water about the room and across Min's robe. Dashing around to the opposite end of the screen, he scooped his hands into the tub and lifted a wave of water directly into Min's face.

She let out a gurgling yelp.

"Why do you always have to be so damn—"

Min spat out a spray of water and swiped her hair from her eyes. "Strong?"

"Yes!" Droplets flew about the room with a jerk of his head. "It is not right. You're mixing everything up. *I* am the man. I am supposed to be the strong and protective one. *You* are the woman. You are supposed to be soft and gentle and—and—"

"Swoon into your arms and allow you to have your way with me?"

"Yes! No!" He slammed his fist into the surface of the water, creating an iridescent wave of liquid. "I would never seek to have my way with anyone but—"

"But you would try when the chance presents itself? Like now? You have a woman clad only in a robe, she is confused and tired and weak—"

"Ah-ha!" He dashed an accusing finger at her, sending a spittle of water across the screen. "So you admit to your weaknesses?"

"Never! I can match any man, any day."

"Take that!" Chance succeeded in flinging a water bomb at Min.

She ducked and the water splashed across the paned window. "Ha! Your battle skills are weak, musketeer. Prepare for a massacre!" She bent to deliver a fatal barrage of splashes.

The tiny apartment was showered with great splashes of water. Puddles flooded into lakes at their feet. Resembling more a drowned muskrat than a musketeer, Chance fended off the water as best he could, but he could not control his laughter. He tottered backward, clutching his stomach in mirth, then suddenly doubled over in a riot of chuckles and fell to the floor.

Not willing to allow her opponent such an easy defeat, Min marched around to his side and kicked the puddle near his head. "Surrender, chevalier—I am the victor."

Chance grabbed her by the ankle, toppling her to the floor. He pinned her shoulders to the soaked floorboards with his big, wide hands. "Now we shall see who is the strongest, my feisty imp."

Min squirmed. But only until her eyes accidentally locked onto his brooding gaze. She was captivated. The look in his speckled blues was not cast by anger—no, it was a strangely lustful look. A look she'd seen in his eyes before. Curious excitement curled through her veins as his face hovered above hers. Would he actually do it? Would he kiss her again? Please, yes, she would let him this time. It had been foolish to pull away from him before. She could no longer deny she wanted him.

His eyes searched hers. Min licked her lips, cleaning away the drops that fell from Chance's face. He touched the soft flesh of her lower lip with his thumb, his eyes curiously heating her flesh. Yes, he was considering it, she could see it in his expression. So wanting and hungry. Oh, but if he would just do it! Her insides screamed for the touch of his lips. The electrifying touch of his fingers to her breasts . . .

"Pardon, chevalier."

Min and Chance froze, their faces inches apart.

The water carrier strolled over to the tub, his hands settled on his hips. Chance had not bothered to bar the door. "Perhaps I should return later?" He casually toed the edge of a puddle, but could not hide his growing smile.

"It is all right, monsieur." Chance rolled off Min and waved a hand towards the empty tub. "The battle is over. I have been defeated. You may take the offending artillery away."

The man bowed and hiked the tub easily over his shoulder, sloshing little of the remaining water on the floor. Folding the screen with his other hand, he gave Chance a wink and left them to their games.

Min pulled herself up and stood silent as she watched the hunchbacked man disappear. She looked down over the wet dressing gown. It clung to her body, revealing each and every curve. She glanced at Chance. He had noticed too. Hiding her body as best she could with crossed arms, she turned away from his hungry eyes. The heat of the moment had been lost; now she was nothing but cold and wet.

"That will be quite enough, chevalier. If you will please find me some dry clothes and leave me to dress in private."

Chance paced past her, and just when Min thought he was going to give in, he turned on her, backing her to the wall, where he barricaded her in with his arms. His words were intense with a hungry passion as he spoke. "Have you never allowed a man to touch you?"

Yes, she thought. But the prospect of giving in to her body's desires frightened her more than a whole army of Lucianos.

Chance squeezed out the ends of his doublet and went on with his gentle but infuriated tirade. "I have come to understand that you were raised by your brothers, and obviously they had no care for your upbringing. But it is simply not right. Women are not supposed to be like you. They are supposed to—to—"

"Please, don't go on about softness and honey," Min interrupted before he could speak. "I never have been, never will be, soft. Now, if you will just lend me some clothes, I can be on my way. I've some things to attend to, as I know you do also."

Chance looked her over, tension pulsing in his jaw. His eyes moved slowly over her face and then lowered over her exposed shoulders. "There is softness inside you, mademoiselle. I know it."

He bit his lower lip as his meanderings took him down

over her hips, caressing her legs, and he was only pulled from his blatant ogling when Min stamped her foot.

"You've already had enough of that!"

"Pardon, mademoiselle." He averted his gaze towards the water-streaked window. "You are correct. How could I ever hope for a *lady* such as you to understand common human longings? Yes, some clothes. Until yours dry. Perhaps you can borrow something of mine until I can procure a dress for you." He turned just in time to catch her impudent lip. "Yes, a dress. I'll not be privy to the scandalous degradation of a woman. I shall go for one immediately. I know a shop where I can purchase a simple gown. Until then, you may rest here."

Stifling the yawn she had fallen into with the back of her hand, Min complained, "I'm not tired. Just the clothes, chevalier, and then I'll be on my way."

A trail of water droplets led to his armoire. Over his shoulder, Min could see there were but a few things inside. Chance turned and handed her a white lawn shirt that tied at the wrists and neck. The rest of the clothes he held bundled in his arm.

"And breeches," she prompted. "Mine are soaked."

Chance raised a finger and backed away from her, his path leading him to the door. "I don't think so. If I'm to ensure you wait here while I find you more suitable clothing, I'll have to do things this way. *Au revoire,* mademoiselle. I shall return."

Min raced to the door as Chance slammed it in her face. "You cannot leave!" The wood slats rattled beneath her pounding fists. "You are soaked to the bone!" Seeing that would do no good, she dashed over to the armoire. There was only his hat with a thick white plume in it and one buckled shoe.

"Damn! You think *I'm* the vexing one?" She picked up the shoe and threw it across the room. It landed with a skidding splash in a puddle of water. A smug smile curled her lips. "Serves you right, Chevalier Lambert."

Suddenly the door burst open and Chance marched back in. He tossed his clothes to the floor by the door, staunch determination setting his path towards her.

Min clutched the robe tightly to her throat. "Did you forget something already?"

"That I did."

"And what—"

A kiss had never served to silence her so quickly. Min mumbled a few protests, but nothing was audible through Chance's commanding motions. Then, as abruptly as he'd taken her, Chance held her back and away. He branded a burning gaze into her own.

"I believe it is high time I taught you the difference between a man and a woman."

Chapter Twelve

Shocked silent, Min watched helplessly as the cloth-covered buttons dotting the center of Chance's doublet were released. She could not prevent her jaw from falling open. His doublet dropped to the floor. What was he doing? He was clearly empty in the head. Undressing before her as if this were all fine and normal. And she standing in only a dressing gown. Madness!

His water-soaked shirt landed in a careless heap at her feet, the white linen forming a puddle that birthed a trickle towards the larger lakes in the room. Try as she might, the very sight of him, his firm stomach, sculpted into rigid bars of steel, his bronzed skin glistening with misty sparkles from their water battle, kept Min from finding her voice.

It was when he reached for the buttons on his breeches that she snapped out of her dumbfounded fog and rushed a staying hand to his.

"What are you—this is—"

Her words were abruptly silenced by the heat of his lips.

In order to keep from toppling backward, Min had to grip Chance's upper arms. The flesh beneath her fingers felt firm and hot and was scented of rugged, powerful man. Strong hands grazed over her shoulders, coaxing the Turkish robe down to expose her bareness to his heated tongue.

Min's mind fought a crazy intermingling of right and wrong. She hardly knew the man. And they were not married. In fact, he was married to someone else, albeit, a dead someone else . . . .

But she could not deny that every pore on her entire body yearned for his touch, every ounce of her being wanted more.

Must she deny her own needs?

Surprisingly, her good sense triumphed. "Are you mad?"

"Merely teaching you a lesson," he muttered against her shoulder.

His breath was hot, July sun hushing over her sensitive skin. Instead of further protest, Min could only gasp.

"The first lesson being . . ." He gave a firm jerk and her robe rippled from her shoulders, slipped to her elbows, and rested in wet folds just above her nipples. Chance drew in a sharp breath at the sight of her breasts plunging from the silk. "That a woman is soft."

His kiss to the corner of her mouth came like a breath of wind. He then floated down with a breeze of kisses over her jaw and to her shoulder.

"I can feel your desire, Mignonne."

And I yours, she thought back to his heated confession. Something irreversible had begun to happen. She sensed it. And the desire to make it stop was not there. Good sense had been abandoned for wanton desire. Hell, it was being kicked out on its posterior, the door slammed behind it. She wanted this to happen. She wanted to know this man in every sense that she could. She needed, yes, *needed,* to be wanted by him. And that scared her more than a whip-wielding villain creeping about in the dark.

"Relax," he whispered, sensing her apprehension. "I've no intention of harming you."

No, he never would. But it wasn't harm Min worried about. It was that she didn't want to lose control. Control was the one thing she still had in her life. Lack of control was the very reason she'd fled her home. Control granted her confidence. Could she concede it to a man? Any man?

Min could not help but let her head fall back as Chance's masterful tongue tingled exciting shivers to the surface of her flesh. All right, so maybe just this once she'd concede. Just a small portion of control could be granted. For this blissful moment, right or wrong mattered not.

Min sucked in a quivering breath as Chance's chest pressed to her breasts, brushing across her beaded nipples beneath the silk.

Soothing whispers reminded her that he was set on teaching her a lesson. "Women speak gently." His fingers strolled lazily across her shoulder and down to the mounds of her breasts, where they circled slowly. "They are demure in their actions and never, ever, best their men."

Min tensed. "Ever?"

"Ever." He searched her eyes. There was an unspoken vow in his blue eyes, a silent promise that he would stop and walk away if she asked. But Min did not. Instead she pushed her fingers up the back of his neck and twined them through his damp hair, gently coaxing him back to her.

"They wear the softest smelling perfumes . . . right here." His lips closed over the lobe of her ear.

A sigh slipped from Min's mouth, a soft release to match the longing groan that tickled her ear. The sweet tingling pressed onward, spreading through her face, blazing a hot path down to her breasts and setting her nipples to marble hardness.

So much for a woman being soft, Min thought with a smile.

Chance continued his lesson, preying with wicked slowness over her flesh. "And on their necks." His hot whispers trickled down her neck to trail a teasing path across her shoulder. "And on such soft places as their wrists . . ."

He lifted her limp hand and pressed a kiss to the aforementioned part. The pressure of his mouth, his hot, wet tongue over her vein, made Min intensely aware of her fleeting pulse.

"Oh, my," she gasped.

"Their elbows . . ." His trail moved upward, slowly swirling and kissing until he lodged his tongue in the soft crease of her arm.

"Oh, no, this is too much." Min squirmed, pressing her legs tightly together to contain the rapturous sensations that threatened to turn her limbs to soggy noodles. Rational thought fled. At once she wanted more, more, and more. But at the same time she wasn't sure if she could handle the teasing pleasure this man invoked in her body. It was as if he were bewitching her body to do things beyond her control.

"And behind their knees."

"What?" Min jerked her arm from the man's delicious pleasure. In order to restore her equilibrium, she had to gasp in a deep breath. "And why, chevalier, would I want a man sniffing about behind my knees?"

With his smile, two sexy wrinkles creased the corners of his eyes. In a heartbeat, Chance was on his knees. He slid the slinky robe up her legs. Min twitched as his tongue touched the tender, sensitive flesh behind her knee.

"Oh!" She had to balance one hand on Chance's head, for her left leg buckled as he pressed teasing kisses behind it. "I—I think I understand n-now."

With a gentle chuckle, Chance stood. "I move ahead of myself," he reprimanded, and resumed his delightful ministrations to her upper parts. "As I was saying, women are . . ." His tongue moved again, slow and intent on its path to her heaving breasts. He tugged at her locked hands. With no more than a moment's reluctance, Min relinquished them, allowing the robe to slip and fall in a pool of silk at their feet.

"Very soft." Chance's growl rose from his groin as he pressed a deep kiss onto the firm mound of her breast. "Mmm, like sun-ripened melons." Soft and delicate as a butterfly's footprints, he tiptoed down the side and pressed wet, lingering kisses to the undercurve of her breast, his tongue slipping out to tease and taste. Min matched his throaty whimpers as he crawled over to pay due attention to the other.

It seemed her hands moved of their own volition as they crept up along his bare, muscled back, slowly tracing the defined rises and tight stretches, as if to imprint a map of his body in her mind. When she had thoroughly navigated his flesh, Min threaded her fingertips up through the soft wet crop of his hair.

She tensed as his tongue drew around her hardened nipple. Teasing wetness puckered the areola into a tingling tightness. He gently nipped, and then sucked with great passion, as a hunger-starved infant from his mother.

Chance suddenly drew back with a great indrawn breath. The fine dark hairs on his chest sparkled with moisture, his rigid muscles glistening beneath Min's shivering fingers. He shook his head and gave a soft chuckle. "I am really getting ahead of myself."

"You said there were two things?" Min prompted, worried that he might be finished just when she had decided to surrender all control. She had come too far to allow him to turn and walk away now. "A woman is soft. And then what?"

"The second lesson being . . ." He slid his arm around and up Min's back, pulling her close so their bodies were like two candles melted together by the sun's heat. "That a man is hard."

His chest was firm against her aching breasts. His arms held her gently. It was then that Min noticed the hard shaft shrouded beneath his breeches, pulsing against her naked thigh. Surely it must be as long and hard as her dagger! "Oh, my."

"And I have every intention of showing you just how hard a man can be."

Stop trembling, she thought, as Chance lifted her hand to his chest. *Keep your wits about you. You want this.* She was reluctant to touch the rigid, sweating flesh that rose and fell over his heart in great passionate sighs. But the heat of his body drew her closer. *Enjoy this. You have always wondered what it would be like. You want this man. Take him.*

Min ran her fingers under the shadowed curve of his breast, up over the hard plane where fire flashes danced across his bronzed flesh, and then explored the forest of soft hair and over the tiny marbled nipple, which caused him to draw in a gasping breath.

Did he feel the same incredible sensations she had? Was it her touch that made him gasp and set his entire body to rigidity? Perhaps he needed her as much as she him?

"Oh!" Min cried as her feet left the ground. Her body was momentarily airborne as Chance tossed her across his bed, and she landed with a soft *pouf* on the mattress. "Chevalier!"

"What?" he growled as he moved across the bed on hands and knees, the glimmer in his eye that of a wild beast on the prowl. He brushed away a thick curl of hair from her face and smoothed the back of his hand across her cheek.

Curious trepidation set Min's heart to a frantic beat. She was frightened of the unknown. What next? She had never lain with a man before. Would she do the right things? Would he laugh and wince at her lack of skill?

Yet at the same time a strange excitement stirred within her veins. She had always wondered what the carnal delights entailed, dreamed of being captured in the naked embrace of a man . . .

Chance whispered a teasing breath across the smooth planes of Min's stomach. "What is it, *ma petite garçon?* Is it that you've finally decided to be the woman you appear to be?" His body hovered but inches above hers, his breath heavy as he leaned into her ear with pleading whispers. "Will you be the soft one, Mignonne?" He drew one finger over her breast and circled her nipple.

Her flesh was hot and soft and so, so delicious. He could drink of her body for all his days and never grow tired of the flavor.

Min drew in a gasp as his mouth sucked her nipple and he began to gorge himself upon her hard bead of pleasure. He curled his tongue around her nipple, teasing and tasting and sucking. Instinctively, she arched her back to encourage his exploration of her body. But he needed no more encouragement than his own desires.

He felt her lithe fingers slide across his back. Not so shy and timid as before, her touches were seeking, knowing in their destinations. He growled as her hands moved lower to the waist of his breeches. "Oh, Mignonne." He pressed his body to hers, crushing his hardness in the valley between her legs.

"Saints in heaven," she cried. "Chevalier, I—I cannot—"

He pressed a finger to her lips. Long, slender lashes

dusted over her dark eyes. Curious and proud, his Mademoiselle Imp, yet still a trifle fearful.

"Of course you say you cannot. What a fool I am! You cannot when I am still half dressed."

Chance stood and loosened the clip behind his waist and unbuttoned his breeches. The tan chamois, soaked entirely through from their Battle of the Bath, shrugged down his legs with little struggle. With a few tugs, his linen underdrawers followed.

Min gasped, drawing her hand back to her breast. She could not tear her eyes from the hard shaft that grew at the base of his torso. It was an exquisite thing to behold. So firm and proud, and wielded by its master as mightily as any sword. Yet it was of flesh and blood, nestled snugly at the base of a curling mass of dark hair. So beautiful. The urge to touch it was almost too much.

"Truly, a man *is* hard, as you say."

With a deep-throated chuckle, Chance pushed her back onto the bed, locking her hands securely in his, up by her shoulders. "Very good, mademoiselle. I think you are finally beginning to learn. And now for a review."

Chance laid a gentle kiss on Min's lips and then moved slowly downward until once again he found her tormented nipple. He pressed lighty, then raised his head just an inch from the pulsing button, then pressed gently once again. He did this over and over until her whimpers became pleading moans. This gentle teasing was madness. Min felt sure she would slip over some invisible cliff if he continued.

"A woman is . . .?"

"Soft," Min said in a release of her held breath.

"Excellent."

She felt his lips smile against her flesh. Min thought sure she would faint if she were subjected to further torture. But she couldn't stand the thought of his touch leaving her body. His was a blessedly sublime torture, commanding her senses and her very soul. She felt very comfortable lying beneath this beautiful musketeer. As if she had known him forever in her dreams.

"And the man?" she offered breathlessly.

A tickling shiver ran down her neck as Chance nuzzled his nose into her hair and whispered, "I thought I was the one asking the questions?"

"Forgive me. I got carried away. But—"

He took her hand and brought it down past their hips. Min closed her eyes as she felt him place her fingers around the firm shaft that plunged from the thick nest of curls between his thighs. "And the man?" he growled.

Her fingers blazed hot around his member. The flesh was of velvet pulled over a dagger handle. Oh, this was a prize of hardened steel and softest suede! "Very hard."

"And now, if you'll allow me to continue with the lesson?"

"There is more?" she inquired, in a daze of passionate fascination and discovery.

"Quite."

Clasping his hand over hers, Chance began to slowly teach her the motions that would satisfy him. At her touch, he began to succumb to the wanton realms of sweet torture she had just learned. His moan was heaven in her ear. Min held the throbbing prize firm, her motions steady and rhythmic. "Am I doing things correctly, chevalier?"

"Oh . . . quite."

He gasped and steadied himself above her, one hand to either side of her head. It seemed he wanted to speak, but with her attentiveness to his needs, Chance could do little more than pant.

"What is it, Chance?" Min pressed on the back of his neck, directing his head down to hers. She suddenly realized she was in control. The way she liked to be. He was virtually unable to speak, let alone complete such a simple task as lowering his head without direction. "Tell me," she whispered, her new power giving her words a wickedly sensuous edge. "What do you want?"

Suddenly his hand clamped over hers, setting her motions to a standstill. The column of steel in her hand pulsed madly, matching her heartbeats in a frantic scream for more. "I long to know the secrets your body possesses, Mignonne." He drew his tongue up her neck and to her lips where it delved deep inside to dance with hers. His actions were no longer the restrained gentleness she had melted to before. He fought some inner pull of a sort she was well aware of. Tormented desire.

Min felt Chance's hand reach down and gently persuade her legs to part. It was time. The hot shaft sprang free from her fingers. It pressed against her dark garden, begging for entry, pleading to be encased by her female scabbard.

"Please," Chance whispered inside her mouth. "I relinquish all control unto you, Mignonne. I am at your mercy. Do not deny me the pleasure I seek, nor deny yourself the same."

She was in control. Yet she had no desire to be in control this time. She had already fallen over the edge of a fantastical oblivion. To stop things now would be madness. Like pulling the wheel pins from a running carriage. She had to know him, she had to possess him, and in turn she wished to relinquish her body to him, grant him possession of her secrets.

"Yes, please," she pleaded.

"It may be painful the first time," he whispered.

"I'm a tough one," she said with a smile. "You should know that by now."

She slipped both hands around his waist to pull him hard to her.

Chance let out a throaty groan as he was enveloped by her hot flesh. Min closed her eyes to the small bit of pain that echoed through her limbs. But it was momentary, swallowed easily by the bliss that followed close on its heels. She dug her fingernails into his back, not willing to let him go as his rhythms became faster and faster.

Chance gorged her with a passionate fury that blinded her to all but the heady sensation of desire and lust and want and need. Then he froze above her, his head tilted back, eyes closed, his body quivering madly as the rapture took his body and echoed into hers. It captured Min in its hold and swept her into an unexpected and dizzying climax. A great flash of brilliance exploded in her body, her inner core released of its inhibitions and set free. This sweet taste of heaven was brief and fleeting, but the aftershocks rushed through her body for long after.

"Mignonne," Chance whispered, and fell slack on top of her. "Oh, *ma petite* imp." He pushed his hands beneath her back and fell to his side, bringing her with him. "The lesson . . . is finished for today."

Chapter Thirteen

Chance drew his finger along the bruise on Min's forehead, careful not to press too hard. He'd just planted tender, healing kisses on her shoulder and knuckles, and at her prompting, moved upward to work his magic. "And so Armand was the first to take to the road?"

"Oui." Min traced her fingers along the raised silvery scar that stretched from Chance's left shoulder down to his nipple. They lay facing each other, beads of perspiration drying on their skin, their conversation quiet and revealing. She had made love to a man. And it had been everything she could ever have imagined. And so much more. She felt safe in Chance's arms. A feeling so new and yet, as welcome as a brotherly hug. So needed, she felt, and . . . so loved.

"Father was away far too much, and when he did come home, his wages did not provide our most basic needs. Armand did not want to work the fields or leave us for Paris. He was fifteen, I believe. Alexandre was fourteen,

Adrian, twelve, and I nine. But he was quite successful from the start. Adrian joined him soon after."

"Hadn't you any relatives to help?"

"No. After Father married my mother, the relatives turned their backs on him." Her voice grew ominously quiet. " 'Tis what Alexandre told me. Besides being a gypsy, Mother was also a Spaniard. It seems the Saint-Sylvestre family was not too keen on anything or anyone from Spain. You understand why, I'm sure, having fought in many campaigns against the Spaniards. But Father did not care; he was in love. One thing he always taught us was to never judge a man you've not broken bread with. Labels such as enemy and fool are too easily hung on all such as the Spaniards. When all are not deserving."

"But what of your Aunt Huguette?"

"Er—" She had forgotten her mention of the cane-wielding nun. "She is Mother Superior at Val-de-Grâce. Not exactly the place to send three boys."

"I see."

With a sigh, Min turned her head and gazed across the puddles, her vision not truly focused. "I wish I had known my mother. Alexandre says I look so much like her."

"Then truly she was a lovely lady." Chance kissed the pads of Min's fingertips as she swept them across his lips and traced them along the line of his mustache. "Any man, I'm sure, would have been enchanted."

Enchanted. Such a magical word. For that was how she felt in this man's presence. Taken. Smitten. Completely at the mercy of his desires. Unwilling to ever imagine a time without him or to think of leaving. Like a spell cast beneath the full and golden sun, his eyes were the noonday sky, his touch the magic that bound them in ribbons of rainbows.

Perhaps this was how her mother had felt in the arms of her father. So safe and protected from the dangers all about her. Free to be herself without fear of rejection because of her origins.

Min swallowed. Though she had no memories of her mother, the question of what their relationship might have been was always there. "She died two days after my birth. Perhaps . . . perhaps that is why I have grown up with this prejudice regarding women. They suffer so much, and for so little. After four children my mother was gifted with death. Is that fair?"

"Mignonne." Chance cradled her close, reaching beneath the rumpled sheet to hook his hand behind her bent knee. He smelled of salty male and musky lust. "I'm sure your mother would have loved you no matter what. It is not your fault that you have become a feisty, headstrong imp. Nor it is your brothers'."

She smiled at his laughing description of her. Truer words. "My brothers wish me to marry. To hand me over to the protection of a husband. As if I need such protection. Ah, but that is a woman's life. To marry and have children."

"And what is so terrible about marriage and children?"

"Nothing. But I would prefer choosing my own mate. Someone I know will love me as I him. Someone I can trust."

Min felt the muscles in Chance's arm tense against her chest. She trailed her fingertip down his arm. His flesh was still hot and pearled with evidence of their vigorous coupling. Ah, but she mustn't speak of marriage so. He had married. And had obviously been madly in love.

If there were a time to satisfy her curiosity, now she must.

"Tell me about Justine? You said you loved her, but then you also said something about it being stupid?"

He nodded and pushed both hands over his forehead,

contemplating the dark-beamed ceiling with a heavy exhale.

"If you don't wish to speak of her—"

"I did say stupid earlier, didn't I? I loved Justine. But it was the stupidest act of lust I have ever committed in my entire life."

"You mean you married her out of lust?"

"I will never know for sure. At the time I thought myself passionately in love. And now, when I have the opportunity to look back over the relationship, I realize it might just have been stupid lust that blinded me to her real nature. She was an evil woman, Mignonne. I can only admit that now, now that she is gone and not staring at me with her seductive gaze."

An evil woman? Too intrigued to grant him solace from a confession, Min remained silent, hoping he would continue.

"The first few months of our marriage were blissful. It was only after I started noticing things—new jewels, fine linens on the bed, exotic face creams sitting upon the vanity that my musketeer's wages could never pay for—that I began to suspect Justine was stealing. She readily confessed when I confronted her. Always, she pleaded boredom. She needed excitement, thrills. What was there for her to do when I was away on campaign or drilling every day? Because I adored her so much, I turned a blind eye. It wasn't difficult to overlook the rows of jewels sparkling around her neck when I was drawn like a spellbound slave to the beauty of her face. The stolen linens were fancy enough, but mere rags when lying beneath a body that would put Aphrodite to shame.

"But her cruelties festered."

Chance's entire body tensed next to Min's. "Tell me." She pressed a kiss to the back of his hand and clasped it in both of hers.

"Less than a month ago, I returned home after dark.

Not unusual, for I've many tasks that require late hours, such as accompanying the captain in pursuit of criminals. I told Justine not to expect me until late, and she promised to wait up for me. There was a candle in the window when I returned home. I stood there for the longest time, out on the street, just staring up at that round glow of candlelight. This is good, I thought. She does love me. Even though I come home late, and cause her great fits of boredom that force her into unsavory acts of theft, she does love me.

"It was not to be. As I entered our bedchamber, the clatter of boots stepping out the window alerted me. I had only time to glimpse the man's hand slipping over the sill before I was stopped with the point of a sword. Justine held me at bay with my very own rapier while her lover escaped. And for the first time, I saw hatred in those steely eyes of hers. Can you imagine, a wife holding her cuckold husband at swordpoint so he'll not impede her lover's escape?"

It was becoming difficult for Min to understand why Chance now chose to avenge his wife's murderer. Why? When she had been so cruel to him!

"I ran out with the intention of distancing myself from the horrid scene, but not before cursing her to hell. I will always regret those words."

"She deserved as much for what she did to you."

"Ah . . ." He drew Min's hand up to his lips and absently kissed the backs of her fingers, his eyes still focused on the ceiling. "I returned the next morning after a night spent sleeping in the corner of a smoky tavern. There was a note speared to the center of the bed with the rapier she'd used to aid her lover's escape. Justine had left for Creil, her mother's home. I couldn't let her go without speaking to her. I left immediately, hoping to apprehend her on the road.

"About five leagues from Paris I found Justine's carriage. As I've said, the seats were bloody, the driver dead. And Justine's body was gone. Why any criminal would take a dead body with him is beyond me. There were no signs outside the carriage that a bleeding body had been moved . . ."

"Then how do you know she is dead?"

"She must be. She has to be. I found a slip of her dress imbedded in the seat cushions, secured behind a musketball."

His palm trembled over her fingers as he drew her hand to his heart.

"I loved Justine with a passion that surprised me. Was it lust? I've often questioned myself in the weeks that have followed that horrendous night. No. Impossible. But it must have been, for I was not able to look beyond the beauty to see the black heart."

"Her heart could not have always been black. She attracted a man like you."

"A man like me." He chuffed a mocking breath through his nose. "And just what is so special about a man like me?"

She studied his profile. Tears slipped from the corners of his eyes. She sensed his need to fight looking at her, a move that might reveal the true pain. "You are brave and true. Honest and devoted. Even after you were deceived, you seek the man who did this in your wife's name."

His voice caught, and Min felt as if his pain leapt out in sizzling sparks and traveled through her veins to pierce her own heart with the intensity of a blazing fire. His breathy whisper echoed Min's thoughts. "I had such great desire for family. A home with a smiling wife and fresh-baking bread, perhaps even a few children scrambling around my legs with dirty faces and laughing eyes. I shall never love again. I cannot."

Chance trailed a finger along her cheek, smoothing back her unbound hair. The gentle reassurance of his kiss was so quiet, so soft after their fierce coupling. Yet bittersweet in light of the pain Min sensed.

I shall never love again.

"This is not right." She rolled away from his touch and stared at the ceiling. "I feel terrible. I am keeping you from your mission."

"Man cannot live without sleep, food, or—"

"Or debauchery?"

"No, Mignonne, don't say it in such a tone. You mean something to me."

She winced at the touch of his lips to her forehead. She had meant something to him all right. He had just explained that even after Justine's cruel treatment of her, he still loved her. He did. Else he would not give her another thought!

"Yes, well, as long as you are lying next to me, Justine's murderer only distances himself further from your grasp. I wonder . . . Do you think it might be Luciano?"

"I had considered that. I was too concerned with seeing you away from Remalard to remain and discover it if was true."

"I'm so sorry, I've been nothing but a distraction—"

He jerked her back to his side and glided on top of her body, securing a hold with his legs to either side of her hips. "A fine distraction, indeed."

"Chance."

He strained against the palm she pushed against his chest. She didn't want this anymore. Not when she couldn't be sure how to take his affections.

"You must find Luciano."

Chance's fingers curled into a tight fist above Min's chest. "Very well." He sprang up on the bed and looked about for his clothes.

Reaching over the side, Min grasped Chance's breeches and handed them to him. "For Justine's sake and the love you two once shared, you must have vengeance."

Chance halted, his breeches hanging upon his finger. They were still soaked around the waistline and knee buttons, but the rest had dried. He dropped them and knelt by her on the bed. "Oh, no, my precious one." He searched her eyes. "Vengeance is only for the weak. I am a musketeer! Honor is my code. I will find the man and bring him to be tried and punished by his peers. He may not have shown mercy for Justine, but it would be a feeble and cowardly thing for me to steal his own life without justice."

Taken by his noble words, Min could expect nothing less. "You're a strong man, Chance. Most would plunge their sword into the villain's heart as soon as they matched eyes."

He nodded, agreeing. His fisted knuckles grew white. "The deuce, if I haven't thought many times of doing just that. Ah, but there is another reason for pursuing him. A rather selfish reason."

"You? Commit a selfish act?"

He shrugged. "I need to see that Justine's body lies under the ground and not beneath the frippery of another man's bed."

"So you do think she is still alive."

"With Justine, anything is possible."

"And then what? If she is alive."

"I . . . don't know."

Min's heart caught on a sharp hook. Their lovemaking had only been a comfort to him. Gentle arms to cradle his head, a heated body to accept his pent-up vengeance, a quiet heart to hear his pain.

His wife might still live. And if she did, he wasn't sure what he would do when he saw her. For as much as he had loved her—he had turned a blind eye to her crimes!—he might return to her arms.

She closed her eyes and fought the regret. It would be hard, but she must try her best to forget this new emotion of love that Chancery Lambert had introduced to her. If he could not love her—well, then, she would suppress the love she had just discovered for him.

For his sake.

He was quietly amused to hear the low-pitched snore rising from the tumble of sheets. Her tiny figure lay curled beneath the thin linens, yet the noise she made was fitting of an army of men. Ha! What a delightful creature she was.

Delightful? Chance clubbed the side of his head with his palm. What was he thinking? She was an imp! An impossibly wild, savage little she-male.

Chance glanced over Min's face. Perfect bow lips pursed sweetly in sleep; her long black lashes feathered a thin shadow across her cheeks. Lower, a few button toes peeked out from beneath the white linen.

Blast! She *was* delightful. Capable of making him do irrational things. Of taking her sweet limbs and stripping them bare, only to appease his own passions. What had he been thinking? She challenged every quality he had ever thought he'd wanted in a woman. The complete opposite of the woman who would fulfill his fantasy, this woman tempted him as no other woman ever had. He could not think straight with her big doe-eyed stare on him. Nor with that sassy smile. It took all his strength to keep from pulling back the sheets and curling up next to her.

And that was exactly why he had to get rid of her as soon as humanly possible.

Love was too dangerous right now.

Love brings nothing but pain. Do not allow yourself to be taken in by her sparkling eyes and delectable body. Fight temptation. Tout mon possible!

Yes. Chance's mind switched to action. He had things to do.

He carefully opened the trunk next to his armoire and reached below the red velvet saddle cloth that he used only for military parades. The watered silk was cool to the touch. Drawing out the gown, he arranged it on the floor by the window and took one last look over his sleeping guest. He could not leave in search of Luciano until he had seen to Min's protection. Yes, he had to either find her brothers today or else bring her to Val-de-Grâce. For if she remained in his presence much longer, he wasn't sure if he could control his desires. Desires that had betrayed him once already.

Protect her from yourself.

A little late for that, isn't it?

He would be a lucky man if he were not tried for *stupre,* the seduction of a virgin. But it was not too late to kill any further emotional attachment. It would be unfair to allow her to believe there could be more, when Chance knew there could not. Love was a sacrifice he could not—must not—make.

Not until he knew whether Justine walked this earth or lay beneath it.

Chapter Fourteen

Sleep left her with a gentle wave and a kiss of dreams. Min's smile curled beneath the warmth of a gentle ray of sun. She stretched her arms out to her sides, smoothing her fingers across the sheets. The bed linens were cool and wrinkled.

She touched her lips, remembering the soft kisses Chance had pressed there. Kisses that had changed to deep, hard, demanding acts of passion. He'd awakened wicked longings in her, and fed them with a kind of emotion she must now learn to suppress.

Love. Love? "Yes, love . . ." Min's thoughts wandered to the hours earlier when she had shared her naked emotions with Chance. So that was what love felt like. "It is a good thing." It was love she felt for the chevalier. She knew it despite her hurt.

But Chance did not feel the same for her. It was obvious from the passion with which he spoke of Justine. She had hurt him, yet he loved her still. Even in her death.

A shudder ran through Min's body to recall the words Luciano had spoken when she lay on the forest floor under his pistol. *It takes a while for the body to cool.* Was that why Justine's body was not found? It was too horrid to even imagine.

Knowing Luciano's twisted fetish allowed Min to feel some mercy towards Justine. But only for a moment. The man she loved was infatuated with the memory of a dead woman.

The heavens had opened up and gifted her with a beautiful love. And now the storms had come, flooding away her dreams and desires into a swirling, murky pool of mixed emotions. Oh, how cruelly life worked its bag of tricks on her! To give her a beautiful and caring man and to allow her to fall in love with him, only to wave an admonishing finger at her and tell her no.

The embers of last night's fire were white powder. Sunlight danced in glistening blues, purple, and emeralds across the shallow lakes on the floor. The buckled shoe she'd tossed in a rage was a growing island amidst a retreating ocean. Chance was nowhere about.

Why hadn't he lain close to her until she woke? Snuggled his body next to hers with the same reckless abandon he'd shown last night? They fit together so well, as if made for each other. So hot his flesh, even hours after their lovemaking, he had still retained an inner heat that drew Min to him like a bee to a golden froth of pollen.

But she knew why. Min switched her thoughts to practicalities. Now that Chance had determined that Luciano was the man he sought, he had to find him and bring him to justice. *Vengeance is not for me.* Honor and chivalry were the sinews that bound his musketeer's integrity. Pride stirred deep within Min's being to know the man she had lain with was of such a breed.

But surely he was in quite a hurry to get to Luciano. He

could have at least waited until she woke and kissed her good-bye.

No, Min thought, *I don't ever want to say good-bye. Not now.*

It was very likely that Chance—still feeling an obligation to her—had left to find her brothers and be rid of her, for she would only be in the way. A thorn in his side. Emotional baggage that would hinder him in his pursuits.

Min sat up, stretching her legs out above the floor, and reached for the Turkish gown. Their late-night conversation reverberated inside her mind, the words *I shall never love again* repeating over and over in vicious vibrations.

Fool girl. Leave without a turn of your head. This man does not need you, nor does he want you.

Min set about to gather her things. She toed the discarded shirt, which was still soaked from last night's battle. But her doublet and breeches were dry enough. Her hat, carelessly tossed, now lay before the armoire. Only one thing remained in the depths of the armoire. Min touched the blue mantle and ran her fingers along the four arms of the cross, each ending in a fleur-de-lis. "His musketeer tunic."

A twinkle of desire prompted her to lift the mantle up over her shoulders. It was heavy and stiff. Min spread her hands over the silver lace cross embroidered on the front. *"Vive le Roi,"* she whispered.

Her dreams had never been more close at hand. She was in Paris, home of the King's Grand Musketeers. The time had come to prove to her brothers that she wasn't the sort to be married off as a breeding machine. She wanted to march for the king. And she would.

Can you handle the battle? Min recalled running her fingers over the smooth scars on Chance's shoulder and torso after they'd made love. He'd flinched and gritted his teeth, possibly from remembrance of the pain.

You must do this. You cannot let your brothers think it only a silly boast. Where is the Saint-Sylvestre pride? You have the letter. It will provide your entrance into the musketeers. Follow your dreams. Prove yourself!

Min hugged the tunic to her breast. "I've no time for love and its silly trappings. I've things to do."

Assuming *en garde* stance, Min pressed her invisible opponent across the floor with her imaginary sword, her mind fixed on the image of herself as a musketeer. To ride a regal horse, her tunic and billowing white plume a proud sign to all that she fought for the king, was entrusted to protect his life . . .

Min's feet slipped on something smooth and soft.

"Where did this come from?" Shimmering Chinese watered silk of palest blue glistened in a slash of morning sunlight. "So lovely." Min lifted the dress from the sill and held it before her. Chance must have left it for her. Had he purchased it as he'd said, or—No, there were signs of wear, the lace turned in at the collar, a smudge of white powder creased into the fine grain.

"Justine's, no doubt." She glanced about and found that indeed, there sat a small wooden trunk on the other side of the armoire. "He has kept her gown. Truly he still loves her even after her cruelty. Else wouldn't he have destroyed her things?"

Min touched the neckline, beaded in shining blue paste jewels. Her brothers had gifted her with far finer jewels, the real thing, most times. Of course, they had been stolen. As most likely this dress had been?

Truly, Chance had loved Justine if he had been able to turn a blind eye to her thefts.

Min pressed the dress to her chest as her thoughts took her into even greater confusion. First that demanding kiss, and then his lesson in male and female differences, which had led to the most incredible lovemaking—and then the tale of his undying love?

Why was he so conflicting in his actions?

"No!" *This is foolishness,* her conscience screamed. *Forget him. For if you remain, it will only pain you more when he pushes you away again. For he will. That is for sure.*

Could she pull off her intentions beneath the eyes of the very man who would be her leader? Dare she? It would only bring shame to him when she was discovered.

"I'll cross that bridge when it comes."

Besides, she knew she meant nothing to Chance. Perhaps it might even serve him well to have the challenge of a woman in his troops. For it would keep him on his toes, for sure. From what she had seen of the household troops yesterday afternoon, her presence would only improve the distinguished ranks.

Setting her hat at a jaunty tilt upon her head, Min marched on to the Louvre to procure a position in the illustrious musketeers. Min was sure she would not run into Chance, because he had no idea of her plans. And if he was anywhere, it would be in search of Luciano. And most likely *her* after he discovered her missing again. Ah, but he would be in search of a young lady in blue silk—not a strapping young rogue in violet damask and Belgian lace.

Delighted at having given all the men following her the slip, Min stepped down the Rue Dauphine and squeezed through the bustle of the Pont Neuf. People were elbow to elbow across the span of the bridge. Hooves clopped and wheels rattled. Hawkers cried their wares and children shrieked in play. Everyone seemed to be flowing the same way Min walked. One had to be careful so as not to get a toe stepped on or rolled over by a carriage wheel.

Pushing her way to the raised sidewalk by the wooden railing, Min stood upon an abandoned crate to see what the ruckus was about. The only bridge unhampered by houses, the view from the Pont Neuf was one of the best in Paris. Min could see for a long distance from where she stood. Drums beat just off in the Croix du Tiroir, a monotonous drone of unchanging tempo. The tops of the wooden gibbets sprung like weeds above the heads of the crowd. Her jaw dropped, her heart growing cold. "An execution."

In all her life she had never seen such a sight, though Armand had once told her of a few he had witnessed. She could not believe the Parisians took sport in watching such a hideous display. Hundreds of gawkers filed around the scaffolds, some cheering, others even singing from what she could make out.

Not able to stomach the hideous gaiety, Min turned and looked across the Seine. Dark waters, crowded with many fishing skiffs, barges, and colored boats, drifted lazily, each having slowed to get a glimpse of the macabre festivities. She tried to close her mind to the busy rush about her, but there had to be hundreds of people on the bridge alone. All headed for the hanging, with nothing in mind other than grisly entertainment.

"I am not yet ready to leave, monsieur! The devil's dandruff, you are in a hurry."

The bones in Min's fingers stiffened beneath the fine lace at the familiar female voice. *No, it can't be.* She glanced over the heads in the crowd, trying to pinpoint its origin. A crew of brightly colored hurdy-gurdy players passed before her, two heads taller than the crowd, for they were on stilts. Finally Min saw the mop of blond ringlets and the heather silk dress that was sorely in need of replacement.

"Sophie!" Min pushed past a gaggle of dirty-faced children playing with miniature gibbets, on which hung strangled rag dolls, and made way to the sedan chair where Sophie Saint-Sylvestre stood staring at her reflection in the oval mirror attached inside the door.

"What kingdom fell and put you here?" Min demanded.

Sophie only returned a blank gaze. Her eyes were underlined by dark half circles and her tiny pout was a solemn O.

"Where is Alexandre?" Min could not believe the woman would be fool enough to be in Paris all by herself. Surely Alexandre would not allow her to come unescorted, let alone leave the children. "The twins? What have you done with them?"

With the mention of her family, it finally dawned on Sophie whom she stared at. Her confusion became a snicker, and then she laughed loudly, her gaiety echoing across the crowd in hilarious guffaws. "Oh, this is absolutely too . . . exquisite," she was finally able to say between muffled giggles. She pointed to Min's lip. "I pity the poor mouse who gave his hide for that. Ha! And you do not think you look the fool?"

Min ground her jaw. If she were smart, she would have avoided this woman. Sophie would only inform her brothers. But it seemed as though she was without Alexandre. "And what of you? Where are your children? You should be home tending them. Does Alexandre know?"

Sophie shrugged and closed the sedan door. She drew on her gloves and groomed her hands down across her wide skirts. "Most likely he does not. The three of them took off with hell in their eyes after they discovered your escape. Armand is quite furious."

Min could picture Armand's raging eyes as he stomped towards her. Hellfire and brimstone come to earth. A rival to Luciano's devilish rage any day.

"You realize you endanger your own brothers by forcing them to pursue you?"

Yes, for wouldn't the *garde* like to get their hands on two highwaymen? "I did not force them to do anything. Armand must enter Paris at his own risk. But what are you doing here? Have you abandoned your children at the first chance of escape?" Min peeked inside the chair. Vivienne, Sophie's handmaid, was asleep, her head lolling at an uncomfortable angle against the seat. At least she'd had the sense to bring along an escort. Not that the dull-witted Vivienne provided much protection.

"You may believe it. I left them with Camille and a good wet nurse. I shall return soon enough. I do want to return before Alexandre discovers I've left. But I couldn't resist this chance at freedom," she whined. "The infants are like a sentence to the Bastille, and Alexandre pays me no mind. Camille despises me, and you—"

"Me?"

"Yes, you," she snapped. "You go traipsing off to adventure whenever you please." She danced her fingers through the air in illustration.

"This is the first time I've ever done this!"

"And just look!" Sophie drew her bloodshot eyes over Min's foppish attire, her disgust very obvious. "I thought maybe this freedom you speak of so often was a good thing. But this!" She spread her gloved fingers in dismay to encompass Min's masculine attire. "And this!" She touched a finger to Min's mustache.

Min jerked away. She was now quite sure she should have walked the opposite way upon seeing Sophie. What had she been thinking? Sophie took such joy in humiliating her. Though no longer living in Paris, or hosting the many salons she was constantly bragging about, it was as though she could not step down from the ladder that she deemed herself to stand upon. A ladder whose bottom rung was barred across Min's throat to impede her ever beginning such a climb to touch Sophie's skirts. They were family—why would the woman not be nice to her?

"Ha-ha! Perhaps the life of a slave, as you so eloquently describe mine, is far better."

Sophie snapped her fan open and fluttered it before her pouting lips. "At least I still look a woman and do not have a dead mouse sprawled on my lip."

"The deuce!" Min marched a few steps away, set on putting as much distance between her and Sophie as possible. But her body, having a mind of its own lately, stopped. Fine, Min thought with a huff. So what was it now? It wasn't as if Chevalier Lambert stood waiting for her. For if he did, she could completely understand her body's reluctance to keep on walking.

Are you going to continue to let this woman treat you as a mindless child?

Pride shimmering just beneath her skin's surface, Min spun on her heels, marched back to the carriage, and matched the woman's defiant stare. "You just don't see, do you, Sophie? What sort of life do you have? To use your own words, you are shackled to the bed and those babies. Is that what you'd always dreamed of? Do you not wish for freedom? Perhaps a bit of occasional privacy? Oh, Sophie . . ."

The woman cast a snide glare down her nose as Min rambled on about the joys she was missing.

"Have you ever ridden a horse through the meadow at dawn? Or run free across the lawn, the wind singing through your hair? Have you ever decided for yourself that you will spend one hour just sitting in a chair, daydreaming, your cares and worries all closeted away? Have you never desired a thing, Sophie?"

"Desires?" Sophie mouthed the words as if a distasteful substance adhered to her tongue. "And how am I supposed to have desires when I've babies screaming from all directions?"

"Exactly!" Min narrowed her eyes on the stupid woman. "You are too perfect an example. Women are slaves, and I choose not to become one."

"Even if that means wearing those hideous breeches?"

"They're quite freeing." Min smoothed her hands down the billowing violet damask. "Far easier to navigate a crowd such as this than with those monstrous petticoats you women wear."

"You women?" Sophie's laughter echoed out across the Seine. "Do you not see? You've already put yourself in the male class. Poor, poor Mignonne. You are so confused. Why, the only thing you'll ever attract with your manners and attire is—is women. Oh." She pressed a gloved finger to her lip and averted her eyes as if she'd just pronounced herself a virgin. "Unless, perhaps—" sly humor shimmered in Sophie's pale gaze—"you *prefer* women to men?"

Prefer women? Min blew out an exasperated huff. Sophie was just too stubborn to see beyond her own little circle of life, which was no more than two feet in diameter. And that circle was lined with mirrors so she could see only herself.

"I must go," Min said abruptly and pulled on her gloves.

"Where to, my pretty *garçon*? Have you a rendezvous with a lovely lady?"

Min clenched her fingers into fists. Chance's proud words kept her from flinging herself upon the woman. *Vengeance is for the weak and feeble-minded.* Oh, but wouldn't she just like an unobserved moment or two to give the woman a good solid shaking.

"I've business across the way."

"Going to watch the execution?"

"No. I am off to the *Hôtel des Mousquetaires*—"The words slipped out too quickly.

"You're actually going through with this nonsense? Mignonne Saint-Sylvestre, now I truly know you are mad. Do you think this silly disguise will work? It did not fool me."

"The deuce, it fooled you! Had I not mentioned Alexandre and the twins, you'd never been the wiser."

An unenthusiastic shrug barely lifted Sophie's shoulders. "Very well, so you did take me by surprise. But you'll not dupe the king's musketeers. Please, *chère,* only a fool would be so stupid."

A fool! Min squared her shoulders and thrust out her chin. She'd show Sophie who the real fool was. "I am going to see Captain d'Artagnan. I shall return a cadet in the king's musketeers."

Min pushed past Sophie's voluminous skirts. The nerve of the haggard woman to call her a fool. Blast! She'd show them all.

"Care to make a wager you don't?" Sophie called.

"What?" Min hadn't made it farther than five feet away, and was now sandwiched between an apple cart and the rotund hips of a peasant woman bearing armloads of egg baskets.

"I'll wager you do not get accepted into the musketeers. Even with that stolen letter you carry with you."

Sophie knew of the letter. Had the woman been snooping in her things? Of course, she would put nothing past Sophie. Min returned to Sophie's side to find the smug reassurance the woman always held painted in a bright red smile across her face. Damn her priggish attitude. "And what if I do?"

Hand-painted turtledoves fanned her sister-in-law's sun-starved face. Sophie suddenly took on great airs. "I am attending a ball at the Countess de Maurepas's this evening. Most all of Paris shall be there. That is, all who matter. When I received the invitation, I absolutely devoured it."

Ah, yes. Min recalled the day the courier had arrived with the letter. Sophie had pranced about for hours waving the engraved invitation in the air like a battle flag, flaunting it and preening over what she would wear. Until Alexandre returned home. He refused to let Sophie go; she had her duties to the children. Sophie had moaned about it for days. "So?"

"This is my wager." The woman's gray eyes absolutely sparkled with intrigue. A fire did burn deep within Sophie's haggard body, Min felt sure. But it was doused daily by cold infant wails and an oft-absent husband. "If you do get accepted, I shall don breeches and doublet and attend the Countess's party thusly tonight. But if you fail . . ."

Min crossed her arms over her chest. The gleam in Sophie's eyes was damned maddening. Oh, but she would love to see the prissy little vamp in breeches and bucket-topped boots and— "The mustache, too?"

About to go on, Sophie paused. "Er, the mustache?"

"That is a part of the costume. It is all or nothing."

" 'Tis not the most appealing thing I've ever laid eyes on."

Min held her jaw firm.

"Oh, very well. The thing *is* dead, isn't it?"

"Excellent. And if I fail? Which I will not."

"You'll wear a dress, have your hair done up, and attend the party with me."

Min sucked in her top lip. She wished only to remove the spiteful grin from Sophie's face and replace it with a mustache. She wasn't that sure, after all, if her disguise really would work. Walking into the Louvre and procuring a position in the king's musketeers was going to be a challenge. She had been practicing her walk; she'd developed a gentle swagger. And lowering her voice in a reasonable impersonation of a man's was not a problem.

Chance would forgive her. She hoped.

"Very well. You have a wager. Where shall I find you?"

"The Hôtel de Lauzun," Sophie giggled. "Oh!" She clapped her hands together, her glee restoring her drawn features to an amazingly healthy glow. "I must be going. I need time to select your ensemble for this evening."

"Fie! You had better look into a suit of men's clothing for yourself."

Chapter Fifteen

Felt hat pulled low and a frothy black plume covering half his face, Armand cautiously strolled the white pebbled walk at the north end of the Jardin des Tuileries. He felt sure his identity was unknown to the average mounted guard. He did not use a disguise when pretending, beyond an exaggerated foreign accent, surplus facial hair, or distinguishing hand gestures. All of his victims had been, and would continue to be, women. He should not be recognized.

There were three large wooden tubs with orange trees sitting about, and many buckets filled with flowers of every imaginable color, though he hadn't the knowledge of their proper names.

In the exact center of the formal garden stood Alexandre—plain as day, no concern for adversity. He looked up from the pile of dirt he was tamping down and nodded to Armand, then laid his spade down and stepped over the uneven earth. Alexandre spread his arms to encompass the gardens. "It's beautiful, is it not?"

Alexandre inhaled a deep breath and Armand did likewise, but all he smelled was the taint of fresh manure from a nearby cart.

"It looks as though your interview with Le Nôtre went very well, brother?"

"I've already been assigned to travel with Le Nôtre to Vaux-le-Vicomte in two days' time. Monsieur Fouquet has a large project he's been working on there. Until then, there are a few lime trees that need replacing, for the winter was a harsh one."

"I am proud of you, Alexandre. The first of the Saint-Sylvestre brothers to make an honest living." Armand threw his arm across his brother's back and kissed both of his cheeks. "You do the Saint-Sylvestre name proud."

"*Merci,* brother. I feel quite proud." He spread his arms wide to encompass the great spans of geometrical hedging, flowers, and trees around them. "I am in my heaven here."

"I have never seen you happier, Alexandre. This is truly a great day." But Armand could not disguise the deep worry in his voice.

"You take great risks coming to Paris," Alexandre observed.

"A necessary risk to find our sister. I don't believe the *garde* has a description of me. Not that I'm aware. If only we knew of Mignonne's whereabouts."

A wisp of wavy hair blew across Alexandre's eyes. He pushed it away. "She has not yet been found?" A rhetorical question, as both brothers knew she would not be found until she was ready.

With a solemn nod, Armand crossed his hands behind his back. The strain of the past days wore heavily upon his brow. "I fear not. We've split up, Adrian and I. Paris is a big city. Min is a small woman. She could be most anywhere."

"Yes." Alexandre studied the pebbled walk along with his brother. "And right under our noses would be the most obvious. Did you check . . . musketeer headquarters?"

Armand snapped his dark gaze to Alexandre's. "How the hell do you propose I do that?"

"Not sure, but it is most assuredly her destination."

"Fool girl."

Alexandre pulled the brim of his straw sun hat down over his eyes. "It is not foolishness that will lure Min to the Louvre. It is a desire deep and heartfelt that burns within her. I cannot believe I never noticed it before. I thought it just a silly whim. A masquerade she played, as a child takes to the wooden sword and shield. But the look she gave me the other night by the fire . . ."

Alexandre's thoughts wandered inward. Yes, he had known the shimmer in her eyes to be more than just a boast to get her brothers to pay attention to her. Whether Min knew it or not, she needed—something—to fulfill the deep inner longing that had tempted her to flee to Paris. Though he thought it was not the musketeers that would answer her longings. No, it was something much bigger, more intense, that would satisfy his *petite* one.

"She truly desires to fight for the king, Armand. Her mind does not accept the inequality of the sexes. It matters not that she has never served in a campaign. She simply wants to gain fulfillment and prove herself."

"Prove herself?"

"What better way than by joining the *corps d'élite* of the king's household? By wishing her to become more feminine and to marry, you took away the pride and respect she desires from you."

"Me?" Totally unprepared for such a revelation, Armand's heart began to race. Him? Respect? But she had his respect. Mignonne was an excellent fencer, a skilled rider, and she had grown to be a strapping young . . . *Mon*

Dieu. Armand suddenly realized that he thought of his sister as another brother. Another man.

"Mignonne is not like other women, Armand. She looks up to you. She sees the way you ran the family in father's absence and have saved our lives from desolation. But at the same time, I know she harbors great worry should either you or Adrian be arrested. There is a fierce pride that carries her head high and glows like fire in her eyes."

Armand swallowed the guilty lump pushing up his throat. "The Saint-Sylvestre pride." All the brothers possessed it in varying degrees. "But she has no idea of the peril she may be in. You think I can get hold of her once I do find her?"

"Not sure. You've threatened her with the confines of a convent." Alexandre shook his head sadly and wandered a few paces away. The red heels of his new shoes crushed the pebbles in squeaking crunches. He turned back to his brother, their gypsy eyes locking in a gentle stare. "That would be like plucking the wings from a falcon and consigning her to a gilded cage."

Chance kicked the opened trunk. Justine's gown lay carelessly arranged on the top. And Mignonne was gone.

"Where is she?" Adrian Saint-Sylvestre's voice jarred Chance back to reality. He'd run into the man on the Rue St. Antoine. Chance had been buying sausages and fresh croissants for breakfast and had been fretting over the proper cheese when the dark-eyed young man offered assistance over his shoulder.

When he told Adrian that he had his sister stowed away at his own apartments, the man insisted he take him there straightaway.

Mindless of his guest, Chance stomped angrily about his apartment. "Such a fool, you are, Lambert!" he chided himself. "To think the imp would stay when you gave her such ample opportunity to leave. The deuce! You need some sense knocked into you!" He stomped over to the thick wooden beam that stretched from wall to wall and pounded his forehead against it. "Oh! Fie!" Stinging pain jarred through his temples and shuddered down his neck and shoulders. "Not only are you talking nonsense, you've gone mad as well and taken to beating yourself."

"Lieutenant?"

Chance pressed the heel of his hand to his pounding forehead, suddenly aware of his guest. "Forgive me, monsieur. As you can see, I am out of my head. Blast!" He glanced around. "Ah, but those damned men's clothes are gone."

"Men's clothes?"

"She had procured a fop's gear, and I found her trying to teach my musketeers fencing."

"Your musketeers?"

"I am lieutenant of the Blacks."

"I had no idea you were such a high officer."

Chance sensed the worry in Adrian's voice. "Fear not, monsieur. My list of worries is far too long to address a wayward highwayman at the moment—once again finding your sister being the most pressing. Forgive me, monsieur. It is all my fault. I had her and I let her slip through my fingers."

But not before you debauched her. Oh, yes, you had to take your pleasures of the helpless imp.

Helpless? Fie!

"No need to apologize, lieutenant. And please, do not punish yourself so cruelly. I shouldn't wish for you to draw blood." Adrian could not hide a gentle smile as he looked over Chance's reddened temple. "It is a great task for any man to keep Mignonne Saint-Sylvestre in hand for more than a few moments at a time. She is a wild one."

"That she is." *But I did tame her for a few precious hours.* His face turned away from Adrian, Chance closed his eyes and instantly pulled the image of Min before him. In the glow of the firelight, her flesh had been a temptation beyond his powers of resistance. And the sweet taste of her kisses far exceeded the quality of the bittersweet chocolates her eyes reminded him of. Ah, she had taken to lovemaking with the same adventure her life followed. She hadn't once cast a shy, fluttered lid away from anything he had suggested last night. *Mon Dieu,* the touch of her hand as it skimmed over his body . . .

"Tell me, lieutenant, why is it you care about my sister's well-being? If I did not know better, I might think you've taken a liking to *ma petite.*"

Blowing out a surprised breath, Chance pushed his fingers back through his hair. He stared at the floor. A liking? Never. Maybe? A liking? Oh hell, it was more than that!

"Perhaps you are right, monsieur." Chance boldly met Adrian's quizzical stare. It was as though he were looking into her dark eyes, tasting the sweetness of her look on his tongue. *Oh, Mignonne, where are you?* "Your sister . . . it may seem . . . has succeeded in stealing my heart." Chance cringed to hear his own thoughts out loud.

How could you allow this to happen?

Adrian chuckled. "Do not fret so, Monsieur le Chevalier. I am delighted to see a man take an interest in my sister. Especially you. But you don't look so delighted."

"I am not sure how I should feel lately. More emotions then I ever thought possible have run through my heart. I am—was—a married man. My wife died weeks ago. Murder."

"I see."

"I hadn't wanted to fall victim to my emotions ever again, but I'll be damned if your sister hasn't changed my mind for me."

"Does she return the same interest to you? Is she aware of your recently departed wife?"

Chance shrugged. "I am not sure what interest she has beyond using my protection to further her advancement towards her final goal. Which I'm quite sure does not include visiting this Aunt Huguette she mentions. And yes, she does know about Justine."

Of course she didn't care about him. She hadn't wasted a moment fleeing his apartment. She wanted nothing to do with him, that was obvious. Why had she worked her bewitchery on him and then fled? And why should he care? He had already decided it best not to encourage an affair between the two of them.

"I fear your sister may never take to being tamed, Monsieur Saint-Sylvestre. She is not the sort who will sit at home and sew up a man's breeches and prepare his meals. She is an adventurous dreamer." Chance stopped. Adventurous? Wasn't that the truth. The last time he'd dashed across a rooftop was—well, never! As for a dreamer, he sensed something when he looked into her eyes. It was as if he were seeing everything for the first time, seeing so much more, imagining, perhaps, his own future.

Justine had once been his future. Could another woman possibly take her place? A place he never wished filled?

Another woman already has.

Yes, Min was a special woman. One like no other. A fierce vivacity danced in her heart. An uncapturable spirit she possessed. Not like the wicked woman who had taken his name. Justine owned a black heart. Mignonne's was golden.

When had he relinquished control of his own emotions? He had vowed never to love again! It was too damned painful.

Mignonne Saint-Sylvestre was a sly one, for sure. To have stolen from him without his being aware until now. Surely she was a most skilled thief. Mademoiselle Imp, the thief of hearts.

"Perhaps you will join me in my search?" Adrian prompted.

"Yes!"

Adrian jumped at Chance's outburst.

Chance cracked an embarrassed smile and began to replay his plans. "Come. We should be off before nightfall. The streets are filled with all sorts of danger. We must find her before the streets are chained up."

"Perhaps we should check the *Hôtel des Mousquetaires?*"

Musketeers? Chance paused at the door and turned an inquiring gaze on Adrian. "Whatever for?"

"Ah . . ." A dark brow rose above Adrian's left eye. "She has not told you."

"Told me what? Why the musketeers?"

"Come, this one may surprise you."

Chapter Sixteen

In the main hall of the Louvre's north wing, cadets wielding blunt-tipped swords and daggers practiced their lunges and dodged straw-stuffed dummies circling on creaking wooden quintains. Beneath the great arched beams caked with dust, muskets were cleaned, packed, and primed, and a few women sewed up breeches and fluffed plumes. Feminine giggles and hearty boasts echoed about the spacious lobby. A welcome respite from campaign always found the musketeers in good humor.

Though she was confident of her disguise, Min kept the brim of her hat low. She felt sure she would not encounter Chance, for she was but three strides from the captain's door. All she had to do was keep her voice low, present the letter to Captain d'Artagnan, and pray.

When she was finally announced, Min drew in a deep breath. "This is it."

Determination carried her across the threshold, through the captain's anteroom, and into the dark-paneled office.

Bowing deeply—but most certainly, stiffly, as most men were wont to do—Min then stood at attention before the eyes of the recruiter for the king's musketeers.

His hair was a pleasing mix of sandy strands and gray, his beard still coal black. Though in his midforties, his eyes were keen and lucid as he gave her a quick once-over. It looked as though he was quite busy, what with the stacks of maps and letters beneath his spread fingers. Hands that were gracefully turned and mottled with a few light brown spots, yet also scarred from years of service to the king, gestured for her to straighten from her bow.

"You wish to join the musketeers?" he said briskly, his attention fleeting up to her and then back over the scatter of papers under hand.

"Yes, Captain d'Artagnan."

"Name?"

"Saint-Sylvestre. Mi—er Armand Saint-Sylvestre." *Forgive me, Armand,* she thought desperately. This wouldn't really be a lie. Just a stretching of the truth a bit. "I've a letter of recommendation." She retrieved the yellowed parchment from her doublet—now water-stained from her adventures—and laid it on the desk within the captain's reach.

He unfolded it and as he read his lips moved.

"Signed by your very hand," Min proudly declared. "My father served under Captain Treville. He was of the *noblesse de l'épée.* Antoine Saint-Sylvestre, Vicomte de Montrichard."

D'Artagnan looked up from his papers. "Yes, yes, Antoine Saint-Sylvestre." He studied Min furiously. "He . . . passed . . . some years ago?"

Blackness squeezed Min's chest. She lowered her head to disguise the pain. It would not due for a potential recruit to cry at the interview. She bit her lip, then stopped, suddenly aware of her actions. Men did not do such things. *Be on your guard. You mustn't let him discover you're a woman.*

No crying. No lip-biting. And keep your eyes low. She thrust out her jaw and held a firm stance, pushing away all female emotion. "Just over a year ago. He was taken down by cutthroats while on a mission for the king."

"An exceedingly brave man, your father. Our paths never did cross, but I have heard of his dealings with the Dutch in efforts to open new trade routes. Unfortunate, the circumstances of his death."

"He was always faithful to the crown, captain."

"And in what regiment have you served, Monsieur Saint-Sylvestre?"

"Regiment?" Why would he expect that she had already served?

"Surely you must realize that even with this letter, the king will not admit an untrained man into his musketeers. You have been honing your skills with another regiment?"

"No, but—" Untrained! She handled a sword as though it was a third arm. Adversity was her calling, the cunning and stealth a soldier must have already in her arsenal of skills.

"Young man, I am not taken to wasting my time. I've many appointments today and tasks to attend to. Now, once more." This time he granted her attention with direct and fierce eye contact that led Min to understand his rumored battle prowess. She would not want to be the enemy looking down this man's musket barrel. "Have you served in campaign or achieved some honor befitting a musketeer?"

"Campaign?" Min bit her tongue. "I, er, well—"

"You're quite young, boy." D'Artagnan squinted as he examined her downcast face. "That's fine dress for a soldier. Come now, tell me, you've no military experience, have you? Perhaps a wild and chivalrous dream of serving the king? It's a glamorous fantasy, but not a reality. Perhaps a few years in the *garde* will give you the experience you need—"

"Oh, but I have experience. And the letter . . ."

"This letter will be honored, I assure you, monsieur. But not until all the conditions have been met."

"Conditions? But they were never clearly stated." Min clasped her hands together and stepped up to the captain's desk, forgetting to disguise her voice. "Oh, please, you must give me a chance. I've come all this way, and I would serve the king well. I would die for him!"

"As any musketeer would. I am truly sorry, my . . . boy?" he faltered, his attention growing more curious.

Min felt d'Artagnan's scrutiny heat her face. She jerked her chin down. *Don't sweat,* she thought, *or the mustache will fall off into his hands.*

"I am sure your intentions are well-meaning," d'Artagnan started slowly. "But there's just no way around it. I'm sure your father has taught you well, but there is nothing I can do. We do not train men with no previous military experience. It's just too risky. The musketeers are the *corps d'élite* of the household troops. Perhaps I can sign you on in a regiment that needs your help? Get your feet wet serving in the trenches, and then we'll see if you've what it takes to come back in a few years. I will be more than happy to honor the granted commission at that time."

What it takes? A few years?

A dark cloud opened over Min's head. In all her dreams she had never imagined things would go so disastrously. Her courage and bravery had failed her miserably. What had she been thinking? She had thought Armand's letter would be sufficient.

To serve in the *garde* just wouldn't be the same. Would it? No. Those were the cadets who were always sent to the vanguard of a battle. Yes, her father had started in the guards, but she had never really thought much on that.

Of course she would have to prove her mettle first. Which wouldn't be difficult. But why not in the musketeers, right under d'Artagnan's very nose, where he could see she was worthy? If she spent any amount of time in the guards, her true identity would surely be discovered, and then hopes of the musketeers would be forever dashed.

Time for a new plan.

"Captain—"

Min turned at the new voice. God's blood—him! She spun towards the window, sucked in her breath, and tucked her chin to her chest. What to do?

Cautiously, she gripped the ends of her wig, gathering and holding two sausage curls together beneath her chin in an attempt to hide. Keeping her back to the two men, she stepped over to the window. Damn! He really was one of those homing pigeons the Cardinal so cherished. Except his home base was her!

"Pardon, Captain d'Artagnan." Chance bowed respectfully. "I had no idea you were occupied. It's just that I've pressing business regarding a young woman who might have been here."

Min tensed. A woman? He was looking for her. How did he know? She could feel his curious scrutiny blaze like a fire on her shoulders. Would he recognize the clothing from yesterday afternoon's debacle in the courtyard? Double damn!

"Alert, chevalier." D'Artagnan gestured with a nod towards Min. "Perhaps you can assist me with a matter that has just presented itself."

Min ran a gloved finger along the dusted windowsill. To hope for the world to stop at this very moment, only to allow her to jump off, was too much, she knew.

"This young man seeks a position serving the king."

"There are positions available in the foot guards," Chance answered helpfully.

Enough. Time for escape.

Things went fine until she reached the door and could smell the brawny scent of the musketeer blocking her way. Min stepped on uneven ground.

Chance gave a disgusted grunt and poked her in the back. "Monsieur! That is my foot. Are you blind?"

Trying to shuffle around him without actually turning her face his way, Min stumbled on her own damask heels. Why did he have to show up here, at this very moment? And smelling so delicious?

Chance gripped her by the arm and spun her around. Her thick wig flapped across her eyes and then fell away to reveal her face. His jaw dropped. "What is going on?" He looked to d'Artagnan.

"Forgive me," Min pleaded and used his frozen astonishment as opportunity to slip out of his grip.

"Stop that woman!"

D'Artagnan bolted upright behind his desk. "Woman? But I thought he—By the love of all that is sacred!"

Min faltered as her slick-heeled shoes missed the first marble step behind her. She turned, focusing her attention on escape, and scrambled down the steps, her wide pantaloon breeches ruffling between her thighs. The white plume in her hat billowed in her face, and she repeatedly blew it back. She finished the first flight of stairs and then completed the second.

Disaster was too insignificant a word for what was happening. Chance's voice carried down the hallway. He followed close on her heels. Were they forever destined to play cat and mouse?

Min raced down the stairs. The sound of a trumpet fanfare mixed with Chance's heavy breaths; he was less than ten feet from her. Frantically, Min looked about for an escape. Someplace to sort out what was happening. Members of the court sashayed by, a snobbish air preceding their footsteps. All were dressed exquisitely, with the most elegant wigs and powdered white faces.

Having never been in the Louvre, Min had no idea what was happening. Perhaps it was a parade of courtiers making their way to the king's chambers for supper. Perhaps a band of musicians sent to entertain that supper. But she hadn't the time to wonder.

"Stop! Why are you doing this?"

Min moved just as Chance's fingers brushed across her arm. She jumped from the bottom step and dashed through the guards in gray livery who preceded the parade. Woman squawked and thonked her on the head with their feathered fans, and kicked at her with little result thanks to their generous skirts. She could lose Chance in the confusion of petticoats and fops. It would be easy. If only—

"Mignonne, no!"

A few misjudged steps sent Min's heels skidding across the slick marble floor. Her breath left in a crush as she plunged into a lady, landing them both in a heap of gold damask, jewels, and ermine fur. As they fell, Min heard a familiar sound whiz past her ear. Her instincts prompted her to look up. A musket ball had nicked the marble wall just beyond her. Shocked to see that if she hadn't fallen, she or the lady beneath her would be dead, Min collapsed with a relieved sigh on the woman's body.

"He tried to assassinate the queen!" Chance yelled. "Seize him!"

A crew of Queen's Guards took off after Chance while Min raised herself upon her elbows. Her hat had fallen. She brushed her hair back over her shoulder. She had little time to determine what was going on, other than the fact that Chance's command had not sent a barrage of guards upon her.

But what she had just heard? Someone had tried to assassinate the queen!

The *queen?*

"Oh, *mon Dieu.*" Scrambling to her knees, Min looked over the crumpled heap of damask and lace that lay between her legs. An elderly woman—perhaps in her sixties—groaned and flashed her eyes open. "The queen?" she squeaked. Her stomach flipped over once and landed with a flat splash inside her gut.

"He's pushed the queen!" someone gasped.

"It's a woman!" another exclaimed.

Everyone stared and pointed. Fear scattered Min's rational thoughts. Not willing to stick around and see what was in store for one who shoved the queen, Min turned, pushed past two frilled ladies, and took to running.

Movements and voices seemed to happen in slow motion as Min rushed forward. She was aware of two or three men, courtiers in billowing plumes and ribboned white doublets, following her. They shouted, but she couldn't take in their words. Right now, she wished for anything other than this. Even to be in the hands of Chance, a man who had just witnessed her greatest dream fall to pieces.

He tried to assassinate the queen!

Her heels slid on the marble steps as she rounded the first corner. Fear gripped her insides as she heard a brute command. "Seize her!"

Chapter Seventeen

The holding cells beneath the Louvre were most unappealing places. Rancid water seeped down the filthy stone walls to muck up the straw that barely concealed a cold stone floor. The skitter of rodent feet sent a shiver up Min's spine. Having been placed exceedingly close to the torture chambers, she cringed with every moan, every slap of the whip, every cry for mercy.

Was that to be her punishment?

"I have orders from d'Artagnan to release her."

She jerked at the sound of the summer-rain voice. Chance! He was here to save her. Again. Oh, she would never again question his unerring pursuit of her safety.

The jailer's ring of keys rattled against the iron bars of her cell. Min scrambled up from her soggy nest and brushed strands of rotten straw from her legs and arms and hair. A dark shadow of silence, Chance stood just behind the lackey twisting the key in the lock, hands behind his back, his eyes lowered.

"Mademoiselle," the jailer said and bowed politely as he stepped aside to allow Min to step out.

Assuming a haughty stance for her jailer, she thrust back her shoulders, prepared to leave with as much dignity as possible. Why the sudden release was a mystery to her. If it had been ordered by d'Artagnan, it could not be a good sign. Min followed Chance's silent direction through the long tunnel that led to the stairway that in turn would return them to ground level. No welcoming hug or kiss on the cheek. Not a single word. He hadn't even looked at her, had only started walking, assuming she would follow.

She had done him wrong. By masquerading in front of his captain, Min had betrayed him far more seriously than she could even imagine. He must take her actions as an affront to his very manhood. Damn, if only he had never found out!

What was she thinking? The chevalier would have found out sooner or later. If she had infiltrated the ranks, would she have been able to pull off the charade forever? Not likely. Perhaps it was better that he had discovered her now. It wasn't as if this new masquerade would change his feelings towards her. He loved a dead woman!

Min walked toward punishment. She must stand tall and take what was served her. If only she had a clue as to what awaited her, perhaps her nerves might stop jumping.

"Chance . . . er, chevalier? I don't know what is going on. Can you tell me?"

"D'Artagnan sent me with your release. Other than that, I know nothing."

Not even a glance of reassurance from him.

"Am I to be tried for harming the queen?"

His bootsteps did not falter as they gained the marble floor of the ground level. "I don't believe so."

Min stepped out of the musty tunnel and drew in a breath of clean air. "Where are we going?"

"The queen wishes to see you."

Oh, great dread.

Min turned her hat round on her finger, the tormented plume dusting the knee of her breeches as it circled. The ends of the feather were beginning to wear thin from the constant turning. As were her nerves. Her jaw was sore from gritting her teeth, her knuckles curled in permanent claws. She needed to relax, to stretch. But she could not move. Chance watched over her, and any motion to stand or even cross her legs was halted by a snide glance from his grave countenance.

Neither dared speak to the other. What was there to say? *Sorry, I almost killed the queen. And yes, I tried to join your regiment, and I much prefer men's clothing, but I really do like kissing you. And making love to you.* And . . . oh, hell. Her life had become a disaster in a period of less than twenty-four hours.

Min went through a number of unthinkable consequences in her mind. She would lose her head for pushing the queen. The queen would have her thrown in the Bastille, chained to the wall, and left to rot with the rats.

And then there was the additional crime of impersonating a male and trying to join the musketeers. After the queen was through with her, Min thought sure Captain d'Artagnan would present his own list of complaints.

If there were anything left of her, Chance could sort through the scraps.

Val-de-Grâce was beginning to look very appealing.

Glancing to the Queen's chamber door, Min was met with a cool-eyed glare from Chance. Nothing like making the pig suffer before the feast. Why don't they just reserve the next available noose and get on with it? What was she thinking? What a fool he was to ever get involved with her.

She had succeeded in betraying his trust in her, only as Justine had done.

"Oh." She caught her forehead in her hands. After witnessing the lynching this afternoon, she had never imagined that *she* would be the Saint-Sylvestre sibling to end up dangling in the wind, her breeches soiled and her boots stolen by the first who could get his hands on them.

"Be brave," Chance whispered.

Min looked up. He granted her an indeterminate nod.

"I do not understand anything that has happened today, but you must be brave, Mignonne."

"How can I do that when I've no one to stand by me?"

He looked away.

"You think me deserving of punishment?"

"No. I'm not sure what to think. I was on a mission to find my wife's killer. But it seems I've stepped from one fire into a raging blaze. Mignonne, Justine betrayed me by not revealing parts of herself that eventually came out to slap me in the face. And now you . . ."

His unspoken words twisted a knife in her heart. Yes, her. She had also betrayed him by not revealing her own desire to become a musketeer. And because of that she had also slapped him in the face. She was no better than Justine.

"Perhaps it would be best if you stepped away and forgot about me."

He shrugged.

Shrugged. He did wish to forget about her. So be it. She did not need a man who was still attached to another woman. Dead or otherwise. He wasn't capable of offering her support. And so she wouldn't ask it of him.

When she was finally announced, Chance excused himself, and left for the dungeons, where he was needed to interrogate a criminal. Min dragged herself to her feet and followed one of the chamber guards through the queen's front apartments, where she was scrutinized by a number of the queen's ladies-in-waiting. Their giggles, muffled by lace-encircled hands and fluttering feather fans, did nothing but increase the count of goosebumps that had sprouted all over Min's body. The private salon—a place reserved, Min had heard, only for the queen's closest of friends—was a welcome relief from the stares and giggles.

This is really serious, Min thought. She absently smoothed her fingers around her neck, her imagined fate haunting her thoughts. Would she feel the rope burns?

As she entered the private rear chamber, Min came to realize why the queen was seeing her there. Anne of Austria, Queen Regent of France, lay on a bed of mahogany covered in red damask and fringed in gold, her head propped against a mass of silk-covered pillows and her arm soaking in a large pewter basin of milky-colored liquid.

Mon Dieu, I've hurt the queen. Min felt her heart slip from her knees to her toes and spread across the exquisite gold and blue fleur-de-lis carpet. Forget rope burns and soiling herself in public; they would have her drawn and quartered for sure.

The queen gestured with her free hand for Min to step forward.

Her stomach doing athletic flip-flops to make even the most skilled tumbler jealous, Min was barely able to make herself bow. Yet, by all means she must maintain the proprieties. She had done enough already to affront the queen. She quickly pulled off her hat. While still down, she begged, "Have mercy on me, your majesty. I knew not what I did. It was madness. Pure and simple madness. I most humbly beg your forgiveness—"

"Forgiveness?"

The abruptness of the queen's voice stayed Min in her awkward bow. She dared a glance upward but saw no more than the top of the queen's head, her auburn curls pulled tightly back from her forehead, as was the fashion. "*Oui*, your majesty." Rising slowly, Min drew her brows together, unable to see why the queen should question her apology. "I'm so very sorry. I am but a fool running about with my head in my—" She stopped abruptly. *No. Don't give her any ideas about methods of execution.* "I pray you will have a small mercy on so meager a soul."

Silk slithered against brocaded satin as the queen sat up, setting the gold lambrequins around the bed canopy to waving.

"So, I am to understand you are before me now begging forgiveness for *saving* your queen from death?"

Min jerked her head up. Saving her? But of course she had!

"Oh, no, your majesty. Not like that. Of course I am only pleased that your life was spared. But I would never— Well, I had no right to push you. You are the queen. I should have been more careful."

The queen waved her good hand through the air and sighed heavily. "My child, you mustn't torment yourself. I am not so fragile as I appear. Attribute that to years of court intrigue. I much perfer a bruised elbow to a musketball in the head. Do you not feel the same?"

"Of course, your majesty, but—"

"But absolutely nothing! I will not forgive you for saving my life—er, Mademoiselle *Mignonne* Saint-Sylvestre, was it?"

Min bowed again. She couldn't help it. She'd never met royalty before. She had dreamed of it many times, and now here she stood in the queen regent's bedchamber! She gave another quick bow just for propriety. "Yes, your majesty, that is correct."

"Are you quite sure?" The queen eyed her carefully, her dark eyes worrying across Min's features.

"Why . . . yes, your majesty. Mignonne Saint-Sylvestre is my name, I am sure."

"Really?" The queen leaned forward to scrutinize her more closely. "You wouldn't prefer *Monsieur* Saint-Sylvestre?"

Monsieur? Had the queen the same ill humor as Chance? "Oh, your majesty. Forgive me." She pressed a hand to her slashed and ribboned doublet, and this time remembered to curtsy. "I know how this must look. I *am* a woman."

"Well, if you are sure?"

A betraying heat flushed Min's cheeks.

"Tell me . . ." Interest sparked in the queen's eyes. "Do you often parade about in men's clothing?"

"Er, well . . . yes, your majesty." Oh, now wasn't this a fine situation? For a moment Min thought she much preferred being chased by a whole regiment of guards than to be standing before the queen admitting to her preference for men's clothing.

" 'Tis not what you may think, your majesty. You see, I was raised by my three brothers." Nervously twisting the plume through her fingers, Min stretched her gaze along the soft pink-and-blue Aubusson rug at her feet.

"Oh, you must stop it, you'll ruin that lovely thing," the queen said suddenly.

The plume broke with a crisp snap in Min's hands. "Forgive me, your majesty." Not sure what to do with the feather fragment, she stuffed her fist under her arm.

"Please, *chère,* you may dispense with the formalities. I quite tire of it some days, myself." Milky droplets splashed into the bowl as the queen lifted her elbow to examine the damage. "I only wish to learn why you prefer male attire to the lovely dresses you should be wearing? And why, pray tell, was I told that you were in with Captain d'Artagnan?"

The devil's toenails, news certainly did travel fast around here. "D'Artagnan? Your majesty, I was, well . . ." Min let out a defeated sigh. "I thought to become a musketeer, your majesty."

"A musketeer?" she wondered with all the disgust one uses when looking over a plate of fish innards. "You? But you are a woman. You just confirmed that fact to me yourself."

Min waved a dismissive hand before her. Confession was in order. For she could not go to the scaffold without a clean conscience. "A nasty twist of birth, majesty. Because I was born without a—" Min's jaw locked. Visions of Chance, naked, standing before her, filled her thoughts. *A man is hard.* Not that sort of confession! "Er, pardon, your majesty. Ahem. For lack of the right body parts, I am cursed forever to be a slave to the men whose freedom I so desire for myself."

Min bit her lip, which she released with a careless sigh. It no longer mattered what they did to her. Bring on the scaffold, the executioner's blade, the Bastille. Her dreams had been vanquished by a simple twist of fate. And the love she had for a brave and dashing musketeer was not returned. Nothing mattered anymore. She was empty, unfulfilled, humiliated beyond belief.

"You see," she began without regard for the queen, though her majesty was quite rapt at Min's words. "I have always dreamed of becoming a musketeer." Her dreams capturing her heart, the broken feather became her rapier as Min stabbed the air and lunged against her invisible opponent. "Oh, I realize now 'twas a glamorous, swashbuckling desire. Fighting, gallant missions, spying. You see, my father was a musketeer. And my brother Armand was forced to rob—er, *do things* to support us. Father was never around."

"No man is ever forced to do a thing, child."

"I know. But I simply wished to restore honor to the Saint-Sylvestre name. I thought perhaps if Armand saw that I could do it, he might have a change of heart. I am so sorry." She gave a careless sigh and sheathed her flimsy sword, watching as it floated aimlessly to the floor at her feet. "I have always dreamed of protecting my king and queen—"

"My dear, then you've already achieved your dreams." The queen slid off her bed.

"What?"

Coddling her wounded arm with the other, the queen approached, her masses of skirts and stiffened petticoats swishing like fall leaves tormented by a cool breeze. Min bowed compulsively and backed a few steps away. *"Chère,* you've just saved your queen. You committed a most brave and unselfish act for your country. And so it seems to me that you have, just today, achieved your dreams."

"I have?" Min said in an amazed whisper. "I have. I—I saved the queen. Me. I really did it."

Searching out the queen's reassurance, Min found a gentle compassion she had never known reflected in the centers of Anne's dark eyes. Was that the look only a mother could give?

The day's events jumped out with renewed strength to wrestle her to defeat. Her shoulders slumped, and Min literally fell into the day chaise behind her. "Oh, I am so confused." She caught her forehead in her palms. "Forgive me, majesty, I do not feel well. So much has happened. So many new and strange things. I've been on the road for days, chased and kidnapped by a vicious brute of a man. I've crossed rooftops and eluded thieves, and then to meet Chance—"

"Chevalier Lambert?"

Min jerked her head up to discover the knowing twinkle

in the queen's eyes. "*Oui,* your majesty. Chevalier Lambert—he rescued me."

He did more than that. A warm quickening birthed in Min's loins at the thought of her gallant musketeer kissing her and exploring every inch of her naked flesh with skilled fingers. *Why must you shroud yourself from love, Chance? Let me love you.* "He's so brave and honorable." Min did not notice the words that slipped out of their own will.

The queen gave an appreciative nod. "That is why he is a musketeer."

"You are saying that is why I am not?" Min bit her lip and set her glance across the floor. *Don't do this. She is the Queen Regent of France. Humble yourself.*

"No, *chère.* Not at all."

Settling her voluminous yards of satin skirts beside Min, the queen gently directed Min's head to her shoulder. Smoothing her hand along the hair that had fallen from under Min's hat, she cooed softly. "It seems you've been through a great deal lately. And now things are crumbling about you. Where is your family, child? Your brothers? Have you not a confidant to share your worries?"

Min absently picked at the embroidered flowers that traveled the length of the queen's skirts. "My brothers are in search of me at this very moment. Armand, the eldest, plans to deliver me to Val-de-Grâce." She gave a lackluster chuckle. "He thinks the nuns can reform this boastful hoyden. Turn me into a marriageable lady. Ha! That is like the pot calling the kettle black."

"My child, if I may give you a bit of motherly advice?"

"Of course. But—I don't exactly know what motherly advice is."

"Well, then, it is about time you've been given some." She pulled Min's hands to her lap.

Min marveled at the gold rings circling the queen's thin fingers, each clasped tightly about large rubies and diamonds. The royal seal was impressed upon one, a tiny bit of blue wax lodged within the crevices.

"These dreams of yours are perfectly acceptable, my child. Dreams enhance a lonely life and enrich a young child's fantasies. But some dreams are not always desirous to others and may only cause you inward harm should they be achieved. For example, the musketeers. They are a fine and gallant assemblage of young men who would die for their king to bring honor to his name. And yet, society does not approve of a woman taking up arms and fighting for her king. Why, it's perfectly ghastly to even imagine. I know that may seem unfair and perhaps a bit cruel to you. Especially one who has been raised by three brothers."

"As another brother," Min added.

"Yes, that is plain." The queen tapped Min's upper lip, granting her a whimsical smile. "But you must persevere. You should not squander your dreams all at once. Some dreams are best kept in your heart. Speaking of your heart," the queen said, suddenly switching from a firm tone to a much lighter one. "Why not marriage? Have you a true love?"

"A true love? You mean . . . a man?" *Of course she means a man. You haven't fallen cow-eyed for a sheep lately, have you?*

"Well . . . perhaps." Min sighed and sank into the queen's embrace. Chance's figure appeared in her thoughts, this time blessedly fully dressed. With his charming smile, the sun-bronzed flesh crinkled at the corners of his sky-blue eyes. "Yes, I do love someone. But he does not know how I feel. And he will never know because he does not want love himself. He loves another."

"A rogue, eh? Seduces you into his arms and then runs before you've a chance to even pull up your stockings? Sounds a proper coil, *chère.* Men can be very unreliable, especially when they are young and so virile as to want the entire female population of Paris."

"But—" Min hardly felt that Chance was the sort to want all the women of Paris. Though she couldn't be sure. She had only known him a few days. Hmm . . . She hadn't even touched her stockings before Chance was gone.

No, no, no. Her only rival remained a dead woman.

"Forget love for now. It will come," the queen said with a desirous sigh. "And when it does, you will know it, for your heart's desire will return equal love for you. As for the musketeers, well, I can see your passion for this dream. Believe me, I can. But it is just not proper for a woman, you see. You must strive to use that passion for something else."

"Something else?"

"Think about your brother's request. Would it be so terrible for you to spend a few months with the sisters to learn the ways of a lady? Open your troubled mind and your heart to the Lord's work."

Min stiffened at the mention of the convent. "Forgive me, your majesty, but I don't think I could ever do that. I know it will only be for a short time, but a convent is just not for me. It would be too stifling, like . . . locking me up."

"Oh, they will not! Why, the sisters go out daily to take the sun. And many help in the community. You must give it some serious thought, *chère.* The church can give you the answers you need. It will fulfill you in a way you never imagined."

"Fulfill me?"

The way a man's touch can fulfill my heart? Oh, Chance, I love you. Why can you not see that?

The queen nodded and squeezed her hand. "I promise I would never set you astray."

"Your majesty?" one of the queen's guards prompted.

"One moment."

Min was suddenly aware that the queen most likely had other appointments. She had most certainly taken up more time than necessary with her silly masquerade. "What will become of me? For injuring the queen, I mean."

"You shall walk a free woman from my chambers. I am alive, and for that I and the king owe you a great debt. Now, go home to your brothers and think on what I have discussed with you. Do not fear the convent. It can only enrich your life. Will you do that for me?"

Min nodded. "I will, your majesty."

The prisoner was not speaking. Even threat of the boot would not pry his lips open. Knowing that death would be this man's punishment, Chance departed the torture chambers in haste as the yowls of imminent, yet slow, death began.

This was certainly not a unique occurrence. Many a man was executed for an attempt on the king's or queen's life. But today this vagrant might have been successful, had it not been for Mignonne.

Taking the winding stairs slowly, Chance's thoughts returned to d'Artagnan's office earlier. At sight of those shocked bittersweet eyes, he had guessed Min's goal. And later d'Artagnan had confirmed the fact. She had tried to join the musketeers.

Damn! What was wrong with that vexing woman? Did she not realize that no female was allowed in the ranks? Did not belong in the ranks? Could never begin to hold her own against the soldiers who served the king?

Chance stopped at the top of the stairs and pressed his fingers to the smooth veneer door, but did not push it open.

He knew damn well that Min could hold her own against any soldier in his regiment. The woman had courage. Why, she'd defeated him in a sword fight and had even escaped Luciano when he had been armed with pistols.

But she'd never persevere in battle. Could she? Perhaps. But he didn't want to lose any sleep worrying about her safety when he much preferred her in his bed than fighting at his side.

There were too terribly many things to think about. Had she thought before, she wouldn't be in such a quandary now. Min wandered aimlessly down an abandoned hallway of the Louvre. Elaborate gilded frieze work curled above and about her, heavy draperies of blue damask sectioned off rooms and other hallways, and the pristine marble flooring caught her heels in a delightful echo.

But she felt far from delighted. Min dashed the sword Lady Godiva had sold her across the hem of a bunched drapery, silently cursing when it did not sever the material.

"I say, you've lost your way, monsieur?"

Min shrugged and trudged onward, not even bothering to turn to the male voice. "Be off. I do not need your directions."

"Is that so?"

She heard the man's boots echo behind her, not so fast as to catch her, but a casual pace to match her own.

"Do not trouble me, monsieur. I am in no mood."

"Perhaps I could suggest a mood for you. One not so offensive to others."

Min paused, and sucked the inside of her cheek. Why her? Had she not suffered enough humiliation as it was today? She did not need this man to further infuriate her. "I will warn you once more," she snapped. "Leave me, or suffer my retribution."

"Ha! Such a boastful *garçon.* Very well." The man's footsteps ceased. "I choose to suffer your retribution. If only so I may have the pleasure of teaching you some manners."

Min swung around, the tip of her sword finding its mark at the base of the man's throat, just above the wide lace collar that smoothed over a fine blue-velvet doublet.

"God's mercy." Her heart stopped beating. "Captain d'Artagnan." She swallowed her gasp and sputtered, "Forgive me, captain, I did not know. I shall leave as quickly as my feet can carry me from your presence."

"So it is Armand Saint-Sylvestre's twin. I thought as much. Well, if you'll not defend yourself, this shall be a sorry match indeed."

Min held the captain's unflinching gaze, searching for the whimsical spark that would reveal his fun, but found none.

"Not up to it?" D'Artagnan looked down the narrow line of his blade as if sighting in a mouse near Min's feet. "Perhaps I am no match for a mere woman."

The hilt of her sword pressed deep into Min's palm. He was baiting her, toying to see if she would show herself a fool. She could not be sure; the captain's face remained expressionless. She could easily match him, she knew it. But would it be wise?

"Cat got your tongue?"

Yes, Min thought. But she had only the one chance to regain a bit of the pride she had lost earlier in d'Artagnan's office. Drawing in a deep breath, Min acquiesced. "Very well." She assumed fighting stance, her sword arm thrust straight out, her other hand at her hip. She was in no mood for a duel, but she was also not in the mood to let another man preach of her weaknesses. Even a man of such high rank. It was time to prove once and for all that she had what it took to protect her king.

A smile touched d'Artagnan's face with the first touch of steel to steel.

"You've quite the thrust, mademoiselle."

"Honed for years, captain."

"A rather new sword," he noticed as Min dashed away his riposte. "Doesn't look like it's seen much fight. Why a gentleman's rapier for one who deems to live by the sword?"

"It is not mine, captain. I was forced to purchase another after my sword was lost on the way to Paris."

"I see. A duel?"

"Of sorts." She dodged a stab to her left shoulder and returned with a quick lunge to d'Artagnan's midsection.

"Who is it you are so angry with, and pray tell, why take it out on the king's musketeers?"

"I am not taking it out on the musketeers," Min hissed. "I simply do not understand why a woman should be denied a position when it is plain that I have what it takes—"

"You most certainly do," the man said while dodging to avoid the fierce sweep of her sword. He jumped into the air to avoid her upswing and masterfully met her next move.

"Well, you shall be the first man who deems me capable," Min said, surprised at his remark. The man was remarkable with the sword. Her anger lessened as their swordplay turned to serious display of skill.

"Where did you learn that?" d'Artagnan asked in amazement.

"My brother Armand," Min said as she stood back from the flèche attack. "Agrippa, I believe."

"Yes, yes," he replied, following her teasing movements down the hallway. "But most do not use his methods, thinking them too old."

"But they are not."

"I agree. So much more precise than, say—"

Min made hasty steps backwards as her pursuer pressed her to the wall. His sword found her heart. Her heart found its voice in a silent scream. She hadn't even seen that one coming.

"Saviolo? Your brother not show you that move yet, I'll wager." D'Artagnan's smile charmed Min's fear into relief. He meant no maliciousness. He seemed to be genuinely enjoying the duel, as did she. "Perhaps too antiquated for one your age. I, on the other hand, claim a much earlier birth, so I am privy to such moves. You surrender your arms?"

Playfulness aside, Min wasn't about to let this man better her.

Much as she should.

The church will fulfill you.

No. This one last time she had to prove herself. And then . . . who knew? Embroidery might not be so terrible as she thought.

"Never, captain." A deft flick of her wrist turned her blade up and under d'Artagnan's sword, knocking it away from her body and sending it flying.

He held her gaze defiantly. Min sucked in a breath and stood but inches from the man's glare. *A sentence in the Bastille, or a quick hanging.* Then he laughed.

But his laughter was abruptly cut short by a very familiar voice.

"Captain d'Artagnan, I've been looking—Mignonne?" Chance rushed over to where Min stood.

"This is madness," she heard Chance mutter, though he seemed at a loss what to do with his fists.

"I do thank you for attending the prisoner," d'Artagnan said to Chance. "Did he confess his alliances?"

"No torture could untie that man's tongue."

"Unfortunate."

"Just as well he'll no longer worry our queen."

Wishing there were a chamber pot close at hand so she could relieve her queasy insides of their gurgling contents, Min slowly straightened her legs. To look into Chance's eyes would surely be the flame set to wood.

"You must forgive me, captain," Chance started. "I hold myself completely responsible for the actions of this woman. She is not of sound mind."

"Not—" Always at the defensive, Min started, but then stopped. Perhaps she was not of her right mind? Who knew anymore? She had just challenged d'Artagnan to a duel. The captain of the king's musketeers! And she very well might have won had her shadow not shown up. Ah! Could the day be any more disastrous?

"Nonsense, chevalier." D'Artagnan gave Chance a hearty slap across the shoulders. "The lady and I have just had the most enlightening conversation. And a delightful match of swords as well."

"Yes, but—"

"Before today I've not encountered such a brilliant and talented young woman. Your skills are remarkable," d'Artagnan said to Min. "Your knowledge of the sword amazing."

"R-really?" Min could hardly believe it. A compliment from one of the most illustrious musketeers ever to serve France. She glanced toward Chance, who stood dumbfounded.

"Yes." D'Artagnan bent to retrieve Min's sword. He handed it to her with a regal bow. "And if the king should allow women to join his musketeers, then I would be the first to come in search of you. Might I have your name, mademoiselle?"

"Mignonne Saint-Sylvestre," Min proudly declared.

"I take it Armand is a brother?"

"Yes."

"Why was it not he who appeared before me today with letter in hand?"

She caught Chance's arched brow, but ignored his silent nudge at her brother's crimes.

"My brother has gone a different road in life, captain. I felt it up to me to continue the family tradition."

"And continue it you have." D'Artagnan retrieved his sword. He sheathed his blade and gestured that he had to leave. "I shall remember you, Mignonne Saint-Sylvestre. A brave heart in the guise of an angel. Chevalier, I shall see you shortly. Good day, mademoiselle."

"Bon jour, captain." Min bowed to d'Artagnan. A satisfied glow spread through her body. He considered her of caliber to be a musketeer! What joy she felt. But her mirth quickly burned away with the angry look on the chevalier's face. "What?"

"You're not actually taking his words to heart? He was only trying to lessen the blow. You do not belong in the musketeers. This is foolish. Do you know how I felt when Adrian told me that I could find you here? Attempting to join my very own regiment? If you believe—"

"I believe"—she started towards Chance, her fingers twisting cautiously about her sword hilt—"that Captain d'Artagnan would not have said what he just did if he did not mean it. At least *he* believes in me."

Chance crossed his arms, defiantly arching his left brow above an accusing glare.

"Which is a hell of a lot more than I've ever gotten from you."

"What? From me? You never once told me of such plans. To become a musketeer? If I had known—"

"If you had known, you would have laughed and then carted me away to the Hôpital de la Salpêtriere! I know you, chevalier. Where are your needle and thread? A frilly dress for you, mademoiselle. You could never allow a woman, much less *me* to prove that I am your equal."

"Nonsense! If I had only known—"

"Do you know that today the only dream I have ever had was dashed? Destroyed!" Min shook her hand in the direction that d'Artagnan had walked. "But be that as it may, Captain d'Artagnan believes in my abilities. He was impressed! And just to hear him say that he would have me be a musketeer in a minute if the king allowed it is enough. I need nothing more than faith, chevalier. And he gave it to me."

"I have faith in you. I just—"

"Enough. I know you care not a trifle for me. For if you did, you would have stood up for me and backed me when I needed you most. Instead you let me fall. But I should expect no less from a man who pines for a dead woman! Excuse me."

Min pushed past the chevalier, flinching when he reached to embrace her.

"Mignonne, do not say those things. You know that I care—"

"No." She turned and faced him. His features twisted with confusion and consternation. The eyes that had once turned her heart to a mushy pulp now only held blame and regret. "I do not know, Chevalier Lambert. I know nothing other than that you've put up a wall between the two of us. What happened to last night? Was I just a means of satisfying your lust?"

"No—"

"I know I can never replace Justine."

"I don't want you to replace that wicked woman!"

"You loved Justine, did you not?"

"I did."

"You still love her. You just don't know it."

She turned and walked out of the Louvre.

Chapter Eighteen

The cheery afternoon sun did nothing to dispel the heavy feeling that had wrapped itself about Min's shoulders. Pushing her way across the vast expanse of the Pont Neuf, Min had little regard for politeness. She squeezed to the edge of the bridge and looked down into the murky water. At the sight of a single piece of paper, an opera billet drifting by, carelessly abandoned by its owner like yesterday's lover, Min's heart cracked and she felt the hot blood seep through her being.

Chance had been so sure of his words, delivering them boldly and without a second thought. *You do not belong in the musketeers. This is foolish . . .*

Min sniffed away a salty tear. How could he be so cruel? To make love to her and make her feel as if he truly did love her, and then to misunderstand her feelings so. Not that he could ever understand her intentions.

You are the only one who knows your desires. And quite unique desires they are. You have never told him. What did you expect?

Sky-blue eyes, sparkling with unpossessable midnight-blue stars, flashed through Min's thoughts. How she cherished those precious lines at the corners of his eyes that only appeared with his sexy smile. And his kisses . . . Oh, those heart-fluttering kisses. Symphonies of butterflies danced within her body at the touch of Chance's lips to hers, coloring her world as vivid and lighthearted as the myriad variety of the winged creatures. But now she must learn to live without his kisses.

How could she care for a man who could not see her inner strife? Could never know her dreams? Could never consider her an equal?

"Adieu, Chevalier Lambert," Min whispered to the floating paper. "I could have loved you. Bosh!"

Though her mind was determined to forget the musketeer, her heart still pleaded to be heard.

"I *do* love you. Even if you cannot see beyond the outside and into my heart. But I will not press myself upon you. A man like you deserves a special woman. Someone who is soft and delicate, and likes to wear dresses, and will do as you say *when* you say. I know that is what you truly want. You need a woman who can heal your wounded heart with femininity and charm. Not someone who would lie to you and do things behind your back without telling you. Just like Justine. *Mon Dieu,* but I have betrayed him using his wife's very wiles! How cruel of me."

It was hard to say good-bye, but so much easier when Chance did not stand in front of her. For Min knew that should she ever see him again, her knees would bend and her heart would melt at his touch.

It was time to release the butterflies.

"Ah, but what of me?"

The church can fulfill you. The queen's words clung heavily to Min's mind. She was the queen, after all. Worldly and wise, she knew much more than Min could ever hope to know in her entire lifetime.

"Perhaps she speaks the truth," Min muttered as she strolled onward, stepping down from the bridge. Paris bustled by in a blur of browns and muted colors, the stench of manure and the cries of boatmen on the river. Though she hated to even consider the possibility of setting foot inside the disciplined walls of a convent, perhaps Armand was right. He had only her best interests in mind. Married life would be good for her. Tame the unwanted heart within. Her future would be secure. She would have no need of worry or want. It had been blind-hearted foolishness her quest, simple stupidity on her part.

To think, a woman in the musketeers!

Her path wove in a directionless trail as her thoughts were ravaged by her foolish actions. Then a solid object jarred Min from her thoughts. Rubbing her sore shoulder, she examined the low wooden cart set on four sturdy wheels. Its wide split-oak tub housed an enormous orange tree, complete with massive root ball and full glorious foliage. There were even a few pungently sweet oranges dotting the emerald head.

"What they won't think of next." She stood back to look over the incredible sight, quite oblivious to the man's toes she stepped onto.

His cry of pain alerted her.

"Alexandre!"

"Mignonne, *mon Dieu,* you are safe! Do you know how worried we have been?" It felt so good to see her brother and to be cuddled in his embrace that Min could easily ignore the smell of manure that always surrounded Alexandre. He had explained once that it made the plants grow faster. "What sort of mischief have you been up to? Armand is furious."

Min pushed a strand of flyaway hair from her brother's

lashes and kissed his cheek. "I am sorry, Alexandre, but you should know that I had to run. I could not let Armand treat me like that. Could you ever in your life imagine me in a nunnery?"

"I cannot begin. Even for a short time. I feel sure it would take less than one day for you to turn the sisters completely upon their heads with your antics. But what, pray tell, have you been up to?" He stretched his gaze down her attire. "Those are fine clothes. And what—?" He pointed to her upper lip.

Min peeled the mouse skin from under her nose and rubbed her tender upper lip, recalling that she hadn't the thought to remove it in the queen's presence. Surely the regent thought her crazed in the head. No wonder she recommended the Church. And what had Chance thought? All hope of his ever considering her a woman again had most certainly been spoiled. " 'Tis a long story, Alexandre." She flicked the tiny patch to the ground. "But tell me, are you going to wrestle me away and turn me over to Armand?"

Alexandre looked past her, his eyes scanning the luscious tree in the cart. Its branches hung heavy with tiny orange balls, each sparkling like jewels set into an overstuffed emerald pillow. "Much as I'd like to, *ma petite,* and *should,* I've work to do."

Min turned to the tree-moving apparatus. A man stood on the other side securing a rope about the base of the gnarled trunk. It suddenly struck her what Alexandre was talking about. "Oh, Alexandre, you've been accepted to work with Le Nôtre?"

He gave a modest nod.

"I am so proud of you!" She embraced him, and the two swung in a merry circle. "The first Saint-Sylvestre to make good of himself. It's simply fantastic. Your dreams have finally come true."

Burying herself in his embrace, Min squeezed tight to let him know how proud she was of his accomplishments. But a sharp stab pierced her breast, as if one of Chance's imagined imps were prodding her with his poker. "Your dreams," she whispered to herself, remembering the queen's words about leaving some dreams untouched. Unfortunately for her, she had not. *But I did at least* touch *them.*

Alexandre smoothed his finger over her upper lip, rubbing away the remaining glue. "And what of your dreams, Mignonne? You do not sound very happy. If I am correct, you've already been to musketeer headquarters. Is that not from where you've just come?"

She nodded, hanging her head shamefully. It was difficult to admit her defeat when he had accomplished so much. Alexandre had taken his dream and made it a reality. He'd invested years and years of hard work studying his plants and poring over the textbooks that Armand's booty had purchased.

A touch of her brother's finger lifted her chin.

"Ah, I see." Alexandre could read her face easily enough. "You tried to use Armand's letter?"

"I was a fool to believe the musketeers would accept an untrained soldier."

She caught his rising brow.

"Yes, yes, and also a fool to even think they would tarnish their ranks with the likes of me. A woman."

"A very brave and honorable woman. *Ma petite,* it matters not that you've no tangible evidence of the fulfillment of your dreams. Would it mean anything to you to know how proud I am of you?"

"You are? But—but what of my leaving without a word?"

"Now, that will take some forgiveness. But you had a dream and you would let no one stand in your way. Isn't that what dreams are for? To pursue, and learn along the way. You have learned something about yourself, haven't you?''

''Only that I have failed.''

''Really?''

She shrugged and turned away, closing her eyes to allow the events of the past days to wash over her thoughts. Adversity had followed her all the way to Paris, and even then it had not released its hold on her. And along with the trials, she had encountered love. Not a free love, one willing to be captured by her, but a teaching love. ''You're right, Alexandre. I have learned some things. And even if I didn't grasp my dream, it touched me. If only for a moment.''

''Some dreams are best kept forever in your heart.''

''That is the same thing the queen said.''

''The queen? And since when has *ma petite* been conversing with the queen and deems to do so casually mention her in conversation?''

''That is a long story. Much too bizarre to believe. But you are both right. I'm beginning to see that now. I was a fool to believe any man would give a woman a chance. The musketeers shall remain forever unblemished by females, I fear. I am doomed to rot in a convent or to marry some fat bourgeois husband who wants dozens of dirty-faced children.''

At the mention of children, Min recalled Sophie, with infants in hand, her darkened, soulless eyes, and her oftentimes tear-streaked face. ''I almost forgot. I've that damned wager to honor.''

''Wager?''

''I've an engagement tonight. With, er . . .'' Could she tell Alexandre that another Saint-Sylvestre had made her escape? His own wife? ''It's nothing. But what of you? Are you to be leaving us?''

Her brother signaled to the man standing by the team

of four horses hitched to the cart. "We leave for Vaux-le-Vicomte in two days. I must see Sophie before I leave. She would never forgive me should I not. But I will send for her and the infants when I am settled."

"Do not worry, Alexandre, I'll see to it she does not raise a fuss. I'll bring her a message from you promising your faithfulness and love."

"And love?" Alexandre cocked his head towards Min, his eyes wondering. "Yes . . . my love. I do love Sophie, trying as she may be. She has given me two lovely daughters. Ah, I cannot leave without seeing her first."

"I think I can arrange that," Min offered. "But go now. Let me take care of things. I shall see you before you leave, and I will have Sophie with me."

"Merci, ma petite." He pressed his palm to her cheek. Min closed her eyes. "Promise you won't ever lose sight of your dreams, no matter what the outcome?"

"I promise."

"I've been unable to pinpoint Luciano's location, though I have talked to some who know him. They say he frequents *la Maison Rouge.* Perhaps we should go there tonight?"

Chance gave Adrian Saint-Sylvestre a good once-over. He didn't even want to know how the man had come to know people who knew Luciano. Min had said her brothers were highwaymen. But gentleman thieves.

Right. Gentlemen always requested your jewels and coin before kissing you *bonne nuit.*

"I cannot tonight." Chance blew out a breath and toed an abandoned potato with his boot. "Captain d'Artagnan has a mission for me."

"Mission?" Adrian could read his displeasure, Chance

was sure, but he wasn't about to jump for joy over this assignment. "You don't seem pleased."

"I'm not. It is foolishness. But d'Artagnan has ordered me, and so I must obey. Seems he's a more pressing matter to attend to."

"What of my sister? You saw her at the Louvre?"

"Yes." Chance squeezed his fist into a tight coil, the frustration building once again. Blast, he had been a fool to treat her so. Why, oh, why had he said such things? He wanted to take her and hug her and kiss her and tell her things—things like *I need you, I care for you, I—* Instead he had only pushed her further away. Perhaps permanently. "I am sorry. I let her slip away again. She didn't want my company. I wasn't even thinking of the danger should Luciano find her."

"We will find her," Adrian reassured him.

"*Oui,* but pray God we do before Luciano gets his hands on her."

Min wandered down the Rue Poulletier, en route for the Hôtel de Lauzun, where Sophie was staying. Her stomach growled and her feet ached for walking on the garishly fancy heels. She checked her purse; there were six sous left. Not enough to purchase boots, but enough for a bite to eat and something to wash it down. Though she'd never developed a taste for spirits or beer, Adrian had tried his best to get her to like them.

She wondered where he was right now. If the brothers had split up as Alexandre had said, then surely she would like to meet up with him first. For Adrian she could talk into anything. It was Armand who would not give her a moment's time. He would whisk her immediately to Val-de-Grâce without allowing her so much as a protesting gasp.

Course it might not be so terrible to go to a convent, after all. How long could it take to learn to sew, and cook, and clean, and dress properly, and hold her head just right, and speak with a womanly air, and . . . ? "No. I cannot do it. They will laugh at this fumbling excuse for a woman."

But must she listen to the queen? Perhaps she could say she had had a momentary lack of comprehension while in the queen's presence and hadn't even heard what she had said to her.

She could not forever roam the streets as a man. Her disguise was not so foolproof that no man would ever discover her true identity. And she was shunned as a woman in man's dress. She fit in with neither the men nor the women!

And what of the irrepressible desire she held for the one man who did not want love?

Like fire to ice, he had melted her resolve with his seductive gaze and tamed her into his arms with a charm so subtle and polished, she hadn't known what hit her. A fleeting shiver combined of scintillating coolness and a fiery glow engulfed her entire being for a sweet moment.

"You've given up on him. Remember?" Min pushed splayed fingers over her temples to ease the throbbing. She'd removed her hat, not caring whether anyone saw her and thought her to be a woman. She was tired of the charade. It was time she did some serious thinking on her life.

"Oh, if only he had never made love to me," Min murmured, romantic visions of her brave musketeer flashing before her eyes. For then her decision would be an easy one.

She couldn't erase the throbbing sensation of Chance's lips pressed to her own, soft and firm at the same time, each subtle movement teasing her deeper into his passionate world. And she could still smell his scent. Woodsy and deep, underlined with that heady note of male. For a few brief hours, he had possessed her. And she had held him in her arms, helpless and tender as a newborn babe. Willing to tell her his deepest secrets, he'd opened his heart, blindly leading her to believe that he had feelings for her, too. He *had* needed her. If only . . . for the moment.

Min pressed her hand to her breast. Her heart started a fast patter each time she thought of the chevalier.

"He does not care for me!" she reasoned with her crazy thoughts. "He will never love again, for he believes I shall betray him as his wife did. He wishes only for the same thing as Armand, to see me married and safely out of his grasp. It was a foolish moment; his defenses were down. It meant nothing more to him than a quick release for his own needs. Maybe . . ."

Maybe you can change his mind?

"Never. I know not how to influence a man. Seduction is certainly not one of my charms."

She looked over her clothes. Not too many men were attracted to her chosen mode of dress. She could never hope to catch the chevalier's eye unless she softened up a little. God's navel, she would need an entire change of character to even attract a man.

"Oh!" Fists shaking near her thighs, Min took the cobblestones in vehement stomps. "Such madness! I cannot do this. Just forget about Chancery Lambert! He's already told you he cannot love you."

Min marched onward. The Hôtel de Lauzun stood just ahead, veed onto the corner of a street by angling stone houses on either side. Much as she dreaded seeing Sophie again, she would never dishonor her word. A gentleman always honored his word.

Gentleman?

Ha! Perhaps Sophie was right.

Taking a sharp corner around a tavern, Min stopped cold. An assortment of rough-cut tin signs blocked her vision, but that did not prevent her from hearing an all-too-familiar voice. She shuffled backward into the shadows and pulled her hat low.

"She wore a pink dress trimmed in lace around here, though it's likely she'll be sporting breeches and doublet by now."

Min stiffened at the sound of Luciano's deep, lisping voice. Lisping? Serves him justly, she thought with a growing smile.

"Five hundred *livres* to any man who brings her to me. Alive . . . or dead." He lingered on the last word, as if savoring the snap of the whip as it bit through his enemy's flesh.

Alive or dead? Min cringed, knowing that the man most likely preferred the latter. And what would he do when he found her? Min did not even want to think of it. Luciano's admonitions regarding how long it took the body to cool churned her stomach. And he had taken Justine's body with him—oh, the horror!

"I will keep an eye out, monsieur."

There came no reply. Feeling the flesh on her back prickle, Min swallowed. A tickling bead of sweat ran down her neck. She dared a quick peek around the corner. The thin silhouette of Luciano hobbled down the street away from her. He was limping!

Pleased that she had done some damage, Min dashed in the opposite direction and ran up the steps of the Hôtel de Lauzun.

Chapter Nineteen

"The girl actually has bosoms!" Sophie joyously declared as she made the final adjustments to Min's new attire. "Who would have thought?"

Min could only rudely mimic Sophie's words, for she felt sure, talking, let alone breathing, was something she could only do sparingly now. After everything she had been through in the last few days, leave it to Sophie to find a way to humiliate her even further.

Sophie stepped away and Min turned around to stare at her sullen reflection in the gilt-edged Venetian mirror. She hadn't any idea what to do with her arms; they were so tightly sheathed in emerald brocade. And her legs felt like two bare sticks shivering in an open field beneath the massive skirt.

"I feel hideous," Min managed. She pressed her hands to the constricting stays, tightened torturously snug at Sophie's evil hands. "Like a squashed melon oozing all over." She breathed heavily, watching her breasts rise and fall like squashed melons from the confines of the greenest dress she had ever seen.

"Ah, but it is your 'melons' the men will like to see." Sophie's head disappeared into the great paperboard chest she had lugged from home.

Min eyed her décolletage in the mirror, thrusting her shoulders back proudly. "I prefer to keep them under wraps than expose them to the entire city of Paris. Where is that shawl?"

"Oh, no, Mignonne, tonight you do as I say." Sophie tossed the embroidered shawl she had pulled out back into the chest.

Sophie's own attire was quite elegant, Min noticed. She must have been hoarding the lace-trimmed cream silk for years, for it still had a farthingale and long sleeves. But she did look better than usual, what with her face powdered to conceal the dark circles beneath her eyes and soft rouge to brighten her cheeks.

"You look perfectly exquisite, dear." The black star pasted on the corner of Sophie's mouth wobbled with each word she spoke. "If only you could see for yourself how lovely you really are, you would never think to look at a suit of men's clothing again."

Min shook her head, causing the thick sprays of dark ringlets to bounce against the side of her face. Whoever thought to wear a wire from ear to ear to hold these silly bundles of hair into such an absurd style must have been half crazed at the time. Min adjusted the hair wire so both sides were even, finding that she didn't really care how she looked, as long as the evening went quickly.

Her reflection still frowned at her, so she stuck her tongue out at it. "This is stupid."

" 'Tis the style," Sophie clucked, her own blond ringlets dancing happily upon their perch. "Now sit. Let's put these on."

Min eyed the high-heeled shoes with horror. They were a good two inches higher than the ones the maid at the inn had given her. "I can't walk on those! I shall fall and break my neck."

"Or worse yet," Sophie said, "you may just fall into the arms of a ravishingly handsome young rogue."

Sophie pulled Min beneath the enormous crystal chandeliers of the de Maurepas ballroom, introducing her to every face she recognized, and even to those she did not. Sophie had lived in Paris before marrying Alexandre, so she was familiar with *le beau monde.* At least it seemed to Min—by the air Sophie had taken on—that she knew what she was doing. The escapee mother brightened like the sky after a spring rain as they drew deeper into the crowd of fops and overstuffed wigs and she recognized one after another of her old friends and familiar faces.

Feeling this was the most embarrassment she had ever had to endure, Min had to force a graceful smile for each woman and man she met, and cast a rebuking sneer towards those men who let their gaze linger longer than appropriate on her melons—er, décolletage.

She winced as Sophie elbowed her in the ribs for the umpteenth time. Her body was sore enough from the tight stays without Sophie making it worse.

"You're frightening all the men away. How perfectly dreadful. It's as if you've the plague."

"I would have gratefully taken the plague over this evening's frippish festivities," Min hissed.

"For this one evening, you must act as a lady. I know it will be exceedingly difficult . . ." Sophie drawled, and at the same time cast a gracious smile across the room to the Duchess de Maurepas. "But that was the wager."

"I do not recall acting as a lady being a part of the

wager,'' Min stomped her foot and nearly toppled over until Sophie provided a rescuing grip. 'Twas a good thing her skirts were long, because Min had yet to learn how to balance on the high damask slippers Sophie had laughingly bestowed upon her. Brushing a coil of hair from her flustered face, Min bravely continued. ''You are always changing the rules to suit your own whims, do you know that?''

''Oh, Mignonne, if that be the case, then why is it I am shackled to those dreadful infants?'' Sophie pulled Min close to the Chinese urn from which a massive fern spilled myriad tendrils. ''Oh, 'tis not as if I do not care for them. I adore the twins dearly. They are my life. But if I had my way,'' she whispered secretively, ''they would each have their own nurse. It is Alexandre who insists the mother should be the principal caregiver. Little does he realize, I've three infants instead of two. Some days the man is impossible. Bring me my ink and papers, Sophie. Do tend to our children, Sophie. Do not hammer on my nerves so, Sophie.'' She waved across the room, receiving a delighted answering wave from a woman swathed in pink ribbons and blue tassels, impressing Min with her ability to hold two conversations at once. ''Believe me, Mignonne,'' Sophie said, lowering her voice conspiratorially. ''I desire freedom as much as you. And it boils my blood to sit back and watch you have all the pleasure.''

''Pleasure? In this silly costume? This is not pleasing in any way, Sophie. This is—''

''Do you not think it pains me deeply to know my husband does not love me?''

It had been Sophie who trapped Alexandre into a loveless marriage by becoming pregnant. And Alexandre, being too kindhearted, wanted only to give a name to his child and see it well cared for. What a further surprise to end up with twins. Min knew her brother did not love his wife as a man who is passionately in love, but he did adore his children.

Sophie set her frustrations free. "What I wouldn't give for the life I once had."

"And do you think Alexandre does not wish for that too? You are the one who trapped him."

"Trapped?" Sophie's colorless eyes sharpened. "How dare you."

"How dare *you!* After only two nights together, you became pregnant. Two nights! That's unthinkable for my brother, Sophie. Alexandre is too kind and gentle."

"*Oui,* he is very gentle, isn't he? He just has this sweet air about him. I couldn't resist—I simply had to have him. Oh, it was I who seduced him. I wanted so desperately to have the favors of a sweet and gentle man. I thought if I shared myself with him, he would not stray. Alexandre is far too kind to be a rogue, and I was so dreadfully bored with all the cavaliers at the time."

"Bored? You seduced my brother into your bed because you were bored?"

"Oh, Mignonne, what is done is done. I do love your brother. There are days I feel blessed to be his wife and mother of his children. I only wish he could love me. In Paris. Whatever shall I do?" Sophie sighed.

"I know not," Min snapped, enraged at the woman's dramatics.

"Some help you are. If it does not involve you, you do not care a trifle. Oh, duchess, it has been so long."

With a wave of her fan, Sophie strode off to mingle, leaving Min open-mouthed over her lack of compassion.

"Bah!" Turning the opposite direction, Min made to stomp off, but instead she blundered into the Chinese vase, setting it on edge. Grappling for the heavy urn with both hands, and struggling to maintain a footing, slick-heeled shoes on freshly polished marble, Min eventually heaved the pottery back into place. Steadying herself against the vase, Min checked over her shoulder. It didn't appear as if anyone had witnessed her clumsiness. Still, embarrassment flushed her cheeks.

In an attempt to sequester herself from the curious gazes of the many feathered and jewel-laden fops who strolled by, Min turned and examined the fern. Its fragile leaves broke under her nervous touch. Nerves? More like high-strung agitation. This was pure hell and torture. Why, oh, why had she ever agreed to such a wager?

Min dared another glance over her shoulder. Sophie spoke in great animation to the diamond-laden duchess, who seemed absolutely rapt at every word Sophie uttered.

Very well, so she owed Sophie this much. The poor woman was jealous of *her*. Jealous? When she seemed to have the entire room at her fingertips? Perhaps this was Sophie's true calling. Socializing. 'Twas not as if half the women in Paris didn't hold the same occupation. Salons were the popular pastime. Sophie did love Alexandre in her own odd little way. Perhaps with him leaving for Vaux, they would have a chance to become close.

The least Min could do was play along with this masquerade for one evening. Let Sophie have her dreams. Soon enough she would be back at the château chained down by bleating infants. It couldn't hurt. Except her ribs. Min pressed her fingers to her chest. "I shall have marks in my flesh from these damned whalebones. And my toes will never uncurl."

Stepping away from the strains of the minuet that encompassed the vast ballroom, Min passed a narrow hall filled with vaporish women resting against the walls, their handmaids fanning them and cooing reassurance. With her eyes glued to the folding limbs of a particualrly hefty woman, Min's shoulder connected with an object that yelped.

"Stupid oaf!"

"Forgive me." Min had barely time to register that she'd walked into a finely dressed lady before she had to throw up her hands to block the barrage of thwacks the woman delivered with her fan. "I surrender, madame! Cease!"

"Oh." The woman drew back with an instant change to her features. Her pale countenance smoothed, and her gray eyes flashed in recognition. "It's you."

It was the woman from the inn, the one who had traded her dress for Petit Feu. "Madame, you must forgive me," Min offered with a bow before the regal woman. "I was preoccupied. I've not been to such a splendid gathering before. There are just so many things to see."

"Apology accepted. Though I must say I'm quite surprised to see you here. After your dip in that foul water?" She drew a bejeweled hand over her fan, snapping it smartly against her palm. Then she touched Min's forehead, and smoothed a rogue curl from her face before looking over Min's attire. "This color is most unappealing on you. It appears as though the bed curtains from the Hôtel Dieu were ransacked to afford such a hideous concoction. Whatever happened to the dress I traded you? The soft color suited you so well."

She'd left scraps of the pink concoction all across the French countryside. "It certainly served many a purpose," Min said thinking of her bruised forehead. "Though the er—travel—"

"You did like it, didn't you?"

"Oh, yes, it was beautiful. If you must know, it was destroyed." The woman had a way of voicing her outrage with a mere lift of her narrowly tweezed brows. "I was apprehended by a most vicious highwayman." Min paused to further gauge the woman's reaction. Tense interest held her rapt. "Needless to say, I succeeded in escaping, leaving him toothless and limping for sure."

"Limping?" As cool as the pale blond appeared in her

sparkling cream concoction of silk and rosettes, she could not disguise a sudden flicker of fear.

"Yes, the bastard thought to have his way with a woman who can well handle herself, thank you very much. I escaped, though I must say your dress did suffer dearly."

"This man—don't you fear his retaliation?"

"Of course I do. I know he pursues me still."

"Why does he pursue you?"

"As far as I can figure, he just doesn't take kindly to dirt."

The woman drew in her lower lip and looked away.

"I'm sorry, I didn't catch your name—rather surprising, considering all you've done to help me."

"Er . . . baroness. Yes, the Baroness de Maurevel."

"Oh, my lady."

"And you?"

"Mignonne Saint-Sylvestre."

"Mignonne. Interesting name. And what will you do if this highwayman should come upon you again?"

"Besides knocking out more teeth and laming him permanently?" she parried.

The baroness nodded.

"I've the lieutenant of the king's musketeers on my side—"

"Chance—er, the Chevalier Lambert?"

"I was escorted to Paris by him."

"Lambert? Oh . . ."

The baroness's face actually colored beneath the layer of heavy powder and patches.

"You know him?"

It seemed from the sudden stiffness of the woman's carriage and her intense gaze that she might know Chance. She'd spoken his first name.

"But of course, who has not heard of the man? He is d'Artagnan's right hand, or so I've heard." She snapped her fan into a rapid flutter before her face, underlining her intense gaze. "Tell me, how did you come upon the chevalier?"

"He rescued me from the highwayman the first time he captured me—"

"The first time?"

"Yes, in Remalard. The nasty buffoon had me tied to his bed."

"Tied!" She stopped fanning abruptly. Min appreciated her sympathy and outrage, but something about the woman's demeanor made her wonder if her outrage was misdirected. Not specifically towards Min.

"Yes, tied. But Chance—the chevalier—rescued me just in time."

"So, the two of you are . . . involved?"

"I wouldn't call it quite that."

"But you wouldn't call it quite *not* that?"

Min shrugged, feeling a flush of heat on her face and neck. "Perhaps," she mused, "I could call it that. We've become close the past few days."

"I see." The woman snapped her fan and cast a glance down the hallway of swooning women. "Is he here with you this evening?"

"Oh, no, he has more pressing matters." Like avoiding her at all costs. "He seeks the Notorious Ones."

"Ah."

"He believes them to be aligned with the very same man who kidnapped me."

Using her fan as a shield from which she could cast a cunning eye or redirect a nervous glance, the baroness circled Min. "Sounds dangerous."

Min couldn't help but feel the ice in the baroness's voice chill her blood. "He also believes him to be the man who murdered his wife."

"Oh?" Layers of ice sealed up the woman's visage. She

snapped her fan shut against her wrist. "Well . . . how chivalrous."

"He still loves her."

"Who?"

"His wife. He doesn't admit it, but I can read in his eyes what his heart won't allow him to see."

"It sounds as if you've become quite close to the chevalier."

"I should like to think so."

The sharp edge of the baroness's fan scraped beneath Min's chin. Feeling like an insect being studied beneath a sun-scorched microscope, Min swallowed and dared to meet the baroness's curious eyes. *Evil,* she thought of the gray orbs. Coated with a slick veneer that allowed others to see a reflection of their own emotions in them. For now, Min saw her own fear—no, not fear. Distrust.

"Well." Dashing her fan hand from Min's chin, the baroness stepped back, her shoulders squaring rigidly. "I sense I've overstepped the bounds of polite conversation. I was in a bit of a dash before you blundered into me."

Min offered another profuse apology. She barely missed being skimmed by the slash of the woman's fan as she lifted her skirts and made a haughty exit.

The baroness had made it perfectly clear that she was upset with Min for . . . something. But what?

She considered wandering over to the buffet to find refreshment, but after a moment's thought decided it would be much easier, if not safer for all around, if she stayed put. Besides, the man standing by the crystal punch bowl was just too much. He appeared even more feminine than most of the women, what with all his powder and rouge and patches. His movements were dainty, his lashes fluttering across death-white flesh with every word he spoke.

Min turned back to her fern, gifting it with her confidences. "Fops. All of them. These women do not know what it is like to be in the presence of a real man."

Real men did not powder their faces. Real men did not smear on the lip paint and rouge. Nor did they prance about like peacocks in a parade. And real men most certainly did not wear bows in their wigs. Real men were like . . .

"Ah, Mignonne, I've a gentleman I'd like to introduce you to."

With Chance's name on her lips, Min turned and toppled on her heels.

The man standing next to Sophie rushed to catch her arm. When she was finally able to regain her equilibrium, Min followed the sleek gray velvet doublet up to sapphires glistening with delight. Eyes surrounded by pasty white skin and a silly wig of black sausage curls. Her tongue suddenly felt three sizes too big for her mouth.

"You see." Sophie giggled. "She's absolutely speechless. I was equally taken," Sophie whispered confidently. "Mademoiselle Mignonne Saint-Sylvestre, I'd like you to meet a recent acquaintance of mine, Chevalier Chancery Lambert, lieutenant of the second company of the King's Grand Musketeers."

"Lieutenant," Min muttered as he took her hand and pressed an all-too-brisk kiss to her knuckles. What to say? *I was just thinking about you.* But instead of speech, all she could manage was a silly sigh.

"It is Mademoiselle Imp," he proclaimed with gentle amusement, an equally gentle smile tickling the corner of his mouth. "And in her most daring disguise yet." His eyes smoothed over her shoulders and landed like butter dripping over hot rolls on her cleavage. Min felt the color ride down her neck and across her shoulders, which were completely revealed thanks to the wide neckline of the dress. The dress also revealed a good amount of her tortured cleavage. Which Chance noticed. Oh, yes, he noticed.

"And I see you have quite a knack for disguises too, lieutenant."

Where had the real man disappeared to? He wore a gray velvet doublet and breeches with black ribbon rosettes tied at the waist and knees. His soft brown hair was hidden by a black periwig, the beautiful sun-bronzed flesh painfully disguised by flour powder.

Had he been kidnapped by fops? Held down and sprinkled with powder and ribbons? Oh, this was not at all to her liking. Where was the musketeer? Had he taken leave of his senses? This was not the place for a real man. He was supposed to be out chasing villains. Protecting his king. Not looking like a fop himself. Not exchanging niceties with a bedraggled housewife and a confused woman who could not decide whether she wanted to be a man in the army or a soft and delicate woman in a musketeer's arms.

When their eyes finally found each other, Min pressed her fingers to her breast. She felt weak, her breath stolen away, her knees threatening to buckle. Hindered by powder and a foppish wig, his wicked eyes still spoke to her the language of desire. It was as if they were alone in his apartment again. Naked. With only the heat of the night between their bodies and the walls closing in . . . pushing them into each other's embrace. . . .

"It seems the two of you have met?" Sophie wondered, painfully sullen for being so obviously left out of their silent conversation.

"Yes," Min squeaked, finding Sophie's voice suddenly not as irritating as usual. Or perhaps it was because she wasn't even hearing Sophie anymore.

Oh, to be in his arms again. Just one more kiss . . .

"The chevalier is here by request of Captain d'Artagnan." Sophie slid her arm inside Chance's hooked elbow, jarring Min from her thoughts at the sight of the woman's comfortable attachment to him. "How absolutely fortunate for us that you are here, chevalier," Sophie drawled in a sickeningly sweet tone. "You add a much needed spark of excitement to a rather tediously boring fête."

Min felt her temperature rise. What was Sophie doing flirting and batting her lashes at *her* musketeer? And the way she pressed her milk-heavy breasts to his side. She was married! With children!

"Not nearly as fortunate as I believe I am," Chance replied, his eyes never leaving Min's. He slipped his arm from Sophie's, not in the least aware of her chagrin. Behind them, a sudden electricity of violins and harpsichord sparked through the ballroom. "Ah, the minuet. Come, mademoiselle." Chance slid his arm through hers. "Let us dance."

"Dance? Er—wait!"

Chance did not seem to notice as Min stumbled gracelessly onto the dance floor.

"I cannot do this," she gasped and proceeded to tumble into his arms. "Not in these shoes."

"Of course you can; don't be silly. If I can endure the humiliation of this foppish attire, then you most certainly can endure the trappings of a female's dress. I've seen you do it once before." He slipped his right arm around her waist and secured her left hand with his. His attitude was strangely cool, his body held stiffly, instead of in the relaxed posture he had presented in the last few days. "Just follow my lead."

Min caught a glance of Sophie pouting near the fern. She would gladly have given this dance to her. But not her partner. No. Death by high heels or not, it was pure joy to be in this musketeer's arms again. To feel the side of his body pressed to hers. To smell the scent of his masculinity hidden beneath layers of flour powder. To rest her trembling hand in his large, sheltering fingers.

"You are the most beautiful woman in the entire room," he whispered in her ear. The heat of his breath traveled down her neck and sent a delicious shiver across Min's breasts, setting her nipples to rigid alertness. Still he held his body erect, far too tense for the music. "No man can keep his eyes from you."

"Really?" Entrancing words, but coming from him, they confused her. Hadn't he sworn to never love again? Then why was he flirting with her? And why wouldn't he relax? He was starting to squeeze her fingers. "Surely you jest, chevalier."

"Look around."

She squeezed his hands tightly and braced herself against his thigh as they stepped lightly. "It is you they stare at. Most ladies cannot resist a beribboned fop. You wear the fashion well. Perhaps I've been mistaken about you all along."

"This was not my idea," he hissed through gritted teeth. "I was given a direct order from my captain. I had no choice but to attend."

"Secret military mission?"

"Call it keeping up appearances," he said. "The Countess de Maurepas has been a staunch supporter of the king's army. Her purse strings loosen at mere sight of a musketeer."

"As do her stays?"

"Are you implying what I suspect, mademoiselle?"

"And what if I were? Would you challenge me to a duel to defend your honor?"

"As you did d'Artagnan? What the hell were you doing this afternoon?"

"I was only defending *my* honor."

"Honor? Against the Captain of the Musketeers? Are you mad?"

"Let go, you're hurting me."

"No." He tightened his grip. "I have taken more than enough of your silly games, but this has gone too far."

"I had no intention of besmirching your reputation," Min defended herself. She hadn't even planned for him to be there. Of course, that was about the only thing she had planned. "Why must you mock my dreams so?"

"Your dreams?" he hissed. "Blast! Women belong in the musketeers no more than elephants belong in the ocean!"

Elephants? He was just like all the rest. Masculine pride ran through his being like a thick syrup. He had no more ability to see past his own self-importance than Sophie in her world. "Oh, I remember, chevalier. Women are soft and should be home sewing up the seat of their husband's breeches. Where are your needle and thread, mademoiselle?" she mocked. "Oh! After all we have been through, how can you possibly believe that I would be happy like that? I was a fool to ever think you could be pleased with someone like me."

Wrenching her hands away from his, Min stumbled to the edge of the dance floor.

"Pleased? But, Min, I am— Wait! Don't leave!"

The baroness clung to the cool Italian marble column, well hidden, out of the lieutenant's sight. He still looked so dashing. So virile in his carriage and long strides. And still he wore his anger with a brute sensuality that steamed her insides to a wanting boil. Chevalier Lambert stormed from the dance floor after the woman in the emerald brocade. Mignonne. Such a ridiculous name.

It had taken less than a month for Chancery to find another.

Tense knotd twisted in her gut. The two goblets of champagne she had sipped since arriving had ceased to bubble delightfully in her head and now pulsed with an angry bite.

She reached out, her grasping fingers far from the retreating gray velvet that passed her by. He hadn't noticed her clonging to the column. His sight was set, like that of a horse with blinders, on that silly dust rag of a woman.

But hadn't the insolent chit said he was in pursuit of the Notorious Ones? Why would she misspeak when he had been there all along? Perhaps she was not as close to Chancery as she claimed.

And what of Luciano? This new information of his having the girl tied to his bed would most definitely have to be dealt with later. But now, with Lambert on his tail there was little time before he would be brought down. That was a certainty. And then what would become of the jewels and fine clothing she had come to enjoy from the booty of her lover's raids? She would become nothing, struck down by Chance's vengeance. And he so unaware of the truth.

"I must inform Luciano."

Chapter Twenty

Mademoiselle Imp sat beneath the double-tipped shadow of a gargoyle's horns, peeling her shoes from her feet with grunting difficulty.

The footmen were inside, dipping into the spiked punch, and so Chance was alone with her at the base of the great marble steps leading up to the de Maurepas mansion. Muffled laughter and the fragrance of pine and freshly scythed grass surrounded them.

"This is hell," Min mumbled. "I cannot wait to get this horrendous thing off."

Neither can I, Chance mused, as he observed Min's struggle with the bodice of her dress. What must it have taken to get this fiery imp into such a dress! She looked amazing. No. Beyond amazing. Absolutely and thoroughly enchanting. The color gave her cheeks an inviting glow and set off her dark hair around bittersweet eyes ablaze with warmth.

Ah, those eyes. Chance felt lustful heat burn in his groin.

Bewitching in their color tonight as she'd danced alongside him, like witch's fire.

Chance stood on the bottom step, scanning the street for an oncoming cabriolet, trying to act nonchalant. As though she were just another female, wearing just another dress, and looking just the same as the rest.

A breath of wind swirled a stray strand of hair across her alabaster shoulders. So smooth, like porcelain. Oh, she was so lovely. . . .

Something, some inner beast, clawed and growled inside Chance's breast to escape. *Go to her! Touch her! Take her in your arms!* "No!"

Min looked up, her expression unchanged from her previous anger. "I should have known." She looked away. "My own private homing pigeon come home to roost."

What Chance wouldn't give to unbind the frivolous curls from their wires and pull his fingers through the silken tresses, to press heated kisses on her bare shoulders, to taste her sweet flavor and inhale her intoxicating scent.

He had to give in before he could bear it no longer. No matter what the consequences. No matter if she should reject him. It mattered no longer that he keep his promise never to have a relationship with her. He had to try. Mignonne Saint-Sylvestre was too precious a jewel to let slip through his grasp. She would never betray him. At least, not intentionally. "I cannot take my eyes from you, Mignonne."

"What?"

Nervous fists shaking by his thighs, Chance stepped down and came within a foot of her. "Er, I mean . . ." *Take it slowly. Do not frighten her away again.* "My apologies, mademoiselle. It seems I've upset you. I was just . . . well . . ." He could no longer hide his confusion. Wearing breeches and doublet, and riding astride and acting a highwayman was one thing. But the musketeers? "Explain to me, so that I may understand. Why the musketeers?"

The thick coil of dark hair that hung over Min's right eye distracted Chance from his concern. *Blast! Control your thoughts, man. Are you so bewitched by this woman that the mere sight of her sends your lust into a frenzy?*

Yes, he thought back to his conscience. *Yes, yes, and yes.*

"Mignonne?"

"Perhaps," Min started with an intake of breath, "it is because every time someone has ever told me I could not do something, the urge to prove them wrong has become paramount." She turned and examined him for a reaction.

Chance remained silent. She had captured his attention far too long ago to stop listening now.

"I have always had this need to prove others wrong, to show them that I was just as capable as the next man in completing a task." She tilted her head and caught the side of her head in her hand. "If I recall correctly, Alexandre—strange as it may seem—may have been the first to set the bravado running in my veins. He was chopping wood out back of the stables. I watched for hours, following the flying splinters, gauging the sweating muscles in his arms as they seemed to swell before my very eyes. I wanted to try. He laughed." Min gave a short chuckle. "That laughter had me on my feet in seconds. I wrestled the ax away as Alexandre mockingly snickered. I could barely lift the thing. But I tried, over and over, until finally the blade fell down across the log. Needless to say, Alexandre was quite willing to give up his task to me."

"I can imagine," Chance said.

"My own brothers never even realized the monster in the making. Adrian taught me how to ride after I was nearly trampled. Armand, after I had sat for many hours, many weeks, watching him practice his fencing moves, finally succumbed to my pleading. He still has a scar across his left forearm from me. But once I began to understand the intricacies of the art, it was Armand who would wake me at dawn to practice."

"And the musketeers?" Chance wondered softly.

"You know my father was a musketeer. I used to watch him as a child. He would bring his companions home for a night or two. They'd fence with my brothers, dressed in tunics and wielding swords with the words *Mousquetaire Du Roi* etched in the blade. They were so dashing and cavalier. I was told that a girl could not do such things. And I accepted that for a time. It was merely a dream. . . ." Min sighed. "Until my brothers laughed at it."

"Ah. I understand." Chance came down the steps and sat next to Min.

"Forgive me, chevalier, for my betrayal."

"Your betrayal?"

"I should have revealed my true destination when first we met in Remalard. I had no intention in humiliating you in front of Captain d'Artagnan."

"You could never betray me, Mignonne. I really do understand."

By proving her brothers wrong, Min had become such a fascinating woman. She did not fear danger; she savored it. She did not walk away from an insurmountable task; instead she dove in headfirst. She knew no boundaries; she refused to settle for the lowest apple on the tree. She aspired for the heavens, and would let no one stand in her way.

"You are quite a woman, Mademoiselle Saint-Sylvestre."

She forced a snickering noise. "Do you know the Saint-Sylvestre name was once looked upon with pride? I only wished to return the luster and the honor to the name. My brothers have no need to rob innocent citizens. Armand would make a fine musketeer, and Adrian too. I simply felt that if I could show them I could do it, they would see the light."

"A most noble effort."

"But I've failed. And I've succeeded in doing nothing more than infuriating Armand beyond all reason, I am sure. He will never forgive me for this. I don't know what I was doing. 'Twas nice for a while, the freedom. I was alone, discovering the world for myself. . . ."

Much as he should have been against a woman in the ranks, things had changed. For the sake of the woman he loved, Chance couldn't help but wish that her dream had been fulfilled. D'Artagnan had been right; should the king ever allow women into the ranks, Min was most deserving.

"Lieutenant?"

"Huh?"

"You're doing it again."

Chance read the teasing tone in her voice and immediately knew what she was thinking. "So I am. Well. And this time it most certainly is not pastries I am looking at. That dress . . ." He could not stop himself. "You are truly the most lovely woman in all of Paris."

"Don't try to change the subject, chevalier." Her shoes dangled with a vicious bounce from her fingertips. "No matter what reasons I may have had, you are still furious with me for the fiasco in d'Artagnan's office. I know."

Chance's smile grew slowly. "You are right. I was furious when I first saw you." He cupped her chin in his palm and tilted her head so their eyes met. He didn't have to taste the bittersweet chocolate. He now knew from experience how delicious they could be. "After you stormed away, leaving me to d'Artagnan, I remembered, *this* is Mignonne Saint-Sylvestre. If the king were to allow women to join our ranks, then surely you could teach me a thing or two. Do you know that you are in every way imaginable completely the opposite of every quality I have ever desired in a woman?"

"And how shall I take such a statement, lieutenant?"

"I have always desired a woman steeped in laces and perfume. Gentle, charming, of a nature that would attract any man like a bee to honey."

"Enough."

"Don't you see?"

She shrugged.

"Instead of lace and perfume you adorn yourself in mud and pride. Feisty and headstrong is your nature. You could never match any of the frivolous females that have paraded through my life. You stand above them all, Min. I wonder now what I ever saw in any of them."

"Including Justine?"

"Most especially Justine. But then . . . this!"

Min crossed her arms over the luscious mounds of her exposed cleavage. A hot flush pinked her cheeks. Chance loved that he could make her feel so. Perhaps she wasn't so indifferent to him after all.

"And what of *this?* Have you never seen a woman in a dress?"

"Every day. But never—" He closed the distance between the two of them, the moonlight casting a shimmer across Min's face, sparking brightly in her dark eyes. "—never have I seen one so lovely. Mignonne, what you do to me." He felt his body betray his longings. If she pressed close to him, she would feel it also.

"What *I* do to you, or what the dress does?" Min pushed past him, and with great effort was able to stand and march to the street. "It is only a costume, chevalier. Be it a dress, or breeches or *armor,* for that matter. It still does not change what is beneath." She spun about, fixing her proud gaze on his, her arms spread wide in display. "*This* is still the same imp who attacked you in the country. I can still match or better you in swords. And I can fight a whip-wielding highwayman off as well. Just because I've donned some fancy silk cut down to my navel doesn't mean I am one bit like those fluff-headed women you so deem to like."

"I know that!" Chance pulled her to him, feeling her gasp at the finely trimmed stubble on his chin. Fire blazed in her eyes. Nor could she hide the burning passion in her kiss. She struggled to push away, but Chance held her firm, commanding her lips with his. He would not allow her to escape this time. He wanted to tame her again—if only so that she might listen to the things he must tell her.

"There's a fire inside of you, Min. I see it blazing in these beautiful bittersweet eyes. It attracts me like moonshine across the river. I must have you, be it in a dress or breeches, or hell . . ." His chuckle echoed across the quiet cobblestones. "Even armor! I want to make you mine."

Her dark lashes fluttered as she scanned his face, her defenses suddenly stripped bare by his revealing confession. "But what of the things you've said? Justine's killer? You said you would never love again. If you've plans to have me without love . . ."

He swallowed. Yes, what had become of his vow? "I'm not sure what to say, what to think anymore."

"It is your gate," she replied. "The doors are locked, the chains rusted. I feel as though they've been slammed in my face."

"My gate doors," Chance repeated, considering her analogy of his heart. How very true that she should describe him so perfectly. Those gates had been erected in hopes of never having to endure the pain of loss again. "I once opened them freely and allowed a woman to enter. What remains is shambles."

"I have seen the disarray in your conflicting actions. Why do you make me feel as if you might love me when at the same time you push me away with your vows to never love again?"

"If I could answer that, I would be a wise man, indeed. I have always loved women, Mignonne. I think that is the one thing that hasn't turned me into a hermit who fears the touch of any female. I don't want to push you away. It is just . . . these gate doors, as you say. And my heart. I believe the lock has become rusty. Perhaps some oiling and a key?" he suggested.

"And who holds this key?"

"But you, of course."

She turned to him, her eyes dancing. "Really. You would allow me control of the keys to your heart?"

He nodded.

"But how can I be so sure that I've the right heart?"

"What do you mean?"

"This," she said with a gesture to his foppish attire. "And this." She laughed as she tufted the ends of his wig with her fingertips.

"This"—he yanked the wig from his head and tossed it to the steps—"makes me itch." He pointed a toe. "And I'm not so certain I've the calves for these hose."

Min laughed. "You do, chevalier, believe me, you do. I should think the ladies will be swooning at your feet at the sight of you."

He pulled her close. "There is only one for whom I desire to fall swooning. My gates are always open to you, Mignonne. With or without a key. I promise you."

The squeaking wheels of a carriage gained the street, yards away from the de Maurepas mansion. Chance nodded towards it. "Come, let's escape this silly festival of fops and powdered faces."

Min looked reluctantly to the carriage. She turned back to him, her eyes searching, delving deep within as if to touch his very soul. What she found there was a genuine and truthful desire. With a growing smile, she nodded.

Chance gave the coachman directions and helped Min navigate the step up and inside with her abundance of skirts.

"What did you say to him?"

He pulled down the linen shades so there was but a crack of moonlight in the carriage each time it hit a bump in the cobblestones. "I told him we'd like a tour of the city."

"A tour? But how shall we see with the shades pulled?"

Chance knelt on the floor at Min's feet.

"You shall have to figure that one out for yourself." Mischief laced his voice. "I told him to drive slowly."

"Oh!" The heat of his fingers trailing up her legs startled her. Min pushed her hands down her skirts to prevent them from journeying any further. "What are you doing? We're in a carriage, on a public street!"

Chance knelt up, pressing his hips between her knees, his lips inches from hers. "I want you, Mignonne."

"I warn you, monsieur, if you continue to impress upon my person, I may take any such actions as a declaration of devotion . . . and love."

He quirked a dark brow. "Chevalier."

"Whatever." Min lowered her voice to a confident tone. "Do you accept my challenge, musketeer?"

"I do."

Overwhelmed by the sheer, brute presence of this man, Min leaned forward, wishing his kiss to come. But he pulled back, teasingly. "Chance." Try as she might, the closer she got to him, he'd pull back, challenging her to beg for what she wanted. Once, and then again, his breath was hot on her lips, but she could not catch it. "Please?"

It took but one of his fiery kisses for Min to forget her worries. Whatever was it she had fretted about earlier? His tongue dared hers to dance with his, taking her lead as soon as she responded. Min took from him with a greedy passion.

She felt the reluctance in his arms as Chance pulled away from their kiss. A spot of powder from her cheek had smudged his chin. Never had childlike innocence and curiosity looked so appealing on a man's face. "To the victor go the spoils."

Chance's battle-roughened fingers caressed her thighs with such delicacy and tenderness that she found it hard to imagine him wielding a sword in campaign. He quashed her defenses with ease, taking command of her troops. She sank back against the cushion and allowed him to lift her right leg and lay it across his shoulder. She wasn't quite sure what he had in mind, but whatever it was, she had no argument. Whenever this enchanting musketeer deemed to touch her, it could only bring the most incredible of feelings.

She wanted only to revel in the precious moments with this exquisite man. He was hers, if only for the night. When she felt the hot swirl of his tongue on her upper thigh, it was more than she could endure in silence. "Chevalier!" she cried out, not caring if the entire city of Paris heard.

He'd found a sensitive button, the innermost core of her being, and worked his pleasures undauntingly, swirling and sucking, teasing her entire body into a shuddering dance of release.

"You are mine, Mignonne," he whispered against her passion-heated thigh.

"Do you really mean that?"

"I do."

They circled Paris completely, their passions also coming full circle, before the coach stopped in front of Chance's apartment.

Min had to pull herself down from the crest she'd been

riding for the last half hour. Chance panted next to her, his breeches now buttoned, his crinkled velvet doublet straightened.

Min teased her fingers through his sweat-beaded hair, mussing it into a reasonable order, the texture of the soft strands sending delicious shivers through her veins.

Three words lingered on her lips. *I love you.* She wanted to say them to him. To unlock his rusted heart and step inside. The moment seemed so perfect, so right.

She took a deep breath, her stays having loosened after their lovemaking, and started to speak. "Chance—" when a man's voice outside the carriage froze her resolve.

A chill riding her spine, Min pushed aside the curtains and spied the man who had spoken, flanked on either side by another man. Anger renewed, she dropped the curtains, set her jaw, and yanked Chance's head up by his hair.

"I cannot believe you would do this to me." He winced as her fist, of its own volition, twisted his hair into a tight coil. Min jerked him away from her. "You trickster!"

"What?" Seemingly unaware of what would set her into such anger, Chance leaned across her and saw Armand, Adrian, and Alexandre waiting outside on the steps that led up to his apartment. "No, I did not know they would be here. Mignonne, you must—"

"You lie!" She pulled her skirts from beneath his leg, wanting nothing of hers to be touching him. How could he? To lead her around Paris, seducing her into a love-smitten bundle of noodle-brained mush, only to turn her in to her brothers. This was the ultimate betrayal. "To think I really believed you were beginning to care for me. Keys to your gate? The deuce! You planned this. How convenient, my brothers waiting for me at the exact moment we arrive. And I had almost thought to tell you—"

"Tell me what?" Chance followed Min out of the carriage.

"N'importe!" she cried.

Armand's eyes widened at the sight of his sister dressed in the brilliant emerald costume. Alexandre and Adrian also dropped their jaws at the sight of her.

Min jumped from the carriage and rustled her skirts down, then snapped a haughty glance across her brothers' stupid looks. "What are you looking at?"

Deep in his cups, he slumped on the corner of the pallet, his head bowed to his chest, the ends of his stringy black hair dipping into the half-filled pewter tankard balanced precariously on his thigh.

"What I ever saw in you is at times beyond all understanding, you know that?" she hissed as she crossed the creaking floorboards of their tiny room and gripped Luciano's hair. "Why didn't you tell me about the girl, you nauseating slip of a man?"

"Pet? Is that you, pussycat? I've been waiting for you."

He groped the air, but she stepped back to avoid contact. Ripping the tankard from his hand, she splashed the contents into his face. He spewed and sputtered and mumbled obscenities about her soiling his clothes. In actuality her dress received the brunt of the soaking; all down her skirts trailed murky, foul ale.

"Damn your clothes," she raged. "Tell me about the girl you had tied to your bed in Remalard. And explain to me now why you insisted I ride ahead and not spend the night with you in the very same village."

"Girl?" Luciano, picking at his soaked shirt, finally gave up on the mess and slumped back, his head hitting the hard stone wall with a dull crack. "Come to bed, pet, I've been waiting—"

She lunged onto the bed and gripped her pouting lover by the throat. "Was her name Mignonne?"

"Unhand me, woman!"

"Not until you tell me why you were swiving that idiotic excuse for a woman!"

"I didn't lay a hand on her! She touched my horse. I wanted to punish her, but some damned hero swept her out of the window before I could satisfy my—"

"Satisfy your stinking hide." She stood and ripped her skirts away from his groping hands. Beyond disgust, she poked her head out the small tavern window that boasted no glass. Why did she do this to herself? Always and every night she found Luciano in a drunken stupor. And always and every morning she forgave him his nasty habit, for she had convinced herself she loved the dashing rider of the road. He had promised danger and excitement, something she had so lacked in her dull life. But never had he been unfaithful to her. Never. "Do you know she is aligned with Lieutenant Lambert?"

"Ah, a familiar name."

She spun away from his winking eye.

"The lieutenant rides in search of the man who murdered his wife, a man he knows to ride with the Notorious Ones."

Luciano appeared to ponder her statement, and then observed with a drawn-out burp and a sniffle, "Chivalrous."

"Fool! Bastard!" She started to gather her things, shoving her cherished Spanish pistol into a saddlebag that lay near the door. "We must leave Paris this eve."

"I go nowhere."

She turned. Luciano had somehow righted himself and now stood over her, arms akimbo, looking almost intimidating. Not even a sway in his stance.

"Did you hear me?" she hissed. "The chevalier is looking for you. And when he finds you, as I know he will, he will then also find me."

"And that frightens you, pet?"

"Oh!" There was no dealing with the man in his condition. Hell, there was no dealing with him sober either. Once set on a course, Luciano stubbornly refused to veer, no matter what the circumstances or danger. He lived for danger and the challenge.

And that was exactly why she loved him.

"What are your plans?" she said, giving up and slumping against the wall. It was fruitless to pack.

"To find the bitch who did this to me." He nicked his missing front tooth with a knuckle. "And if I should encounter the infamous Chevalier de Cuckold Lambert in the process . . . then all the merrier."

Chapter Twenty-One

Chance paced the mud-speckled cobblestones before his apartment steps, kicking aside a rotten melon that the hawkers and rats had left behind. The sun had set to his right, and with that, his heart was wrenched into a chasm of darkness.

Armand had asked that the brothers have a few moments alone with their sister. He wasn't sure, but Chance thought he'd seen a resolute acquiescence in Min as she'd followed the trio up the stairs. She seemed quite calm, almost willingly compliant, after being so upset with him.

She couldn't possibly believe he would plan such a ruse as delivering her to her brothers?

Certainly that had been his intention days ago when he had no mind for anything but seeking justice against Justine's killer. But no longer. Now he could not bear to part with this woman. Vengeance could wait. Mignonne Saint-Sylvestre was too elusive to chance losing again.

A twinge of regret pulsed in Chance's heart. He

smoothed his fingers along his stubbled jaw. *I should tell her. You almost told her when you slipped and said she was the complete opposite of everything you had ever desired in a woman. And damn, but those differences were so exquisite!*

No. He mustn't interfere with her brothers' plans. They knew what was right for her. Besides, Mignonne was a free creature who should not be restrained by any man or by bonds of love and commitment.

So why are you allowing her to be taken to a convent? Would that not be the ultimate betrayal of her trust? Her freedom? She does not want that. She cannot.

"She wishes to speak to you."

With words of regret tickling the back of his throat, Chance turned to see the three brothers emerge from his building. Adrian toed the splattered melon seeds, while Alexandre snorted a spot of snuff from his forefinger and scanned the horizon.

Wary of Armand's anger over seeing him descend from the carriage with Mignonne earlier, both of them disheveled, Chance approached the eldest.

"I must apologize."

Armand pinned him with an accusing glare, but it quickly faded to a sigh. "You expect me to forgive you for what you've done to our sister?"

A swallow lodged in Chance's throat. "No, of course not. But I do—" No. *You cannot tell them you love her. You mustn't interfere.* "What has come to pass?"

Armand folded his hands behind his back and stepped aside. "She will tell you."

With a weary heart, Chance climbed the stairs to his third-floor apartment. Surely after all he had witnessed of her irrepressible spirit, Min would never agree to go to the convent.

He tossed his hat to the bed, the sheets still rumpled from their union. The water had long dried, though the residents below had caught him this morning to complain about their leaking ceilings. Min stood by the window, her gaze focused high on the darkened clouds, her emerald satin-encircled arms crossed before her.

She'd taken her hair down. Well, finished taking it down, after what was left from their stolen tryst in the carriage. Soft tendrils of blackest mink curled about her exotically colored cheeks. Warm candlelight flickered across her face, kissing her lips with an ethereal softness. She was an emerald in the sand, sparkling seductively, waiting to be claimed by a treasure seeker.

Their coming together in the carriage had only fueled his desire. Desire that had not been quenched in the least. Chance had to repress the urge to run to her and kiss those angel lips, to finally show her that she truly meant something to him. To tell her . . .

I love you.

No. He gritted his teeth and steeled himself against possible betrayal. Aware of the thick vein pulsing in his clenched fist, he spread his fingers wide. It was too late. The look she gave him now, her eyes so empty and bleak, was enough for him to know she had conceded to her brothers' wishes.

"Forgive me for my hasty assumption after we arrived. I know now that you were not involved. Sophie left the party and promptly ran into Armand. It was then she revealed she had last seen me speaking to you. I must thank you for all you've done." Her voice was as weak as the lax expression on her face. "If it had not been for you, I might still be lying in the forest, my dead body being debauched by Luciano. I—I'll never forget you, Chevalier Lambert."

She was going to leave him! And her choice seemed so effortless. As if she were merely thanking him for a meal and then preparing to depart.

"Nor—nor I you." Chance faltered, then crossed the room and took Min's hand in his. She shivered, a subtle quake at the touch of his hand. He dared to touch her cheek, so soft and faintly warm from the nearby candle. If only he could imprint the texture of her flesh in his mind, like a ripe summer peach, or the sweet smell of her body, the softness of her lips, the sparkle in her bittersweet eyes. "Is this what you truly want, Mignonne?"

She nodded and gave a shrug, turning to the window where the spire of Nôtre Dame spiked the sky in the distance. "Armand has convinced me. And besides, how can the queen be wrong?"

"The queen?"

Dismissing his query with a sigh, she paced past him, taking the length of the room with swishing steps. "Oh, Chance, it does not matter. My brothers are delivering me to Val-de-Grâce tonight. I think it best that I not dally any longer." She turned to him. "Don't you?"

"Huh?" Chance jerked his gaze up from the soft rise of her breasts. They had been so receptive to his touch, those soft mounds of heaven. It took all his strength now to keep his hands at his side. "Of course."

No! It is not. A dozen proud warriors plundered the rough casing that surrounded Chance's heart. But their efforts were fruitless. He could not go against the wishes of Min's brothers. "If that is what you really want?" he asked again.

Min paced past him, her fingers to her lips in thought. "It is." She spun around, her skirts dusting across his legs, and locked eyes with him. A deep sigh from her mouth teased Chance closer. "Some dreams are better kept to yourself."

"Dreams?" *Like the dream of possessing the women he loved.* For the first time in his life, Chance was suddenly aware that he had a dream. And he was about to let this emerald slip through his fingers like so many grains of sand. "Of course, dreams . . ."

She had probably been easily swayed by Armand. For if she cared even a little for him would it not be harder for her to leave? Would she not even ask his feelings for her?

Chance followed the spark of white light in Min's dark eyes as they searched his own. He wanted to tell her, to proclaim his love for her. . . . But she had already made up her mind. She was willingly going to Val-de-Grâce tonight. And she seemed not in the least upset about leaving him.

Twice now a women he loved had left him.

It had to have been a difficult decision. To choose the convent over the freedom she now had. Not that her life of masquerading would get her anywhere. Yes, it was a good decision. Armand only wanted her to stay long enough to learn to be a lady. He would see her again . . . someday. To tell her his feelings now would be to make things much harder than they had to be. He did have a mission. A mission he'd virtually ignored the past few days.

Min tilted her head quizzically. "What is it, chevalier?"

There was a hopeful note in her voice, as if she waited for him to impart some great advice upon her. But Chance knew nothing to say that would make her decision any easier. His throat dried and he had to swallow.

She does not even know how much you love her. She can never know that you would die for her happiness.

Chance drew his eyes across her features, imprinting their softness and beauty in his mind. Beauty to rival even Raphael's imagination. Her eyes widened and she tilted her head. Oh, to never taste those dark sweets again. *Don't look too long. You will never see what you need, only what you desire.*

He had to at least let her know that he would never forget her. "Perhaps, mademoiselle, it is only that I was trying desperately to forever remember the taste of your lips on mine. The memory . . . it is sacred to me."

She turned to the window. Her delicate fingers played fretfully with the sash. "Do not say that. You must forget me, chevalier."

"Words spoken but a month ago by my wife."

"Oh, forgive me, I didn't mean to—"

"But this time it is not the same." He spun her about by the shoulders, her hair slipping softly through his fingers. *So easily she is slipping from my life.* Oh, to possess the heart of such a lovely woman. A privilege he would only be granted in memory. "I shall never forget you, Mignonne."

Min watched from the narrow window of the tiny cell as her brothers left the vast grounds of Val-de-Grâce. A forest paralleled the convent on two sides in dark and jagged cutwork against the gray, cloudless sky. The midnight sky would never again be the same color. From this moment on, the night would be gray, her days equally as colorless.

Closing her eyes, Min felt the darkness permeate the glass and touch her heart. She bit her lip, wishing away the traitorous feelings. But they came as water rushes down the river. She fought to suppress her emotions, but when Alexandre did not even look back, she gave in to her pain and let the tears stream in sad rivers down her cheeks.

She turned and sat on the plain roped bed, her slippered feet feeling the cold stone like ice on her flesh. She shivered beneath the sheath of white cloth that covered her body. The sisters who had helped her change had politely averted their gazes as she stripped her body of the gaudy emerald damask. It felt odd to have the gown of the church pulled over her shoulders. Not unlike the nightdress she had worn to bed, but so very different, cold and stiff and . . . proper. Virginal.

What comfort to have known the pleasures that her body could receive from a man. She must never forget—for after today, they would become pleasures she'd never be privy to again. Until, of course, Armand could secure a betrothal. Thank God she had learned what love was before being forced to endure a loveless marriage.

Images of the only man she had ever loved came rushing forth. His gentle, charm-you-madly smile, those commanding eyes and the smudge of beard quivering beneath his lower lip. Min pressed her lips tight together, hoping to recall the warm sensations that had rippled through her body as her kiss drew Chance's arms about her waist and he pulled her close.

She pressed her fingertips to her mouth. The remnants of Chance's kiss were so distant, so faint. Like butterflies on the breeze, so elusive, yet if captured, a precious memory of a life lived in freedom. "I shall never forget you, Chevalier Chancery Lambert."

She would prove to Armand that she had what it took to attract a man and then be done with the entire fiasco.

Instead of telling Chance her true feelings, she had stubbornly consented to her brother's will and walked away from the musketeer. Why, why, why?

Oh, she knew why. There was only one reason why she had agreed to Armand's wishes after resisting so futilely. Only one reason that mattered.

Chance had not tried to stop her from leaving.

Chapter Twenty-Two

Chance was surprised to see Adrian Saint-Sylvestre back at his door early the next morning.

"And your plans now?"

"I've a villain to apprehend." Chance ground his fist into his opposite palm. "The leader of the Notorious Ones. He endangered your sister's life and . . . took my wife from me. He must be brought to justice."

Adrian nodded. "Luciano, yes. I wish I could have been more help to you yesterday. I am sure he's in Paris somewhere. I can feel it. Be assured my brothers and I will help. We're due back at Val-de-Grâce in an hour to bid Mignonne adieu before we return home."

"Whatever for? Didn't you take your leave last evening?" Capturing the man's gaze, Chance discovered a bitter darkness in Adrian's gypsy eyes.

"Armand is furious over this whole situation. He has decided against her marrying. He's going to pay Mignonne's dowry to the church." He shook his head.

"Not at all what I would want for my sister, you understand. But Armand is the word in our family since Father's death."

"But he cannot. Min would never stand for it. She will take this as a punishment for something she must not be punished for. She was only following her heart!"

"The church is not a punishment."

"You agree with your brother?"

Adrian sighed. "You know I do not. I don't know how to change Armand's mind. Perhaps after a few weeks, he'll see the error of his ways."

"By then it will be too late."

Sadness turned to curious mirth as Adrian lifted a thick brow. "For Mignonne or for you? Admit it, chevalier, you are in love with my sister."

Chance paced to the window and scanned the smoky horizon of ragged rooftops. He had vowed never to love again. But he could no longer deny his feelings. Feelings that had been there since first meeting her. He had known since first laying eyes on Mignonne that his life would never again be the same. Why had he denied it for so long?

"Of course I love the vexing little imp. I wanted to tell her last night. But I didn't want to make her decision all the harder—though I thought her only going to Val-de-Grâce for a few months. Ah, but it matters no longer. After her cool good-bye last evening, I am sure she does not feel the same for me."

"How can you be so sure?"

Chance blew off the question with a careless sigh and a wave of his hand. "She hasn't said anything."

Hooking his elbow on the window sash, Adrian tipped up the brim of his hat with one finger. "And since when have you known Min to express an emotion other than wild anger or adventurous curiosity?"

True. The girl was excellent at expressing her wild moods. But she seemed to clam up and take directions quite well when in his arms. She never protested his kisses. In fact, she took to them with a hardy assurance and a vigorous willingness. Did she really love him? Had he been blind to her feelings all along?

A full minute passed before either of them made a move.

Finally a smile drew across Adrian's lips. "How soon do you think you can have her out of there?"

Chance retrieved his hat from the bed. Mischief sparked in his eyes as he smoothed his palm over the brilliant white plume. "You keep an eye on Armand. Make sure he's not too early. Myself . . ." He rubbed a finger across his mustache. "I've work to do."

Chance stepped from the barber's chair precariously positioned in the center of the bustle on the Pont Neuf. He lifted the silver-backed glass that hung on a rusty chain from the wooden cart, pouted his lips, then thrust his chin up to examine the clean skin. It had been years since he'd seen his naked upper lip.

"Is good, monsieur?" The barber's reflection looked expectant.

"Sure." Chance handed him three sous. "How soon before it grows back?"

The barber gave a hearty chuckle.

Alexandre fumbled with the Belgian lace that caressed the tops of his soft leather boots. He pulled the wide interlaced threading straight and checked to be sure it hung properly. A smudge of dust was easily removed with moistened fingers. He sat back, stiff as a board, against the soft wing-backed chair outside the Queen Regent's chambers.

She had commanded an interview with him. And the hairs on the back of his neck still stood upright. Why?

What had he done? He hadn't even known she was aware of him. Had Le Nôtre said something?

"Her majesty will see you now."

Shocked into a tense rigidity, Alexandre cleared his throat and bowed to the lackey who then led him through the doors to the queen's chambers. A heady mist of lavender engulfed the room, threatening to overwhelm Alexandre's precise senses. The queen sat at her vanity, yards of silver damask splaying over the chair and flowing like wind-rippled water across the carpet. Her chambermaid pushed long fingers through the queen's soft mass of burnished curls, following with a tortoiseshell comb inlaid with gems. The maid gave Alexandre a double-take as he slowly approached.

He averted his eyes, thinking perhaps he had interrupted the queen's *lever.*

"Monsieur Alexandre Saint-Sylvestre, your majesty," the lackey announced and then disappeared with a formal bow.

"Come closer, young man." The queen gave a slight, bored wave. "I'll not bite."

Alexandre bowed with all the grandeur of a courtier—he'd had opportunity to observe how it was done in the last two days—and stepped over to the vanity. The maid cast him a brazen summation, her long lashes shading her curious eyes. She was very pretty, her shoulders delicately rounded, her bosoms so—

"Watch yourself, Simone," the queen gently reproved. Her voice was like cool melon to Alexandre. He liked it. It took his mind off the deafening perfume. "He's mine right now. You may busy yourself with him later."

Alexandre felt the heat rise in his cheeks. Later? As far as women were concerned, he—well, he had Sophie.

"You work in the gardens with Le Nôtre?" The queen looked to Alexandre in the mirror.

"Yes, your majesty." He spoke to her reflection, thinking that if he should look directly at her, he might lose what little self-control he had left and make a fool of himself. He was in the queen's bedchamber. This was madness! "Just yesterday I was hired."

"You are happy?"

"Yes, your majesty."

"Your sister is Mignonne Saint-Sylvestre?"

Min? Alexandre remembered Min telling of a conversation she had had with the queen. He thought her simply spouting nonsense. Another one of her far-off dreams. But now . . . "Yes, your majesty. Is there . . . something amiss?"

"I fear there is. Enough, Simone." She sent her maid away with a flit of her time-withered fingers.

Alexandre acknowledged Simone's flirtatious wink with a nervous nod.

The queen stood, and Alexandre bent to his knee.

"Please stand." Bother and urgency vied in the queen's voice. "I fear I've committed a grave error against your sister, Monsieur Saint-Sylvestre. I've told her things . . ."

The muscle in Alexandre's jaw tensed. A grave error?

"Things that in the circumstances of any ordinary woman would have been reasonable and quite acceptable. But your sister is not an ordinary woman." She startled Alexandre by touching his chin and directing his fearful gaze in line with her own gentle eyes. "Is she?"

Though his insides shuddered with humility at being touched by royalty, Alexandre could not suppress a smile. So Min's feisty spirit had reached even the queen. Perhaps she was destined to achieve the dreams that haunted her. With such friends in high places, he could not doubt it. "No, majesty, ordinary is certainly not a word I've ever used to describe *ma petite* Mignonne."

"I see you are proud of her." The queen strode before Alexandre, pacing a length of about five feet back and forth. Her skirts slithered across the carpet, forming luscious notes of multicolored music in Alexandre's mind. "As you should be. Did she tell you what she did for me only yesterday?"

The queen held up her arm. Soft burgundy velvet hung in sensuous curves around it. She pulled the billowing sleeve back to reveal a great bruise that covered her elbow and spread down to her wrist in spidery splotches.

Alexandre's heart thudded against his chest. What did Min have to do with this? Unless . . . "Oh, majesty, no, my sister did not—she could not!"

"She did."

In the silence that followed, Alexandre thought sure the queen could hear his own heartbeat. He felt like a mouse looking down the lion's throat. *Oh, Mignonne, you've dug your own grave.* How could his sister have done such a thing? She was not violent towards others. Never. And the queen! It was too terrible to imagine.

The queen gave a soft chuckle at the sight of Alexandre's horrified features. "Do not fret, my boy. She saved my life. Did she not tell you? Modest little thing. Had she not pushed me to the ground when she did, I would have a hole in my head right here." The queen tapped her skull. "Nasty assassins. They scurry about as thick as rats in a dungeon."

Alexandre's jaw fell lower.

The queen ignored his dread. "I wish to speak to her. It is of utmost urgency. I've already spoken to Le Nôtre. You may take leave of your duties until Mademoiselle Saint-Sylvestre is delivered to my presence. I'll arrange for your travel to Vaux when you have completed your task. That is all I can tell you, I'm afraid. Now I've other matters to attend to. Good day, monsieur."

Alexandre bowed out of the queen's chamber, his mind spinning with a myriad of fantastical scenarios. What was his sister up to? Saving the queen, and she hadn't even mentioned it to him. And what was so urgent that he had been given leave to deliver her to the queen? Oh, this court intrigue was not for him. He hated being involved in the like. It gave him a maddening pain in his right temple, which had nothing to do with the overabundance of scent shrouding his mind. But if it involved his sister, he would do as he was told, immediately.

Mignonne had saved the queen's life?

"You have had quite the adventures lately, haven't you, *ma petite?*"

"Tout mon possible, Min. I will have you again."

Chance tiptoed carefully down a pristinely scrubbed hallway in search of the woman he loved. The walls of Val-de-Grâce stretched into gothic arches above him, meeting in the center of the cathedral beneath the great lead-and-gilt dome. Here and there, his steps took him through a smattering of colors reflected on the floor from the stained glass in the high windows. He stared into the Virgin's downcast eyes, feeling quiet settling deep in his gut. "Blessed Mother, forgive me, for I am about to sin. I must. You see . . . I am in love."

Chance spied a door down the hallway. It appeared to be an exit, set into the outer wall. Good. He made a mental note of its location. Another escape option should his first be spoiled.

Up ahead, just a few doors away, he heard what could only be the *shush* of a scrub brush across a stone floor. A flash of sunlight caught his eye as he dared a glance inside the small chamber. A white-robed nun knelt over the floor, rocking her hips back and forth. An intense quickening shuddered within him. He could sense her presence, feel her proud heartbeat in his blood.

It had to be Min kneeling on the floor.

Just then, the door down the hall opened and out walked a nun, followed by a man. Chance immediately recognized Armand from the wide lace that rimmed his doublet and cuffs. The nun had to be Aunt Huguette, the mother superior.

"Ah, hell—er, blast." He averted his gaze upward and directed a mental forgive me to any holy being that might have heard his oath. "I guess this means I must do things the hard way."

With that, he dodged across the hall and slipped inside the room opposite where Min was, and waited.

Chapter Twenty-Three

When presented with the option of scrubbing floors or beginning with a few basic needlework patterns, Min had vacillated. Too long. Aunt Huguette—who must now be addressed as Mother Superior, and don't forget it, child—decided she should begin her lessons in domesticity from the bottom up. Besides, daylight would be soon upon them, and Aunt Hugu—er, Mother Superior so liked the reflection of the sun on a freshly scrubbed floor.

Min felt she had gotten the better of the bargain. This mindless scrubbing had actually helped to erase the erratic events of the past few days from her mind. Now she felt relaxed, more in tune with her inner voice. A voice that was pleased to have nothing demanded of her beyond the simple cleaning of a floor. No villains could harm her within these walls. Nor could a musketeer threaten her emotions with the mere flash of his smile.

In fact, Min had almost decided that a few months inside the quiet walls of the convent were exactly what she needed.

She could rethink her dreams, come to grips with the fact that not all dreams were attainable, and maybe even resign herself to marriage. What could be so terrible about having a man care for you and see that all your earthly needs were met?

Min's hand slipped from the scrub brush and she bruised her knuckles. She stuck her fist against her lips and sucked at the stinging flesh.

All right, so she still hadn't come close to resolving the issue of turning over her freedom to a man. But she had months to work on that. And she would need it.

A goose was being strangled within the sacred halls of Val-de-Grâce.

In search of the odd sound, Min peered out the doorway to see Aunt Huguette's black gown. She stood talking to another nun, and someone else who was hidden by the wall. The nun she spoke to was an interesting nun at that. Min stood and eased a crick out of her back. Now she could see that the other person was actually Armand. What was he doing here? And looking so damn solemn. Min took a step back and discovered that Adrian also stood talking to their aunt—and looked as though he'd just eaten a horse.

What was going on? They had bid her adieu last evening. Had Armand changed his mind, decided she could come home and learn domesticities from Sophie? A notion Min might even consider.

"We need a moment alone with this child," Aunt Huguette said to the other nun as she directed a gesture toward Min. "Is there something I can do for you?"

"Do?" came the nun's deep voice. The sister bit her lip and pressed her shrouded hand to her mouth, cleared her throat, and then spoke again in a different voice. "There is. There has been a mistake!" she said in a strangely high and shaky trill. "This child must come with me. The

Ursulines have sent explicit orders that she is needed there."

Min quirked a brow at the odd tension stringing the woman's voice into a hoarse mixture of high and low tones. How curious. Why did another convent wish her presence?

"I was not informed." Aunt Huguette glared into the strange nun's eyes, her own gaze, Min knew, possessing all the power of a mountain cougar's. "I spoke to the Mother Superior of the Ursulines but three days ago. She mentioned nothing of it. And we've only just received Sister Mignonne yesterday. Besides, I know this child, she is my brother's daughter. She belongs here, nowhere else. She's to take her vows—"

"What!" Min slammed the scrub brush into the bucket of murky water. Iridescent soap bubbles floated up around her shoulders.

"Mignonne," Armand chastened, "it is for the best."

"The best?"

Adrian rushed in to cradle Min into his arms, but she pushed out of them and backed away. "You trap me here and then do this? Adrian!"

"You cannot force this child to take vows against her will," the gruff nun threw in as she pushed between Armand and Min's aunt.

"Who *are* you?" Armand and Aunt Huguette both demanded at the same time.

Min darted glances from Adrian to Armand, and then to the strange nun's face, though there wasn't much to see. Her wimple covered her cheeks and neck and was pulled low to her thick, bushy eyebrows. With further scrutiny, Min found the face of the nun rugged and angular. An ugly woman if there ever was one. Perhaps that was why she had given her life to God.

"Who am *I?*" The Ursuline sister fumbled with her rosary with such frantic vengeance that her thick fingers got tangled in the black beads. She gave a curt pull and a nervous chuckle. "Oh, dear me." The beads held her fingers captive. She tried to act nonchalant but found no place to hide her bound fingers.

"What is going on?" Armand demanded. "I've had no contact with the Ursulines. You are quite mistaken, sister . . . what is your name?"

"Er, I am . . . Sister Margarite, er . . . of the Heavenly Sword! Yes, that's it. The Heavenly Sword. Come, child." The nun gestured impatiently with her trapped fingers. She strained and tugged, and with an abrupt snap she succeeded in freeing them. Black glass beads tinkled across Min's scrubbed floor.

Funny, Min noticed, the Ursuline held her sleeves down over her hands so that only her thick, scarred fingers showed.

"What is the meaning of this?" The mother superior echoed Armand's words.

Scarred? Min leaned closer and gazed hard at the stranger's face. For a brief moment, their eyes locked. Min could almost count the tiny azure spots that speckled the nun's eyes. Speckled blue eyes?

"Come," he hissed between his teeth.

Armand stepped over the soap bucket, his hand on his sword hilt. Aunt Huguette demanded to know the meaning of this outrage.

Using the confusion as a diversion, Min slipped between the two of them and gripped Chance's sweaty fingers.

"Don't stop," he whispered as they sped down the hall.

"Halt!" cried Armand. Steel seared across leather as he unsheathed his sword. Adrian followed close behind, but he slipped on the black beads, bringing Armand and their aunt down in a crash of arms, legs, heavenly robes, and soap bubbles.

"Why are you doing this?" Min called as they took a corner in the endless maze of corridors in Val-de-Grâce.

Chance ripped off the wimple and tossed it over his shoulder. His hair stood spiked at odd angles on his skull. One quick motion and he had her pulled tight to his chest. His lips seared a deep desire onto Min's consciousness. She felt her knees weaken. Her arms gripped the sleeves of his borrowed gown as her legs began to give way.

"You don't want this," he said. "I know you do not."

"Oh, but I do want your kiss."

Another one she did receive. Quick, but enough to prove to Min that Chance had come for her because he wanted her. Because he needed her. Maybe even . . . because he loved her.

"Come."

A smile gracing her lips, Min lifted her skirts and scrambled behind Chance. They ran through a red haze beaming down from the stained glass. Just ahead, she could see a crack of daylight shining between the thick wooden door and the floor.

"This is madness!" yelled Armand as he rounded the corner.

"You cannot force me to remain here. 'Tis not what I want, Armand," Min yelled back as the door flew wide open and Chance hefted her into a waiting carriage. Chance jumped to the driver's seat, coiled the reins about his fists, and with a lash of the whip, the horses galloped away.

Min poked her head between the red damask curtains to see Adrian run headlong into Armand's body, toppling the two of them to the ground outside the convent. He was never so clumsy, but she had to admit, his clumsiness today had aided her escape. A press of nuns appeared outside the door, waving and screaming.

"Are you all right?" Chance called.

Min pulled her head inside the carriage and spread her arms back over the seat. "All right? I've never been better."

The horses did not slow until they'd gained the Rue Cuvier, just outside the box-hedged yew walls of the Jardin des Plantes.

Chance jumped from the coach and opened the carriage door. Min sprang forward, wrapping her arms about her savior. She pushed her fingers up through his hair, devouring his essence as he twisted his lips across hers. Silently, she apologized to the heavens. The only one she wished to ever give herself to was this man who held her now. Yes! was her silent answer to his unspoken statement—you are mine.

Min kissed him long and deep, wanting never to lose touch of this exquisite man. "You're going to have to stop saving me," she whispered between passionate kisses. "I might start thinking I need someone to look after me."

"Armand had no right to do such a thing. I intend to suffer the entire brunt of his anger over this, for I know he will come looking for me. It would be too stifling for you and . . ." Chance spread a handful of her hair through his fingers.

Min saw that he had fallen speechless, his actions intent on her, his mind lost somewhere she knew not. The strange screeches of the garden's monkeys caught her attention. The air was fresh and smelled of rosemary and other herbs she hadn't names for. The scents suffused her senses, clearing her mind of her worries.

"What?" she asked when Chance jerked her chin to center and burned a longing gaze into her eyes. "What are you looking at?"

He nodded, as if satisfied with what he saw. "My future," he whispered.

Min knelt back upon her legs and rested her chin on

the ledge of the carriage. He'd rescued her again. Her hero, her knight, her cavalier musketeer.

But he is not really yours! Min felt the sinking weight of her heart as reality crashed her fantasies and daydreams to a billowing dust. No beautiful garden, no exotic-smelling herbs could change things. For her rescue changed nothing. She was right back where she had started. Alone, confused, and not fitting in anywhere. And would she still have to battle the dead ghost that haunted Chance's emotions?

"I'm not sure anymore what is the life for me," Min reflected. "The musketeers won't have me and I do not want the church, though the queen thought it would be good for me."

"The queen?" Chance pressed a finger to his lips and ran his sparkling blue eyes over her. "What have you been up to, Mignonne? Impersonating a man in hopes of joining the musketeers. Leading the most notorious villain all about the Paris countryside. You've crashed Val-de-Grâce, and now, the queen? I know she pardoned you of any crime, but you speak so casually of her."

Min gave him a bewildered shrug. As she looked at Chance, standing delightedly amused at her adventures, he the brave musketeer who fought danger daily for his king, her eyes fell on the nun's habit he wore. It stretched across his shoulders and chest and the top of the hem was caught up in his left boot.

Sister Margarite of the Heavenly Sword?

Min tried to stifle the giggle, but it was too hard what with the way Chance just stared incredulously at her. He had completey forgotten his attire. "You speak of me parading about as the opposite sex!" She jumped from the carriage and lifted the hem of Chance's gown, taunting him gaily as she danced from side to side. "Does Monsieur le Chevalier prefer the woman's dress to a man's? Hmm?"

"Nonsense!" In proof, Chance pulled at the neckline and succeeded in ripping the gown clean down the center, revealing to Min his sun-bronzed, muscular chest.

"Oh." Min felt the carriage suddenly support her. Standing only in breeches and boots, the sun played across his sculpted body, accenting each hard line and firmly powered muscle. Had the king's greatest military advisor designed him as a fighting weapon, he could not have improved upon nature's work.

Her slippered feet left the ground as Chance gripped her arms and lifted her to sit on the edge of the carriage floor. Bedroom-bound lids fell over his eyes and he drew in a deep breath. Min could not find her breath for the pounding in her throat. It was her heart, ready to catch his love if offered.

Chance twined two fingers through the ends of her hair, relishing the texture, the pure softness for a moment. It was a long time before he could draw his eyes up to meet hers. And when he did, he was all seriousness. "To even think of you in a convent made my blood run frigid. Why did you even agree to go there in the first place? I have known you only a short while, but I feel sure the convent is no place for such a spitfire as you. 'Tis like putting the devil on a block of ice and telling him to sit tight."

He knew her mind as well as her body. Oh, and did he know her body! Min looked down at the fingers he had twined through her hair, recalling the slow, painfully delicious journey they'd taken across her sweat-beaded flesh.

And the queen's words had echoed in her head. *Some dreams are better left alone. The church can give you the answers you need; it will fulfill you in a way you never imagined.*

"Mignonne? Your leaving last night . . . It was so . . . effortless. Don't you . . . Don't you care for me?"

"Chance?"

"What?"

"Now you say such things!"

"What do you mean?"

"I agreed to go to Val-de-Grâce only because . . ." She pulled away from Chance's grasp and crossed her arms before her, suddenly offended by his apparent lack of compassion regarding her destiny. "All my dreams have been dashed! And well . . . you did not seem to care one way or another when I took my leave of you. You did not try to stop me, Chance! Why didn't you?" her words ended in a tiny gasp.

"Oh, Mignonne." Unable to meet the truth in her eyes, Chance hung his head. "If only I had had the courage. I did not want to interfere with your brothers' wishes. I thought sure it would make your decision that much harder. And I stupidly believed that you did not care for me. That you could not."

"But—"

"It should not have mattered. I should have never let you go."

He tilted her chin up and brushed his thumb along her cheek, smoothing away the teardrop that slid over her skin. His thumb skimmed across her lower lip, wetting the flesh. "Jewels from an angel's eyes."

Clutching his hand in hers, Min kissed the scarred knuckles. "What do you mean it should not have mattered? You really wanted me to stay?"

"Min, I—I love you."

"You—"

He pressed a finger to her lips. "I wanted to tell you yesterday. But I did not want to contradict your brothers' wishes. But then, when Adrian revealed Armand's plans this morning—well, that was simply too much. I could not bear to think of losing you forever. May God forgive me for what I have done."

"You really love me?" she said in delighted wonderment.

"*Oui, ma petite fille.* I love you. I believe I may have loved you since that first day you fell from the trees and wrestled me to the ground."

It took a deep swallow to prevent her heart from exploding. This feeling—so enormous and encompassing—was amazing. It was as if with Chance's simple declaration, all the years of not knowing, of feeling that something was missing, were simply erased, blown away like dandelions in the breeze. Everything felt so right. And yet . . . it was simply overwhelming.

"Chance, I don't know what to say."

He kissed her cheek, and then the corner of her eye, brushing away the remainders of her tears. Min nuzzled her nose into his hair, delighted in the gentle tickles across her flesh.

"You once told me love was the greatest sacrifice."

"Yes," she whispered, a sharp twinge clutching her side as she recalled his ill-fated declaration the night they had made love. "And you told me you wished never to love again. What about Justine?"

"I was a fool, Mignonne. My heart has been broken. Justine—the love I had for her—is different from what I feel for you. You and I . . . what you give to me is like nothing I've ever felt before. I feel your presence in my life is a gift. A precious gift."

He pressed her face between his big hands and brought her to him for a long, deep kiss. If all kisses were as bewitching as this, Min thought, then may the spell never be broken. For no matter what sort of wicked sorcery Chance Lambert practiced, she wished to be forever in his arms.

"As for the greatest sacrifice . . ." he whispered into the thick folds of her hair. "I sacrifice myself willingly if only to have the affections of the sassiest masquerading imp this side of heaven."

Like the flames of the sun stretching through the sky, an enveloping warmth radiated through Min's body. She was full and complete. Her desolation after her recent defeats vanquished. Her mind was swept clean of all worry, and she began to see and think clearly.

Could this be what she had been searching for? The void deep inside, once gnawing and wide, was no longer empty. Thinking to fill it with the satisfaction of a cadet's position in the musketeers, she had followed her dreams. Only to have them shattered. Perhaps it was this particular musketeer she had needed all along. In fact, with every whispered *amour,* with every soft touch of Chance's fingers on her flesh, Min felt the fulfillment stir deep inside. And she knew that it was to be.

"Oh, Chance." She kissed him quickly, and then pressed her lips to his again in her excitement, wanting to sear her devotion to him like a brand. "I love you, too."

Chance nuzzled his face into her hair and whispered in her ear. "I think I have always been in love with you, Min. It just took the queen and your brothers and the nastiest villain in all the country to make me realize it."

His chest was hot beneath her palms. Min drew a teasing finger down the center of the burnished flesh. "And Mademoiselle Imp?"

"I believe she might have been instrumental in convincing me, too. Mignonne—" Chance fell to his left knee and held her hand with both of his. "If you can love me, I shall never ask you to change or to wear silly dresses and idiotic hats and ridiculous shoes. I love you as you are. Whether in breeches or silks."

Feigning consideration for a moment, Min cocked her head teasingly. "What of armor?"

"Armor?" Chance leapt to his feet and pulled Min from the carriage. "Anything!" A breeze of exotic herbs and fresh greenery spun through Min's hair as they twirled in a circle beneath the thick, glossy leaves of an orange maple.

"You are too generous, my love. I don't know what I ever did to deserve you."

He gave a deep-throated chuckle that sent delightful shivers up Min's arms. "You knocked me around, insulted me, and beat me, that's what you did."

"Ha! I promise to take it a little easier on you from now on. On one condition."

"That is?"

Min traced his upper lip, smoothing the pad of her finger over it. "I much prefer the mustache."

"So do I." A sexy smile drew across his handsome face. "But it was a sacrifice I had to make. I don't think Sister Margarite of the Heavenly Sword would have been quite as effective. You're not the only master of disguise."

In a burst of relieved laughter, Chance encircled her waist and lowered her back across the carriage floor, his kisses setting her body ablaze, as only his kisses could.

"*A jamais.* Forever, my love," came his heated whisper. "And always."

Forever. Min held fast to the word, repeating it over and over in her mind. Forever with this lovely man. Forever in his heart . . .

Chance startled suddenly. He sat up and leaned back, his eyes scanning the street.

"The devil!"

Min scrambled up, a task in her long robe, and peeked over Chance's shoulder. A band of riders wove between the people milling about the entrance to the garden. There were six. Min recognized them from her debacle in Remalard.

"Luciano's men!" she cried.

"The Notorious Ones!"

"My sword." Min patted her hip where her sword should have hung. "I need a sword!"

"No!"

At the touch of Chance's hand over hers, Min froze in her frantic search. He folded her fingers gently in his big, rough hands. "Please." His eyes pleaded far more eloquently than any words. "My love, let me do this."

He wanted her to sit back and let him do all the work. Fight the villains. Save the damsel in distress. He needed to show her his bravery, to prove his manhood, his love for her.

A silly thing. But . . .

Perhaps it would be best if she held back and allowed him to do what he must. *Take the woman's position just this once. If you truly love this man you will allow him this victory.*

Luciano's men were but yards away. One had jumped from his horse and reached for his sword belt.

It took all her strength to gently fold her hands in her lap, hands that itched for a sword. "You are right," Min said, urgency fighting her suppressed calmness. "This is a man's job." Min clenched her fists. This was so hard. But she could do this. "Please, chevalier." She pressed a hand over her pounding chest and borrowed a few lines from Sophie. "My heart absolutely flutters. You must rescue me from these—er, these vicious villains before I am completely taken by um—er, the vapors."

Chance smiled. She was overdoing it, but he took it in stride.

"You must go." Chance drew his sword. He graced her lips with a brief, yet possessive kiss, then pushed her to the other side of the carriage. "Follow the Rue Jussieu. Go to my apartment. You'll be safe there."

"Chevalier!"

Armand and Adrian rode up behind the carriage. Min had never been happier to see them. "My brothers." She pressed a reluctant hand to his heart. "I will go, I promise. Use my love for you, Chance. It can keep you strong."

Min watched until she was sure Chance and her brothers would be all right. There were six men against the three of them. She wanted to stay. To help. But a wave of calmness lowered her itching sword arm. *He will persevere. Do as he says. He loves you.*

Yes, Chance had fought in many campaigns. A few villains should prove little challenge to him. She hoped.

With one last heart-wrenching glance over the man who loved her, Min ducked behind a stack of hay and filed down a narrow alleyway that ran parallel to the hedged walls of the Jardin des Plantes. Behind her, Armand called out as his sword clashed with the deadly sabers wielded by Luciano's men.

Min froze, her ears pricked.

Go, he will be fine. Chance is with him.

When she heard her brother's voice again, it was to call to Chance. He was not hurt.

Min emerged from the narrow tunnel only to find her path blocked by a carriage and four horses.

"Damn these Parisian streets. Always such a clutter." She lifted her skirts and stepped gingerly around a puddle, her head hitting a low-hanging sign. "Ouch!" She backed away and bumped into another immovable object. But this one was not swinging in the air.

She spun around.

"Fancy meeting you again, my feisty little *garçon.*"

Min opened her mouth to scream, but her voice was stolen away as Luciano's fist came crashing across her jaw.

Chapter Twenty-Four

"She's gone!"

Chance stepped over the last of the fallen highwaymen and came up behind Armand, panting and heaving. "What? She was just here! I saw her watching." Breathless and bleeding in assorted places on his body, Chance scanned the street, his mind screaming louder than the death cries of Luciano's men. *No, please God, I just got her back. Not now!*

"Where's Mignonne?" Armand slid his sword inside its scabbard and smeared a blood-stained glove across his forehead.

The street rumbled with gawkers who found the fight much more interesting than the herb gardens. A member of the Watch—after Adrian explained that these men were notorious criminals—arranged to have their bodies carted away. Of course, he'd neglected to mention that he, too, was wanted before quickly slinking away.

"We must leave now. There are too many guards

around," Adrian hissed as he kept an eye on the men from the watch. "Where is Min?"

"I don't know."

A carriage ambled slowly past the crowd, the creaking wheels echoing sharply across the muffled observations of the crowd. It was when the driver cast a glance over his shoulder that Chance pushed Armand ahead of him and they began the chase.

"It's him! Luciano. He must have Min!" He rushed onward, pushing men aside, and stumbled across the bloody cobblestones. "Make way!"

"What is it? the general of the Watch called.

"The leader of these men," Chance yelled. "I am a musketeer. We'll apprehend him!"

Seeming to prefer to deal with six dead men than one live criminal, the general waved Chance on.

Luciano's whip lashed the air above the horse's heads as he realized his pursuit. The crack of his pistol did not dissuade the brothers, but the musketball caught Chance in the shoulder. He stumbled, his hand slipping down walls of stiff shrubbery, but caught himself, his knee scraping the cobblestones. He gripped the searing pain in his shoulder, feeling the hardness of the musketball against his palm. "Go on!" he yelled to the brothers. "Don't lose him."

Finding it odd that he had to stuggle to keep hold of his sword, Chance leaned against a stone column for support. He'd taken many a bullet before but had never felt such instant numbness. He switched hands, curling his left fingers about his sword hilt. Left or right, neither side was less than the other.

Luciano cracked his whip over the horses' backs as he saw the two following him. A mangled scream was abruptly cut off as the carriage skidded and slid into a man standing on the street corner.

Chance saw the carriage send the man flying to the

ground ten feet beyond where he had stood to land across a fish hawker's cart. "On him!" he called to Armand and spied a saddled horse just ahead. *"Arrêtez!* Stop! I demand in the name of the king!"

Armand ran to the fallen man and lifted his shoulders into his arms. "God's blood—Alexandre!"

"Your brother?" Chance reined the horse closer. He narrowed his eyes on the fallen man. Indeed, it was the one who studied botany. Such a frail man. It appeared his leg might be broken for the way it lay. He muttered a brief prayer for his safety.

"You go!" Armand insisted. "Save our sister."

Chance gave a firm nod and took off, steeling himself against the pain that ripped through his upper body. *Use my love for you . . . it can keep you strong.* Yes, he would not let Mignonne down. His life meant nothing without her by his side.

"Alexandre, can you speak? Say something."

Adrian joined Armand and pressed his palm to his brother's neck. "He's alive."

"The . . . queen," Alexandre muttered. He inhaled deeply and choked on the blood that spilled from his mouth. His fingers wavered before him. "Must find . . . Mignonne."

"She's dead."

Luciano toed the woman's chin, easing his boot toe along the patch of burgundy-colored flesh. "I barely bruised the skin. She's merely in a faint."

"What purpose does this woman serve you? You don't intend to mete out some idiotic revenge by having her beneath you, do you?" Bent near the inert body, the baroness smoothed away a dark veil of hair from their victim's face.

"I do." A snap of braided leather punctuated the statement with a sharp *thwack.* Luciano jerked a nod towards the rickety stairs the baroness had followed him up. "I need fetch my brandy. Also, the lead horse has taken lame, and I'll need to unharness him for our escape. I want to be long gone from Paris before the midnight owl flies overhead. Watch her. She's a cunning wench."

As well as herself, the baroness thought with an evil smirk. Spreading her skirts in preparation to nestle into a cross-legged position near the girl, the baroness froze at her lover's bark. "You'll dirty your skirts!"

Why she'd chosen the cream satin this morning was beyond her. The prospect of a carriage ride hadn't precluded the turn of events that now found her squatting in a dusty hayloft deep within the Marais. She and Luciano had been set on heading north, with Belgium in their sights. They needed to distance themselves from the rest of the Notorious Ones until things settled down in Paris. But now her enigma of a lover had only further twisted his fingers into the brew of intrigue.

She had no regrets, though. This was the sort of adventure that stirred her blood and made her feel alive. No man could excite her need for constant adventure and skullduggery as did Luciano. Nor could any man brew up the giddy desire that bubbled within her every time he stood near. Her body reacted to Luciano's seductive voice before her mind had a chance to comprehend the spoken word.

Ah, but what sort of sticky brew had her lover stirred his whip into this time?

She fingered the rough white cloth circling the girl's arm. A nun's habit? Rather curious considering that she had last seen her in vivid emerald brocade. And before that, men's clothing. Must be yet another costume. For a brief moment, envy flared in her cheeks. This woman lying unconscious before her had adventure and excitement and . . .

She'd thought her an innocent, a fresh-faced young adventuress intent on gaining one peek at the world before being chained into marriage and children. But now the baroness recalled their conversation at the countess's party just one night before. *I've the lieutenant of the king's musketeers on my side.*

For the moment, this beautiful young naïf had adventure and freedom, and . . .

And she had Chancery Lambert.

A delicious chill of darkness coated the innocent streak of envy and stirred it into a simmer of jealousy and desire. A triple strand of pearls, draped from shoulder to shoulder, clicked smartly as her fist tightened about the scratchy wool habit. The baroness leaned over the woman's body and whispered in her ear, "He was mine first. And he can be mine again."

Chapter Twenty-Five

Like a diver rising for air, Min surfaced from unconsciousness. A dizzy wave washed inside her skull. She felt as if she had run headfirst into a brick wall. "What happened?"

Dry, dusty air tickled her nose. Flashing her eyes open, Min saw that she was no longer outside the Jardin des Plantes. The faint scent of burning peat lingered . . . somewhere. The rapid chirps of a swallow flying overhead bit into Min's throbbing brain.

Where were Chance and her brothers? They had been behind her, so close, fending off Luciano's men . . .

Remembrance shocked her alert. The deep voice that had grated chillingly up her neck, before darkness had blackened her consciousness, echoed between her ears. "Luciano," Min whispered. *"Mon Dieu,* no."

Attempts to prop herself up on her elbows were futile. Min wrenched her bound wrists against one another.

Damn! She worked at the knot with her teeth, but to no avail. *I must get out of here.* But where was here?

Thick charred logs supported a thatched roof with a massive network of dust-coated cobwebs clinging to it. Swallows had made a nest high above. It seemed their chatter pinpointed her presence, and they were not in the least pleased. A mound of hay towered at the opposite end of where she lay, and she felt beneath her partially exposed legs thin shards of the same golden straws.

A hayloft? From what she could see, lying prone, two sides of the loft were open to the bright afternoon sun, with only a few wide rough-cut logs supporting the roof. Sparse treetops dotted the view out, and a few tufts of smoke billowed from distant rooftops. Min thought she could make out the graceful sails of a windmill in the distance. They were in the country somewhere, but . . . no. Carriage springs groaning against their cargo sounded very close. The clatter of wooden pattens click-click-clicking across the cobbles, and the reverberating echoes of a nearby church bell joined in the symphony of city sounds. They were still in Paris.

Luciano must have thrown her into the carriage that had been blocking her way after delivering what felt to her jaw now like an iron fist. But she had no idea how long they had traveled or how long she had been out. They could be anywhere.

Min groped at her hip, pressing into the nun's robe, but found no sword. As for the dagger she frequently carried in her boot—Min wiggled her toes—thin slippers only. "Fie."

"Ah, she awakes!"

Min jerked her head around in search of the woman's voice. She'd expected Luciano; instead it was the baroness who had lent her the pink dress. What was she doing here?

"Pity it is you who riles my lover's blood," the baroness

offered in silky consolation. A long strand of knotted pearls clacked against her breast with the sweep of her hand. "I rather favored you. Save your fashion sense, of course. Ah well, what must be done, must be done."

Min released a heavy breath. "What must be done?"

Cream satin crinkled in buttery waves down the woman's narrow arms with a lift of her shoulders. "Only when my lover has been satisfied that you have paid for your crimes will we then be able to finally vacate the city."

"My crimes?" Infuriated beyond the limits of her bounds, Min struggled frantically. "I committed no crimes!"

"You do not consider mortally wounding a man a crime?" The baroness clucked derisively as she adjusted the black velvet cuffs that rimmed her long sleeves. "My lover limps like a wounded goat because of you. And his smile . . . such a pity. What did you do with the gold?"

Her proffered sneer did not rile the woman as Min had hoped. No, this woman was as cool as a man two weeks dead. She doubted there was any chance of winning the icy baroness over to her side. But right now anything was worth a try.

"I've it stashed."

"Where?"

Gauging the glitter in her aggressor's steely eyes to be greed, Min asserted her only trump. "I'll show you if you take me back to Paris. Without your partner."

"We are in Paris."

"Then untie me and I'll take you there."

"Impossible. 'Twas a mere nugget. Nothing is worth betraying Luciano."

"Really? Even if your lover has plans to debauch me?"

"Even so. Besides, he won't leave me out of the pleasure." She drew a manicured nail below her parted lips, obviously savoring every bit of discomfort she could induce in Min. "I'll be the one holding your arms above your head."

Oh. Joy. Well, at least someone was going to enjoy her death. Min gulped.

Boot steps pounded up a staircase that Min judged to be just to the right and behind her. Step. Drag . . . clunk. Step. Drag . . . clunk. Indeed, she had done some damage earlier. The devil had arrived. And standing guard with chains of pearl, one of the dark lord's satin-shrouded demons. What Min wouldn't have given to be locked behind the stone walls of Val-de-Grâce right now.

Black-gloved fingers snaked across the baroness's pale skirts and journeyed up to caress the curve of her breasts. Evil reigned in the cold darkness of Luciano's countenance. He nudged a kiss against the baroness's neck, all the while eyeing Min. "She is a pretty little morsel, isn't she, pet?"

"I wouldn't quite say pretty."

"You are jealous, pet? You, who are nothing less than exquisite, are jealous of a mere pretty?"

"When you put it that way . . ." The baroness turned in Luciano's embrace and pressed a hungry kiss to his lips.

Min couldn't bear to watch. But she daren't avert her attention from the two people who held her fate in their slimy hands.

"Confound me!" Luciano pounded the floor with a shiny boot. "I shot the damn horse, but I forgot the brandy. Retrieve my flask, will you, pet?"

"Where is it?"

"Under the driver's seat. And do something about the smudge on your skirts. 'Tis making me ill. I'm the only one who wears white in this outfit. You know that. Me and my horse."

The baroness skittered out of Min's sight, mumbling

something about the damned horse getting more attention than she, and silently descended the stairs.

Black polished jackboots toed the straw near Min's right shoulder. The devil's hooves plowing the sacred ground. She looked up to the evil shadow dressed in angel's white. It seemed blasphemous to her that he should wear such a color. From neck to knee he was a match to his horse. Clean and deadly. Luciano's smile curled in wicked satisfaction, revealing a square void in the row of pearly whites he once possessed.

"Looks like you're in need of some cork plumpers," Min quipped, trying to make light of a situation she'd rather not be in. Inwardly she cursed herself. *Do not even give him the pleasure of knowing you are frightened. Stare the dog down.*

"No thanks to you." His lack of tooth made him lisp. Hands crossed behind his back, Luciano paced in short, limping strides. "You're a headache from hell, wench. I should shoot you dead right now."

"Then why not!" With a few twists and grunts, Min found the strength to stand, making a firm stance against her abductor. If he was going to kill her, she had no intention of making it easy for him. She'd fight to the death. Not that death would dissuade her aggressor from seeking his pleasures— No, no! She mustn't think like that. Not when the situation demanded a clear head.

With an amused roll of his eyes, and a shrug of his narrow shoulders, Luciano announced, "I am not in mind to waste a maidenhead."

"Humph." With a toss of her curls, she straightened her shoulders. "A bit late for that, I'd say."

"Is that so?" The mocking blackness of Luciano's stare shot a chill down Min's spine. The beady black orbs seemed cold tunnels that could suck her very soul from her body. "Your musketeer?"

Battling the scream that vied for escape, Min stiffened her jaw and nodded proudly.

Luciano gave a casual tilt of his head. "All the same, I will save on musketballs if I take you alive."

"If I recall correctly it does not matter to you whether I am dead or alive."

"Well now, this is entirely true." Luciano's boots crushed the shards of straw to dust as he paced calmly back and forth. "But sometimes the struggle can be *so* amusing." He stopped, toe to toe with her, his lecherous grin inches from her face. Garlic had been replaced by plain old rotten breath, yet still the fragrance of lilacs lingered. "Promise you'll kick and scream and put up a great and glorious fuss?"

Min steeled her shoulders and thrust her chin proudly. "And if I lie like a dead eel?"

Another infuriatingly casual shrug. "Won't be as amusing." His whip cracked the air, causing Min to nearly jump out of her skin. "But I shall oblige you just the same."

"What about your woman?"

"She likes to watch."

"She doesn't know about Remalard, does she? You had every intention of enjoying your pleasures solo that night, didn't you?"

"If you're thinking to turn my pet against me in your hour of need, wench, think again. My precious baroness is devoted. She's proven her alliance to me many times over."

A scourge of horrible thoughts raced through Min's head. It was two against one. One of the two wielded a whip and the other a twisted allegiance to her partner. She was no match for either.

She backed away as Luciano gained on her, his long fingers caressing the whip in seductive cruelty. The welt on her shoulder pulsed with renewed pain with each step she took. Her toes curled about something hard. Min couldn't stop herself from tumbling backward into the scratchy depths of a hay pile.

At its master's command, the leather snake clawed the floorboards, inches from her ear, sending splintering hay floating about in a glittering scatter.

"M-maybe we could talk about this?"

"I'm not much for talk. Especially since I've not such a lovely smile anymore." Luciano stretched his thin lips wide and thrust the tip of his tongue through the space, teasing her with his hideous new expression.

She held Luciano's gaze as he approached, watching for hesitation, a momentary slip. Unfortunately, he knew exactly what he wanted and would not let her out of his sight until he had her. Maybe it would be better to be dead, Min thought. At least then she'd not have to look into those hideous eyes or endure the torture of having his body on top of hers doing things only Chance—

Where is he? My musketeer. I need you, Chance.

He would be halfway across the city, still fending off the remainder of Luciano's coven of demons.

Luciano was on her like a ravenous dog on a blood-dripping carcass. His growls shivered through her system as he secured her hands upon her stomach. She squirmed and kicked her legs, trying to spread them wide enough within the confining habit to get in a good kick.

"It seems to me you are as eager as I, my masquerading little wench." Luciano mistook her actions. "Ha! Today a nun, yesterday a *garçon,* what next?"

"How about that eel?" she squeaked.

Another growl curdled in his throat. "I adore seafood."

Min held the villain's stare. She felt her heart rise to her neck, but at the same time, sensed that she had the dog frozen in her gaze. Exactly what she needed.

"Arrgh—"

A momentary lack of attention. Enough for her to ram her knee into Luciano's gut. But the move did little more than suffuse his face with the deep color of blood and start the drool forming at his mouth. Damn! Min cursed inwardly. Should have gotten him on his wounded leg.

"Witch!" Luciano wrenched Min's hands above her head and anchored them deep within the hay. The flesh of her inner thigh pinched as his knee wedged between her legs and began to spread them. The bile rose in Min's throat as the devil-come-to-flesh slid his snaking fingers down her body, his foul breath inches from her lips. She struggled against the burning rope, but it was too tight, and her wrists were beginning to numb from lack of blood.

"How thoughtful of you to choose a comfortable spot for our afternoon of debauchery," he growled near her ear and blew a straw of hay from her forehead. "A roll in the hay? An intriguing notion."

"Aren't you going to wait for your partner in crime?"

"She's on her way up," he reassured her with a jaunty chuckle. "Of course, first there's that nasty stain on her skirts she must tend to. Now, where were we?"

"No!" Min tried to wedge her knee up to kick him in the groin, but he foresaw her plans and succeeded in keeping her legs pinned by kneeling on each of her thighs. His bony knees pressed deep into her flesh; she could not even rock him off balance.

Sun-cracked lips fell upon Min's mouth with an odor so foul, she gagged. Twisting her hands only succeeded in burning welts into her wrists. Her struggles upset the loose hay, and a great mound of gold straw fell over the top of them, blacking out the daylight.

"You prefer the dark, mademoiselle?" Luciano spat out a straw with a curt chuckle. "All's fine with me. Now, do not be such a prude." He reached down and pulled up her skirts. "Spread those pretty white legs, or I'll break your neck."

Min screamed as the hot pinch from Luciano's fingers caused her to involuntarily jerk her leg away. His hand between her legs shocked her silent. *This is not happening! It couldn't.* She closed her eyes and prayed that this could only be another of those dreams the queen had told her to keep shelved. 'Tis only a dream . . . only a dream . . .

Hell, this was a nightmare!

There was only one man she would ever allow between her legs, and he was painfully absent from the scene at the moment.

Luciano's body suddenly took to the air, accompanied by his hoarse yelp. Squirming out from under the scattered straw, Min spat out a dry sprig of hay and pushed up to see the back of Luciano's white shirt slashed wide to reveal a deep, oozing gash.

Standing Luciano off, another man wavered into her vision.

"Chance!"

Bare from the waist up, his body glistened with streams of crimson. He wiped a fist across his mouth, leaving a streak of blood across his jaw. A staying glance from Chance's bloodied and bruised face told Min to stay back. This was his fight. Min fell back into the hay and closed her eyes. All would be well now; her musketeer had come to save her.

The two men engaged in a sword fight, Luciano wielding his rapier and whip, Chance only his sword. Min tensed as a lightning-swift lunge tore a clean slash through Chance's breeches. His sword swung backward with no care for direction. His eyes seemed barely focused. His entire right arm was bathed in a wash of blood and dangled at his side. *Mon Dieu,* he was badly injured. Could he withstand Luciano's wrath?

"Is it really worth all the effort for this breeched harlot who doesn't even know whether she is a man or a woman?" Luciano chuckled and stopped Chance's lunge with crossed rapier and the handle of his whip. He returned a swift riposte, the long tongue of his whip kissing the air near Chance's thigh.

Rage pulsed in Chance's jaw. His fingers tightened to white coils about the sword hilt. "I'll see that you are brought to justice and swing at the scaffolds as you so deserve!"

"What crime would lure me to the scaffolds?"

"Murder!"

"Bah! Too easily you label every petty criminal for death, musketeer."

"A trial shall determine your fate. And murder can hardly be construed as petty, despicable blackguard!"

"Speaking of despicable"—Luciano nodded in Min's direction—"have you heard the foul words that cross that one's lips?"

The tongue of Luciano's whip had only licked Chance once or twice. But he couldn't hold up forever. And Luciano showed little sign of weakening, even with the blood oozing from his back.

Min looked about for a weapon. Something. Anything. A sword or a stick she could hold with her bound hands. She could not sit back and watch Chance succumb to Luciano's torture. Hay, twine, and scraps of burlap were the only objects lying about. Nothing that would prove a worthy weapon. A rope, secured to a supporting beam, swung in the breeze above her head, perhaps used to hoist the hay up from the ground. Min inched across the floor on her thighs and glanced over the edge of the loft. A haphazard stack of hay grew up from the ground, and a wooden cart filled with more of the useless hay waited nearby. But there! Sticking tines-up in the cart was an abandoned pitchfork.

She stretched her arms over the wooden floor but didn't even come close to the weapon. Min's hope sank.

Where had the baroness slunk off to? The carriage waited just below, the unharnessed horses tied to a nearby post. No sign of movement on the ground.

"Blast!"

Chance's oath pulled Min from her search for the baroness. She straightened against the loft wall and watched the duel, helpless.

Luciano, suddenly in command, forced Chance backward across the loft with a darting rapier, his whip snaking through the air above his head. The clashing duo moved dangerously close to the edge. Chance's back jarred a supporting beam. A snap of the whip sliced his knee. With a tortured yelp, he jumped. His right leg hovered in the air, his body swaying close to the edge.

"No, please." Min's heart slammed into her clenched teeth.

Teetering, pining to answer the seduction of gravity, Chance's body swayed towards the ground.

Min bit her lip so hard that tears blossomed in her eyes.

With a heave and a guttural moan, Chance thrust his body forward, rolled across the floor, and stood with an abandoned scrap of burlap in hand. He wielded the tattered cloth with his right hand, the arm dead but the fingers still able to clutch and somehow fend off Luciano's next lunge with a snap of the cloth.

Min released her breath with a thankful sigh.

"Give up, Luciano." Chance drew in an exhausted breath. "Your men have already been defeated. Turn yourself in to the *garde* and face the consequences."

"Ha—you think I am such a fool?" Not a single bead of sweat had formed on the villain's brow. "I've had more of the Paris elite beneath my sword than your dead king Louis XIII had mistresses in his bed. Every man in Paris will be waiting around the gibbets to see me swing in the breeze."

"In the name of the king, I command you!"

"Pompous musketeer." Luciano's snake slithered at his feet, waiting for the strike. "Your kind think a man is not fit to breathe your precious waste fumes unless he has served the king. You think all musketeers are brave, honest, and proud? What of the musketeer that killed my father?"

The tip of Chance's sword clinked across the wood floor. Min stiffened, feeling as though the blade had been drawn across her throat.

Chance stood swaying on his feet, his brows drawn to his nose in confusion. A splatter of blood dripped from the whip lash on his forehead and splashed across the toe of his boot. It seemed he was contemplating what Luciano had just said, leaving himself wide open to attack.

"Oh, yes, musketeer." Vivid hatred burned in Luciano's eyes as he stayed Chance with an erect sword. "And for nothing more than standing in the king's way during some sanctimoniously pompous parade. He ran his sword through my father's heart without a thought as to his family."

Chance ran a hand across his forehead, wiping away the bloody sweat, wincing when his fingers accidentally grazed his arm. "I abhor senseless bloodshed. But that is no reason for you to run wild, killing and robbing innocent citizens."

Luciano pressed the tip of his sword to Chance's chest. His eyes narrowed into thin black slits. "My father was innocent."

Panic lifted Min to her knees, her back stiff, her fingers curling into her palms. Chance could barely stand still, let alone concentrate on Luciano's blade, which had already bored a blossoming red stain in what little clean flesh remained on his chest. The villain's fingers worked about the grip of the bullwhip, charming the snake into a macabre dance of death.

She spied the rope dangling an arm's length away and quickly traced its origin up to the rafters where a thick twist of knots held it securely. The villain stepped backward and raised his whip before the staggering musketeer, the black snake circling the air.

"You don't remember me, do you, lieutenant?" the villain mocked icily.

Chance faltered. "What do you—"

"Take a close look." Luciano flipped his hair over one shoulder and resumed a grand stance.

"Yes, I . . . do remember." Chance squinted. "But I have known since Remalard. You had every intention of raping Mignonne."

"Ah, yes, your precious Mignonne. How quickly the man abandons his heart for another. But you went from exquisite to mere pretty, fool musketeer." A slippery grin spread beneath Luciano's glittering eyes. He paced side to side, ready to fend off Chance's advances, but not challenging in any way. "You don't remember that night a month ago when I slipped from your wife's bedchamber?"

Chance's sword fell slack.

Min tensed. No! Did he not see that he was unguarded!

"But of course not," Luciano resumed, "I was already out the window when you came barreling in. Slid down the roof tiles and gained my horse in the next breath. Wasn't the first night I cuckolded you, musketeer."

No, this was too horrible. Min opened her mouth to scream to Chance, but she could not form a sound.

"It was you . . ." Chance swayed.

"Delicious white thighs . . . wrapped round my hips like a scorpion's tail securing a hold around a snake . . ."

Blood ran down Chance's arms in dark rivulets. He staggered forward, and then back. "My Justine. W-why would you kill your own mistress?"

"Ah." Luciano raised a thoughtful finger and lowered his gaze in wicked glee. "Our ruse was successful. You believed the bitch dead. *A moi,* my pet!"

From behind the haystacks where Min now teetered stepped the baroness of ice and pearls.

Chance's sword clattered at his feet. "Justine!"

Chapter Twenty-Six

And all this time she and Min had crossed paths so unaware of the connection they had to each other. What havoc this must be stirring behind Chance's bland expression. Not a brow moved, nor a muscle flinched. To know that the wife he thought dead was not.

Why wasn't she dead? What was going on?

Min studied her surroundings as the baroness slowly crossed the hayloft. The fact that Chance had dropped his sword caused her no amount of worry. He now stood before two of his enemies completely unarmed and seemingly ready to black out.

But was one really the enemy?

Exchanging a knowing glance, Luciano then stepped two paces back as Justine approached Chance's wavering figure.

Min honed in on the rope dangling from the ceiling. Just one more step and she would have the upper hand over Luciano. But she must bide her time, wait for the perfect moment. Much as she knew it wrong, the voyeuristic urge to allow Justine and Chance this meeting of two parted hearts was too great. And perhaps Chance needed this opportunity to wrench out the demons that tormented him—demons that Min had only glimpsed, but was well aware resided in her lover's soul.

Pulling herself straight, fragile fists balled near her thighs, Justine approached Chance. Satin brushed the loft floor in rhythmic beats—*swish, swish*—as loud as the blood rushing through his veins. Menace glittered in her gray-velvet eyes, a place where once he'd imagined love had lived. Fool that he had been.

"I had suspected as much," he muttered.

"Really?" So easily she embraced evil, masking her features with a cool calm, even finding a smile as simple as betrayal. "What of the blood and the torn skirts left in the carriage?"

"Initially very convincing, I must say." Chance winced. Every movement of his arm screamed with pain and threatened to blacken his sight. "But I was never one hundred percent sure. I have come to learn you would stop at nothing to have your way, Justine. Just as you lured me into your arms, so did you escape. With lies and trickery. How did you do it? Where did the blood come from?"

She shrugged, casually deflecting his bitterness with her ice shield. "The coachman provided the theatrics. Though I do believe the fabric wedged behind the musketball was an exceedingly delicious notion." She cast a glance at Luciano, and the villain granted an acknowledging bow of gratitude towards her appreciation of his cleverness.

"You're a cold woman, Justine. Why was it necessary to make me believe you dead? Wasn't it enough that you flaunted your twisted passions before my very eyes? Did you not think you'd be granted the freedom you so obviously desired after what I witnessed?"

"I couldn't bear to leave the marriage knowing you'd suffer endlessly for my betrayals. I do have feelings."

"Don't give yourself so much credit."

"I thought if you believed me dead, it would serve as a fitting payment for my betrayals in your heart. You would forget me, and I could go on without worry that somewhere my husband still pined for me."

"You think damn highly of yourself, don't you, Justine?"

"As do you. You still love me, Chancery. I know you do. Your new plaything has said as much."

"No—"

"Pet!"

"Wait!" Justine's eyes flared, stopping Luciano's approach. A silent warning flashed between her and the villain, curbing the man like an admonished puppy. Sure that she would be granted the main stage, Justine then turned and slinked closer to Chance. The foul scent of her cunning dulled any desire he feared might emerge. "You do still love me. What man who claims he no longer loves pursues his wife's killer?"

"My only reason for pursuing the Notorious Ones was to ensure that you lay six feet under."

"You love me!"

Slender fingers gripped his shoulders, and the click of her pearls brought flashes of happier times to mind. Laughing and loving, tumbling upon a feather bed with wine in hand and passion in heart. "The pearl of my heart," he recalled her whispering in his ear on the eve of their nuptials. "That is what you are to me, Chancery Lambert."

No! Chance gripped her arm and twisted her round in a swirl of cinnamon and satin, easily capturing both hands behind her back. Jerking her head back against his own, he hissed, "I despise you."

Luciano pulsed his bullwhip in waves near his side.

Behind him, Min carefully approached the swaying rope. *Be careful, precious one,* Chance sent a mental prayer to her.

"Liar." Justine did not struggle. Instead, her body conformed to the rigid defiance in Chance's bones, threatening to melt his stance with just the right touch. "My kisses haunt your dreams just as the warmth of my body taunts your desires. You love me now as you loved me months ago. I am still your wife!"

"Only on paper. Never in my heart. Hold steady!" Chance barked at the whip-wielding bastard who stepped closer. "Unless you wish her dead."

"You haven't the boldness to take her life." Luciano curled the thick base of the braided whip about his fist. "Even now you rub your hands over her body, recalling the frenzied lust she stirred in your loins."

"Luciano, wait," Justine called. "It is my turn."

Turning her round, Chance gripped Justine's shoulders. The slippery satin slid from her body, leaving his palms sealed to her bare flesh. A pearl-festooned hair comb sat askew upon her disarrayed tresses. Many a time he'd pulled that very comb from her hair and nuzzled kisses against her neck. No! He squeezed her shoulders until the memories fled and he thought he saw fear in her eyes. But he instinctually knew better. It was all a game to her. Fear could be painted on as easily as laughter or cruelty, or yes, even love.

"True, I loved you once, Justine. Foolishly, blindly. I did love you. But the heart that beats beneath this deceptive mask of satin and pearls is black. That will always be so. I can never paint it the color I wish it to be."

"You will never love her as passionately as you did me," she purred with a wicked smile and a nod towards Min, who now stood silently listening. Luciano had yet to realize his captive even stood, but his impatience grew in the angry waves of his whip.

"Wrong again. I know the color of her heart, and it is a match to mine."

"I've had enough of this—" Luciano's voice emerged in a bark as Min's body suddenly plunged into his. Her bound hands held above her head, she clutched the rope. The force of her body knocked Luciano from his feet. His sword clattered to the floor and Luciano flew over the edge of the hayloft.

Min's feet swung through the air, her body swaying with no floor beneath it. The rope burned across her palms. But she did not swing back over the floor as expected. Something was wrong. The rope twisted and jerked above her. Luciano struggled to keep hold of his whip.

Min looked up the line of braided hemp. The leather snake had wrapped about the rope, though it was uncoiling, slowly, with each movement Luciano made. She kicked hard, her sweating palms sliding in painful burns down the rope. She couldn't hold on much longer. "Damn you! Let go, you buffoon!"

Luciano's frantic jerks served Min far better than he. The tip of the whip lashed over her body, releasing the villain in a bloodcurdling scream. Min swung her legs and succeeded in swaying back over the floor.

"Insolent wench!"

Chance was pulled from his stunned observation at Justine's angry outburst. He lunged forward and gripped her about the waist just as she tried to grab Min on her return swing. "Let go of me! She has murdered my lover!"

Min skidded to a landing in the hay with a shout that she was not hurt. The angry she-wolf scrambling to free herself from his arms managed to kick Chance in the shin. He released his wife and she stumbled towards the loft's edge. Crimson pain shot through his leg, but it did not exceed the damage he had already received.

One demon had been eliminated. Now there was just the one. Beautiful, deadly bitch that she was.

Securing a hold against the battered supporting beam, Justine scanned the ground, only to turn back to Chance with a triumphant gleam in her eyes.

Impossible. Chance dashed to the loft edge. Below on the ground, Luciano wrestled with the pitchfork that had pierced his thigh. Damn, that bastard surely was a demon, for he defied death as if it were nothing more than a pesky insect.

"I'm coming!" Justine called and took a stride. Chance extended a foot, successfully felling his wife in a pouf of creamy skirts before him. Wrangling her arms behind her back, he chuffed out in exhausted breaths. "You're not going anywhere until I know that man answers for his crimes."

"You thought him a murderer," she choked through her struggles. Long curls of blond hair scattered across her jerking face. Skirts ripped and pearls snapped at his knuckles. Chance had to lay all his weight upon her body to secure a hold. "He no longer holds that title. What crime must he commit to appease your lust to see him hang?"

"He has attempted more than once to debauch Mademoiselle Saint-Sylvestre, and would have murdered her days ago had she not escaped. From the information I have concerning the Notorious Ones, I'm sure theft and assault will figure in as well."

Justine stilled. "As well as cuckoldry?" A triumphant flame flickered madly in her eyes.

Chance gasped in a breath. Below him lay his wife, defying him with a mere look. Deceptive. Cunning. Adultress. *Alive.*

He hated her for every breath she drew. And only now did he finally see clearly.

"You cannot hurt me anymore, Justine."

His breaths heaved across her hair, each intake drawing in her cinnamon perfume. Much as he despised the closeness of her presence, squeezing his eyes tight did not erase the flash of memories that scurried before him. There had been good times. Happy days filled with laughter and love. Perhaps he should have tried harder to steer her misdirected boredom into a more fitting hobby?

Forget it all, he thought. *Yes, think with the knowledge of your being, not the blindness of your heart.* Adoration and desire were now only bitter regret and spite. "May God have mercy on your soul."

Below, the stir of hooves on the ground alerted Chance. The demon had risen again. "Mignonne, he is escaping!"

"He's badly wounded. He won't get far," she said. "He clings to the horse's mane, while his legs drag on the ground." She held up a length of rope that Chance took to be used to secure the baroness's hands. "What are we going to do with her?"

"Bait."

"Oh, no, you don't." Justine snapped her teeth as Min handed the rope to Chance and he tied her up. "You cannot do this to your own wife!" were her final words before Chance tore off a chunk of her sleeve and stuffed it in her mouth.

Suddenly gifted with a moment of relief, Chance gave in to inertia, rolled to his back, and expelled a heavy breath.

"My love!" Min pressed her body along the length of his, and a gusher of tears opened across her cheek, streaming down to mix with the blood on Chance's forehead.

"My arm," he gasped. "I can barely feel it."

"I must get you to a surgeon." Min tenderly touched his shoulder, smoothing the bloody remnants of his shirt aside to reveal the lacerated flesh. A stunning chill of want shuddered through him at her touch. And behind that, solace rode in, blanketing his body.

Min prodded the slimy pistol ball wedged in his shoulder with the tip of her finger. "How did this happen?"

"Luciano," Chance groaned, and pulled himself up on his good elbow. "When I gave chase." He gave his head a conk with the heel of his hand and shook it vigorously. He had not gained his equilibrium. In fact, the notion of just lying back and closing his eyes grew more appealing with every blink of his lids.

"Don't try to stand."

"We must give chase." He felt so depleted. Blast, that he could not rise and finish this now! "If you say he is barely mounted, this may be our only chance."

"Not until I tend this wound. Besides, we do have her. Much as I'd prefer we did not."

"Can you get it out?" came his breathless gasp.

The ball sat deeply imbedded in flesh and possibly bone. "If I were a surgeon."

"Don't tell me . . ." Chance sucked in a deep breath. "The fearless Mademoiselle Imp has not yet tackled that profession?" Despite the obvious pain, Chance was still able to smile his chivalrous musketeer smile that sent a delicious shiver racing through Min's body.

"Not yet." Min gingerly touched the skin, her finger slipping through the bloody mess. "Is that a challenge?"

"It is," Chance groaned.

"Then I accept. But my hands . . ." She displayed her bound wrists.

"Use my sword."

Securing the sword between her knees, Min sawed her bound wrists over the blade. The words carved into the steel, *Mousquetaire Du Roi,* flashed at her. A dream lost. She glanced at Chance. A new dream found.

Perhaps it was *this* musketeer she had needed all along.

But there was one problem. The woman squirming on the floor. Would Chance reconsider his feelings towards the two of them? Whom would he love now?

No, she mustn't be possessive. Not at a time like this. He would make the right choice. And if that choice did not include her, then . . . ah, hell! What was she thinking? She wanted him to choose her. And yes, she might even wish that Justine was really dead. Might? Why couldn't the woman be dead? It would make things so much simpler.

Ah, but when had she ever chosen the simple route?

The rope snapped, her wrists springing free. Min plied the pad of her thumb over the tip of his sword, wishing there were another way. But it had to be done. There was no telling how much blood he would lose before they could get him to a surgeon and have it sewn up. And with all the other whiplashes and cuts, he could die if left untended for too long. With a brave intake of breath, Min reached for Chance's scabbard and pressed the leather to his lips. "Bite on this."

He obliged her with a painful moan and clamped down as she pressed the steel to his flesh.

Min dug carefully around the ball, wincing as each movement cut deep into his flesh and released new spurts of blood. Chance's groans made her pull back but, spurred by a get-it-done-with jerk of his head, she forced herself to finish the task. One firm push sent the bloody ball rolling across the floor. Released from its knotty tension, Chance's shoulder fell back across the wooden slats. If his eyes had not been open, Min would have thought he'd fainted. She ripped off a portion of her skirts and bandaged him up as best she could.

"God's angel," Chance muttered, teetering on the edge of consciousness. His fingers blindly traced the air. Min moved closer and pressed her lips to his searching fingertips. "I love you, Mignonne."

"Until she betrays you."

A cringe of pure undiluted hate surged through Min's veins at Justine's nasty comment. The gag lay on the floor near her lips. Without thought for permission or justification from Chance, she drew back a fist and connected with the ice baroness's jaw.

"Forgive me," she said, softening her mood for her lover's surprised gasp. "What were you saying?"

He crooked a finger to lure her closer to his face. "I love you."

Her relief was so great, she wanted to close her eyes and become forever lost in the warmth of Chance's embrace. To never lose touch of him. Always in his arms . . .

Shaky fingertips traced her lips, and a smile blossomed on his blood-spattered face. "You belong to me forever."

She smiled behind his fingers, but could not help glance towards Justine.

"She no longer resides in my heart. She means but one thing to me."

"Bait?"

He nodded. "We must find Luciano. I want this nightmare over."

Chapter Twenty-Seven

It was a shock to hear that Alexandre had been hit by the very carriage Luciano had used to spirit Min away. But her brother was doing well. He'd received a nasty cut on his forehead and the fever was just now leaving. Other than that, the surgeon believed there to be no broken bones. Amazing, but the pile of fish he landed in had broken his fall.

"He's been mumbling all day of the queen," the tavern maid who had been watching over him informed Min. "Something about the queen's mistake. Must be fixed? You've got me." She shook her tumble of age-wearied red curls. "He's delirious, he is."

"Perhaps we should leave him to rest," Chance suggested from the doorway.

"You'll be my next patient, chevalier," the maid said to Chance as she looked over his haggard condition. "Come with me. I'll fix you up, then I'll fill your belly with roast pork and ale before the evening patrons eat it all."

"Yes, go with her, Chance. Give me a moment with Alexandre, please."

Having no choice but to follow the redhead who had hooked her finger inside the waist of his bloodied breeches, Chance closed the door, leaving the two alone.

Through the window, Min placed the stables behind the shop. She envisioned Justine, bound, gagged, their helpless bait squirming impatiently in the carriage. Chance would most likely see to her after he'd been bandaged.

Min felt her heart catch at the base of her throat. Much as she trusted Chance, Alexandre would be a quick visit.

She went to her brother's side. Seeing him lying so helplessly stung her deep in her breast. Of all the people who least deserved such violence, it was Alexandre. Sweet, softhearted Alexandre who saw the world as a rainbow of colored voices and scented sounds.

"Alexandre? It's Mignonne." A bruise purpled his right temple and his shirtsleeve had been cut to bandage his arm. His brow felt warm, but not alarmingly so.

Alexandre's dark eyes fluttered open at the touch of her hand.

"Petite one." His voice cracked. He wrinkled his nose distastefully. "Do I smell . . . fish?"

"You mustn't speak, Alexandre. Save your strength. We must give thanks to God, for a pile of market catch broke your fall."

He whispered a *merci Dieu,* and then, "The queen regent . . . I spoke . . . to her."

"Really?"

"Her voice . . ." He managed a weak smile. "It was like melon. Cool and soothing."

"That's wonderful. But rest now, Alexandre. You've taken a terrible spill."

"No . . . you must . . . go to her. She wants to speak . . . to you."

"Me?" Again? "What have I done now?"

He smiled. "It seems the q-queen . . . is a trifle . . . worried. Oh . . ." His breath spilled across his lips in an exhausted hush. "I am so tired. Everything is hazy and dull. I don't like this clang of sharp colors that pulses in my arm. I need . . . Sophie."

"Yes, Alexandre, I'll send for her immediately."

"Thank you. Be a good girl and go to the queen . . . will you?"

"I will. Chance and I have a few things to take care of first. I'll send for the maid. You could use more blankets. I don't want you to catch a chill. And perhaps some lavender oil. You smell horrible. Sophie mustn't see you this way." She kissed his cheek and smoothed his soft hair across the pillow. "All will be well, Alexandre. Rest peacefully."

Silently she thought to herself, *I hope.*

Chance's boot heels scraped the cobbles, and every step or so an involuntary gasp eased out of his mouth. There weren't too many places on his body that couldn't produce a stab of pain. The only thing that wouldn't hurt would be lack of movement. Utterly impossible at the moment. He had things to take care of. The carriage ceased rocking as he approached it.

There she sat, out of view, on the other side of the black laminate door, curtained for privacy with faded azure fabric. She knew he stood just outside the purloined vehicle, her breath held, her ears pricked to catch every subtle movement, pick up every single thought. Justine had a way of sensing her opponent's moods, emotions, and thoughts. It was as though she could look through to his heart with that steely gaze. Touch him without lifting a finger.

A chill touch, hers. One he had initially thought warm and inviting. But no longer.

Having procured a clean shirt and bandages from the innkeeper's wife and a quick meal of rosemary pork roast and wine, Chance felt his strength renewed, as was his mood. Though he wasn't in the least cheery.

Not when hell sat in wait on the other side of this carriage door.

The clang of a tin apothecary sign slapping against a stone storefront beat rhythmic vibrations through his head. How natural that the world should continue its pace, absorbing change and adversity and trial without fanfare, without blazing sparklers or public announcement. While inside, Chance felt his entire world had been gripped and shaken upside down. So many suffered, and because of such trials, learned to endure. He was no different.

He just felt alone. Even knowing Mignonne loved him could not chase away the chill of despair that had resurfaced upon seeing his wife standing before him. Alive. Grinning like a pigeon-fed cat with feathers sticking out of its mouth.

Always those damn pearls. They snaked about her curves, accentuating and luring with every click.

What to do now? Justine was still his wife. He no longer loved her. It was certain she harbored no love for him, only a false mask of sincerity that she used to her own best interest.

"Yes," he whispered on a heavy breath. "Remember her wiles." And he pulled the carriage door open.

" 'Tis high time you saw to me. Do you know I'm near expiring from the heat and the tightness of these wretched shackles?"

She twisted her wrists, which Chance had bound with strips of Mignonne's robe and then tied to the opposite doorframe. He drew back the thick black fur that cuffed one of her sleeves, saw there was a minute bit of slack, and, satisfied, settled onto the seat opposite his wife. As the cushion received his body, he pulled a mask of indifference over his features, raked his fingers through his hair, and blew out a sigh. "Tell me where Luciano hides out and I shall release you."

"He has no permanent home. He's no fool."

"And neither are you, Justine, so I know you'll do your best to conceal your lover's whereabouts. But if you wish freedom, you will have to talk. It nears dark, but I wager with the rising sun tomorrow morn, the heat can become unbearable in the confines of your prison. That satin and fur . . . a most peculiar selection for a rest beneath the sun, or rather a morning spent baking in a tiny wooden box."

"You mean to keep me here? You've become a heartless cad within a month's time, Chancery."

Justine had a way of casting daggers with her eyes. One particularly sharp blade nicked Chance in the heart. He stiffened, determined to never again fall victim to her slippery charms. "Call it as you see fit, but between the two of us, I bet you lose the race of humanity, Justine. So what'll it be? Freedom, or starving inside a baker's oven?"

"I can go without food."

He quirked a brow. He'd never known Justine to forgo sustenance in the name of morals. She adored the sensuous pleasures of food—had once ordered in fresh mussels from the coast for an afternoon picnic.

"I can suffer the heat also."

"Is it really worth it for that gape-toothed bastard?"

"What makes you think he'll return for me? For all you know, he's long gone from Paris."

"I don't think so." Chance leaned forward and stroked a finger along her cheek. "Pet."

Her lips fell slack, her eyes softened in the growing haze

of early evening. Yes, any man would surely prize her fine skin, her plump lips, her knowledge of pleasuring a man. . . . Chance drew the side of his forefinger over her lower lip, remembering their own journeys into lust and frenzy and yes, love. She had been so easy to love. So giving and open to new experiences. Instant adoration. On both their parts. He'd snatched her into his arms as if she were a prize he must hoard and keep secret from all other treasure seekers.

And he had kept her to himself. Exclusively. Until . . .

Delicious heat drew along the length of his finger. Chance snapped out of his reverie to find Justine snaking her tongue in a leisurely pace down to his palm. Heavy lids blinked. One flash of her icy eyes, then another. Each motion a hypnotic charm that enticed him to remain. Cling to the past. Watch. Feel. *Enjoy,* coaxed her eyes.

"Remember," she whispered in her kitten-soft tone, a tone visited only after heady lovemaking and long mornings spent lazing in bed. She pursed her lips and kissed his fingertip.

No, Chance's consciousness muttered. She deceives you. There is another . . . That other woman. Waiting . . . somewhere . . .

"You are cruel, Justine." Somehow he'd risen from the seat and now knelt on the floor before her. Chance gripped her chin and jerked her gaze away from him. "Your eyes promise one thing, but your heart is already cuckolding me once again. Know this—I forsake our wedding vows from this day forward and shall always consider you six feet under the ground. For you are dead in my heart."

She twisted out of his grip, but her countenance remained stubborn. Triumph glistened in her eyes. "It isn't your heart that still desires me, husband." The pressure of her touch, a slender thigh cloaked in satin, eased along Chance's leg. He did not move. "I can do things for you that dirty-faced wench can never dream to know. Only I can satisfy your needs. Needs you are well aware of. Remember . . ." She closed her eyes and whispered, ". . . the feeling of being inside me?"

Her knee brushed his groin and the memories of their lovemaking gushed into his mind. Hot and tight and endlessly driving, pushing, pulling him to the brink of ecstasy. In her arms, inside her body, Chance had found a home. Yes, she had answered needs he'd not known he had. The scent of her desire, all passion-laden musk and cinnamon and masterful, demanding kisses . . .

The touch of her lips ignited a forgotten cinder, and as he pressed hard against her mouth a flame sparked. Siphoning her moans into his soul, Chance sought out the passion he had once possessed. Perhaps he had judged her too quickly. Misunderstood her intentions. He pushed an arm around her waist and pulled her to his body.

"Yes," she moaned into his mouth. "You still love me."

"Yes," he answered without thinking. He did.

No. Wait.

The squeak of the carriage door shattered the moment. While Chance was just straightening out his conflicting emotions and still had his lips pressed to his wife's, the sound of the slamming door jarred him back to reality.

"No!" He stumbled backward, struggling to untangle his boots from the froth of satin skirts. "Min!" He pushed open the door just in time to see her round the corner of the inn. "Blast!"

"Where is it? It must be around here somewhere." Min dodged sideways through a shoulder-wide alleyway and onto a street littered with stacks of shattered kegs. "Where the hell am I?" She paused, scanned the buildings around her, yet found no street identification carved into the stone shop fronts. It was a business district judging from all the wooden signs hanging from rusted metal hinges, but she never had been too good with her letters—

"Mignonne!"

No time to begin an education now. Slipping between a couple linked arm-in-arm, Min barely missed getting her elbow nipped by a frou-frou concoction of poodle nestled in the woman's arm. Most likely theatergoers, though there was no sign of others and it was still too early for the nine o'clock performance.

"Right bank," she muttered and headed towards the stale scent of the Seine. From there she could assimilate her position by keeping Nôtre Dame in sight. "Ouff! Out of my way, monsieur." She instinctually reached for her dagger, but the tree of a man she'd bumped into gripped her arm and pushed her against the wall of an apartment building just as a carriage spun by, licking spits of mud across their ankles. "Chance. Let go of me. If you don't mind, I'm in a hurry."

"To get where?"

She ripped her arm from his grasp and pushed her hair from her eyes. Twilight masked his features in eerie shadows, but it did nothing to disguise the scent of lust that lingered like a wraith about him. And she knew where that scent had been born. Back in the carriage with his wife.

"There's a woman I know, Lady Godiva—"

"What?"

"Oh, yes, now I know for sure there's absolutely nowhere else I could possibly belong. I've no chance to serve the king. Val-de-Grâce would sooner say a prayer for the devil than admit me, and you—"

"Me?" He gripped her by the shoulder and rammed his bandaged arm against her opposite side. "Mignonne, what you saw back there—"

"What I saw back there is entirely beside the point. She is your wife, after all. You have every right—" The sudden threat of tears forced Min to choke. She struggled to remain stone-faced, though her jaw began to quiver and her shoulders shook under Chance's firm hold. She could taste the tears at the back of her throat. "Your lips were on hers!"

Her words worked like a fist to his face. Chance reared back. Min glanced down the street but decided she no longer wished to become a prostitute. For the moment, anyway. Not until she heard his explanation. Then . . . she'd think about it.

"Yes, I suppose they were."

"You suppose? And would that be akin to stating you suppose you are a man, and you suppose a horse has four legs, and you suppose—"

The sudden intrusion of his kiss only infuriated Min further. She pushed and squirmed and finally succeeded in biting.

Chance touched his lower lip, intercepting a trickle of blood. "I suppose I deserved that."

"You suppose rather much lately, monsieur."

"Chevalier."

She opened her mouth to retort, but grew further incensed at his reference to their previous banter. This was no lighthearted conversation. "I had thought you'd declared your love for me."

The muscle in his jaw flexed. He nodded.

"And even though now there is this difficulty involving your wife—oh, what am I saying?"

"Mignonne—"

"Of course you must remain true to Justine. She is your wife. Less than a month has passed since her disappearance. But . . . but hadn't she been so cruel to you?"

Why was it so difficult for Chance to see that he was

only walking into another sticky web, woven with skillful cunning by the ice baroness?

And why could Min not just mind her own business? This was Chance's life. He must decide what was right or wrong for himself.

He caught her in his arms as she slumped backward. No resistance this time. Min allowed herself to be folded close to his chest, heartbeats rampaging beneath his shirt. "Forgive me. I'm nothing but a spoiled little imp who always wishes her way, and when it isn't handed to her on a silver platter, I throw a tantrum. Of course, that is what husbands and wives do . . . kiss."

His heavy exhalation drained her last ounce of defiance.

"It is not what you thought you saw, Mignonne. Please, you must believe me."

"Yes, well, I suppose it was a rather simple task for her to kiss you unawares, she being tied up and all, and having quite the range of movement so as to make her attack unexpected."

"I kissed her."

If she had thought her world shattered to pieces in d'Artagnan's office just yesterday afternoon, surely now oblivion had swept in to carry it away.

While the warmth of Chance's hand smoothing along her cheek and tilting her head up reminded of tenderness and closeness and a night shared in heaven, Min dared not hope. Not now.

"I have told you before that Justine is conniving and cruel. Yes?"

She nodded. Behind Chance another carriage ambled by, two horses blinded to the world save what they saw straight ahead. If only she had the ability to see straight ahead and not all around and behind into the past of the one man she cared for.

"I do not love Justine. I will never forgive her for her

treatment of my emotions. I kissed her . . ." His hold on her shoulder tightened as he gritted his jaw and closed his eyes. And when he opened them, the sky-brilliant orbs were soft with the threat of rain. "I kissed her because she did it to me again. I got caught up, ensnared in her brilliant web. Don't you see, Min, my own emotions are so tormented, so delicate right now. I just wasn't strong enough to resist. Justine thought she could lure me into releasing her. And if you had not come when you did, I might have."

"Just how much luring might it have taken? Had I not opened that door when I did, perhaps you might still be back there. Tangling your limbs in her *web.*"

"Mignonne."

"I'm sorry. I have no right. But you must realize it is difficult for me too. So much has happened within a short period of days. Where is Justine, by the way?"

"Still in the carriage."

"Are you sure? Knowing her, she might have found someone else to help her escape."

"This is true."

Chance turned towards the street, but Min pulled him back to her and spread her arms around and up his back. "Forgive me? I acted a fool. I had no right to forget that I am not the only one struggling with my emotions and dreams. I will help you, Chance. I promise that from this moment forward, I'll set aside my selfish desires. They were foolish desires anyway."

"Not so, precious one. Never have I known a more courageous, brave woman. Indeed, the musketeers would benefit to consider your commission. But I must say myself, I'd much prefer they did not. If anything were ever to happen to you—"

"You've no need to worry about that. But if you think about it, a soldier is no more in dire straits than any civilian walking the carriage-addled streets or, shall I say, flying from lofts and landing on pitchforks?"

"He'll come looking for Justine. We should return to the carriage. But first . . ."

He threaded his fingers through her hair and lured her into his kiss. Beyond exhaustion, releasing herself to the power of his kiss was incredibly easy. The skim of his fingertips danced scintillating tickles across her scalp. The night grew heady with the moist threat of rain and caressed her senses.

Crushing her body against the hard lines of her musketeer, Min surrendered to a new desire. One that did not involve bravery or honor or fighting skill. This desire simply demanded her heart. And it was given freely.

Midnight. Nôtre Dame's bells settled their dulcet vibrations like a gentle cloak across the city. Candlelight flickered in windows. Few travelers ambled through on horseback and those on foot scurried quickly over the cobbles, always on the alert for footpads.

Clutching Chance's good hand as if the contact alone could keep her safe from the unseen eyes lurking in the darkness, Min skittered behind him down the Rue des Pyramides. She'd yet to procure clothes of her own. Whether a gown or men's breeches, anything would be better than this nun's robe.

Make it a gown, she thought as she silently followed Chance. He would like a gown. And perhaps she would too.

"Just as I thought!" Chance broke into a jog as Min sighted the carriage. The next thing she saw was a dark-haired figure pulling Justine free. "Stop!"

Drawing his sword, Chance charged forth, while Min frantically patted her hips and thighs. She would never get used to traveling unarmed! "No weapons. A poor musketeer you'd make, Saint-Sylvestre."

Already the clang of swords signaled that Chance had engaged with Luciano. Visibility in the shadow of a long stretch of apartments was minimal. But Justine's ivory skirts flashed with a telling luminescence. Chance had already had one close match with Luciano tonight. Both men were wounded. But Min laid all her bets on her musketeer.

She hiked up her skirts and dashed around the carriage where she crashed into Justine, and the two women fell to the refuse-crusted cobbles. Satin tore and curses abounded from the baroness's perfectly colored lips. Her hands were still bound, which made Min's task a bit easier. But the woman's legs were free and kicking. One good blow hit Min square in the back and forced the air from her lungs. She collapsed on top of her aggressor, but something sharp clamped onto her shoulder.

Min shot upright and slapped Justine's face. "You've the bite of a beast, you horrible woman."

"You haven't seen anything yet, wench."

The snap of the whip ignited the air above Min's head. Chance's luck had just taken a dive.

One moment of inattention to her captive was one moment too long. From out of nowhere, a sharp talon tore across Min's throat. She gripped her neck, felt blood ooze between her fingers, and heard the clank of steel upon the cobbles. Justine's hair comb. Min staggered. In the next moment a heel to her jaw sent her tumbling backward, her skull jarring against the hard street.

"You're no match for the best," Justine spat as she stood and shook out her skirts above Min's head.

Min had not lost consciousness, but the voices, the sounds of fighting, the click of pearls, and the smells of the city began to waver. . . .

* * *

A flash of glowing satin appeared in his peripheral view. He'd heard Min go after Justine, and now the fact that Justine stood and Min was nowhere to be seen—

Luciano's whip bit the air near Chance's shoulder. He dodged and redirected his attention to the villain. In the feeble light it was difficult to judge movement, but the whoosh of the snake's attack was unmistakable.

"Don't harm him!" Justine shrieked.

Undaunted by his wife's change of alliance, Chance lunged forward to slice the tip of his blade through his opponent's breeches, revealing the bloodied and bandaged wound from the pitchfork. Obviously it was a great fount of pain, for Luciano's yowl could have woken the dead. Indeed, a shuttered window high above their heads swung open and out popped the heads of two yawning youngsters.

"I do not need your mercy," Chance growled as he gauged Luciano's next strike, while keeping Justine also in view. "Where is Mignonne—what have you done with her?"

"She lies on the ground."

"The deuce! I'll see you in hell, Justine, if you've harmed her!"

"I believe you'll be going there first, musketeer. Justine, stand away—I've had enough of this feeble sword fight."

The tip of Luciano's whip slapped Chance's boot, minus its bite. He'd abandoned his weapon, which could only mean—

"Time to die, musketeer."

"No!" came Justine's cry.

The click of a pistol cock snapping into position registered in Chance's mind. No time. His sword was useless. Mignonne might lie dead—

An amber sizzle of sparks ignited Chance's thoughts into a dizzying display of his future. Mignonne kissed the meat of her palm and blew him a kiss, her smile brightening behind the delivered morsel. *Come to me in heaven, my chevalier,* floated the voice in his head. *We can still be together . . . .*

The expected jolt of pain—right in his heart—did not come. Instead, a heavy mass of satin and long, streaming hair fell into Chance's arms. Before he could register what had happened, Luciano's shrill cry echoed up and over the rooftops. The sudden realization of what he had done plunged the villain to the ground before him, where he gripped and tore at the cream satin skirts.

"Justine." She hung in Chance's arms, limp, bloodied, and lifeless. She had jumped in front of the bullet to save his life. *"Mon Dieu."* Chance fell to his knees, bringing his wife's body down with him. The fresh scent of blood filled his nostrils. Luciano's shuddering whimpers lapped at his ears, and the soft flow of Justine's luxurious hair rippled like a cool stream through Chance's fingers.

"She loved you."

Chance looked up. Min stood with arms akimbo. *Bittersweet,* he thought. *Yes, this moment was so very . . . bittersweet.* Min touched her throat, smearing a dash of blood across her chin, and shook her tangled tresses from her face. Her contemptuous glance poured over Luciano's agonizing form, and with a single look Min told Chance she would take care of the wounded snake. She leaned over and delivered a silencing fist to the bastard's jaw, then dragged him away by his feet. "Take all the time you need," she called. "I'll be here waiting for you. Always."

Always.

The difference between Mignonne Saint-Sylvestre and Justine Claudette Lambert. Justine had granted him a moment of her time. Min had given him always.

A *splat* of warm rain nicked his brow and dispersed into the shimmering strands of Justine's hair. A steady stream began to fall upon his head, washing the salt of tears from his face, the dust and grime from his body, the blood from his wounds. The crimson flower blooming upon Justine's breast began to spread and saturate her bodice.

Chance pressed a finger to her lips, as cool and beautiful in death as she had been in life. It was too late for regrets. Life had become so very bittersweet.

Chapter Twenty-Eight

He gently laid his fallen angel upon the floor of the carriage. Crossing her hands over her stomach, he then leaned forward and kissed her cool knuckles. He kissed her breast where she'd bravely taken death so that he might live, and he kissed her closed eyelids, peaceful in their rest.

Her sacrifice was the first unselfish act he'd ever witnessed from her. Fitting that his final memory of her should be such. And he would remember just that—that Justine had died for him. Nothing else. Her crimes of deception and betrayal no longer reigned in his heart. He owed her that much for her sacrifice.

Drawing a fingertip along the line of pearls that bloomed around her neck, he toyed with the cold marbles that would forever remind him of Justine. "You are a pearl, Justine. Perfect, cold beauty. I will keep these to remind me of the good times." He loosened the strand and coiled it into his hand.

Already the street had begun to stir behind him. With forced indifference, Chance directed a damask-robed apothecary to care for Justine's body; he would return in the morning. The *garde* was directed to Luciano, whom Chance discovered tied and bound on the opposite side of the carriage. The villain was livid, his eyes fixed to the ground as the king's men carried him away. Justine's name echoed in his hideous moans through the street. Only once did he complain about the mud that had smeared his breeches.

All was done. His mission was complete, his question regarding his wife's death answered.

The rains showered cold light upon Chance's shoulders, promising a new and fresh beginning. He spread his hands out before him, allowing the heavy drops to fall between his fingers.

Why did these fingers looked so unfamiliar to him? Rough and swollen, slashed and bruised. They needed something. What, he did not know.

He tilted his head back so that the rain plummeted onto his face and arms and soaked his clothing to his body. He felt heavy, wasted, defeated.

Until the darkness gave way to a beam of moonlight down the street. And in the beam of silvery shadows stood his salvation. She held her arms high above her, her head tossed back as if to suffuse her pores with the cool elixir of renewal. The nun's robe clung to her body. The tips of her bare toes sparkled in the ethereal light.

As he neared her, his boots sloshing through the puddles, she turned. Streaming rain washed over her face and down her neck, cleaning away the final traces of blood. She lowered her arms and held out one hand. Surrounded by an aura of goodness and right, she truly was an angel standing in heaven's light.

Chance stepped forward. He did not touch her. *How*

could he with these horrible, different hands? But their closeness sent a slow, surging roil of heat from his head to his feet. Her essence was palpable in the shock of being that coursed through his body. She was alive. She loved him. He loved her.

Always.

He opened his mouth, hesitated, and then, "I need you."

Clinging to her body, her arms embracing him, Chance felt this feisty imp encompass his every pain, his every need, his every desire. She filled him with love and hope.

He would do better than endure. In this woman's arms, he would thrive.

And then he touched the back of her head with his big clumsy hands.

And they didn't feel so horribly alien after all.

The quiet scrape of the door closing behind him didn't warrant investigation. A lone island perched on the end of his bed, his boot heels cocked in the curled iron frame, Chance heaved a sigh.

"They've taken Luciano to the Bastille. He'll be tried for Justine's death, and for various thefts as well," Min offered as her voice drew closer. Comfort hummed in the resonance of her voice. "What of you?"

The mattress swayed behind him as it accepted her weight. The press of her cool fingers on his shoulder stirred his need. He lifted his head. "I will survive."

"Will you?" she whispered against his ear. Oh, the sweet pain of her lips barely brushing his flesh. Torture it was. She slipped from the bed and came around in front of him, placing her hand against his chest. Chance fought the urge to push her away, as he desired to push away life, the urge to feel, the very need to breathe. "You've been wounded very deeply," she continued, "right here." Her palm pressed over his heart. "A love wound can be deadly if not tended to."

He looked up and fell into her bittersweet eyes. Deeper and deeper he felt his body falling, plunging, flailing without sign of bottom into the chasm of her soul. "This wound has scarred over," he offered. "But only because of you."

"I want to erase it." Softest whispers caressed his mind, luring him forward, closing his eyes. "You made love to me the other night. You selflessly gave of the few pieces of your heart that were spared the scars. I want to make love to you now, Chance. Let me trace the scars . . . maybe cover them."

He eased his head to the side to receive her nuzzling kisses. Slipping along his jaw, rising to his earlobe. Utterly unable to resist, for he was tired and weak, he surrendered with a moan and a gasp that secured him only air, for he could not comprehend space or time at the moment. Only pain and desire and raw exhaustion roiled within him. A dizzying mixture that could conquer, and would.

"You trust me?" whispered into his mind.

Hell, what was trust? After everything he had been through with Justine, he didn't even know anymore, didn't want to know. Except he could not overlook the fact that he felt as though he were exactly where he should be at this moment in his life. Right here, right now, with this woman spreading her fingers over his body.

"Tell me you do, Chance. Tell me again how much you need me."

"I do," he rasped out as she brushed her lips along his shoulder blade, the exquisite sensation masking the pulse of pain that tormented his opposite shoulder. "I need you, Mignonne."

"As I need you this very minute. I wish to spend forever kissing you and touching you and learning every pore of your body. But I think right now I just want to feel you inside me. Lie back."

No arguments there. The pressure of her lithe body pushing his to the bed sank Chance's shoulders deep into the wool coverlet. Tendrils of moist dark hair danced across his lips, his eyelids, his neck, followed by the urgent fire of her mouth. He sensed the rain-cool breeze from the window across his arm as she stripped the soggy shirt from his left arm, a deft move that did not break her kiss from his mouth. Sucking her lips, her tongue, softly, harder, more soft and then demanding, Chance drew the urgency from Min into his own body.

Yes, now. He must have this woman.

She broke contact for a moment, straddling his hips and tossing her hair back like a proud summer-goddess who worships the sun. The tattered nun's habit slid over her head and sailed to the floor in a soggy puddle.

Blessed mother, it truly was a goddess perched upon him. Chance throbbed beneath her weight, aching for admittance between the lily-white thighs that embraced him. With a grand motion, she pushed her fingers up through her hair, lingering as she pulled them through, releasing a fan of dark angel wings about her shoulders. Misty droplets spattered his chest like angel kisses.

With his good hand, Chance reached for her breasts, proud and heavy, gifts against his palm. The sound of her moan and the wanting clasp of her hands over his drilled the need for satiation deep into his groin. He arched his hips, barely grasping a sane thought as the pressure of their connection bruised along his hardness. "Now," he managed through a tight jaw.

She freed the buttons on his breeches and pulled the chamois down to his knees in less than a heartbeat. He lit like a blazing torch as her fingers wrapped around him and guided him to the entrance of paradise.

Abandon sorrow all ye who enter here, he thought blissfully. This was heaven. If only for the moment. And for every moment thereafter.

An animal growl clawed from his tense mouth as he sheathed himself deeper and deeper inside her walls. "Hold me forever. . . ."

"I will."

He followed as she directed his hands to her hips. Surrender was mindless and richly delicious. The soft hiss of her breath tasted sweet upon his eyelids; the steady pulse of her hips, grinding against his, was just as things should be. Always. Here was home—lying beneath Mignonne, the curled tips of her hair drawing wet trails around his nipples, her fingernails grazing his biceps, her thighs hugging his waist, her hot cream slathering him like butter over porridge.

The thick vein that drew along his member was milked and filled and milked and filled with every slide of her body. Tremors started in his center, rapidly building, spreading through his limbs and up to block all rational thought from his mind.

Heat. Bliss. Ecstasy. More. Always . . .

As words ceased to register, his body arced towards heaven, drilling high inside his lover, and triumph spilled from his throat. *"Yeeesssssss."*

He was faintly aware that his partner shuddered upon his hips. Reaching out, he pulled her to a tight fit against his panting chest. Her flesh was wet and hot, her heartbeat thumping against his own heart. He remained inside her for a long time after. Here was home.

Always.

"I want the whole world to know," he whispered.

"What?"

"I love you. And I need you," he said as he ran the back of his fingers along her downy smooth cheek. "You once told me you were a lady, no matter what your attire, and I laughed at you. I beg you, Mignonne, forgive me, for I was wrong. You truly are a lady." He curled his fist beneath her long fingers and pulled them to his lips. "After the last few days, I can never imagine letting you go. I should truly be lost without you, Mignonne Saint-Sylvestre. I know I must speak to Armand about this, but I will ask you first. Will you do me the honor of becoming my wife?"

Min let out a sigh. "You wish to so quickly tie yourself to another woman after what you went through with—"

He pressed a finger to her lip to silence the voicing of that wicked name. "Remember once I told you I had distinct impressions of what sort of woman I wanted?"

She nodded.

"And then I told you how you were the complete opposite of all I desired, all I ever hoped to find in my perfect woman?"

Another silent nod behind his admonishing finger.

"Well, you taught me a lesson, Mademoiselle Imp. I find I much prefer a woman who follows her own heart, a woman who'll not sway to society's preachings, a woman who even prefers to wear the breeches once in a while—"

"Once in a while?"

He shrugged. "All right, as often as you desire. But what I have come to know about you, Mignonne, is that you need no man by your side. I admire your independence. Dammit, I adore your feistiness too."

"So why would you want to be with a woman for whom you deem a man unnecessary?"

"Perhaps it is because I crave a marriage of equals, neither of us the master over the other, and yet . . ." He looked down towards their joined bodies and smiled. "I rather enjoy being mastered by you."

She twisted her hips, stirring up a moan from deep

within Chance's gut. "I think I could get used to this mastery notion, myself."

"So will you marry me?"

The answer came quickly and with such ease, she knew it was the only thing to say. "Of course I'll marry you. For I myself have realized that the fulfillment I sought in the musketeers has been filled to overflowing by the lieutenent of the musketeers. I could never go on without you, Chance. Yes, yes, and yes, I'll marry you! That is . . ." A mischievous smile spread across her face, and she tickled the pad of her fingers across his lips. "If you can handle me?"

Chance's eyebrows rose to the challenge.

Chapter Twenty-Nine

The following morning, her brothers awaited her on the street in front of the ale shop where they'd spent the night and Alexandre's wounds had been treated. Chance sat on an overturned ale keg, nursing a tankard of the same brew. He'd seen to Justine's burial arrangements as soon as the sun graced the sky. She would be laid in the ground at Creil, between her mother and father.

Adrian greeted Min with a firm bear hug. "I'm so happy for you, *ma petite.*" He beamed from ear to ear, and when he noticed Min's dismay, explained, "Chevalier Lambert let us in on the upcoming nuptials. It's simply marvelous."

She looked over Adrian's shoulder to catch Chance's sheepish shrug. "I hope you do not mind? I had to ask your brothers' permission."

Mind? Mind becoming Madame Chancery Lambert? Mind being this dashing musketeer's wife, in and out of his bed? Not in a cat's lucky lifetime.

"Not at all. I love you, and I want everyone to know it."

And when her eyes met Armand's, his expression spoke volumes. He wasn't happy. But he wasn't angry either. Min approached him slowly.

"You've been through hell," he said in a soft, yet commanding voice.

"But no worse for the wear."

He touched the bandage secured loosely around her neck. A raised brow was all he dared muster. "I am convinced that the convent can teach you the skills you lack."

Min bowed her head. "I know. But—"

"But." Armand tilted her chin up and a smile curved his lips. "If the lieutenant will have you, I couldn't be happier. You've a good man in the chevalier. I only hope the two of you can both forget my foolishness and put these past few days behind you."

"Oh, Armand," Min pressed her arms around her brother's body and hugged him tightly. "Thank you. Thank you. But it was not foolishness that pressed you to secure a future for me. You've always seen to the well-being of the family. You were only doing what you thought right." She stepped back and threw up her arms to encompass the width of the streets. "But do not fret over these past few days. Look at the adventure we've had. I wouldn't have missed it for the world."

"Perhaps I would have," Chance said slyly as he draped his good arm over Min's.

"I believe we have all learned a bit about listening to what our women say," Armand said, as he squeezed Min in his embrace. "But come now, what is this cryptic message Alexandre has been muttering on his sick bed. Something about the queen?"

"Oh, yes." Min looked over her torn and bloodstained nun's habit. It would not do at all for an audience with the queen. "It seems the queen wishes to see me. I should leave right now. It sounded urgent."

"The queen?" Chance looked up from his tankard and cleared his throat. "What is this . . . business between the two of you?"

Min smiled at his dismay. "I'll tell you about it sometime. Perhaps after we've settled into our own home with a big roaring fire and a stable of horses?"

"She has big plans," Adrian echoed over her shoulder, with a wink to Chance.

Pressing his cheek next to Min's, Chance kissed the corner of her mouth. "Plans that I shall fulfill."

"But I really should be going," Min said. "You'll come with me? And my brothers too." She looked over Chance's shoulder, and the men in question agreed. "There is one thing before we go."

Chance waited with eager eyes, her brothers as well.

"I am in need of a dress."

Min turned and sauntered away. She did not even look back. She knew that both of her brothers' jaws fell in unison.

This time Min was allowed immediate admittance to the queen regent's private chambers—though not without a warning that she had better make haste, as the queen was due for an appointment within the hour.

"There you are, *chère*—oh, my!"

Min curtsied grandly, lifting her soft daffodil skirts with elegant grace. Generous curls danced atop her head, much to the delight of her brothers. Chance had eagerly selected the yellow silk, saying it complimented her dark skin tone wonderfully. She felt like a princess, and not a bit uncomfortable, for the seamstress had loosened her stays at her request.

"My child." The queen approached her with wide, delighted eyes. "Can this be? You are so lovely!"

"*Merci,* your majesty." It was much easier to keep her balance wearing flat slippers than the high heels Sophie had laughingly bestowed upon her. "I rather like it myself."

"Oh, I cannot believe it. Such a transformation." The queen clucked her tongue and couldn't keep her eyes from dancing over Min. "Lovely. Simply lovely. Oh, but I shouldn't go on. You know you look lovely. It's obvious by the glow. You're simply radiant. Come, *chère.*" She motioned for Min to sit beside her on the damask day chaise. "I've only a few minutes, for I am due in the courtyard. There is an initiation ceremony this afternoon for the new musketeers."

"New musketeers?" Min's heart sank. *I should have been one of them. I could have!*

But then she remembered she no longer had any reason to feel lonely or unfulfilled. She had learned that desires come in many different forms. And her greatest desire had been found. Chance. Her true love. From this point on, everything would be right. No matter what she did, she had her musketeer. A man who loved her with all his heart.

But you really did want the musketeers. You did! You know deep down inside this is true.

"*Chère,* I must beg your forgiveness."

"Mine? Oh, no, majesty, there couldn't possibly—"

"Now listen." The queen silenced her with a firm hand bejeweled with heavy rings. "I was a fool before, sending you away with such stern words. I've regretted them since and couldn't sleep for the thoughts that ran through my head. I had no right to tell you the things I did. Sometimes I do not realize the power a queen's words have over her subjects."

"And a faithful one I am."

"Yes, well, I should have never said those things about seeking a vocation. At least not to you! Oh, my dear, it was the look on your face after I had spoken to you. Such sadness, as if I had ripped your dreams from your heart and pounded them into useless pulp. It took me a while to realize that you are a very unusual girl. Heaven knows, with the clothes you wore!"

Min blushed to recall how the queen must have viewed her in full men's wear, slouch-topped boots, sword, and mouseskin mustache. She would definitely have to make some changes in her wardrobe. But . . . slowly.

"I want you to forget the things I said," the queen said with a squeeze of Min's hand. "I now know it would be impossible, unthinkable, to tame a wild and glorious heart such as yours. Please, you must not take up a vocation."

Royalty had never pleaded so grandly.

Min laughed. "Your majesty, I have already tried the convent."

"Oh dear! You mean to tell me—"

"Oh, no, I lasted no more than a night."

"Thank God." The queen pressed a delicate palm to her décolletage. "Such relief washes over me. Ah, but I have something that will restore that happiness to your face. Though . . . if I'm not mistaken . . ." The queen looked over Min's face with a gleaming curiosity. She clapped her hands and was suddenly gay. "So the rumors are true!"

"The rumors?" At court that could mean numerous things. Rumors ran as quickly and frequently as a raging river. "You mean—"

"You are to marry that wonderfully handsome soldier of *Les Mousquetaires Noir!* Oh Mignonne, my dear, I am so happy for you. He is such a prize. You will do me the honor of marrying at the Louvre?"

"Here? Your majesty, I would be honored, but—"

"Then it is settled." The queen signaled over her shoulder to the guard at her door. "My chamberlain awaits. I must be going. You'll inform me of your plans as soon as they are settled. But now for your surprise."

"Surprise?" Everything was happening so fast. One more wonderful thing was piled upon another. To marry at the Louvre? Min felt light in the head. "Majesty, you have already been far too kind. What could you possibly—"

"I want you to attend the ceremony this afternoon. Please. You've brought your fiancé? Of course, how foolish of me—he will be in the ceremony!"

"Yes, and my brothers—"

"Splendid! It shall be a family affair. Now, I've a maid waiting for you. You'll have to change first. I shall see you outside in a little bit."

"Change?"

And with that the queen bustled out of her chambers, leaving Min standing in stunned silence.

Min navigated her passage back to the outer chambers with a mindless ease. Perhaps she would fit in well at court, she mused. She felt almost graceful in her wide skirts, and the slithering silk sounded feminine and seductive. But it was only a brief thought. No, the yellow silk was just for today. It would take a while to become comfortable in a dress, and Min had no intention of throwing out any of her breeches.

It was Chance's kiss that finally brought her out of her wandering thoughts.

"Mignonne? Is everything all right? You look lost. It's not the dress, is it? Is it too tight? Damn these Parisian fashions."

"I'm not sure." Completely oblivious to Chance's worries, Min tried to make sense of the Queen's hasty invitation. *You will have to change?* "I'm to attend the ceremonies this afternoon."

"I must be there also to present the new recruits to the king. You are not . . . angry?"

"Angry? Whatever for?"

He hugged her into his embrace. "You would have made an incredible musketeer, Mignonne. I will always believe that."

"Then that is all that matters. As long as my husband has faith in me."

"I do."

Min noticed that Chance had changed to his musketeer tunic and breeches. His boots were polished, and a thick white plume billowed in his hat. He was so dashing. And he was all hers. She kissed him again and again, until she knew nothing else than his flesh upon hers and his sweet, manly taste. "Mine. All mine," she whispered.

"What was that, love?"

"I was just laying claim to you."

"Ah, that was done days ago, love. When I first held sight of these luscious bittersweet chocolates." He kissed her eyelids gently, lingering on each one. "They are truly priceless."

"Do you know why the queen would want me at the ceremony?"

"I've no idea. From all I've heard of your adventures lately, perhaps it is that you are the queen's newest friend and she wishes you there. I will introduce you to the new recruits afterwards. Your brothers are already outside. I noticed Armand and Adrian speaking to Captain d'Artagnan."

"Really?" Relief flooded her senses like a spring rain. "Maybe something good has come of this after all."

"Something good? You mean to say that our betrothal is not?"

"Oh, no, it's just that now perhaps my brothers can turn their lives around for the better."

"I shall do all I can to help. Shall we go?"

"Mademoiselle?"

Min looked over Chance's shoulder. A meek young girl stood with hands gracefully folded before her. It was the maid the queen had mentioned. "Um . . . you go ahead. I've one more thing to do."

"You're sure?"

Chance's midnight gaze locked onto hers. Yes, it mattered not that she hadn't achieved what she had come to Paris for, for she had gained something far greater.

"I'm very sure, Chance."

Epilogue

"Dreams do come true," the queen regent whispered in Min's ear as she kissed one cheek and then the other in front of Chance, her brothers, the king and his new queen, d'Artagnan, and the entire assembly of courtiers and newly commissioned musketeers.

This time the blue tunic was not heavy upon Min's shoulders. She felt she could support the entire world right now for the joy in her heart. An honorary position in the King's Grand Musketeers had just been bestowed upon her. "Honorary" meaning she had earned the tunic, but still would not be allowed to fight in campaigns.

But that was perfectly fine with Min. For her other commission as the queen's lady-in-wating—with the understanding that she was really more of a personal bodyguard—would keep her very busy, and satisfied.

The entire crowd burst into uproarious applause as Min turned around. Beneath the long blue and gold streamers, Armand nodded and granted her an approving wink. Alexandre, sitting in a specially fashioned chair with wheels, held Sophie on his lap. They kissed beneath the storm of waving multicolored ribbons. Adrian, flanked on either side by two lovely young girls who were suspiciously lacking in jewelry, cheered and hooted the loudest.

Wine was brought out and the music began. Min found herself circled within the crowd in the arms of her fiancé. The rhythm of the dance spun Min's heart into its grasp, and she twirled around and around beneath Chance's raised hand. The noise of the crowd did not enter her head. Each was tuned only to the other.

"I am very proud of you, Mignonne," Chance said, pulling her close so she could feel the fierce strength of his heart pounding against her chest.

"It does not bother you that your wife will spend most of her days guarding the queen?"

"Your duties do not begin for a fortnight." He smoothed a lingering finger down the side of her cheek. "We've plenty of time to get settled."

Min raised a brow. "A fortnight? And how would you know? I've not been told that."

His sexy smile warmed his face and lit the stars in his eyes. "I've the queen's ear myself, precious one."

His smile was irrepressible. And Min could see, deep in his eyes, that it mattered not that his wife-to-be stood in his arms dressed in breeches and tunic and bucket-topped boots. All that mattered was that she stood in his arms.

Always.

AUTHOR'S NOTE

Alexandre Dumas created a hero for all ages in d'Artagnan, star of *The Three Musketeers.* But did you know d'Artagnan really existed? Dumas based his character on Charles d'Batz Castlemore, a young man from Gascony, whose dreams took him to Paris where he signed on with the king's guards using his mother's maiden name, d'Artagnan. Born somewhere between 1620 and 1623, the real d'Artagnan would still have been in infant skirts during the time Dumas based his story. I have used a more exact age for him in *Tame Me Not.* He's in his late thirties, possibly forty. I did promote him to captain about seven years early for my own purposes.

I hope you enjoyed Mignonne's story. Next it's Min's eldest brother Armand's turn to face his past crimes and try to make a better life for himself in *Betray Me Not.*

Readers can write to me at:

PO Box 23
Anoka, MN 55303

mihauf@aol.com

http://members.aol.com/mihauf/Scarlet.html

Put a Little Romance in Your Life With
Janelle Taylor

__Anything for Love	0-8217-4992-7	$5.99US/$6.99CAN
__Forever Ecstasy	0-8217-5241-3	$5.99US/$6.99CAN
__Fortune's Flames	0-8217-5450-5	$5.99US/$6.99CAN
__Destiny's Temptress	0-8217-5448-3	$5.99US/$6.99CAN
__Love Me With Fury	0-8217-5452-1	$5.99US/$6.99CAN
__First Love, Wild Love	0-8217-5277-4	$5.99US/$6.99CAN
__Kiss of the Night Wind	0-8217-5279-0	$5.99US/$6.99CAN
__Love With a Stranger	0-8217-5416-5	$6.99US/$8.50CAN
__Forbidden Ecstasy	0-8217-5278-2	$5.99US/$6.99CAN
__Defiant Ecstasy	0-8217-5447-5	$5.99US/$6.99CAN
__Follow the Wind	0-8217-5449-1	$5.99US/$6.99CAN
__Wild Winds	0-8217-6026-2	$6.99US/$8.50CAN
__Defiant Hearts	0-8217-5563-3	$6.50US/$8.00CAN
__Golden Torment	0-8217-5451-3	$5.99US/$6.99CAN
__Bittersweet Ecstasy	0-8217-5445-9	$5.99US/$6.99CAN
__Taking Chances	0-8217-4259-0	$4.50US/$5.50CAN
__By Candlelight	0-8217-5703-2	$6.99US/$8.50CAN
__Chase the Wind	0-8217-4740-1	$5.99US/$6.99CAN
__Destiny Mine	0-8217-5185-9	$5.99US/$6.99CAN
__Midnight Secrets	0-8217-5280-4	$5.99US/$6.99CAN
__Sweet Savage Heart	0-8217-5276-6	$5.99US/$6.99CAN
__Moonbeams and Magic	0-7860-0184-4	$5.99US/$6.99CAN
__Brazen Ecstasy	0-8217-5446-7	$5.99US/$6.99CAN

Call toll free **1-888-345-BOOK** to order by phone or use this coupon to order by mail.

Name ____
Address ____
City ____________________ State __________ Zip ______________

Please send me the books I have checked above.

I am enclosing $____________
Plus postage and handling* $____________
Sales tax (in New York and Tennessee) $____________
Total amount enclosed $____________

*Add $2.50 for the first book and $.50 for each additional book.

Send check or money order (no cash or CODs) to:

Kensington Publishing Corp., 850 Third Avenue, New York, NY 10022

Prices and Numbers subject to change without notice.

All orders subject to availability.

Check out our website at **www.kensingtonbooks.com**

Put a Little Romance in Your Life With

Fern Michaels

__Dear Emily	0-8217-5676-1	$6.99US/$8.50CAN
__Sara's Song	0-8217-5856-X	$6.99US/$8.50CAN
__Wish List	0-8217-5228-6	$6.99US/$7.99CAN
__Vegas Rich	0-8217-5594-3	$6.99US/$8.50CAN
__Vegas Heat	0-8217-5758-X	$6.99US/$8.50CAN
__Vegas Sunrise	1-55817-5983-3	$6.99US/$8.50CAN
__Whitefire	0-8217-5638-9	$6.99US/$8.50CAN

Call toll free **1-888-345-BOOK** to order by phone or use this coupon to order by mail.

Name____

Address____

City ____________________ State ________Zip______________

Please send me the books I have checked above.

I am enclosing $______________

Plus postage and handling* $______________

Sales tax (in New York and Tennessee) $______________

Total amount enclosed $______________

*Add $2.50 for the first book and $.50 for each additional book.

Send check or money order (no cash or CODs) to:

Kensington Publishing Corp., 850 Third Avenue, New York, NY 10022

Prices and Numbers subject to change without notice.

All orders subject to availability.

Check out our website at **www.kensingtonbooks.com**

Merlin's Legacy

A Series From
Quinn Taylor Evans

__**Daughter of Fire** $5.50US/$7.00CAN
0-8217-6052-1

__**Daughter of the Mist** $5.50US/$7.00CAN
0-8217-6050-5

__**Daughter of Light** $5.50US/$7.00CAN
0-8217-6051-3

__**Dawn of Camelot** $5.50US/$7.00CAN
0-8217-6028-9

__**Shadows of Camelot** $5.50US/$7.00CAN
0-8217-5760-1

Call toll free **1-888-345-BOOK** to order by phone or use this coupon to order by mail.

Name ____
Address ____
City ____________________ State ________ Zip ______________
Please send me the books I have checked above.
I am enclosing $______________
Plus postage and handling* $______________
Sales tax (in New York and Tennessee) $______________
Total amount enclosed $______________
*Add $2.50 for the first book and $.50 for each additional book.
Send check or money order (no cash or CODs) to:
Kensington Publishing Corp., 850 Third Avenue, New York, NY 10022
Prices and Numbers subject to change without notice.
All orders subject to availability.
Check out our website at **www.kensingtonbooks.com**

Put a Little Romance in Your Life With

Hannah Howell

__My Valiant Knight 0-8217-5186-7	$5.50US/$7.00CAN
__Only For You 0-8217-5943-4	$5.99US/$7.50CAN
__Unconquered 0-8217-5417-3	$5.99US/$7.50CAN
__Wild Roses 0-8217-5677-X	$5.99US/$7.50CAN
__Highland Destiny 0-8217-5921-3	$5.99US/$7.50CAN
__Highland Honor 0-8217-6095-5	$5.99US/$7.50CAN
__A Taste of Fire 0-8217-5804-7	$5.99US/$7.50CAN

Call toll free **1-888-345-BOOK** to order by phone or use this coupon to order by mail.

Name ____

Address ____

City ____________________ State ________ Zip ______________

Please send me the books I have checked above.

I am enclosing $____________

Plus postage and handling* $____________

Sales tax (in New York and Tennessee) $____________

Total amount enclosed $____________

*Add $2.50 for the first book and $.50 for each additional book.

Send check or money order (no cash or CODs) to:

Kensington Publishing Corp., 850 Third Avenue, New York, NY 10022

Prices and Numbers subject to change without notice.

All orders subject to availability.

Check out our website at **www.kensingtonbooks.com**

Put a Little Romance in Your Life With

Rosanne Bittner

__Caress	0-8217-3791-0	$5.99US/$6.99CAN
__Full Circle	0-8217-4711-8	$5.99US/$6.99CAN
__Shameless	0-8217-4056-3	$5.99US/$6.99CAN
__Unforgettable	0-8217-5830-6	$5.99US/$7.50CAN
__Texas Embrace	0-8217-5625-7	$5.99US/$7.50CAN
__Texas Passions	0-8217-6166-8	$5.99US/$7.50CAN
__Until Tomorrow	0-8217-5064-X	$5.99US/$6.99CAN
__Love Me Tomorrow	0-8217-5818-7	$5.99US/$7.50CAN

Call toll free **1-888-345-BOOK** to order by phone or use this coupon to order by mail.

Name ______________________________
Address ______________________________
City ______________ State ________ Zip ______________
Please send me the books I have checked above.
I am enclosing $______________
Plus postage and handling* $______________
Sales tax (in New York and Tennessee) $______________
Total amount enclosed $______________
*Add $2.50 for the first book and $.50 for each additional book.
Send check or money order (no cash or CODs) to:
Kensington Publishing Corp., 850 Third Avenue, New York, NY 10022
Prices and Numbers subject to change without notice.
All orders subject to availability.
Check out our website at **www.kensingtonbooks.com**